KU-797-332

'A brilliantly convincing and gripping dystopian vision.
Fantastically detailed and assured'
Elizabeth Buchan

'A gripping, chilling, dystopian fantasy:
think Atwood meets Orwell'
Mail on Sunday

'*Widowland* is fabulous! A very exciting counterfactual'
Adèle Geras

'Brimming with crackling detail, a gripping thriller'
Miranda Carter

'The power of words is at the heart of this terrific
and sometimes terrifying novel'
Sci Fi Bulletin

'Revelatory'
Observer

'Resonant and timely . . . a creative and colourful
story that entrances the reader'
The Lady

C. J. Carey is a novelist, journalist and broadcaster. She has worked at the *Sunday Times*, the *Daily Telegraph* and the BBC, among others. She also writes novels under the name Jane Thynne and lives in London. *Widowland* is the first novel she has written as C. J. Carey.

WIDOW LAND

C. J. CAREY

QUERCUS

First published in Great Britain in 2021 by Quercus
This paperback edition published in 2022 by

QUERCUS

Quercus Editions Ltd
Carmelite House
50 Victoria Embankment
London EC4Y 0DZ

An Hachette UK company

PB ISBN 978 1 52941 200 0
EB ISBN 978 1 52941 201 7

10 9 8 7 6 5 4 3 2 1

Typeset by CC Book Production

Printed and bound in Great Britain by Clays Ltd, Elcograf S.p.A.

Papers used by Quercus are from well-managed forests and other responsible sources.

For Caradoc King

It might seem amazing that women and girls should return to work at spinning wheels and weaving looms. But this is wholly natural. It was something that could have been foreseen. This work must be taken up again by women and girls . . .
Alfred Rosenberg, 1936

Widow: Origin: Old English widewe, *from an Indo-European root meaning 'be empty'; compare with Sanskrit* vidh *'be destitute', Latin* viduus *'bereft'. Printing: a last word or short last line of a paragraph falling at the top of a page or column and considered undesirable*

The art of editing lies in exercising taste, making aesthetic judgments and attuning oneself . . . to the sensibility and psychology of an author.
Peter Ginna, *What Editors Do: The Art, Craft, and Business of Book Editing*

PART ONE

CHAPTER ONE

Monday, 12th April 1953

A biting east wind lifted the flags on the Government buildings in a listless parody of celebration. All the way from Trafalgar Square and down Whitehall they rippled and stirred, turning the dingy ministerial blocks into a river of arterial red. The splash of scarlet sat savagely on London's watercolour cityscape: on the dirt-darkened Victorian facades and dappled stone of Horse Guards, the russet Tudor buildings and ruddy-bricked reaches of Holborn, and around the Temple's closeted, mediaeval squares. It was a sharp, commanding shout of colour that smothered the city's ancient greys and browns and obliterated its subtleties of ochre and rose.

The big day was approaching and there seemed no end to the festivities. All along the Thames decorations were being hung. Bunting was entwined between the plane trees, and ribbons twisted through the Victorian wrought-iron railings of the Embankment. The House of Commons itself was decked out like a dowager queen in a flutter of pennants and flags.

Every shop had its royal picture posted in the window, tastefully framed, and every taxi that passed up Whitehall had a patriotic streamer dancing on its prow.

Flags were nothing new in the Protectorate. When the Anglo-Saxon Alliance was first formed, its emblem – a black A on a red background – was displayed in front of every building. No sooner were they run up the poles, however, than the flags were vandalized, ripped to ribbons and left in puddles in the street. Disrespecting or damaging the flag was swiftly made an act of treason, punishable by death, and the order came down that people found guilty of tampering should be hanged from the same flagpole that they had attacked – a deterrent that was as grisly as it was ineffective. After the first shock Londoners took as much notice of the bodies suspended above them as their forebears had taken of the heads that used to be stuck on spikes on London Bridge.

But that was then.

A lot can change in thirteen years.

It had been threatening a downpour all day. The chill in the air, and the absence of anything cheerful to look at, meant people shrouded their faces with scarves and huddled into their coats, keeping their eyes down, skirting the craters in the potholed roads. *March winds and April showers bring forth*

May flowers. Wasn't that how the saying went? Judging by the regular deluges that had drenched the past few weeks, April was certainly shaping up to be a traditional English spring. At least (as some older people thought) there was something traditional about it.

High above Whitehall, in a block that had once been the War Office, Rose Ransom stared down at the tops of the buses and the heads of the pedestrians below. She was a solemn-looking woman of twenty-nine. Her eyes were dreamy and her face, poised above the typewriter, was pensive, as though she was seeking inspiration for the page she was composing, though nothing could be further from the truth. Rose was fortunate enough to possess the kind of physiognomy that gave nothing away. It was an untroubled demeanour, not so much serene as enigmatic. She had a perfect oval face framed by neat dark blonde hair and grave eyes of indeterminate blue, like a lake that reflects back precisely the colour of the sky. From her mother she had inherited a smooth, peachy complexion that meant she could pass for a decade younger and from her father an air of unreadable composure that belied whatever turmoil stirred within.

'Come and see this, Rosie! It's amazing!'

Rose turned. Across the office, a commotion was going on and Helena Bishop, a lively blonde, was predictably at the centre of it. Any event was enough to distract most office workers, but that day's novelty was exceptional. A pair of technicians had wheeled in a squat box of wooden veneer encasing a bulbous fisheye of screen with two dials set beneath. Once a technician had plugged in the set and switched it on, the glass spattered with static before brightening to a monochrome glow. A murmur of excitement went up as every worker abandoned their desk and crowded round, nudging and jostling to get a better view of the tiny screen.

Like most people in the English territories, they had never seen a television close up before, and were eager to get a good look.

At first it was nothing more than a snowstorm, but after warming up, a picture emerged, sliding upwards in horizontal lines until someone twiddled the tuning button and it shuddered to a stop.

'Would you look at that!'

The entire office was transfixed. The murky image resolved into a man in evening dress, reading aloud with patrician jollity.

'*Anticipation is mounting in London as the first crowds begin to line the Coronation route. Early birds are pitching their tents to ensure they get the best view of the royal couple as they make their way from the abbey.*'

All across the nation, the same scene was being played out. The Coronation of Edward VIII and Queen Wallis was scheduled for 2nd May and the Government had announced that every citizen in the land would have access to a television to watch it. To that end thousands of sets had been installed: in workplaces, factories and public houses. In schools, offices and shops. For the first time in thirteen years, every adult and child had been given a day off to see the royal couple crowned. There was more than a fortnight until the big day, but excitement was already at fever pitch.

'Come *on*, Rosie!'

Rose grinned across at Helena with appropriate enthusiasm and shook her head. In a split-second calculation she judged it safe to linger at her desk rather than join her colleagues across the room. She bent over the typewriter and pretended to write.

Television was nothing exciting to Rose. Unlike the others, she had seen plenty of TV sets close up, due to her friendship with the Assistant Cultural Commissioner, Martin Kreuz. Friendship with Martin meant not only television shows, but entry to special access exhibitions and theatrical premieres. Art exhibitions at the top galleries. VIP parties and meals out. Martin Kreuz may be Rose's superior and twenty years her senior, but he was a cultured man and endlessly generous in sharing the benefits of his position with her. There were numerous advantages to knowing him.

And the disadvantages? She tried not to think about them.

Her gaze drifted restlessly back through the barred and smeared windows to the street outside. The Culture Ministry building itself was a monstrosity, scabrous with soot and girdled with an iron fence laced with barbed wire, but a few metres along from it the Palladian columns of the Banqueting House retained something of their original dignity. This was the place where, as every schoolchild knew, three hundred years previously, Charles I had been beheaded. The famous occasion when the English killed their king was on every school curriculum and the place was constantly beset by throngs of kids milling around as their teachers held forth, chatting amongst themselves and pricking up their ears for details of the beheading.

Some of Charles I's more recent descendants, King George VI, his queen, Elizabeth, their two daughters and a rabble of minor royals, had been accorded far less ceremony in their demise. But as far as Rose was aware, no child learned their fate in school.

Most people had no idea what had become of them. Or cared.

It was Protector Rosenberg who featured in the history lessons now. The Leader's oldest friend, who had been with him in the beer halls and marched alongside him in the earliest days of the movement. The man dubbed the Leader's Delegate for Spiritual and Ideological Training, who had guided and shaped the development of the Party, its philosophy and its ideals. The thinker who embodied the Party's connection to the past and the future. Rosenberg was a visionary, and when the Leader made him Protector, he had resolved that his dream of a perfect society would find its ultimate expression in England.

Now, more than a decade later, Rosenberg's vision was complete. A whole generation was growing up who had never known anything but the Alliance. German came as easily as English to their lips. As Martin was so used to explaining, the Alliance was the perfect fruition of the history of the Anglo-Saxon peoples. In a way, he liked to say, it was the end of history. The ultimate 'special relationship'. Two peoples who had once been a single race had come together again in a seamless join.

As neatly as if King Charles's head was restored to his body.

Not that anyone cared about history. The only thing that mattered was that order was restored, and whatever people thought of that order, it meant that life ran smoothly. Food appeared on the table and the buses and trams arrived on time. The blossom on the horse chestnuts in Green Park turned up as punctually as ever and birds still sang each spring.

'I see the march of technology leaves you unmoved.'

The sardonic voice emerged from Oliver Ellis, who occupied the desk next to Rose. He had a dark, unruly thatch of hair, a brooding demeanour to match, and a wit that was acid enough to eat through shrapnel. Generally, Rose appreciated Oliver's barbs; they were mostly aimed at hapless colleagues or at diktats of more than usual idiocy from the Cultural Commissioner's office. But sometimes, she guessed, she must be the target of his humour too.

That was how men like Oliver worked.

He stood up, adjusted his horn-rimmed spectacles and frowned. 'Aren't you coming to look at our marvel?'

'I've seen a television already,' she replied coolly, adjusting the paper in her typewriter.

'Of course you have. I forgot. Friends in high places.'

He followed her gaze out of the window, where it was raining harder, and pedestrians were raising their umbrellas against the sky, as if seeking protection from something fiercer than an English spring.

'God forbid it rains on the big day.'

'There ought to be a law against it,' said Rose.

'Probably is.' Oliver unhooked his jacket from his chair and pulled it on. 'Alliance regulation number 8,651. Prohibition of Precipitation on Coronation.'

She smiled. 'SS Stipulations on Sunshine Standards.'

'Rain Restrictions Regarding Royalty,' he countered.

She couldn't stop herself laughing. Oliver was good with words. But they all were.

That's why they were here.

Oliver had been an undergraduate at Cambridge before the war and, when the fighting began, he was given a desk job in the old dispensation that meant he missed any action and survived to serve the new regime. Men of Oliver's type were unusual. Many males between seventeen and thirty-five who hadn't died resisting the Alliance had been sent to work abroad, causing a notable gender imbalance in England.

The country now had two women for every man.

Perhaps this was why, as the Leader put it, 'Women are

the most important citizens in this land.' And lest anyone forget, his comment was carved into the pediment of a vast bronze statue erected on the northern end of Westminster Bridge.

It was an impressive installation. Where once the chariot of Boudica had stood, now the Valkyrie figure of the Leader's niece Geli was planted, heavy thighs draped in a classical toga, head encircled with a laurel crown, staring broodily out at the muddy waters of the Thames. Just as France had its Madeleine – a representation of perfect womanhood – England had her Geli. Geli was young, intelligent, talented and beautiful. She symbolized everything that was fine about femininity. She was the apogee of womanhood. In essence, she embodied the spirit of England.

Just a shame the woman had never set eyes on the place.

'You don't want to miss this, Rose!'

Helena's excitement was contagious. All around her, more Culture Ministry staff were emerging from their offices and cubicles – her friends in the Film division, girls from the Astrology Office, young men from Advertising in their braces and red ties, Press department staffers, a gaggle of people from Broadcasting, even some stragglers from Theatre and Art, who were relegated to a couple of back offices on one of the building's lower floors.

Rose was about to give in and join them, when from across the office she became aware of a Leni bustling towards her desk with an air of self-importance. She was a dumpy, matronly figure, steel hair gripped into a bun and an upper lip disfigured by a badly mended cleft palate. She wore no make-up – she wouldn't dare – but her cheeks were flushed with a bright disc of pink and her eyes glinted in the fleshy folds of her face. Encased in thick wool stockings and a pewter-grey suit in the kind of crusty, hard-wearing tweed favoured by her type, she might have been a crab, scuttling towards her prey, carrying a clipboard pincer-style. Generally, Lenis believed themselves to be the essential cogs of any factory or workplace, and no matter how low level their actual function, they regarded themselves as the glue that kept the economy running. They were probably right. There was plenty of dogsbody work in the current administration and it required an army of women to carry it out.

This woman, Sheila, had a desk right outside the Commissioner's office and believed she knew everything that was going on in the Ministry. She smiled blandly as she sighted Rose, certain that the message she was conveying would bring a shiver down anyone's spine.

Rose steeled herself, summoned an expression of polite enquiry and refused to turn a hair.

'Ah, Miss Ransom. An important memo for you.' Sheila detached a piece of paper from the clipboard and floated it onto Rose's desk.

'The Commissioner wants to see you. He's away at the moment but he's back on Friday. You'll report to him first thing.' She leaned closer, bringing a waft of unwashed clothes and cheap perfume. 'Little word of advice. Be punctual. In fact, I recommend you arrive ten minutes early. The Commissioner despises bad timekeepers. He takes a *very* dim view. And no one likes to see him angry.'

CHAPTER TWO

'Aren't you excited? I am. I've never seen a king crowned. It's like a fairy tale.'

'Not my kind of fairy tale,' said Rose, wiping a porthole in the window's condensation and peering out.

The bus was packed and stuffy with tired commuters making their way home. Rose and Helena always shared the journey and they liked to take seats on the upper deck so they could look down on the passers-by. It was a kind of free entertainment, watching the crowds trudging up Whitehall in their shabby clothes and worn shoes. They poured like a polluted river up the Strand, the Magdas in their cheap coats and hats, the Lenis, with their heels and pencil skirts and buttoned jackets, and the Klaras, pushing enormous prams, usually with a couple of children hanging off the handles. Sometimes a trudging Frieda, encased in compulsory black, scurrying home before her curfew. Widows suited black, because they were, effectively, a form of shadow themselves, the sooty remnants of a married life snuffed out.

The detailed regulations on clothing worked through a system of coupons, with the number of points given varying according to caste. Because textile and leather production was geared towards the needs of the mainland, all shoes were made of plastic and rubber, their soles from cork or wood, and most clothes were fashioned from the same rough materials. Yet even with these constraints, it was not hard to distinguish a higher order woman from her sisters.

The differences between men were more subtle, marked less by appearance than by demeanour. Foreigners carried themselves with a natural confidence and swagger, whereas natives remained buttoned up, modelling their famous stiff upper lip.

On the corner of Adam Street, a group of elderly men rolled out of the pub and deferred obsequiously to a pair of officers monopolizing the pavement two abreast.

In a flash an image came to Rose. Her father, in one of his rages, when the Alliance was first announced.

It's a failure of leadership. We were led by fools and charlatans. No wonder we caved in so quickly with leaders like ours.

Her mother, white-faced and flustered, explaining that Dad was ill and didn't know what he was saying.

The chief advantage of the bus journey was that it offered the chance for Rose and Helena to talk out of earshot of their office colleagues. You could never talk completely freely, because surveillance was notoriously easy to carry out on public transport, and watchers were hard to spot, so it was as well to shoot a look over the shoulder before speaking. But the Leni behind them – plain with plaits and thick spectacles – was buried in a paperback called *A Soldier's Love* and the two Magdas on the other side, their hair tucked under turbans, were engaged in fervent bitchery about a friend.

Helena rolled her eyes.

'I forgot. You're the expert on fairy tales. How's it going?'

'Fine. Fairy stories are easy really. Better than the Brontës.'

'I don't know what you're complaining about. I'd kill for your job.'

'Says the girl who goes to every movie premiere in the land.'

'I know it sounds fun, but you can't relax. I'm there to check inaccuracies. Anything that's slipped through the net. If political errors remain, it's on my watch. Imagine how stressful that feels. I'm not just sitting back eating chocolate.'

'Chocolate. I remember that.'

Helena grinned. It was as though she could not help the good humour shining out of her. Everything from the milky blonde tendrils spilling from her hat, to the smile always hovering at the edges of her mouth, was irrepressible. Short of being German, Helena had been gifted with all the blessings the gods could bestow, chief among them a sense of the ridiculous – a vital attribute in Government service.

'Don't tell me Assistant Commissioner Kreuz doesn't bring you back chocolate from all those foreign trips he makes. I bet he has huge boxes tied with satin ribbon hidden in that briefcase of his.'

'Don't know what you're talking about.'

'Oh, come on. Give me credit for having eyes in my head.'

'And . . . ?'

'He adores you. I've seen him around you. You'd have to be blind to miss it. And I know full well you're mad about him too.'

She gave Rose a gentle nudge with her elbow.

'I can keep a secret, you know, Rosie. We are best friends, remember?'

The bus shuddered to a sudden halt. Peering out, Rose saw a series of army vans blockading Waterloo Bridge. White tape had been hoisted across the carriageway, and a policeman was directing traffic with officious semaphore, as though conducting an especially bracing marching band.

'There's been an incident,' murmured Helena.

'Where?'

Helena checked swiftly over her shoulder.

'In the office they were saying it was the Rosenberg Institute. It happened right in the middle of a Classification procedure. As if that's not nerve-wracking enough. Remember?'

Back in the early days of the Alliance, shortly after the Time of Resistance, every female in the land over the age of fourteen had received a letter summoning her for Classification. The procedures were staggered to cope with the numbers, but in the event, the processing of more than half the population was carried out with military efficiency. Sixteen-year-old Rose, along with thousands of others, had reported one Saturday to the Alfred Rosenberg Institute, the former County Hall, on the South Bank of the Thames.

It was a bright, sunny morning, and the consignment of women being processed that day was held in a strict line that snaked out of the building and all the way across Waterloo Bridge. Guards with dogs patrolled, and Rose noticed the younger men staring hungrily at one girl about her own age, whose beauty and natural confidence marked her out. She had the glossy pedigree beauty of a racehorse, with long, coltish legs, wide-set pale blue eyes, gleaming hair and a light dusting of freckles. She was tossing her head, aware of the men's glances and knowing her looks were precisely the kind that the regime loved. They called such attributes Nordic – the highest praise – and Rose had no doubt that her neighbour would be instantly assigned to the top caste.

For a moment she had considered hanging back, in case proximity to this beautiful girl affected her own chances, before she checked herself. Systems in the Alliance never worked on whim. The Rosenberg Assessment Procedure was scientifically rigorous and in case of doubt, the Institute walls were plastered with charts showing precise comparative measurements of head size, nose shape and eye colour for each different racial type. Every minute calibration would be translated into a precise position on the scale of caste, from ASA Female Class I (a) to ASA Female Class VI (c).

The method had been trialled on the mainland and was highly reliable. Since 1935, people had been measured, not only to distinguish between Aryans and other races, but also to assess young women who wanted to marry into the SS. There was no reason at all why the practice should not be expanded to classify an entire female population.

No amount of reasoning, however, helped when the procedure itself made every woman flinch.

First the craniometrist fitted a steel device like a giant claw around their heads and assessed their other dimensions with a series of metal rods. Then the anthropometrist, seated between a tray of glass eyes in sixty shades and an array of sightless plaster skulls that looked uncomfortably like death masks, measured the angles of their jaws and noses and brows and noted them down. The endless queues of women shuffled slowly through a hall pungent with a school gym smell of sweat, unwashed clothing and fear.

When it was the pretty blonde's turn to have her profile measured with a contraption that looked like a pair of giant compasses, she rolled her eyes at Rose, and it was all Rose could do not to giggle. The girl seemed to brim with anarchic hilarity and mischief, as if the two of them were sharing some outrageous private joke. Amid the tense and nervous throng of women filing through the packed hall, proximity to this larky woman seemed the best way to get through the ordeal.

Charting every facial feature, then weighing and measuring each female took a good half hour, after which they all trudged into an adjoining hall to face the second level of selection: the questionnaire. This required them to provide a host of information about their family, their ancestry, past health and mental conditions. Eventually, when all the boxes had been ticked, the women were assigned the classification that accorded with their heritage, reproductive status and racial characteristics. This label would determine every aspect of their life, from where they should live, to what clothes they would wear, what entertainment they could enjoy and how many calories they could consume.

Although each classification had its official title, nobody bothered with a mouthful like ASA Female Class II (b), when they could use the inevitable nicknames. Members of the first, and elite, caste were popularly called Gelis after the woman most loved by the Leader, his niece Geli. Klaras – after the Leader's mother – were fertile women who had produced, ideally, four or more children. Lenis were professional women, such as office workers and actresses, after Leni Riefenstahl, the regime's chief film director. Paulas, named after the Leader's sister, were in the caring professions, teachers and nurses, whereas Magdas were lowly shop and factory employees and Gretls did the grunt work as kitchen and domestic staff. There was a range of other designations – for nuns, disabled mothers and midwives – but right at the bottom of the hierarchy came the category called Friedas. It was a diminutive of the nickname *Friedhöfefrauen* – cemetery women. These were widows and spinsters over fifty who had no children, no reproductive purpose, and who did not serve a man.

There was nothing lower than that.

Many of these classifications changed, as women became mothers, for instance, or failed to. Women were regularly screened, and an entire division of the Women's Service was devoted to the business of reassessments. Yet in a way, the labels became self-fulfilling. Certain occupations favoured a particular class of female. Poorer food, clothes and housing reinforced women's differences. Without meat, fresh fruit and vegetables, Friedas and Gretls grew sickly and their complexions dulled. Deference became second nature. No one needed to ask if a woman was a Leni, or a Gretl, or a Magda, because you could tell at a glance. And a Geli, whose rations and work were enough to put a spring in her step, would always walk taller and hold her head that little bit higher.

A Geli card was the golden ticket.

When the two girls left that day with ID marking them as ASA Female Class I (a), Rose's new friend locked arms with her and gave a little spontaneous whoop.

'I'm Helena Bishop. How about we go and get our pictures taken?'

It was becoming a tradition, among young women classified as Gelis, to have their photographs taken beneath the statue of the original Geli that had been newly erected on the Embankment. Photographers had set up shop there, with instant cameras, producing Classification Day pictures on request.

'OK then.'

The two girls were friends from that day onwards.

Yet Rose and Helena were the lucky ones. Some young women, having their life chances radically diminished by Classification, abandoned common sense and created mayhem, weeping, screaming and attacking the guards. Such hysterics were always hustled quickly away, to have their caste downgraded yet again on account of antisocial behaviour.

The bus lurched forward again, leaving the traffic jam behind.

'So, this incident, what happened?' asked Rose quietly. 'Was it a girl?'

'A man, apparently. Walked in quite calmly and shot one of the guards.'

'An angry father?'

'No.'

'Who then?'

'I heard it was, you know . . . one of *Them*.'

Helena jumped up and grabbed her bag, as though relieved to have reached her stop.

'Better get going! See you tomorrow!'

All eyes followed her hourglass figure as she sashayed her way down the stairs.

Two stops later, the bus came to a halt and Rose made her own way into the shadowy streets.

Although street lighting was installed in elite zones, its hours of operation were strictly limited, and it would be another few hours before the dim wattage of the lamps, haloed in the evening mist, pierced the murk. Rose didn't mind. It was still twilight and besides, she preferred shadows. They obscured the everyday gloominess of the streets – the potholed pavements, cracked windowpanes and pallid, malnourished faces – and in the crepuscular light, the dirt-darkened brick buildings and cobbled alleys had a historic feel. The fanlights above ancient, narrow doors and the glint of stained glass transported her to a different age. Sometimes she allowed herself to fantasize that she was going back in time, before the Alliance, even to Victorian times.

Instantly, she checked herself.

Nostalgie-Kriminalität. Nostalgia crime. Any suggestion that the past was better than the future was strictly outlawed. *Sentimentality is the enemy of progress. Memory is treacherous.* The sentiments every half-diligent schoolchild knew by heart.

Citizens of the Alliance were not encouraged to think about the past, except in the way that the Protector wanted them to think of it, as a mythical story. History with a capital H, like something out of the Bible.

When Rose was first allocated housing in Bloomsbury, the name sounded curiously familiar, and it was a few moments before she registered why. Then she remembered that the name had once belonged to the Bloomsbury Group, a circle of subversives who had lived here some decades before, producing degenerate art. From what she knew, their ring leaders had been arrested early in the Alliance and their homes turned over to elite citizens.

Which fortunately included herself.

A blast of stale beer and light emanated from a pub, and a couple of Magdas approached, their exchanges brittle on the evening air.

'She says she can't find a man for love nor money. I said, why don't you get a transfer to the mainland? There's plenty of choice for your sort there. You wouldn't believe the look she gave me.'

They dropped their conversation instinctively as they drew level with Rose and, with obligatory deference, gave way to let her pass.

Rose pushed open the door to her block. The hall was floored with linoleum and to one side stood a shabby deal dresser strewn with a haphazard collection of letters and leaflets. A notice pinned to the wall declared *Females Class III to VI inclusive are forbidden entry to these premises after 6 p.m.* A sour smell hung in the air and instinctively she tried to separate out its components, detecting alongside the usual cabbage and floor polish a tang of vinegar and a top note of oily fish. That was a dangerous smell. In the absence of meat, citizens were sometimes tempted to catch their supper in the Thames – unauthorized fishing was prohibited, but hunger and the need to supplement meagre rations was often enough to drive amateur anglers to try their luck under cover of darkness. Generally, they were picked off by the patrols who waited in the arches of the bridges or concealed themselves by riverbank trees, and their corpses would be found floating alongside the other detritus of society – suicides, desperate women, drunks. But if they returned and cooked their catch, there was still the chance that a vigilant neighbour or caretaker would detect the crime by odour alone.

Snapping on the light, Rose shut the door behind her and leaned against it, looking round. Her room was simple. A bed, a chair and a small partitioned section for a kitchen stove and cooking ring. Tattered photographs of London in the Time Before: a leafy square with smart railings, cheerful shopfronts, and a street scene featuring vans painted with advertisements for bread, sausages and tea. A worn orange rag rug lay before the gas fire. And against the window, a rickety, wood-wormed desk looked down over the tops of the plane trees in Gordon Square.

The furniture was cheap. Like food and clothing and everything else, it was made of the least valuable materials. The best cuts of wood – the oak, ash and cherry – were needed elsewhere on the mainland, together with the highest quality food and building materials. Citizens of the Alliance had to make do.

Rose didn't care. This was a room of her own, and she knew how lucky she was to have it.

Retrieving the teabag she had left out that morning to dry, she set a kettle on the stove. Once she had made a cup of tea, she fed an Alliance mark into the gas meter, kicked off her heels, and drew her legs beneath her in the armchair.

It was only when she was gazing into the cracked bars as they flickered violet, then gently glowed, that she finally allowed her mind to focus on the question that had been haunting her like an ill-concealed shadow.

What did the Cultural Commissioner want with her?

Fat, florid, fifty and prone to random acts of spite, Commissioner Hermann Eckberg's foul temper was partly the gift of genes and partly the legacy of a horse-riding accident in Hyde Park that had wrecked his back and for which he held the whole of England responsible.

As Cultural Commissioner for the Protectorate, Eckberg reported directly to Joseph Goebbels, the Controller of all Culture back in Berlin. Since SS-Reichsführer Himmler had been promoted to deputy Leader, following the defection of the traitor Goering to Russia in 1945, the Culture Ministry was seeded with SS men, and they were not a natural fit. Eckberg in particular loathed his job. As an unashamed Philistine, he detested art and music, let alone literature or theatre, and like the Romans before him viewed England as a distant outpost of empire. The food was disgusting, the weather worse, and the political circumstances surrounding the Alliance meant that employees had to be treated with a veneer of respect that was not accorded to the citizens of other subjugated nations.

All of which was enough to put Eckberg in a perennially bad mood.

Rose had a deep, panicky urge to call Martin. She imagined his handsome face reassuring her, like a kind family doctor. His smooth tones and his husky voice with its attractive

German edge. So, she had been summoned for a meeting? Why worry about that? It was not as if she had been stealing paperclips, for God's sake. What possible grounds could an innocent person have to fear?

She lifted a hand towards the telephone, then immediately dropped it. Not only had Martin forbidden her from contacting him by telephone, but he was away on a trip abroad and not back for two days.

Besides, something told her that the summons concerned Martin himself.

CHAPTER THREE

Adultery.

Of all the double standards practised so fervently among the upper echelons of the regime, the favourite concerned their approach to sex. Unofficially, adultery was rampant. Most senior men had a girlfriend and they had their pick of the Gelis, married or not. Officially, however, it was taboo, and recently the disapproval of adulterous relationships had intensified at the highest levels. As he aged, the Protector's already monkish tendencies hardened, and he had publicly declared that he would not feel comfortable dining with any woman other than his wife. Despite his name, Rosenberg was not Jewish, but the aura of Jewishness that had dogged him throughout his life only intensified his obsession with blood purity and fortified his conviction that adultery deserved the death sentence. The regime was all for increasing the birth rate, but the sanctity of marriage was paramount.

Rose didn't like adultery either, but that was no help on the day, almost a year ago, when she first came to the notice of Assistant Cultural Commissioner Martin Kreuz.

Subliminally she must have detected the ripple of interest before she saw him. An almost imperceptible current of turned heads and whispers as he strode through the clatter of typewriters and the ping of telephones as he approached her place in the typing pool. His smart uniform with its perched eagle above the breast pocket and armband with the black letter A on its red background drew glances and giggles from all sides. What was a VIP doing at the desk of a lowly young Ministry staffer? Especially the handsome Martin Kreuz, whose smiling, suntanned face was so different from the potato-faced Bavarians and humourless, thin-lipped Prussians, with their wire-rimmed glasses and efficiency targets, who dominated the upper ranks of every Government ministry. With his imposing height and muscular frame, Kreuz had a rugged masculinity and a touch of the Italian about him. If he enjoyed opera, it would be Verdi, not Wagner.

To add to the mystery, unlike other Ministry officials, who made a point of conducting all conversations in German, Kreuz addressed her in English. While nobody was attempting to erase the native tongue, German was the language of officialdom, of school and workplace, and most Government staff stuck to it rigorously.

'Could I have a word, Miss Ransom? In private, please.'

'Shall I bring my . . . ?' She held up the stenographer pad for dictation.

'What? Oh no. Nothing like that.'

He led her down the dingy marble corridor, past the uniformed secretary outside his office, Ludwig Kohl, a porcine Saxon with closely shaven hair who failed to contain his obvious curiosity when Kreuz ushered Rose through the door and closed it firmly behind him.

Martin's office was one of the most luxurious in the building. It was thickly carpeted, with a drinks trolley, a monumental mahogany desk and a sweeping view of the Thames. A Renoir bust stood on a side table and the walls were decorated with a selection of Old Masters – Constable, Vermeer, Titian, Rembrandt – picked out from the National Gallery. It was a perk offered to all senior officials, but this charming arrangement was not without its drawbacks. Inspiring though it was to be surrounded by the master works of Western civilization, Ministry rules stipulated that each office wall must also be hung with a regulation picture of the Leader, and the latest version, in which he appeared stumpy, putty-skinned and badly aged, looked all the more ridiculous juxtaposed with a Bronzino portrait of a young man, whose delicate features and Renaissance gaze were as ravishing as the day they were painted four hundred years ago.

Steepling his fingers beneath his chin, and crossing his jackbooted legs, Kreuz gave her a quizzical look.

'Do sit down, Miss Ransom. Cigarette?'

'No, thank you.'

'Mind if I do?'

She shook her head, still mystified, and pulled her tweed skirt down further over her knees. Kreuz lit a cigarette with a heavy silver lighter, inset with a gold Alliance emblem, then replaced it thoughtfully.

'I've asked you here because I have a task that involves books. I wonder, are you the kind of person who likes books?'

Did she like books? She certainly had once.

She had grown up in a rambling house in south London, with a father whose wartime injuries precipitated unpredictable outbursts of anger and a mother whose life's work was to placate him. Whenever a row erupted, and until their father's rage had burned itself out, Rose and her elder sister would escape – Celia to her bedroom to play with her dolls, and Rose into the orchard to climb the boughs of a pear tree with a book. She could still hear the soft call of the wood pigeons as they rustled in the branches around her. The drowsy hum of bees. The tiny plop of a pear falling to the grass. At that age, the books she read concerned adventures and animals and hearty girls in boarding schools who turned detective and solved crimes. But they were her refuge and her sanctuary.

'I used to like books,' she admitted. 'When I was young.'

'I guessed so. I thought that about you.'

Rose blushed at the idea that he had thought anything about her at all. She had certainly never thought anything about him. Other than his name and the fact that he was the Commissioner's deputy, she had registered absolutely nothing about Martin Kreuz. She had certainly never looked past the uniform to the man who wore it. Now, regarding him more closely, she saw a man in his early fifties, sturdy and fit, with an expression of benign jocularity. Yet behind the smile, there was worry, and sadness too. His face was as craggy as a mountain range and stress had carved a ravine between his eyes. She had the fleeting conviction that the bump on the nose had been obtained in a fight. A jagged slash of scar ran diagonally down one cheek. The aura of inner turmoil that haunted him, however, was overlaid by a surface of impeccable grooming. Kreuz's hair was combed back from his forehead, his nails were buffed and he exuded the faint smell of a masculine pomade. On his desk she noticed a picture of a woman and four children: the woman – Frau Kreuz, she assumed – square-jawed and handsome, the little girls with flaxen plaits, and the boys in lederhosen.

'And do you still read?'

'I'm far too busy,' she replied blandly. All citizens knew to be guarded about their personal lives. Reading was not expressly forbidden – indeed, a list of 'educationally bene-ficial' books was issued by the Ministry every year – but too much private reading, outside of a school or institution, was transgressive for a woman. It smacked of subversion. It was the kind of thing that raised eyebrows and got you talked about.

'If I have any spare time, I tend to run up clothes on my sewing machine.'

He shrugged.

'Sure. We're all busy. Berlin has just sent a crateload of new instructions to be put in place and I can't imagine how I'm going to find time to do it. They want to relocate half of the Foreign Office archive to London with no extra provision for it. I'm to find space for hundreds of boxloads of documents, as if I can magic up staff and shelving space with a snap of my fingers.'

A short laugh.

'But you don't want to hear about my personal troubles.'

Rose remained sitting rigidly, alert yet unjudgemental.

'All this bureaucracy. But it's what we poor pen-pushers have to work with. Stick to the rules and don't question them. There's a line from an English poet, Tennyson, about some disastrous Russian battle where the soldiers say, "*Ours not to reason why . . .*"'

'"*Ours but to do and die,*"' she murmured, before she could stop herself.

'Precisely!' A triumphant gleam in his eye. 'You told me you weren't a reader, but you *are!*'

Rose cursed herself. Kreuz had been testing her. His jokey complaint about bureaucracy was a trap into which she had neatly fallen.

'I'm not. It's my father. He loved poetry. He used to recite it. I didn't understand most of it, but the words stuck.'

'I see. Anyway . . .' Kreuz stretched backwards and smoothed his hair with the flat of his hand. 'I'm sure you know that literature is a great interest of the Protector.'

'I don't know much about him,' she said, erring on the safe side.

It was a plausible response. The Protector was rarely seen. Sometimes it was possible to catch a glimpse of him, in tan fedora and trench coat, climbing into a Mercedes in Downing Street, and those who did found it hard to believe that this was the most powerful man in the land. An academic, architect and a keen believer in homeopathy, Alfred Rosenberg was sixty, but looked a decade more. With his sickly complexion, perpetual scowl and deep-set dark eyes, the Protector was more mortician than politician. It was difficult to credit that such a frigid temperament should nurse warm feelings for anything, let alone this land, yet Rosenberg's passionate love affair with England was said to have begun in 1933, when he first set foot on English soil.

Possessed of a long-standing obsession with the story of King Arthur and the Knights of the Round Table, the English, Rosenberg saw at once, were fellow beings with Germans. Both nations were Anglo-Saxons, bred of the same blood and bone and ancestrally intertwined in the mists of the Dark Ages. Only an accident of history had separated them, and back in the 1930s Rosenberg saw a chance to put that history right. When the opportunity arose, he asked the Leader for the gift of the Protectorate, and the Leader was only too pleased to oblige.

Martin smiled at Rose's caution. He understood.

'Not to worry. But I assure you, the Protector is a deeply

literary man. He's a bestselling author himself, as I hardly need point out.'

Rosenberg's masterwork, *The Myth of the Twentieth Century*, was second only to the Leader's autobiography in sales. It had sold ten million copies in Europe alone. It was displayed in every bookshop window. It lay open on a lectern at the entrance to Westminster Abbey.

'So I don't have to remind you about the Rosenberg Regulations regarding books.'

Along with the wide-ranging changes to every aspect of British existence, the creation of the Protectorate had brought an avalanche of regulations. Average citizens had found themselves bombarded with a blitz of rules and strictures on every conceivable area of daily life.

Including books.

On the mainland, back in 1933, when the Leader had come to power, degenerate books had been burned on pyres. Jubilant people danced as the evening air was lit with flakes of fire, and the words of Jews, Slavs, communists, liberals, homosexuals, freemasons, Catholics and every kind of subversive turned to ash.

The English, however, prided themselves on doing things a little differently. Native academics and librarians winced at the melodrama of their mainland allies. Although the regulations stipulated an outright ban on all the same categories of books, these degenerate texts were not burned on public bonfires, but loaded into industrial incinerators. Teams of civil servants combed libraries and archives, professionally cleansing them of problematic texts and disposing of them hygienically.

This wasn't the Middle Ages.

And this was England, after all.

'Actually, it might interest you to see this.'

Kreuz pulled back a drawer of the desk, extracted a small volume and held it up. It bore the title *Informationsheft GB. Gestapo Handbook for the Invasion of Britain*.

'Ever heard of it?'

She shook her head. 'No, sir.'

'Bit of a museum piece now. But back in 1939 it was drawn up by the head of counter espionage, Walter Schellenberg, in the event that England might have to be forcibly invaded. That never happened, thank God, but this little book outlined detailed plans on establishing an occupation administration. How to run the economy, transport, language and so on. Who to arrest.'

He frowned and continued flipping through.

'Yes. Here's what I was looking for. The *Sonderfahndungsliste GB*. Special Wanted List. To be handed over to department IV B4 of the Central Reich Security Office. The arrest operations to be headed by Colonel Professor Dr Frank Six. Two thousand, eight hundred and twenty people.'

Another list. The Alliance liked lists. There were lists for everything.

'Noël Coward, Vera Brittain, Aldous Huxley, J. B. Priestley, Sylvia Pankhurst, Stephen Spender, Rebecca West, Virginia Woolf. Have you heard of these characters?'

'A couple,' Rose said cautiously.

'Virginia Woolf?'

'Don't think so.'

'Me neither. Nor Schellenberg either, I daresay. Still, what does Herr Schellenberg need with Virginia Woolf when he's married to Coco Chanel and has a ski chalet in Switzerland, lucky devil.'

Kreuz broke off from this musing to unlock his legs and swing himself to his feet.

'But that's not the point.'

Crossing the office, he paused at the drinks trolley to pour himself a generous whisky and gazed down at the Thames below.

'If I can speak to you frankly, the reason many of these reprobates featured on Schellenberg's list is because they wrote novels. And their novels are dangerous.'

'Dangerous, sir?'

'Sure. Our Protector believes that books are every bit as dangerous as bombs. Words are weapons, aren't they? They're a conduit for spreading propaganda against the Alliance. Back in the beginning, as you know, we tackled this problem with a fairly blunt instrument. We banned them.'

He remained at the window, shoulders hunched, staring absently downwards.

'Personally, I have never been a fan of the broad-brush approach, and nor, it now seems, is the Protector. He prefers something a little more nuanced. Say what you like about him – though I advise you not to . . .' Here he turned and gave her a wink. 'But the man's a genius.'

'Is he?'

'Without doubt. Now recently, his people have been working on ways of addressing the "woman question".'

'I see.'

'The whole woman question is a far-reaching issue, but the part that's landed in my in-tray concerns fiction. Obviously, you know that novels portraying a subversive view of females are outlawed. Unruly women, those who challenge male authority, degenerate sexual preferences, all that.'

'Yes.'

'But we can't make all books illegal, can we?'

'Can't we?'

He glanced sharply to check for insubordination and Rose returned a polite gaze.

'No, we can't. Rosenberg accepts that there are some texts that cannot be banned. Famous novels. Stories that are woven too deeply into the popular imagination. Unfortunately, a very high proportion of these novels are written by or about women. You must know what I'm talking about. Name one.'

Her mouth dried. Was this another trap? To name a famous title was to admit to having read it, or at the very least having heard of it.

'I'm not sure.'

'Come on now, Miss Ransom. I'm talking to you as an employee of the Culture Ministry. This is official business, not an interrogation. Nothing you say will go beyond these walls.'

'*Pride and Prejudice*?'

'Good example. Jane Austen. One of England's most cherished writers. Elizabeth Bennet and Mr Darcy, am I right?'

'From what I recall.'

'Everyone knows Lizzie Bennet. And that annoying mother of hers. I read the novel as a teenager in English class too many years ago. It didn't mean much to me then. It seemed a small, domestic tale of social climbing, centred around snobbery and various English gentlemen taking too long to make up their minds about their romantic affairs. Yes?'

'It's a comedy of manners, I think. We did it at school.'

'Precisely. But it's not until you reach adulthood that you appreciate what Miss Austen has to say. She's saying that Elizabeth Bennet is intelligent, yes? That marriage can subject women to degradation. That masculine superiority should be questioned.'

'That never occurred to me.'

Kreuz came towards her, perching on the edge of the desk so that they were uncomfortably close.

'The thing is, Rose – if I may call you Rose . . .'

She smelled the aroma of his pomade, and the hot, animal scent of him. From his uniform came a faint odour of horses, suggesting he had been out riding before he came into the office. Close up, his eyes were a warm hazel, splintered with gold.

Despite herself, she felt something inside her buckle. An involuntary kick.

'We can't just erase *Pride and Prejudice* or *Middlemarch* or *Jane Eyre* or any of these novels. They're too famous. They're ingrained in the culture. Cleansing them from the popular consciousness will take a generation. But we *can* do something about them now.'

His voice was low and confidential, as though they were caught up in an enterprise that involved just the two of them. A personal conspiracy.

'I can't take credit for this, it's Rosenberg who had the idea. He says, far better than destroying these books is to correct them. To edit them.'

'*Edit* them? Classic texts?'

'Updating, is the word he uses. There's nothing irrational about it. Scientists update their theories as new discoveries are made. When Galileo discovered that the earth moved round the sun, everyone had to adjust their textbooks, didn't they? Mapmakers correct their charts every time a new island turns up. Are you saying they're wrong?'

'No, but . . .'

'So why not novels?'

'It's just . . . That would be a huge enterprise. To rewrite the classics.'

'I agree. And no one's suggesting that. What's required is something far more subtle. An adjustment of ideology. An abridgement really. A slight, minor correction to some characters and themes.'

'What do you mean by correction?'

'I mean that books, like people, need discipline. Not only the discipline of grammar and sentences, but the hard discipline of meaning.'

She steeled herself to maintain eye contact.

'So I'm talking about excision. Rephrasing. Carving out the rotten and diseased meanings, the subversive suggestions that trigger disturbing thoughts and infect young minds. The necrotic attitudes that have the potential to rot an entire nation. Shaping books, like a sculptor shapes stone.'

The way Martin Kreuz put it, it sounded almost like art.

'How would one know what's subversive?'

He smiled, mock stern.

'Well, Miss Ransom. I might say, a citizen of the Protectorate should have the correct attitudes written on her heart. But I won't insult you. Let's just say, I can see that you're intelligent.'

'But if . . . there was a specific issue. Of ideology . . . ?'

'In that case, I suppose, you would ask the question that every Culture Ministry employee should ask themselves.'

He waited, eyebrows raised, for the answer, and when none came, supplied it himself.

'What would Minister Goebbels do?'

Standing up, he thrust his hands in his pockets and looked down at her.

'I've got a whole Fiction Correction team to assemble, not to mention teams overseeing portrayals of women in advertising, wireless and film and so forth. But to begin with, I need someone to update a series of classic texts for the school curriculum. Think you can do that? It's quite a task, but I hope you'll see it as an honour and I'm sure you're equal to it.'

Perhaps it was the hush in the carpeted office or some unspoken instinct that told her Martin Kreuz would not penalize her for questioning him. She looked deeper into the gold-brown eyes.

'Why me? I know hardly anything about literature. And apart from press releases and digests of speeches, I've never written anything in my life.'

'Because I have faith in you.'

He reached out a hand and drew it slowly down the skin of her cheek. When he felt her flinch, he withdrew.

'And because unlike Miss Austen's gentlemen, I have never been one to ignore the attractions of a beautiful woman.'

Rose jerked awake from her doze. The fumes from the gas fire had made her drowsy and she had pins and needles where her head had pressed on one arm.

Did Martin know about the Commissioner's request to see her? Surely, if he did, he would never have allowed her to endure this nail-biting tension. Even Martin must understand the cold undercurrent of fear that haunted every citizen of the Protectorate. The anxiety that was fuelled by the knowledge of surveillance and informers. The fear that functioned as an invisible force – a kind of electric field that contained its victims and ensured they policed themselves.

Wrapping her hands round her knees in a foetal clasp, she reassured herself that she had no good reason to fear the meeting with the Cultural Commissioner.

But then, no one needed a reason to fear anything anymore.

CHAPTER FOUR

Tuesday, 13th April

'Mummy! Rose has been reading to me about the Snow Queen!'

Hannah was six years old. Her legs were like string with knots at the knees, her face was as freckled as a fresh egg, and Rose adored her.

Rose's sister Celia and her husband Geoffrey lived in an elegant four-storey Georgian house with a russet-brick facade and striking long windows that overlooked the north side of Clapham Common. The house was far beyond Geoffrey's means, but it had come available in the early days of the Alliance – like much other desirable property whose owners were no longer around – and one of Geoffrey's golf club friends had pulled strings. Celia's natural good taste ensured that the house was outfitted with gleaming Regency furniture, chintz sofas, fresh flowers and all the latest appliances. A stack of Deutsche Grammophon discs sat next to their machine, and the mantel was festooned with a clutch of silver-framed photographs of Hannah.

Hannah was their only child and despite all efforts to the contrary, this was unlikely to change. The problem was Geoffrey's, Celia confided, but Rose suspected that her sister reckoned she had done enough for the birth rate and banished Geoffrey from the bed. Either way, Rose tried not to think about it. Hannah was quite enough. She loved babysitting her niece and Celia shamelessly exploited it.

'I chose a story with a queen in it because of the Coronation,' Rose volunteered.

'How appropriate,' laughed Celia. 'I can just see Wallis as the Snow Queen, swathed in white ermine. What do you think she'll wear on the big day? My girlfriends are going crazy discussing it. The King's robes have been designed by Hugo Boss, but apparently Wallis's outfit is top secret. My money's on something madly stylish from Dior. That would be so like her. What do you think?'

'I haven't a clue,' said Rose absently, running a hand through Hannah's silky hair.

'I bet you *do* know and you just can't tell me. Classified information.'

'Hardly,' said Rose shortly. She could just imagine Celia's girlfriends dissecting Queen Wallis with their mixture of snobbery and social cruelty. It was a peculiarly English virtue – to admire and disdain at the same time – and while they despised Wallis for being American, they envied her undeniable style. That a Baltimore socialite should marry into the British royal family and challenge centuries of gilt-encrusted protocol was plain wrong, yet Wallis had injected a glamour and edginess into the House of Windsor that had been sorely lacking.

'Marjorie Stevens played bridge with her, back in the day. Says she's frightfully clever.' *Clever* was not a compliment among Celia's friends. 'Apparently, she's simply longing to go back to America. She finds being royal an absolute bore, and she says all those stuffy courtiers are stuck in the past. The King won't hear of it, of course.'

Rose glanced down at the copy of *Vogue* sitting on Celia's coffee table. Perhaps because fashion belonged to the elite, or maybe because their other diversions were limited, clothes were an obsession for Geli women. Rose was not the only one who spent hours bent over her Singer sewing machine, running up skirts from old curtains, or turning cotton sheets into little blouses. The Queen, of course, had no such constraints, and the women's magazines pored over her clothes, her hair, her shoes, even her interior decorators. That month's edition carried a cover photograph of the Queen in the garden of Fort Belvedere, the couple's getaway cottage in Windsor Great Park, wearing a cerulean silk Ferragamo suit, pussy bow blouse and a pair of pugs.

'Can I have another story?'

Emboldened by her aunt's presence, Hannah was dancing up and down and tugging at Rose's hand.

'I suppose . . .'

'No, you can't!' snapped Celia. 'Aunt Rose has been working all day. She's tired. Get up those stairs before your father arrives.'

Once Hannah had retreated sulkily, teddy dragged by one arm, Celia flung herself down on the turquoise sofa, looping her slender legs over the end and running one hand through her shining hair, which was dyed a popular shade called Nordic Gold.

'Don't know how you manage it. Even reading one story bores me to tears. Children are so exhausting.'

'I enjoy it. Really, I do. And I've been thinking about the Snow Queen a bit recently.'

For the past month Rose had been correcting a version of stories by the Grimm Brothers to be distributed in schools and kindergartens, as well as bride schools and mother training centres. Fairy tales were an important part of childhood conditioning and Rose had attended a lecture at the Ministry for Early Years Propaganda in Malet Street to learn the acceptable adjustments for the educational syllabus. Most changes were simple. Princes wore stormtrooper uniform. Dwarves were subhuman. Cinderella's Ugly Sisters were Scots.

Monarchs were problematic. Despite the forthcoming Coronation, the regime was generally against kings and queens. Royalty was a symptom of a corrupt and archaic society, and Rose tended to replace them with regime functionaries. Gauleiters. Mayors. When she came across a king she would insert an Obergruppenführer.

Queens, though, were something special.

'Can't think where Hannah gets it from,' said Celia, rolling her eyes. 'I never liked fairy tales. Or any kind of books really. They're always trying to teach you something.'

She gave a light laugh, revealing her perfect teeth. It was a laugh that could shatter a heart at a hundred paces and had indeed caused numerous men to fall in love with her before Geoffrey won the prize. Not for the first time, Rose asked herself the same question.

Why Geoffrey?

Like so many other women, Rose's sister had coped with the drought of men in the Alliance by dating one many decades older than herself. Tedious, humourless and balding, Geoffrey had been forty-five and working in an accountancy firm when the Protectorate was formed, and because he had never taken up arms, he was at an advantage when it came to serving the new regime. His transition, indeed, had been practically seamless, and if Geoffrey harboured a resentment for the foreigners who had been placed over him, his innate, pasty-faced dullness was the perfect cover. Not to mention the toothbrush moustache that, like so many others, he had adopted in the Leader's honour.

The occasional dinner or dance with Geoffrey was just about understandable, but to actually marry him, a man who was more like a distant uncle than a husband? To listen every day to his ill-informed opinions and kneejerk prejudices. How could Celia bear it?

Even as Rose contemplated this, there was the sound of the door slamming and Geoffrey arrived. He handed his umbrella and briefcase to the Gretl and came over to dispense a sour-breathed kiss.

'Rose. Lovely to see you. We must have you over for dinner sometime soon.'

Rose knew exactly what he meant. On the one hand, he despised her for consorting with Martin Kreuz, a married man, but on the other hand, it was useful to have a brother-in-law – even an unofficial one – with such impressive connections. She could just imagine Geoffrey hosting such a dinner, smiling greasily, adjusting the position of the cutlery, as he resolutely social-climbed. And Martin, endlessly courteous, flirting with Celia, laughing with Geoffrey, privately despising them both.

'Rose has been reading fairy stories to Hannah.'

'Hmm.' Geoffrey grunted and picked a strand of tobacco from his moustache. 'I'm not sure I'm keen on all these stories.'

'It's harmless, darling.'

'It's not going to do the child any good.'

'Rose keeps it ever so simple, don't you, Rose?'

Why must Celia always try to placate him? Rose wondered.

'Very. It's only fairy stories and they do those in ideology classes.'

'The next thing you know, she'll be trying to read herself.'

Reading for females was strictly banned before the age

of eight, and when they were taught to read, girls learned at a more basic level than boys. Under the Rosenberg rules, females should have a limited vocabulary – ideally two thirds of that of a man – and the risk of reading was that it could accidentally expand a child's use of language. It might enchant and intoxicate her. Help her express herself in new and exciting ways.

Rose was saved from further discussion by the wail that floated over the bannisters from the floor above.

'Rose! I want Auntie Rose!'

'I'll just pop up and say goodnight.'

'We don't do that, Rose. Giving in to her is spoiling.'

'Oh, let her, Geoffrey.' Celia rested a hand lightly on his pinstriped arm. 'Just while you mix me a drink.'

When Rose entered Hannah's bedroom, the little girl was sitting up in bed triumphant, teddy under one arm, and her other toys arranged in a semi-circle in order of size, their fur combed and their button eyes glinting beadily. Celia, with her clever eye for decor, had made the room into a young girl's dream with candy-striped wallpaper, a bright patterned rug by the fireplace and white-painted furniture that was just the right size for a child.

'Give me another story, Rose.'

Rose settled herself on the low, chintz-covered chair beside the little girl's bed and opened a volume of the Grimms' fairy tales.

'What shall we have then? *Sleeping Beauty*?'

'No.'

'*Cinderella?*'

'No.'

'*Hansel and Gretel?*'

'No.' Hannah settled back expectantly. 'Want one of yours.'

She placed her thumb in her mouth.

Rose got up and closed the door.

When she had told Martin she knew nothing about writing, she had not told him the truth.

At first it had been more a feeling than a conscious thought, a kind of energy pushing up, straining at her fingertips, as though the edges of her skin would burst. She had no typewriter – all machines were strictly controlled and you needed a licence to own one. Hearing a typewriter through the wall or floorboards was one of the most frequent complaints to the authorities. But one day a couple of years ago, quite on impulse, she had bought a couple of plain brown notebooks and, tentatively, set them in front of her, pen in hand. Before long it was cascading out of her, ideas and phrases that she herself barely understood, thoughts that emerged from somewhere deep within, which had never before been given expression. Words rolled around her mind like playthings. She wrote and wrote, recklessly, like a galloping horse that could barely be reined in. She wrote about everything – her life, her experiences, her dreams. Short stories, descriptive fragments, journal entries, poems. Bedtime stories for Hannah.

Soon enough, she found if she didn't write, she didn't feel properly alive.

When each notebook was full, she peeled back a flap of wallpaper that had come loose at floor level behind her bed. The wallpaper was hand-printed and exquisitely pretty, its pale green background stencilled with darker green leaves and flowers, writhing upwards in naturalistic abundance. It was a legacy of the previous degenerate occupants that had often piqued her curiosity about them. Beneath the wallpaper was a splintered plank, and carefully levering it upwards, she revealed a soot-caked cavity where a fireplace had once stood. The flue had been bricked up, but the gap for the grate remained, and instead of wasting valuable bricks, the builder in charge of the renovation had merely filled the vacancy with rubble and nailed over a couple of pieces of wood.

There, Rose stored the notebook, along with six others.

Now she put a finger against the soft bow of Hannah's lips.

'Shh. It's our secret, remember? Just for us?'

Hannah nodded solemnly and settled back against the pillow.

Rose pulled a small brown notebook out of her pocket and opened it up.

'As it happens, I did just write something for you.'

'Is it the Kingdom of Ilyria?'

Recently, Rose had created an imaginary kingdom, Ilyria – the name meaning happiness – where there were no female castes and girls were free to become princesses or dragon-riders or artists or whatever they chose. Hannah, as expected, had the starring role.

'Yes. So, settle down.'

When she came downstairs again Celia and Geoffrey were conferring, their heads close together. They moved apart when they saw her.

'She's going to sleep now, I think.'

'Thank you, Rosalind.'

Celia was one of the few people in the world who used her original name. When she was born, Rose had been named Rosalind, but in the past thirteen years Rose had seemed more appropriate. It sounded a little like Rosa and everyone wanted German names now. As for their children, there were plenty of little Adolfs and Alfreds and Evas running around the kindergartens, but names that began with H, after the Leader and deputy leader, were by far the most popular.

Celia only used Rosalind when she wanted something.

'Do you have time for a G and T?'

'Thank you. Yes.'

Geoffrey busied himself with administering the drink, titrating a thimbleful of gin into a glass and topping it up with tonic in the fastidious manner that put Rose's teeth on edge, before handing it to her like a dose of medicine.

'Drink up.'

He disliked her, she realized, and he didn't quite know

why. Geoffrey often remarked on the disparity between the two sisters, as though baffled that Rose lacked Celia's insouciance and Botticellian beauty. His antipathy only made Rose more watchful and reserved, which was one reason he disliked her in the first place.

'If you two girls don't mind, I have a few papers to see to. The elections for the chairman of the golf club are coming up and I've been landed with the application process.'

Before the Alliance, the Germans had code-named the verdant British Isles 'Golfplatz' – the Golf Course – and the nickname was increasingly appropriate. With a nation of ageing men, golf had overtaken football as the national game, and each village club's green was maintained with the same meticulous pride men used to devote to burnishing their Morris Minors and Austins. The golf club was Geoffrey's life, and as he bustled off to his 'den' – a leathery sanctuary that Celia never entered – Rose had no doubt that he would soon be securing the chairman's role for himself.

'Ciggie?'

Celia pushed a silver box towards her and Rose helped herself. They were National cigarettes, limp and dusty, but other brands were rare to find. Celia leaned towards her conspiratorially.

'Lovely stockings. I can't imagine *where* they came from.'

'They're Aristoc,' said Rose neutrally.

'So, how's Martin?'

There was a sly edge to her voice, salacious almost, as though she was vicariously savouring Rose's affair. In reality, Rose realized, her sister would far prefer the life that Martin offered than she did. Celia had always been intensely feminine and loved dressing up. Since the Alliance, fashion had taken on a greater importance than ever because only Gelis had the means to experiment. As all other castes had severely limited clothing rations, it was left to elite women to compete on colour and style. Despite the shortages that saw leather shoes replaced with plastic, and natural fabric with synthetics, Gelis harvested their coupons and combed the fashion glossies obsessively. Rose, like other women who knew high-ranking men, was able to supplement this allowance with the gift of lace underwear and nylon stockings that she frequently passed on to her sister. Celia complemented this with a natural dressmaking talent, hand-stitching elaborate beading in macaroon colours of violet and peach, pistachio and rose, running up floral-print skirts and embroidered blouses, and fashioning evening gowns of mock satin.

Any kind of glamour, however, was wasted on Geoffrey's ancient golf club friends, with their fading eyesight and dimming libidos. It was an irony that while Celia would adore the parties and events and meals, Rose had never felt comfortable in public with Martin.

'We're having dinner at the Savoy tomorrow night.'

'The Savoy!'

'It's where he always goes. His office canteen, basically.'

When the Alliance began, the Germans had immediately commandeered all the top hotels. The Ritz went to the SS, the Dorchester to the Abwehr, and Grosvenor House to the Office of the Protectorate. Joachim von Ribbentrop and his wife, who had spent time in London in 1936 when he served as English ambassador, took Claridge's. The Culture Ministry, virtually at the bottom of the pecking order, got the Savoy, and over the past year, Rose had been treated to numerous meals there. They gave out tiny mint chocolates wrapped in gold foil with the coffee and she always slipped hers into her bag to pass on to Hannah.

'Sounds romantic,' cooed Celia.

Rose shrugged. 'Not particularly. He probably wants to talk about work.'

'Sure that's all?'

'What are you getting at?'

'You are twenty-nine, after all, Rose. And no children. We had hoped it would work out with you and that journalist chap, Laurence.'

Laurence Prescott was a dashing and universally popular feature writer on the *Echo* whose looks and relative youth made him popular with Gelis in the Culture Ministry. Rose had accompanied Laurence to a year's worth of press screenings and dinners. She had even met his family. But somehow, she never felt comfortable with him. Perhaps because, like all journalists, Laurence gave the impression that he was noting down everything she said for future reference.

'Geoffrey's worried about your status. We're both surprised you haven't had a visit from the Family Promotion people.'

Rose had. She had found them waiting at the door when she arrived home a few months ago. A man and a woman, in the navy and red uniform of the ASK – the Amt für Sozial- und Kinderpolitik – the office charged with raising the national birth rate. The ASK was known colloquially as the Association for Screaming Kids. The English loved nicknames and giving a monstrous proposition a funny name lent it a subversive edge, as though they were taking ownership of it.

The ASK came armed with a sheet of questions and veiled threats about Rose's still unmarried status. She remembered the stout Leni with the mole on her chin staring enviously around the room as she ran through the standard mix of threats and inducements.

Rosenberg Regulations state that marriage is the appropriate state for adult women. Spinsterhood puts your elite privileges at risk. There are plenty of Class I women who would love a flat like this.

'If you wait much longer, you might stay single and have no children,' said Celia. 'What would happen then? You don't want to get reclassified.'

That was entirely possible. A woman's status was downgraded if she committed a crime or behaved in an aberrant way. Refusing to have children was placing self above state and a *prima facie* example of asocial behaviour. One might be moved to less attractive accommodation: probably a block where the kitchen and bathroom was shared between several families.

'God forbid you end up in Widowland.'

Even as she spoke, Celia's eyes widened like her daughter's did when a fairy tale took a frightening turn.

Widowland. The word itself was like a howl of wind across its own bleak facades. The Widowlands were the desolate residential districts where Friedas were housed. They were derelict areas, as crumbling and unkempt as the women who dwelled there, tucked away on the stained edges of the towns, their littered streets ringed around with tangled wire. Ramshackle terraces of Victorian brick and barren blocks of weeping concrete where nobody wanted to live.

Celia chewed a fingernail, and then brightened.

'If nothing comes of Martin, there's a friend of Geoffrey's who would adore to meet you. He's a nice chap, a dentist actually. Or he was before he retired.'

Of course he was retired. They always were, the men who Geoffrey proffered. The hands that plucked at Rose were kippered with nicotine, their eyes yellowing, their scalps pink beneath wispy hair. Frequently they were deaf too, not that it mattered because they did most of the talking, yet despite the woes of age, Geoffrey's friends were upbeat about their situation. Usually, they opined that things were not so bad. *It could be so much worse.* That was a favourite refrain.

And it was true. The system suited older men. Most had accepted the classification of females without protest and they had their pick of young women, with their satiny complexions and firm flesh. Although a man's choice of official consort was determined by her caste, nothing stopped them casually patting the bottom of a young Gretl, or running a proprietary hand across a Magda, if she appealed.

As for the women, what were they expecting? Romance?

'A dentist. Is that what you wanted to talk to me about?'

'Not exactly.'

Celia twirled a curl of hair between two fingers and gazed at her sister speculatively.

'There's something I need to tell you, in fact. It's about Dad.'

Rose felt a jolt of alarm. She jerked upright and put her drink down.

'Daddy? Is he all right?'

'Yes, of course. Or rather, no.' Celia had found a small snag on her skirt and was picking at it. 'Geoffrey, that is to say both of us, think he'd be much better off in a facility.'

'A *facility*? What kind of facility?'

'A nursing home. A hospital type of place. Where they can look after him properly. Those rages he has are too much for Mum to cope with now. Her nerves are in shreds. She's utterly ground down.'

'You're not thinking of shutting our father away! There's nothing wrong with him. Mentally, he's absolutely sound. Considering what he went through in the trenches in 1918, is it any wonder that he occasionally gets upset. It's nervous stress, that's what the doctor told us. There's a name for it. It's called shell shock.'

Celia pouted.

'Doctors always have names for things. But names don't

change what things are. Those fits he has. It's madness. And it's been getting worse.'

'So what are you saying?'

Celia avoided her eyes and remained fixed on the snag on her skirt, her fingers delicately plucking.

'You're not telling me you've done it already?'

Celia looked up, her tranquil blue gaze entirely un-apologetic.

'I'm afraid so, darling. A place came up and we took him in yesterday. Geoffrey and I drove him down there.'

'Why didn't you tell me?'

'We didn't want to bother you, what with your important work. We're allowed to go and visit next week. When he's settled in.'

Rose felt the blood rush to her face. She stood up, her heart pounding.

'How could you be so selfish?'

'It would have been selfish not to. Think what it means for the family. Madness is hereditary, you know.'

'Dad's *not* mad. He's probably saner than any of us. He was injured in the war . . .'

'These things get around. And I have Hannah to think of. What's going to happen when she goes for her assessment if they discover that her grandfather is mentally unbalanced? How is she going to be a Geli if she has madness in the family? Her whole future is at risk.'

'So you've sacrificed Dad's future instead.'

Celia shrugged.

'Motherhood's all about sacrifice. As you would know, if you ever got around to it.'

Rose couldn't stand to hear any more. She snatched up her handbag, her mind whirling, and headed for the door. The thought of her brave, sensitive father confined in an institution and deprived of his dog, his garden and everything he cherished brought tears to her eyes. But she could not bear for Celia to see them.

'Think about it,' called Celia, as Rose, her cheeks burning, departed down the path. 'It's so much better for Mum. It means she can come up in two weeks and watch all the excitement with us. You can't begrudge her that, now, can you? Everybody wants to see the Coronation.'

CHAPTER FIVE

It hadn't always been that way between them.

As Rose walked back through the streets of Clapham to the station, allowing the red mist of indignation to subside, she thought back to the day the Alliance was announced.

Thinking about, let alone discussing, the Time Before was officially discouraged. Yet for Rose, as for every other citizen, the events of that day were etched as though in acid in her mind.

The weather was beautiful. A late September afternoon that contained the dying breath of summer. The sky was a high, porcelain blue, the apple trees were bulging with fruit and she and Celia had been playing badminton in the garden. She could still feel the gravel under her plimsolls and the sweatiness of her aertex shirt as they came in, cheeks flushed, to find the adults gathered around the wireless, their faces tight with anxiety.

The drawing room, with its floral wallpaper and patterned

pink and green carpet, seemed like a natural extension of the garden. The scene was bathed in mellow sunlight and every object, from the eighteenth-century clock on the mantel to the Chinese vase on the card table with its indigo scrolls and cracked glaze, felt as though it had been there forever.

The voice of the announcer emerged, so smooth and patrician that you could practically see the dinner jacket that he apparently wore to broadcast. Only that afternoon, his voice betrayed a quiver of fear, and a note of something deeper. Desolation.

'*Air supremacy over Britain has been achieved. Prime Minister Halifax is shortly to sign a treaty of a Grand Alliance with Germany and the formation of a Protectorate is being discussed in London. Citizens are urged to remain in their homes. A temporary curfew has been imposed and will remain in place until further notice.*'

Then, in an addition that sounded unscripted, the announcer added, firmer and more boldly, '*God save the King.*'

For a few moments, the family sat in silence. Then, from a distance out in the streets, unfamiliar noises arose: the low rumble of trucks and the tinny echo of a megaphone. Everyone strained to make out what it was saying.

'*Stay in your houses. Do not go out.*'

Suddenly, from another direction, a series of small, sharp cracks, like fireworks, filled the air. Their father switched off the wireless, and as if in slow motion, went out to the cupboard beneath the stairs in the hall, where he kept an air rifle. The gun was meant for pigeon shooting but Dad was so gentle he could never bear to use it – he could hardly kill a wasp, let alone blast a bird out of the sky. Now he weighed it in his hands, assessing its weight and unfamiliar dimensions.

Impotently, Rose watched his long, delicate fingers deftly loading the ammunition. Then he plunged some spare bullets in his pocket and pulled on his coat.

'Where are you going, Dad?' demanded Celia.

'You stay here.'

'We've been told to keep inside, Frank!' pleaded their mother.

'All the more reason.'

'Don't go, Daddy!' said Rose.

He touched her cheek with his finger, then was gone.

The three of them stood, stunned. The dog began whining, tail down, and Rose put her hand on his head to quieten him. The room was filled with the stillness of expectancy. She was acutely aware of the scent of mown grass coming in from the French windows, mingled with the fragrance of star jasmine on the wall.

A few moments later came a crash and shouts of motion, and despite their mother's protests, Rose and Celia ran out of the house. On their quiet tree-lined street nothing stirred, except for the twitch of curtains. Most homes were firmly closed, but others had their front doors swinging open and peering inside one house, they saw a couple crouched in their hall, a half-packed suitcase beside them spilling with clothes.

When the girls arrived at the high street, however, a different sight greeted them. A rudimentary blockade had been constructed, haphazardly compiled of parked cars and tyres and planks. Pub signs had been dragged down and added to the barricade – The Duke of York, The Queen Victoria, The King's Head – like a line of the nation's own family photographs, gazing wanly out from a nest of timber and masonry. Figures darted from behind the rampart into nearby shops and houses. Neighbours and other men had taken pickaxes to the road and were tearing up bricks and rubble to use as projectiles.

Their father was nowhere to be seen.

The megaphone came nearer, its harsh, metallic voice issuing the same bark, over and over.

'*Stay inside. Do not go out. Everything is under control.*'

'We should go back,' said Celia.

'No. We need to find him!'

Moving in zigzags, they dodged left and right, crouching to avoid the threat of missiles flying through the air, until the howl of a mortar sent the greengrocer's shopfront collapsing to one side, unleashing a glittering shower of glass, and just yards away a Morris Minor burst into a sheet of flame. Rose felt the boundaries of the known world collapsing around her.

They ran.

Two hours later, their father returned. He sat down in his usual chair by the fireplace and refused to speak a word.

★

The next day, Lord Halifax himself addressed the nation. As head of a unity government, Halifax had taken over in May from Neville Chamberlain, his elderly predecessor with his wing collar and scrawny chicken's neck. The gaunt, colourless Halifax may have reminded Rose of an old heron, but he had been savage in demoting troublesome voices like Winston Churchill, who found himself instantly sacked.

Was it fear, or merely fatigue, that haunted Halifax now? In leaden, patrician tones he explained how King George had called him to Buckingham Palace and reminded him that the royal family had German blood themselves. With Poland and mainland Europe gone, would it not make sense to make some kind of accommodation with the Germans? America was also in favour. The American ambassador, Joseph Kennedy, had urged the formation of an Alliance. The United States had no desire to intervene in an unnecessary war. The only alternative was for Britain to fight on alone with no food supplies, help, or contact with its empire.

'*Guided by God and the love of my country, I have authorized an Act of Emergency Powers,*' said Halifax. '*All future law-making will be under the auspices of a Protectorate.*'

Then silence fell, like dust after a bomb blast.

For a week, the radio waves were full of static while jams on all foreign stations and publications were put in place. Newspapers vanished from the racks, and no mail was delivered. Foreign travel was banned, and all letters passing in and out of the Protectorate were censored.

But there was no ignoring the arrests. Hospitals, schools

and holiday camps were commandeered as detention centres. The Tower of London reverted to its ancient status as a prison. Swathes of politicians, local councillors and public figures were detained while others were swiftly promoted. Those members of the ruling class who had forged valuable links with the regime by visiting Germany back in the 1930s and taking the trouble to form friendships with the leading figures were handsomely rewarded. Within days, Halifax was ousted and Oswald Mosley was named Prime Minister. King George, Queen Elizabeth and their two little princesses disappeared.

Rose and her family grew accustomed to the sight of canvas-covered trucks making their early morning round-ups in the streets as strangers, neighbours and friends were collected and detained. Shuffling rows of detainees were escorted by men on motorbikes and soldiers in steel helmets. Along terraces of bleak brick, curtains were lifted, then closed again. The authorities must have their reasons. The rule of law would prevail.

The Vanishing was even harder to ignore.

The authorities didn't call it the Vanishing. They used innocuous terms like 'exit', or 'evacuation', or 'relocation', but the Vanishing was how it came to be known.

Swiftly, over a period of months, men were conscripted. Thousands of males between the ages of seventeen and thirty-five were transported to workplaces on the mainland for Extended National Service. Women were assured that their menfolk would be in touch once destination details were finalized. They would be working in those provinces where labour demand was highest as part of the general relocation. And often they did write – short letters, devoid of detail, with occasional black pencil where words had been redacted.

Yet no bald abstraction could express the howls of high grief that accompanied their departure. Fresh-faced teenagers, no more than children, were marshalled at railway stations or collected by troop carriers at designated street corners. Wives and mothers stood wailing, like cows whose calves had been removed.

Rose's mother constantly gave thanks that she had no boys.

As the months went on, however, people decided to let bygones be bygones. *Let's not spend our lives looking backwards*, that was the refrain amongst the friends of Rose's parents. We're lucky to be in the Alliance. Look at France, look at Belgium. Look at anywhere else in Europe.

People began to call it the 'phoney Protectorate' and everyone assumed that things would pretty much carry on as normal.

'That's politics for you,' said the greengrocer, sliding potatoes into their mother's shopping basket. 'Ain't that what they say? Whoever takes over, Government's always in charge.'

Others pointed out that Canadians, Indians and Australians had always been content to accept a head of state who lived on the other side of the world, so why should Britain object? Political alliances were normal.

But Celia had been desolate as the world closed in. No holidays abroad, no wearing slacks, no make-up. No smoking in public places. No more education, because she was seventeen and university was now out of reach for females. No fun. As the realities of life in the Alliance dawned, she wept constantly, and the house resounded to her tempestuous cries and stamped-foot demands.

So it was all the more extraordinary just how well she had adapted.

CHAPTER SIX

Wednesday, 14th April

'You're tense.'

Martin's usually genial face was clouded and he was chain-smoking, yet even then, the stress barely dented his good looks. He was the kind of man who only grew more handsome as he aged. Though he had gained a few middle-aged pounds, his torso was muscled rather than plump, and everything about him exuded an animal vitality. He shunned the shaven crops of other senior men and grew his hair as luxuriantly as possible while keeping within the prescribed length. It was jet black, now lightened with flecks of grey, but the effect was only to make his naturally olive skin appear healthily tanned.

That evening, however, despite the soothing surroundings of the Savoy's River Room, with its mirrored, sugared-almond walls, pink and gold furnishings and crimson table lamps, Martin was drinking heavily and his cheeks had gained a faint alcoholic flush.

'Tense? Am I, *Liebling*? I suppose I am. Things are difficult.' He ran a hand through his hair and looked distractedly at the menu. 'Between ourselves, I was not only in Germany for family reasons.'

Rose stared down at her plate. It appalled her that Martin felt able to discuss his family openly with her, and she was horrified at herself for consorting with a married man. She had never dared tell him so, but she always shut down his attempts to discuss the inadequacies of Helga, or his hopes that he and Rose could soon be 'properly together'.

'Matter of fact, I was mainly in Wilhelmstrasse planning the Leader's visit.'

'But that's an Interior Ministry responsibility, isn't it? Nothing to do with Culture.'

'There are aspects that concern our department.'

'What aspects?'

He screwed his cigarette stub into the ashtray and immediately lit another.

'You know the Leader is obsessed with libraries?'

'I know he has the biggest library in the world.'

The Leader's Library in his home city of Linz was a vast neoclassical warehouse of dazzling Italian marble, modelled on the Great Library of Alexandria and known as the Eighth Wonder of the World. Informally, the fact that every surface was covered in marble cladding had earned it the nickname the Leader's Lavatory. It had taken thirteen years to build and boasted a collection transported from universities and institutions all over Europe. Protector Rosenberg himself had headed a task force from 1939 onwards amassing treasured works from Paris, Rome, Florence, Prague, Budapest and Vienna. All the major libraries of Europe had contributed their patrimony, and many prize pieces from Britain – the Lindisfarne Gospels, an early edition of the Tyndale Bible – were also on show. There, visitors could stare down at the Magna Carta, dense with the twirls and flecks of Latin calligraphy, sealed by the wax of seven-hundred-year-old bees, drawn up by the barons of England to curb the draconian power of a tyrannical leader. *No man can be imprisoned, outlawed or dispossessed except by judgement of his equals or the law of the land.*

Every British schoolchild studied photographs of the Leader's Library, even if travel restrictions meant that was as near as any of them would ever get.

'It's all he thinks about now. He spends all his spare time overseeing the re-shelving and reordering of his books and personally annotating texts. Books. More books. Always books. Reading. I don't know what he sees in it.'

Martin blew out his cheeks in puzzlement and drained another sip of Pouilly-Fumé.

'Anyhow, while he's here, he plans to make a tour of England's most celebrated libraries. He's singled out the British Museum Reading Room and the Bodleian in Oxford. The Wren Library in Cambridge and the Gladstone Library in York. I'm compiling the itinerary and you wouldn't believe the interest his office is taking. They're never off the phone. They're requesting daily updates. To be honest, I get the impression this library tour is the highlight of his trip. Perhaps the whole reason for it.'

'I thought the reason was the Coronation? That the King and Queen didn't want to be crowned unless the Leader could be there?'

It was touching and admirable, English citizens were told, that King Edward and Queen Wallis should have waited so long to be formally crowned.

Though Edward had abdicated the English throne in 1936, because of his insistence on marrying an American divorcée against the wishes of his bourgeois family, he returned keenly from exile in France once his brother George VI had been arrested and deposed.

For a tricky few months immediately after the Alliance was formed, the Protectorate had functioned without a royal family. With the nation deprived of its ancestral royals, the mood among the people had turned ugly, expressing itself in outbreaks of street fighting and petrol bombing. Every city in the land was riven by guerrilla attacks. Troops on the street were picked off by snipers hiding in the roofs of buildings. Train tracks were blown up and public buildings burned. Rumours abounded of possible foreign intervention. All that ended when Edward and Wallis were installed in Buckingham Palace, and a cheering crowd was marshalled along the Mall to salute the return of the House of Windsor.

Martin downed his fourth glass of the evening and

signalled to the Gretl for another. A red-headed girl of about eighteen hurried over and removed the bottle from the ice bucket, but when she tried to pour the drink, her hand trembled and she spilled a little on the tablecloth.

He slammed his fist on the table.

'For Christ's sake, girl!'

He must be stressed. Although his status intimidated people, Martin normally behaved with impeccable decorum, even to the lowest castes. The little Gretl, flustered, made the mistake of looking at Rose in appeal. That was a transgression. Lower caste women were forbidden to make eye contact, and it was enough to make Martin snap.

'Lower your gaze and keep your eyes on your work!'

Rose frowned and glanced around, monitoring the neighbouring tables. The drink was affecting Martin and restaurants were notoriously risky places to talk. Not only were many staff on the Security Service payroll, but occasionally the tables themselves were fitted with concealed microphones. As the band lurched into a mournful rendition of Perry Como's 'No Other Love', Martin flinched.

'Where do they learn this stuff? The office lift?'

It was never sensible to talk in public, but the quality of the band, coupled with the fact that it was a week night, meant the place was sparsely attended. Rose judged that they were safe.

'I've always wondered why the Leader hasn't come here before,' she said. 'I mean, it's been thirteen years since the Alliance was formed and he's never visited England.'

'He's like that,' said Martin shortly. 'He was enchanted by Paris before we took it. He possessed a gigantic scale model of the city and he would spend hours discussing it with his architect, Speer. What he would do with the place. What he would build. Then the country was taken, and do you know how many times he visited?'

Rose shook her head.

'Once. Just once. In 1940. And he stayed sixteen hours. Long enough to visit the opera house and the Eiffel Tower. He said he'd seen everything he needed. It was all inside his head.'

The Leader was unusual in this respect. Most of the other VIPs of the regime had taken to Britain with relish. Von Ribbentrop, who had always admired the rocky cliffs of the Cornish seaside, had built a mansion there, and co-opted thousands of acres for his personal domain. Goebbels had taken Apsley House, the former abode of the Dukes of Wellington, for his London home, along with Cliveden, a magnificent Berkshire estate he had appropriated from the Astor family. Rudolf Hess had a place in the Scottish Highlands.

'So how's the planning going? For the Coronation?'

He sighed.

'Not good. The Leader's in fair shape, of course, but he's sixty-four and he tires easily . . .'

He paused as a replacement Gretl approached and slid a plate of steaming salmon *en croute* and green beans before him. Then he leaned closer.

'And there's another problem . . .'

Martin hesitated, almost as if he didn't trust Rose with the knowledge. She noticed that his nails, rubbing against the material of his napkin, were bitten to the quick.

'As if we didn't have enough to contend with, some charlatan astrologer has told him his life's in danger.'

'His *life*?' Rose hesitated as a raucous group of uniformed officers with a selection of young Gelis passed by, no doubt on their way to a nightclub. Each young man, with a buzz cut and a wide, impeccable smile, had a girl hanging on his arm. 'You're not serious?'

'Unfortunately. I can't imagine how these people are allowed to operate. I assume they're being controlled by Himmler. They feed the Leader messages and he swallows it hook, line and sinker.'

'Surely he isn't that easily deceived?'

'He believes these people, and they know it. If I had my way, all psychics and mystics would be shot at dawn.'

'Don't let the people in the Astrology Office hear you say that.'

'Oh, the Protector encourages that nonsense for good reason. It relaxes people, thinking things are predetermined . . .'

Martin forked a mouthful of salmon into his mouth and chewed it joylessly.

'Anyway, the upshot is, the whole thing has thrown a huge spanner in the works.'

'Why should it?'

'The Leader's as jumpy as hell. As if things weren't complicated enough with the parade, there's talk of it being cancelled.'

'Cancel the parade! They can't do that. Everyone's dying to see him. There are people camping out on the route already and it's two weeks away.'

'You think I don't know? Originally the plan was that he should ride in the golden state carriage instead of the King and Queen, but now he won't hear of it. The official message is that the Leader despises that kind of pomp and prefers a modest Mercedes. In reality, he's put his foot down. He says he couldn't possibly ride in the carriage.'

'Because he's not royal?'

'Because it's not armoured. He's never forgotten what happened to Heydrich.'

When he was Protector of Bohemia in 1942, Reinhard Heydrich had insisted on making his regular drive to work through Prague in an open-topped car. Czech assassins had taken advantage of this carelessness by concealing themselves en route and throwing a grenade. Heydrich died of his injuries. The Leader's retaliation was to raze the assassins' home village of Lidice, killing every male and sending the women and children to camps. But the after-effects lingered. Always unpredictable, the Leader became more nervous than ever, prone to last-minute prevarications that drove his security detail mad.

Martin lowered his voice, even though the band had moved on to the third of three tunes in their repertoire, a syrupy rendition of 'When I Fall in Love' that more than drowned out their conversation.

'The plan is, the Leader spends the night before in his official residence at Blenheim Palace. He chose that place because it's the birthplace of that old loudmouth Winston Churchill – remember him?'

She tensed. 'Faintly. A politician, wasn't he?'

'Sure. The less said about him the better. Anyway, the Leader's only ever seen it on postcards, so they're pulling out all the stops. The place needs to live up to everything he's imagined, down to the last detail. Swans in the lake, golden cutlery, the works. Then, in the morning, he and his entourage head to London. But frankly, the whole thing's turning out to be the biggest security headache since the Protectorate was formed.'

Unbidden, a flash of images ran through Rose's brain of the Time of Resistance. The bombings and street fighting. Shots ringing out at night and arrests at dawn. People corralled into vans, arms raised, disappearing to God knows where.

A dessert trolley approached, but Martin waved it away.

'We've had enough. Unless you . . . ?'

'No, it's fine.' Rose shook her head, salivating at the glistening confections as they sailed off to the next table. She had a sweet tooth and loved puddings, but with so little sugar and fat available, the cakes on offer to most citizens were hard and dry. The only ones to be found in bakeries were rock cakes, as tasteless as a piece of rubble in the mouth. The Savoy's patisseries, by contrast, were flown in from Paris and oozed with fresh cream, sugar and fruit.

'Actually' – Martin folded some notes and placed them under a saucer, then drew back his chair – 'I think I'd prefer to continue this conversation elsewhere.'

He led the way out of the back entrance of the hotel, causing the guards at the door to shudder into a hasty salute, and walked down towards the Thames.

The river was drowned in darkness, glinting liquid mercury where the water caught the light of the moon. Crossing Westminster Bridge the previous evening, Rose had seen a white, spread-eagled shape and her heart had lifted, thinking it was a swan, but it was only a corpse, bobbing in the water's muddy flow. Tonight, though, it was an empty, fathomless drift.

When they reached a gap between two pools of street light, Martin stopped, leaned back against the granite balustrade of the river, and passed his hands across his face as if he could rub out all the strain and fatigue written there. The momentary humour vanished and beneath the tight, silver-buttoned jacket his muscular frame seemed to sag.

'The fact is, those psychics I mentioned might be on to something.'

'The fortune tellers? I thought you said they were charlatans.'

'They are. But truth be told, we *have* heard rumours of an assassination plot. No idea where it's coming from. The army's on red alert for a terrorist attack. The Gestapo and the police are working overtime. You've seen the threat status has been raised?'

A board in every ministry lobby announced the alert level from terrorist attacks. Green meant no danger, and Rose had never seen it green.

'So let them. There's no need for you to be stressed. It's not your affair.'

He sighed. 'You're right. It's not. I can't spend my life thinking about the future. Unless, it's my future with you.'

He reached out and drew her into his arms. She breathed in a gust of the familiar metallic cologne he wore that always reminded her of belt buckles and guns.

'Come here. I've missed you.'

Normally, Rose relaxed into his embrace, but that night she stiffened at his touch. Perhaps it was the thought that just a few hours ago Martin had been playing with his children and maybe making love to his wife, the unwitting Helga. Or perhaps it was due to the deep resistance that had been building inside her for some months now, rising to a tide of self-hatred when she saw the gleam in her sister's eye, or heard Oliver Ellis's sardonic mention of *friends in high places*.

She had to brace herself not to recoil as Martin bent to nuzzle her neck and ran a hungry hand down the curves of her dress.

'Out there in Berlin, you were the only thing I was thinking of. What were you up to while I was away?'

'Nothing. Work.'

She had been correcting a version of Jane Austen's *Emma*.

It was a useful text for schoolchildren because of a plotline in the story where Emma attempted to matchmake her low-born friend Harriet Smith with a man above her social status. The matchmaking ended badly and the message was that women like Harriet Smith should not dream of marriage beyond their caste. Yet the way Jane Austen had written it, the effect of the lesson was nuanced. Harriet gained self-confidence through her mistaken romance. She came to understand that a high social class did not necessarily imply a finer character. Indeed, Jane Austen seemed hell-bent on undermining traditional class divisions and suggesting some difference between mere accomplishments and the deeper understanding that signals self-knowledge.

It was going to take a lot more clarity and editing to be suitable for sixteen-year-olds.

'We're impressed with your dedication, you know. You're the star of the Correction team. Everyone admired what you did with *Wuthering Heights*.'

Emily Brontë's masterpiece had nearly defeated Rose. It was degenerate on so many levels with the matching of its dark-skinned, low-status hero, Heathcliff, and the outspoken, aggressive, unconventional heroine, Catherine Earnshaw. Eventually, Rose had been obliged to correct Heathcliff's skin colour and background, Aryanize his status, and tone down Catherine's more outspoken assertions. Yet it remained a troubling text, one that sat badly with the Protector's idea of romance as a union between a man and a woman of correct caste and race.

'Thank you.'

'Is that all? You seem quiet, darling. Were you pining for me?'

Rose wanted to share her worry about her father, but she knew Celia was right. Any suspicion of madness in the family was dangerous. Telling anyone was risky. Even Martin. Perhaps especially Martin.

'I saw my niece. My sister's worried that if I read to her, I might expand her vocabulary.'

He laughed shortly. 'Then don't. You know the Party believes there's no shame in illiteracy. We discourage reading for lower orders. It's hardly revolutionary. American slaves weren't permitted to read. For centuries Catholics held the mass in Latin. Besides, most people don't actually *want* to read. They'd rather listen to the wireless or go to the movies. Once this new television gets off the ground, reading will wither away in a generation, you'll see. People will fall out of the habit, and once that happens, the mere act of reading will be harder.'

Rose knew what he meant. It had been hard for her. To someone unaccustomed to them, the long, archaic rhythms of Victorian literature were tricky to grasp. It required dis-cipline to summon the sustained concentration necessary for novels that often ran to six or even seven hundred pages. In a way, her correction work was almost superfluous. No doubt Martin was right, and reading would soon become a specialized interest, like Sanskrit, or Ancient Greek, with no relevance to everyday life.

But while anyone in the Alliance was still interested in literature, she had a job, and with a perfectionist like Protector Rosenberg in charge, she needed to get it right.

'Is that all that's bothering you?'

Rose looked up the river towards the darkened neo-Gothic shell of the House of Commons, the mother of parliaments and the ancestral home of English democracy. Or as the Protector had recently described it, 'Disneyland'.

'No.' She braced her shoulders. 'The Commissioner has asked to see me.'

'I heard.'

Rose jolted out of his arms and scrutinized him anxiously.

'You *knew*! And you didn't tell me!'

'He mentioned it last week.'

'What does he want?'

'I don't know.'

'You must know something! You're his deputy.'

'Honestly, darling? I've no idea.'

He reached out to her mouth and rubbed the lipstick roughly off with his thumb.

'But I'll tell you one thing. If you don't want to be sent to a re-education centre with a recommendation for hard labour, don't go into Eckberg's office with a faceful of cosmetics.'

CHAPTER SEVEN

Thursday, 15th April

Since the restriction of religion, there was only one place to which the populace reliably turned for consolation, contemplation, relaxation and human companionship.

The cinema.

It wasn't only human warmth the citizens craved. The general lack of heating meant people welcomed any opportunity to huddle together in an enclosed space, and the chance to forget their vicissitudes with a couple of hours' laughing and dreaming. Technically, escapism was frowned on, because who would want to escape the Alliance paradise? But paying tribute to the gods and goddesses of the cinema was an acceptable diversion, providing that those deities were politically correct, in private as well as on screen. In the old days, before the Alliance, film stars were the staple of every women's magazine, and so it continued, though now a different breed of film star, like Hans Albers, Kristina Söderbaum, Zarah Leander or Lilian Harvey, was available for worship. And if the cinema was the new church, then the Odeon, Leicester Square, was its veritable cathedral: a vast, plush art deco temple of black polished granite and blue neon, smelling of wet tweed and stale cigarette smoke.

Rose, Helena and their friend Bridget Fanshaw from the Press department were ensconced in the elite section, separated by a crimson velvet rope from the seats reserved for lower orders. For a decade after the Protectorate was established, all places of entertainment had been barred for lower caste women, just as they had for Jews and other underclasses on the mainland. Recently, however, the regime had decided that the cinema was a useful conduit of propaganda and for certain categories the banning order was relaxed. Magdas and Gretls predictably flocked to the cinemas, where a steady diet of romantic comedy and thrillers were specifically designed to distract them from their ongoing privations. Spy thrillers in particular were hugely popular. In a nation rife with paranoia, where every action was circumspect and no neighbour could be trusted, the idea that spies lurked at every turn was actively encouraged by the authorities. It helped to keep the populace watchful and alert – that was the Ministry thinking – and the idea of a faceless enemy deflected criticism of the regime.

As the lights went down, the newsreel began. The news always came before the feature, and while the words changed, the theme was always the same – great strides had been made in international friendship treaties. Record harvests were seen, record productivity, record scientific achievements. Generally, cinema-goers let this information flow over them in a soothing tide of white noise. No one chatted – they wouldn't dare – and everyone knew that watchers were placed in the auditorium to report any disrespectful or dissenting view, but nor did anyone pay the slightest regard. The women – because it was mainly women – occupied themselves with lighting up cheap cigarettes, kicking off their shoes and relaxing their aching shoulders against the worn plush of the seats.

That evening, however, the newsreel opened with a genuine news story – the funeral of Joseph Stalin, who had died the previous month. The event took place in Moscow's Red Square. Hundreds of troops lined the route as a team of black horses carried the hearse, draped with a Soviet flag, followed by wreaths the size of cartwheels. Solemn music played as the cortège progressed to the mausoleum where the mummified corpse of Lenin, in waxen solitude, awaited him.

At one point the camera panned upwards to where a line of dignitaries could be seen on a balcony above Red Square, muffled against the cold, surveying the melancholy scene. In pride of place was the Leader, his face noticeably pasty, even in monochrome, hunched and insipid, clutching the rail in front of him to disguise a trembling hand.

Helena gave her a nudge.

'Looks like something off a fish slab, doesn't he?'

'For God's sake. Careful.'

'Don't worry. No one's listening.'

Despite herself, Rose could not help shooting a quick glance around her. The seats for the lower orders were packed but the elite section was largely empty. Helena continued, unabashed.

'He's half dead. It should be him in the coffin. Wonder if all those people queuing for the Coronation parade will even recognize him.'

She had a point. In the early days of the Alliance there had been no end of newsreels of the Leader, hair flopping over his forehead, glistening with sweat, chopping the air with an angry hand as his voice rose. His image was seared on every retina. Yet in recent years he had cut a diminished figure, pasty-faced, shuddering, shrunk inside his clothes as though afflicted with a wasting disease. The camera no longer focused tightly on him, and he was filmed only in long shot, conferring with world leaders or meeting children as he strolled on Alpine paths.

Beneath them, through the soft fug of smoke, the lower castes watched attentively. Because it was illegal to listen to unauthorized radio stations, or to meet foreigners or read any publication that had not been previously censored, no one in the Alliance had much idea of life beyond their shores. Newsreels were the main source of information, and very dull they were too. Yet that evening's film was no propaganda melange about increasing steel production or advances in the African colonies. This was a glimpse of the exotic. Foreign travel was forbidden for the population – a Strength Through Joy trip to the Lake District was the most anyone could hope for – so the imposing beauty of St Basil's Cathedral, and the panoramic expanses of Red Square, were a glimpse of something miraculous, beyond imagining.

'*In spite of the death of our esteemed ally, friendship between the Soviet Union and the Alliance remains as firm as ever,*' proclaimed the announcer. '*As a mark of our continuing co-operation, Soviet troops will be deployed to fortify positions on the Asian front.*'

The BBC logo flashed up, and finally the movie began, a tepid romance from the state-controlled UFA studio starring an elderly Kristina Söderbaum and Emil Jannings. But even as it cranked into action, Rose's attention remained fixed on the newsreel. With international news heavily censored, and most foreign mail forbidden, this was the only conduit for piecing together an idea of lands beyond their shores. Even for those who tried, it was a pointillist endeavour, in which tiny scraps of information must be amassed to create an image of the outside world. What did the death of Stalin signify? What might happen to Poland, which Russia and Germany had carved up between them? Might the Russians now look to the Leader, as the rest of Europe had, so that Germany stretched even further, over the Russian steppes, bringing ever more people under the control of the Party?

And what about America, who, like Germany, possessed an atom bomb that kept an uneasy mutual détente?

★

When the credits eventually rolled, the three friends went out and stood for a while, sharing an illicit cigarette under cover of an umbrella. A thin drizzle was falling, and passers-by, their faces muffled with hats and scarves, emerged and disappeared like phantoms through the damp mist. The blinking neon of the billboards shivered in the puddles and the taste of soot hung in the air, penetrating everything.

'I assume you've seen that movie already?' said Bridget.

'Of course,' said Helena. 'I passed it. Hope you didn't notice anything bad.'

'Only the script and the acting.'

Helena grinned. 'I have no say over that. Otherwise I'd be banning every UFA movie I see.'

While Helena had, in terms of looks, been gifted all the blessings the gods could bestow, Bridget was far from the Nordic ideal. So much so, that even she openly wondered how she had managed to qualify as a Class I (a) female, and put it down to the fact that her father was a minor aristocrat who from the 1930s onwards had favoured an Alliance and had reaped the benefits in the form of a senior position in the Government hierarchy. She had an angular face, gold batwing spectacles and a spiky personality to match. Her hair, which coiled and sprang naturally out-wards unless it was tamed, was beginning to frazzle in the moist air.

She smiled and plucked at Rose's sleeve.

'Why don't you come for a cocktail at the Café de Paris? Some girls from the Press department will be there. Then

x

we're going on to the 400 Club. Snakehips Johnson is playing.'

Even if no one was permitted to travel to America, American music was wildly popular, so long as it stayed within prescribed limits and avoided swing rhythms or jazz.

'And we are dressed up, after all.'

She wriggled her hips in her new swing skirt, patterned with birds on a sky-blue background.

'Thanks, but no.'

'Might be some nice men,' coaxed Helena. Although she herself was still single, Helena was protected from the scrutiny of the Family Promotion department by an arrangement with a senior man in Radio Censorship. Rolf Friedel had a face that looked as though God had given up, and his conversation dwelled heavily on wireless frequencies and signals technology, but he left Helena largely to her own devices, requiring her attention no more than one night a week.

'Except they're all British at the 400 and that usually means trouble.'

It was not only the absence of so many men on Extended National Service that left the women of the Alliance forlorn. It was as though those native men who remained had been bled of their masculinity. Defeated, and unable to protect their homeland, their bitterness was all too often ignited by alcohol. Plenty of men were prepared to risk prison for the chance to unleash their anger and abuse, and women out in public often found themselves the targets.

'Sorry, I can't,' said Rose.

'She thinks Martin would disapprove,' laughed Bridget.

Martin would. He disliked Helena and Bridget, dismissing them as 'not good enough' for her. *They're shallow, Rose, and vain. I'm amazed they have Ministry jobs. They have no proper allegiance to the Alliance.*

'Actually, I need an early night. The Commissioner wants to see me first thing tomorrow. As soon as he gets back.'

She could tell by the way her friends started that they had no idea.

'God, Rose.' Helena reached out a hand and touched her arm. 'What's all that about? What's so urgent?'

Rose smiled numbly.

'No idea. But if you don't see me again . . .'

Vehemently, Bridget shook her head.

'Don't be dramatic! It's a promotion, I bet.'

'Someone has said something,' muttered Rose.

Helena squeezed her hand harder, worry wrinkling her flawless brow.

'You know not to trust anyone, don't you?'

'Of course, I know that.'

'What could they possibly say?' demanded Bridget.

'Nothing.' Helena turned on her fiercely. 'As if that mattered!'

Bridget summoned a bright smile. 'My guess is, the Commissioner wants to take Rose out for a drink. He's a randy old goat, I've heard. I just hope Martin doesn't find out.'

Rose didn't bother to correct her, but instead kissed her

friends and made her way back through Leicester Square to the tube.

As she threaded her way through the crowd, the wail of sirens rang through the air. Sirens were everywhere now – on lamp posts, on the corners of buildings, attached to apartment buildings and redundant church towers – and mostly, no one took the slightest notice. When they sounded, people registered the volume, calculated the distance, and like a bomb dropping from the sky, thanked God it was not coming for them.

This siren, however, was accompanied by a commotion just a few yards away, at the northern corner of Leicester Square. From where she stood, Rose could make out barely anything more than the screech of wheels, followed by the clatter of police boots and the sound of doors thumping. Then, a sudden, sharp crack of gunshot sliced the air.

The pedestrians around her flinched and fanned away, like a flock of pigeons dispersed by a stone. A man in the uniform of a senior officer approached rapidly, parting the crowd like a knife, and from a doorway emerged a huddled figure slumped between two policemen, hands cuffed, before he was bundled into a van.

Rose recalled what Helena had told her about the incident at the Rosenberg Institute a few days earlier.

I heard it was, you know . . . one of Them.

Back in the Time of Resistance, street clashes had been a constant feature of city life, yet, as the years passed, they were replaced by a pattern of chronic, low-grade, sporadic disruption: isolated incidents of terrorism, chiefly shootings and grenade attacks on Alliance buildings. Stones through windows and train derailments. At one point a bomb was detonated under a London bridge. Nobody discussed these incidents. Nobody wanted to know. If they had to be mentioned, due to transport or traffic disruption, the perpetrators were referred to only as 'Them'.

Them. The grit in the Protectorate's jackboot. As invisible as antimatter in the Alliance's smooth universe. They merited no name but a pronoun.

Who were they? Was this man one of them? Normally, these questions would not detain Rose for an instant, and she knew there was only one reason for her anxiety now.

Her appointment with the Commissioner.

It was not about a promotion. And nothing Hermann Eckberg asked her would be as genial as her choice of drink. In her bones Rose knew that the summons meant only one thing. Someone, somewhere, had informed.

Life in the Alliance was a process of continual observation. Universal Surveillance, it was called. Eyes followed you everywhere, seen and unseen. In offices, cafés, stations, hotels and shops, an array of unofficial watchers noted every detail: what cigarettes a person smoked, which magazines they bought and what drinks they ordered. Watchers reported on their own family and friends for a vast range of infringements. Infidelity. Religiosity. Use of make-up. Sex outside of caste. Joking. Writing. It was almost impossible to keep to all the rules.

Overseeing the whole system was the Alliance Security Office, which dealt with all types of espionage, terrorism, subversion and insurgency. The ASO was famed as the best in Europe, more efficient even than the one established in the 1930s in Berlin, and its chief officer, Ernst Kaltenbrunner, had been installed when the Alliance was formed. Kaltenbrunner, a thin-lipped Austrian with a long, brutal face and a scar that lifted his mouth to a perpetual snarl, had risen up the ranks in Austria, where he ran the SS and assisted in the annexation of the country, before moving over to Berlin and, in a dazzling ascendancy, rising to Security Chief. It was said that his favourite place was still the interrogation cell.

Universal Surveillance was Kaltenbrunner's creation and his genius. It made some citizens edgy, but most shrugged off surveillance like weather, a natural phenomenon no more or less ubiquitous than rain.

Rose was about to hasten down the steps of the underground when a voice floated from behind.

'Enjoy the film?'

Out of the vapour emerged the figure of Oliver Ellis. He was wearing a trench coat with an upturned collar and a hat tilted down over his face, and in the harsh light of the tube station his blanched features reminded her of some ancient Athenian bust from a museum gallery.

He was as cool as marble, too. As ever, he was alone.

There was always, if not loneliness, then a suggestion of solitude about Oliver Ellis. If you thought about it, which Rose didn't, he was something of an enigma. Few enough young men of marriageable age remained in England, so how come he was still single? He was good-looking enough to draw the glances of women in the office, yet he always deflected their interest. Bridget Fanshaw had spent many months flirting energetically with Oliver, to no avail.

'Not wasting any more time on him,' she had vowed. 'He's obviously not interested in women.'

Could that be true? Was Oliver Ellis one of those men whose desires could get them locked up?

Now, she forced a smile onto her face.

'I thought it was a lovely story. Very touching.'

'Really?' His eyes seemed to dance with suppressed amusement, as though he was trying not to laugh, and as usual, she got the impression he was laughing at her. 'I thought it was a disgraceful mishmash of anodyne schmaltz that sounded like it had been translated from Chinese.'

'Kristina Söderbaum's always good,' said Rose automatically. The film had melted from her mind like the candyfloss she remembered from childhood, the kind that vanished in seconds leaving only a sickly-sweet residue.

'What did you make of the newsreel? Stalin's funeral?'

She gave a slight shrug, concealing her astonishment.

Nobody ever discussed international events in the street. She wondered if he was drunk.

'I wasn't watching actually. Too busy chatting.'

'Ah. So you went with Helena Bishop.'

'She was checking the film for anything politically offensive.'

A grin flitted across Oliver's lean, sardonic face.

'Don't think she needs to worry about that. Aesthetically offensive, certainly. And not suitable for anyone under twenty-one.'

'You think?'

'Not suitable for anyone over twenty-one either.'

Rose laughed guardedly. Oliver's flippancy made her cautious, even though Helena was just as irreverent, and she was one of the Ministry's rising stars.

'Did you see the kerfuffle?' he asked. 'Over in the square? The police?'

The drizzle had lent an unexpected intimacy to their encounter, bringing them close and muffling their senses. Rose glanced from side to side. The 'Alliance Look', it was called. A gesture familiar to every citizen who made conversation in a public place, as automatic as breathing.

'I must have missed it. Too busy avoiding the rain.'

Why had she not noticed him in the cinema? The elite section was only thinly populated, and a man of Oliver's height was not hard to make out.

'Looks like they arrested another one.'

Pointedly, Rose checked her watch.

'Are you going home on the tube?' he asked.

She toyed with saying no, in case he was too, but she realized she had no idea where he lived. The southwest of the capital, she vaguely believed. Obviously, it would be an elite area. Knightsbridge perhaps?

Sensing her hesitation, he added, 'I'm walking. I need the exercise. See you in the morning, I suppose.'

Turning on his heel, he vanished abruptly into the misty air.

When Rose reached her block, she entered the hall as silently as possible and crept up the stairs. It was late, but judging by the trace of cigarette smoke and mothballs that lingered on the landing, the occupant of the next-door flat, Elsa Bottomley, had only recently returned. Elsa Bottomley was a squat Geli with hair dyed the colour of mahogany furniture, and a selection of shapeless wool skirts. She had a husband who worked abroad, a wall-eyed son in the Alliance armed services who came and went, and a job in the Transport Ministry. Maybe it was her work with timetables and punctuality that made Elsa so particularly attuned to the tiniest details of Rose's routine. 'Not late for work, I hope!' she would observe, as they passed in the hall. Or in the evening, eyes flickering across Rose's dress or shoes, 'Going out again, Miss Ransom? I'm sure I'd be exhausted with all the socializing you do. I don't know how you manage it!' When Rose was editing the Grimms' fairy tales, she had come across descriptions of witches with hearing as keen as animals and the image of Elsa Bottomley's suspicious, twitching face had sprung irresistibly to mind.

Shutting her door, she stood still and assessed the quality of the silence. Filtering out the distant rumble of the street outside, she could hear only the occasional creak of timber that was to be expected in a tall, Bloomsbury terrace, and the flap of slippers on floorboards, followed by the metallic clink of a teaspoon stirring late-night tea that signalled Elsa Bottomley's ironclad routine. Still motionless, Rose surveyed the furniture around her minutely, as though it had been moved in her absence. She had started doing this occasionally when she returned, though she had no idea why. Habit, she supposed.

Going over to the sink, where her breakfast teacup stood upended, she touched the kettle. Then, moving across to the table, she checked that its leg still covered the same knot of wood in the floorboard, before shifting her bed from the wall, removing the flap of green wallpaper and reaching into the cavity where she kept her notebooks.

The current notebook was made of thin, cheap paper that tore easily. Paper was increasingly scarce in the Alliance, and it had lately been announced that newspapers would be reduced in size to account for the shortage. Nobody in the Ministry could decide if this was an attempt by the authorities to reduce the flow of information, or a genuine reaction to the fact that increasing quantities of raw materials were diverted to the mainland. Yet the notebook was good enough for its purpose. Rose had a fresh story in mind and was keen to get the outline down, so she settled herself at her table, lit the lamp, and stared down at the treetops in the darkened square.

Normally, the act of writing was an immediate salve. It created a distance between the hurry of her day and the stillness of her mind. It seemed the antidote to everything: magical in its ability to transport her to different worlds and surround her with other beings whose lives and loves she had conjured from her own mysterious depths.

Yet now, bent in the pool of light, pen in hand, the encounter with Oliver Ellis refused to dissipate.

There was no avoiding it. Something about him troubled her.

It had started at work — not only in the office, but in the canteen, in the pub after work, and at official functions. Although Oliver's job concerned the correction of history, rather than literature, they both had privileged access to the same library stacks of degenerate texts, and often, when she looked up from browsing the shelves, she noticed Oliver Ellis close by.

She sifted through her memories of the recent past, panning for glimpses of the inscrutable, bespectacled face and the brush of dark hair that he never oiled properly out of his eyes. Unlike some of the other men in the Ministry, who wore patterned braces and brightly coloured ties to signify the cultured nature of their employment, Oliver's grey suits were nondescript, as though he went out of his way to avoid attracting attention. He seemed to possess the ability to merge into any crowd, and in every crowd she could think of, there he was. Whether at departmental staff meetings, or gatherings in the pub, his enigmatic figure was never far away. Was that because he enjoyed the company? Or was it, as everyone said, because he was ambitious? Martin himself had commented that Oliver Ellis was 'going places' and everyone knew his work was highly thought of. As she pondered, another recollection rose to the surface of her mind: a moment during the recent reorganization of the office, when the Correction team had moved to a new floor and Oliver Ellis had arrived at the adjacent desk. The tight, compressed smile he gave her as he arranged his pens and files. Did he ask to be seated right next to her, or had he been ordered? Was he, in fact, a watcher?

Someone, after all, had informed the office of her minute infractions of behaviour. She had received an official reprimand for wearing lipstick to work – an old tube of Max Factor Sweet Cherry that had belonged to her mother. Someone had reported the joke she told about the Alliance's ideal man: 'He's as slender as the Commissioner, as handsome as the Protector, as blond as the Leader.'

Yet even as the thought arose, she dismissed it. Oliver Ellis probably *was* a watcher. After all, every office worker was encouraged to spy on their colleagues as part of the job. But as she had told Bridget and Helena, there was nothing much about her that anyone could discover.

The slam of a door outside and the tramp of feet on the

pavement distracted her. She was tired, and the least she could do to prepare for the next day's meeting with the Commissioner was to try to get some sleep. She shut the notebook and put it away.

Hannah's new story would have to wait.

CHAPTER EIGHT

Friday, 16th April

He was on the phone when she entered. A conversation consisting of short, impatient barks. '*Ja . . . Ja . . . Jawohl.*'

A few moments later he replaced the receiver with an aggressive sniff and turned to face her.

The Commissioner of All Culture in the Anglo-Saxon Alliance had the girth to match his inflated title. In another life he might have been a butcher heaving sides of ham and splintering bones with a thwack of his meaty forearm. He had a shiny bald pate, with strands of ginger connecting the distant outposts of scrub on either side and a roll of flesh bulging over his collar. He spoke solely in German. In thirteen years he had not bothered to learn more than a couple of English words, the chief one being 'fuck'.

'*Fräulein Ransom. Komm.*'

There followed no invitation to sit down, so she

straightened her shoulders attentively. She had barely slept. Her face was as scrubbed as a kitchen floor and she had chosen her dullest, most conservative worsted suit for the occasion, a plain blouse underneath and no jewellery. If the Commissioner noticed, however, he wasn't showing it. He continued to sift through a series of papers on his desk, occasionally tossing one aside like a bad hand of cards.

Rose glanced around her. The walls were free of Old Masters because Eckberg was proudly ignorant, rejecting most culture as pretentious claptrap and liable to take against anyone purely on the grounds that they liked music or sculpture. God forbid that any of his subordinates nursed an enthusiasm for theatre. The sole decorations were a photograph of himself, looking absurd in lederhosen, and one of his family *Schloss*, a turreted monstrosity in Bavaria, hanging above the desk as if a mocking reminder of where he would rather be.

After a short pause, the bloodshot eyes swivelled towards her and he uttered a single word.

'Kreuz.'

So she was right. Her stomach lurched. Knowledge of her relationship with Martin had reached the Commissioner's ears and she was here to face the music. How had she ever expected otherwise? Official penalties for adultery were harsh. Imprisonment. A camp. The rules were so widely flouted that people had grown complacent, but still the authorities could choose to invoke them at any moment.

Eckberg, however, was still speaking.

'Kreuz is much given to talking about you. He admires you, it's clear. What is also clear . . .' – here he allowed a pause to stretch, freighted with the knowledge that she was terrified of what he knew, and feared some retribution – 'is that you're a discreet woman. Able to keep your head down and your thoughts to yourself. You're of good family, I gather. You have a sister? And a niece?'

Rose understood. This was entry level procedure. A polite, seemingly courteous enquiry, disguised as small talk and designed to establish a vulnerability. Your family could always be used against you. Not even the most hardened dissident wanted to see their loved ones come to harm.

'She's called Hannah, sir,' Rose said, adding pointlessly, 'Six years old.'

Eckberg could not care less what age Hannah was. He couldn't care if she lived or died.

'Very nice, but forget all that. It's your discretion I'm interested in. I have a task for you. Somewhat beyond your usual remit. It's to do with vandalism.'

'Vandalism, sir?'

'That's what I said, isn't it? I hope your language is up to scratch, girl. Now, this vandalism has arisen in the past month. There have been sporadic outbreaks around the country. In fact, the call I just had was notification of another one. In London, this time. Come with me. I'll show you what I mean.'

Eckberg's car, a tank of a Mercedes that had once belonged to the traitor Goering and had been shipped over from the mainland after a departmental haggle, cruised through the streets with unchallenged ease. People tended to look away when a ministerial car passed and the dearth of petrol meant very few private cars were around, so it took no more than five minutes to make the short trip from Whitehall to Great Russell Street, where the Portland stone facade of the British Museum gleamed palely in the morning air.

Designed in Greek revival style, the nineteenth-century south entrance of the museum celebrated the civilization of man, and from its pediment the muses of science, geometry, architecture, drama, music and poetry had for a hundred years gazed impassively down, inspiring those who passed beneath to cherish the highest ideals that mankind could attain.

Now, between the monumental ionic columns, arc lights had been strung, lending a theatrical air to the scene, as though it was the set of a UFA movie, and a gaggle of workmen in heavy duty clothes moved around the portico industriously, wielding hoses, nozzles and plastic piping.

Across the top of the pediment in violent red paint a single sentence stretched.

Strengthen the female mind by enlarging it and there will be an end to blind obedience

A shiver ran through Rose. It was the kind of electric thrill that she could not explain, as though something deep within her had momentarily stirred. As though the words had reached inside and kindled there, as hot and as urgent as flames.

'Who was it?'

Beside her, Eckberg snorted.

'That's what we're trying to find out.'

'I mean, who wrote it, sir? Who wrote those words originally?'

'Christ. What kind of question is that? Nobody. A woman called Mary Wollstonecraft.'

Woll Stone Craft. Rose repeated the name silently, letting the syllables sink deep into her brain.

'Dead,' he added. 'And if she wasn't, she would be.'

'How did it get there?'

'The vandals climbed up last night apparently. Using ropes. I'll be using ropes on them when we catch them. I'll hang them here, right in front of their pathetic stunt.'

She didn't doubt it. A shudder at the forthcoming atrocity seemed to carry up through the soles of Rose's feet, but Eckberg was already on the move, the exertion of mounting the museum steps causing his breath to come in laboured, asthmatic grunts.

'This has cropped up in different areas of the country over the past few weeks. At first, we took them for unrelated incidents, but now our esteemed Gestapo chief has concluded that they're linked. A co-ordinated insurgency pattern, he called it. It could be a co-ordinated fucking knitting pattern for all I care. I wouldn't give a fuck if it wasn't my Ministry being targeted.'

'Culture, sir?'

A frown creased Eckberg's meaty brow, as though the very word made him want to reach for his gun.

'Unfortunately. Every incident has taken place in or near a library.'

Rose stared, astonished.

'This used to be a library, apparently. The Jew Marx wrote *Das Kapital* here. That should have been enough to qualify it for demolition.'

'And it's just graffiti?'

That was a mistake. Eckberg cast her a vicious look.

'Graffiti not enough for you? Did you want something more? Well, sometimes they scribble inside too. On corridor walls.'

'What do they scribble?'

'Rubbish. Degenerate rubbish.'

The foreman of the building squad approached unctuously, fingers twisting in apologetic knots. While Eckberg delivered a bad-tempered harangue, Rose watched the sentence being erased with a chemical wash, the letters bleeding pinkly down the stone. There were no other onlookers. The roads around the museum had been closed off with police tape to prevent the offending words being seen more widely and in a matter of minutes, it would be as though they had never been written.

Woll Stone Craft.

Eckberg strode back towards her, scowling, brushing past the parts of the courtyard that had been roped off in order that policemen on their hands and knees could grub for microscopic fragments in the cobbles.

'Useless. They have no leads. And each time they erase

one, another crops up. They're throwing soldiers and police at it but they've got no trace of the perpetrators, and guess who'll get the blame if this kind of embarrassment occurs during the Leader's visit.'

He cast a morose glance upwards, as if God himself had a personal hand in his vexation, then seemed to pull himself together.

'Only theory they have is, the culprits are coming from Widowland.'

Into her mind came the run-down, decrepit streets, the desolate fringes of towns inhabited by the Friedas. Useless old women fit only for cleaning or factory work. The lowest of the low.

'The Friedas are known to be keen on reading. We regularly lock them up for flouting every goddamn regulation that exists regarding literature. You know the rule – books may not be discussed by groups of more than three, except under regulated conditions. We've picked plenty of them off for that. Not to mention discussion of subversive texts. If this is where it's coming from, it makes sense. Trouble is, the Gestapo have already gone in hard but they've found nothing, despite their most persuasive methods.'

Eckberg ran a finger around his collar. Even at this time in the morning it was damp with sweat.

'The fact is, these old Friedas fear nothing. And without husbands or children, it's hard to get a lever on them. They're difficult to crack.' He scratched the place where an angry shaving rash was spreading across his neck, as though his personality was erupting from within in physical form. 'That's where you come in.'

Rose recoiled. Images flashed before her of an elderly woman in an interrogation cell, the policemen by turns persuasive and threatening, with the prospect of torture hanging always behind their dead smiles.

'Sir . . . ?'

Eckberg flattened a cigarette stub beneath his boot and spat on the ground for good measure.

'Listen, would you. I have a plan. It's to do with the Protector's history. You know about that, of course.'

Everyone knew. Protector Rosenberg had for some years been toiling away on a vast history of England that would prove beyond doubt that the English and German nations stemmed from the same blood and bone. Geographers, biologists, historians, anthropologists and even fairy tale experts had been roped into the venture, which had its very own office in London and a dedicated academic staff. The book was Rosenberg's private obsession and he was said to devote far more time to it than he spent administrating the Protectorate. Its central contention was that several centuries ago the two peoples had been one, until war and conquest took the Germanic tribes east, and the English receded to the safe boundaries of their small island. The most profound, motivating quest of Rosenberg's life was to discover the evidence that proved his theory.

'From what I know,' ventured Rose, 'the Protector believes that the nations of the Alliance—'

'I'm not asking what you know. I'm telling you what I want. The Protector needs some research done and he's asked me to send some of my people out to question citizens about their heritage, that sort of thing. Folklore. An insight into the ancestral traditions of this miserable country.'

They had reached the pavement where the Mercedes stood, engine idling. A chauffeur sprang out to open the door and Rose climbed reluctantly in after Eckberg, who was still speaking rapidly.

'So here's what's going to happen. You're going to go into the Widowlands posing as a researcher for the Protector's book. You will assemble a group of Friedas and question them about their lives, their experiences and their memories. Family traditions, local folklore, superstitions. Harmless stuff. Old women love gossiping about their pasts. It's all they have.'

He blew out his cheeks and cast a filthy glance at a milk cart whose horse had inconsiderately caused the Mercedes to slow down. A policeman on a motorcycle who had been escorting them sped towards the milkman and began shouting, but the horse gave only a languid, insolent flick of its tail.

Eckberg pivoted his bulk towards her with effort.

'The Leader arrives in exactly two weeks' time so I want your answers on my desk before then. Effectively, you're my spy. And you tell no one. That includes Kreuz. You report directly to me. I suggest you start in the Widowlands outside Oxford. There have been a couple of incidents there and the Bodleian Library is the first stop on the Leader's itinerary.'

'But, Commissioner—'

'Don't *Commissioner* me.' He brought his face close to her, so that she could almost taste its sweaty sheen and breathe the rank odour of his breakfast sausage.

'Listen. I don't give a damn what you and Kreuz get up to in your squalid little lives. The Protector may believe in beheading for adultery, but I couldn't care less, so long as you keep your fornication to yourselves. However, I do care about my career and anything that might affect my chances of ever leaving this godforsaken rain-soaked dump, so if you don't want to end up in a camp, it's in your interests to make this work. Go to the Widowlands. Root them out. Bring me the names of the culprits and I will deal with them. We've got an entire nation wanting to see a beautiful queen and her king being crowned. Let everyone see what happens to old crones who try to get in the way.'

A trace of a smile flicked across his florid countenance but was over before it had begun.

'Those people in the Amt Moralische have a touch of the mediaeval about them. Apparently they're launching a fresh drive on public purity and moral pollution to coincide with the Coronation. They're longing to make an example. Who better than the Assistant Commissioner and his little courtesan to encourage the others?'

Rose could barely breathe. Would the Commissioner really subject Martin to public disgrace? Was it perhaps an act of pre-emptive envy, against a deputy so much more vital and talented than himself?

His lizard tongue licked its lips.

'Any questions?'

Hundreds. No end of them.

'No, sir.'

'Get out then.'

The car pulled to a sharp halt. Eckberg gave her a little push and Rose was unceremoniously ejected onto the Tottenham Court Road.

CHAPTER NINE

Monday, 19th April

Westwards from Paddington, through the city's stained, concrete outskirts and rows of drab streets, the train ran. Rose stared out. This was England: flat, denuded, grey. The high streets were all alike. Each had their grocer's shop whose windows were stacked with fake goods to disguise the shortages: loaves made of cardboard, milk bottles filled with salt, cereal packets with nothing in them. Each had a police station where citizens must register and report to have their identities checked on a regular basis. Each had a pub, with spittle and sawdust on the floor and tankards of mild Alliance ale. Each had a post office with a back room where Alliance officers would sift and censor mail. And in every town was a church which, since Rosenberg's Drive to Eliminate Christian Influence, rang not with hymns but the hubbub of sturdy female parishioners fundraising for the Alliance Winter Festival.

It was the kind of anonymous English morning that was blanketed by bone-grey cloud. Traffic was light, only the odd bus and tram passed in the streets beyond the track. She caught a glimpse of a road sweeper shifting dirt from one end of the curb to the next. There were no park railings anymore, just as there were no stair rods or brass plates outside doctors' offices, because all kinds of metal were required on the mainland. Everything was monochrome. Even the sparrows seemed to have dust on their wings. The only unusual aspect was the strings of pastel bunting draped across the Victorian terraces in anticipation of the Coronation.

A tattered poster of the Leader flapped on a hoarding, torn at the edges and dampened by rain. His was the face that everyone knew, hung in schools and shops, theatres, swimming pools and community halls. It was more familiar than family and greater than God, both instantly recognizable yet strangely evanescent. If you tried to focus on it, the image slipped away, like a malign *Mona Lisa*, as though it could never quite be captured. In this poster, he stood against a mountain backdrop, mouth downturned, eyes averted to an idealized distant land that, while unknown, seemed unlikely to be the English territories. It was hard to guess what he was thinking.

Advertising hoardings flashed by – *Rowntrees Fruit Gums, Chesterfield Cigarettes: Man-size Satisfaction*. Once, between towns, Rose caught sight of concentric rings of barbed wire surrounding a series of high walls with watchtowers, and electric searchlights fixed to them. There were all kinds of detention centres – Correction Centres, Re-education Centres, Enlightenment Centres – but most people just called them camps. She shuddered, and the Commissioner's threat throbbed in her mind like a physical pain.

If you don't want to end up in a camp . . .

What went on in a camp? She had never seen inside one and she knew nobody who had either, though there were always stories. Of people who disappeared from the workplace, or their home, and never came back. Or of those who did return, hollow-eyed and silent, and never talked about it. Sometimes, walking along the street, or shopping, you might see a collection truck pass, and glimpse terrified faces staring from the grille of a window. Yet most people turned away, as though even to look was forbidden. More often, the security forces deployed disguised vehicles, done up to look like bread or milk or grocery vans with a steel floor and a cramped cell space in the back, so as not to disturb citizens unduly.

She picked up a newspaper that had been left on the opposite seat and read through it in a desultory way. With newsprint restricted, the papers had all grown leaner in the past decade, both physically and in content. Just as radio journalists were assessed for ideological bias, broadcasting transmitters guarded and monitored and foreign stations jammed, so newspapers were obliged to run the gamut of the censors, and most editors operated by a motto of 'If in doubt, cut'.

The *People's Observer*, a red-top, with large, shouty font, was the sister publication to Germany's most popular daily, the *Völkischer Beobachter*, and Rose knew the kind of stories she would see even before she had read them. It was news by the yard, as cardboard as the bread in the shops, as cheap and garish as gummy bear sweets, produced in reams in the Press Ministry located directly below her own office.

On the mainland, journalists would be summoned to the Propaganda Ministry in Berlin for the morning news conference and be told what to write. Any deviation merited instant punishment. The system worked so well that after the Alliance was formed it was swiftly transferred to England. Every day journalists from all the daily papers – the *Express*, the *Mail*, the *News Chronicle*, the *Echo*, the *Manchester Guardian*, *The Times* – would queue up to enter the conference room and be briefed by officials, or if it was important, the Commissioner himself, on what the news was, what it wasn't, and how it should be reported.

It was like making a cake, Bridget Fanshaw said. First you took the raw materials. A man had discovered that his wife, a Leni, was carrying on with a Hauptsturmführer in her office. He comes home from the factory and stabs her with a bread knife. The body of a woman is fished from the Thames, identifiable only as a Gretl by the tattered remnants of her brown clothing. Police are appealing for witnesses. Two Gelis have been killed in a car driven by a Sturmbann-führer. A new musical, *A Girl in Every Port*, is opening at the London Palladium.

These ingredients are sifted to remove the grit – the

details of the Leni's lover, for example, the name of the Sturmbannführer driving the crashed car, any impropriety in the musical that might offend the Morality Office – then sliced, diced and blended to the tastes of individual readers. A little more spice for readers of the *Daily Mail*, a dryer mix for *The Times*.

Today was no different. The splash concerned the country's record munitions production. Three new factories had been opened and thousands of relocated Gretls and Friedas drafted in to staff them. The good news was illustrated by a picture of the women, turbans on their heads and their shapeless forms draped in workers' overalls, bent over their machinery, making bullets. Rose had given up wondering what or who the bullets were for. Apart from some skirmishes in the Far East, the Alliance was not at war, but as the Government repeated with wearying regularity, *Defence is the backbone of a strong and stable society*. For anyone who didn't know, the motto was regularly emblazoned on boards in the lobby of every ministerial building, even Culture.

Plenty of newsprint was given over to the Coronation, including blurry shots of the royal families of Denmark and Romania arriving at Heston Aerodrome, and a feature on two of the grey geldings, Donner and Blitzen, who would pull the four-ton gold state coach.

Before the Coronation a dinner was to be held at Clarence House with celebrated socialites invited, including the Mitford sisters, Unity and Diana, not to mention Diana's husband Oswald Mosley, the former Prime Minister. The

Londonderrys and assorted aristocrats would also be in attendance, along with a selection of faceless MPs who presided over Alliance business in the House of Commons. A set of new stamps had been issued to mark the Coronation, the Leader's disembodied profile floating gothically above the happy couple.

Rose turned the page, flicked through the horoscopes, and her eye ranged casually across the advertisements.

Come to Clacton, Britain's Gold Coast! Sea and sun at all-inclusive Alliance resort. (Class III females and above)

Celia had been to Clacton the previous year and was entranced. She returned telling Rose she couldn't care less about the foreign travel ban when the English seaside offered that kind of attraction.

Felixstowe. Gateway to Glamour.

In the midst of the classifieds was the dating column, the doomed hunting ground of Magdas and Gretls who of all the castes had the hardest job finding a man. These women brought fewer rations with them and were restricted as to where they could live and the places they could frequent. No smart restaurants or cafés for them. Their clothes were drab and their looks frequently ruined by hard physical work.

One thing they did come with, however, was a womb.

Blonde female (Class IV b), energetic, considered attractive, seeks man, any age, for love and reproduction.

Beautiful, blue-eyed, healthy Class III a girl, excellent cook, nursing skills, wishes to bear children for a male companion.

Respectable young woman hopes to produce a son for the Alliance.

Rose scanned the lumpen prose with a cool, professional eye. What might Jane Austen or Emily Brontë have made of these desperate advertisements? How might they have viewed these guileless pleas?

Alongside the classifieds, in almost mocking proximity, was a photograph of a beautiful woman, with a heart-shaped face, high-arched brows and implausibly milk-white skin buffed to a dewy studio sheen. The caption said that the American film star Sonia Delaney was visiting London to present a documentary movie about the Coronation of Wallis Windsor called *American Queen*. There followed a few paragraphs about Miss Delaney, some lines in which she explained why Queen Wallis had 'a special place in every American heart' and a list of the actress's most recent movies – two spy capers, a couple of thrillers and a romantic comedy.

Rose's attention quickened.

Not because she had any interest in Sonia Delaney or her films, but because Martin had recently mentioned that the Culture Ministry was to host a reception for a delegation of American film-makers and the authorities were cock-a-hoop. Relations with America had been cool over the past thirteen years, despite Ambassador Kennedy's initial enthusiasm for the Alliance, so the prospect of a posse of Hollywood powerbrokers, ready to discuss a slate of proposed co-productions, had prompted the Culture Ministry to roll out the red carpet. Queen Wallis was widely credited with these friendly overtures, which was, Martin said, just one more reason to love her.

Rose didn't care why the Americans were coming. All she wanted was the chance to meet them.

Americans were a byword for worldly sophistication and as most people had no chance of ever encountering one, this legendary status was never dispelled. Everything British citizens knew about America came from the movies. America was a Shangri-La, full of impossible quantities of food; it was the home of Coca Cola, milkshakes and glistening cocktail bars with mirrors and black marble. Of gleaming Chevrolets and good-looking young men. Dean Martin. Eddie Fisher. Perry Como. The regime itself did not encourage this vision. America was not an ally, after all, but a neutral country, and Jews there were allowed a quite disproportionate influence on government. Yet the very adjective *American* had come to signal sophistication and chic in the way that once, incredibly, *Parisian* had been used.

As the train travelled further, the towns fell away and they entered the countryside proper. Spring fields stretched out in corduroy furrows and kestrels hovered high above. A herd of russet cows lay in the shade of a tree and a haze of young green tipped the distant woodland. Willows trailed leafy fingers into streams. Lush banks of bluebells, cowparsley, the clotted cream of hawthorn and saucers of elder blossom fringed the train track. After the drab homogeneity of the towns, this landscape was like another England, an ancient, sleeping land that lay deep and undisturbed just below the surface.

A line ran like a ribbon of music through her head.

When that Aprille with his shoures soote/The droghte of March hath perced to the roote

Where did that strange incantation come from? Those enchanting, archaic words? Faintly, into her mind floated a poem about a pilgrimage. It must be something Dad had told her. Dad loved to recite poetry; he knew acres of it by heart. He had an 'office' – in fact, a converted garage at the side of the house – overflowing with books, papers, jam jars of pens and nibs and pencil sharpeners, all rich with the smell of pipe tobacco and a faint, lingering tinge of motor oil. He would sit there, one hand stroking his chin, occasionally leaning towards her with a spark in his eye.

Do you see, Rosie? Do you see what the poet is doing there?

Even when she didn't understand the words, when they were essentially meaningless to her, their magic still reached inside her and made the air between them tremble. The poetry her father read seemed exhilarating, as though its cadences could affect your life, and maybe even transmute it.

The thought of Dad brought back the encounter with Celia, and a fresh jolt of sorrow assailed her. She could imagine Geoffrey bundling his hapless old father-in-law into the back of his Jaguar, talking heartily of a day trip or some other concocted lie, as the car sped towards the faceless institution where Dad would sit in a chair, knowing no one, out of contact with everything he held dear.

What would Dad make of her mission today? She dearly wished she could ask him.

She hadn't dared tell Martin about the Commissioner's threat.

She'd managed to see him briefly over the weekend. He rented an apartment in Dolphin Square – a handsome red-brick set of mansion blocks in Pimlico on the north bank of the Thames, largely occupied by single men rather than families, SS and Ministry civil servants and their women friends. He had given Rose a key, but she had never used it and was nervous of calling on Martin unexpectedly; it breached some unspoken rule between them that said his private territory was sacrosanct, to be visited by invitation only, whereas he might call on her at any time. The Commissioner's request, however, had left her in a state of anxious desperation.

Martin was wearing a dark green dressing gown, luxuriously silky and flattering against his tanned flesh, the neck revealing a glimpse of curled chest hair that was damp from the shower. A towel was draped around his shoulders and he had a razor in one hand. He looked so attractive, Rose wondered immediately if he had a female visitor, but on his bed was only his uniform laid out: black tunic with silver buttons, white shirt, black jodhpurs, peaked black cap with silver braiding below the death's head, and on the floor beneath, black leather boots polished to a mirror shine.

He glanced rapidly up and down the corridor and quickly ushered her in.

'This is a pleasant surprise, *Liebling*.'

'I'm sorry, Martin.'

She only realized she was trembling when he put a steadying hand on her arm.

'I wouldn't have come, only the Commissioner's ordered me to visit the Widowlands outside Oxford and interview some Friedas for the Protector's book. I'm to go on Monday. But I haven't the first clue where to start. And I've no idea how to find anything out.'

'Hey. Calm down.'

'But I was thinking—'

'Trouble with you, my darling? You do too much thinking.' He tapped her forehead, mock stern. 'What else did he say?'

'Nothing much.'

'Then what are you worried about?' He went over to his desk and scribbled on a piece of paper. 'I have a colleague who lives in Oxford. Detective Bruno Schumacher. We were at school together. When I went off to study law, he, poor fellow, joined the police force, got divorced, then was drafted over here for his sins. If you have any problems, give Bruno a call.'

'Really?'

'Of course. Tell him I sent you. And don't worry!'

He tipped her chin towards him.

'This isn't like you, Rose. What are these Friedas going to do? Attack you with their knitting needles? They're old women. What is there to be frightened of?'

Martin was right. What was she frightened of?

After all, she rarely had cause to see or speak to a Frieda. When the Alliance was formed, the office that regulated women on the mainland – the Frauenshaft, or Women's Service – was rolled out in Britain. Each caste was overseen by a division of the FS that did everything from administering ration books to running Mother Service classes and policing adherence to clothing and behaviour rules. Once women were assigned a caste, FS officers instructed them in appropriate behaviour. Those who violated any kind of ordinance faced deprivation of rations, imprisonment, downgrading of caste and worse. Klaras who behaved inappropriately risked having their children taken into the care of the state.

Women in the Alliance faced regulations for everything – where to go, shop, eat, live. How to style their hair. Their identity cards specified the precise number of calories each category of woman would be allocated – 2,613 for Gelis, 2,020 for Lenis, 2,006 for Magdas, Gretls 1,800, and Friedas 879. All these calculations were based on guidelines drawn up on the mainland.

Yet even more plentiful were the regulations for what was forbidden, and the list for women of Class VI was the longest. Friedas were forbidden to walk in public parks, to attend cinemas, theatres, hospitals or restaurants. They could not keep pets. They were allowed no meat or eggs. They could shop only after five o'clock, when most of the produce was gone.

They were not to associate with men.

For some reason, into Rose's head came an incident shortly after the formation of the Alliance, when she had accompanied her father to the Royal Albert Hall in Kensington. It was Ransom family tradition to attend a concert at Christmas, and their father always booked the tickets well in advance, yet when they arrived at the box office that day, everything was at sixes and sevens. The venue had been co-opted as a 'designated collection point', someone apologized, as a posse of uniformed men strode through the foyer past the winding queue. On impulse, while her father waited, Rose slipped away along a corridor, up some steps, and parted a crimson velvet curtain to peer inside.

It was an astonishing sight.

The auditorium was filled with hundreds of Friedas in spiralling lines, waiting to be interviewed by a row of officers behind desks, each with a pile of manila folders to hand. It seemed that the women were being given the details of their relocations and instructions as to what clothes and possessions they could take. A large board had been erected with the instructions.

2 x black dresses
2 x underwear
1 x black coat
1 x pair boots
2 x towels

As she watched from behind the velvet curtain, Rose could not tear her eyes away. The Friedas' faces were sallow moons above a basalt sea. Although none of them spoke, they milled anxiously like the crawling mass of a beehive, exuding insect energy. They seemed, in their ubiquitous black, almost inhuman. Repelled, and a little scared, Rose let the curtain drop.

Now, the memory disturbed her. She rarely gave Friedas any thought. A Frieda was not allowed to address a Geli directly without permission and there were very few occasions in which their paths would even cross. So why did she feel trepidation, almost revulsion, at the idea of entering Widowland, and a sinking dread of what she might find?

With an effortful screech of brakes, the train pulled into Oxford station and almost immediately, it was clear something was happening. The platform was crowded with excited children, girls in the sky-blue and white uniform of the Alliance Girls' League and boys in the chestnut-brown shirts of the Alliance Boys, hurrying past. Others, with trays of tin badges, were stationed at each side of the exit, making it impossible for commuters to avoid a donation.

It was only when Rose had produced an Alliance mark and had a tin badge thrust into her hand that she understood.

How could she have forgotten? Tomorrow was the Leader's birthday.

The 20th of April was a special day across the whole of Europe, marked each year by rallies and brass bands in town squares, readings in decommissioned churches and school plays re-enacting scenes from the Leader's life. Workers in factories and offices would sing the national hymn and a relaxation in rations was allowed – either an extra packet of National cigarettes or a small quantity of sugar per family.

Judging by the instruments and sheet music they were carrying, these children must be practising for the next day. As their instructors shepherded them towards the city centre, the faint thump of brass instruments and drums could already be heard.

Rose allowed herself to be carried along in the stream of children, swallowed up in their bubble of excited chatter, gazing at the honey-coloured buildings around her. Long ago, her father had studied here for a year, at a place called Ruskin Hall, established for working men who could never dream of the traditional university route. His reminiscences of the mediaeval quadrangles, the domes and spires, and the neo-classical Sheldonian Theatre designed by a young Christopher Wren had percolated their childhood. In Rose's father's mind, Oxford was the most exquisite city in England, a lost kingdom of beauty and culture and learning for its own sake. She had not for a second expected the place to match up to Dad's rose-tinted memories, but now she saw that he was right. Even though the sandstone was dulled with soot and the pillars and pediments were crumbling with age, there was a harmony about them, and the way they seemed to fit together, that enchanted her. Above the towers and pearl-grey cupolas, a filigree of leaves unfurled against a soft blue sky.

Many of the colleges had been commandeered for VIPs in anticipation of the Leader's visit, and each ancient stone door was manned by a brace of sentries in field-grey uniform, to the obvious disdain of the traditional college porters, who could be seen, in their black coats and familiar bowler hats, moving officiously around their lodges just inside the gates.

Outside the Sheldonian Theatre, a ring of square stone pillars topped by head and shoulder busts of ancient sages had for centuries stood guard. Yet now the Roman emperors and philosophers had been replaced by busts of the Leader, his deputies Hess and Himmler, Joseph Goebbels, Heinrich Müller, and a couple of other senior men. Their freshly carved faces stared balefully out from their pillars, like decapitated warriors in some ancient and bloody battle. Fleetingly, Rose wondered what her father would make of the renovation. Martin had explained that what people like her father saw as a reverence for culture was really only a small-minded attachment to the recent past by people who had no ability to innovate, but still, it was a small mercy that Dad was not here to see it.

The children were congregating, unpacking their

instruments and being assembled into lines. Before long they had begun a rendition of 'Land of Alliance Glory', a song whose music never failed to stir the blood, even if many people could not bring themselves to mouth the words. The children had no such qualms, their high, pure voices wavering into the clear April air.

Rose stood for a while among the onlookers enjoying the sight until, out of the corner of her eye, she noticed something less harmonious going on.

In the grip of three policemen a black shape that appeared, on closer inspection, to be an old Frieda was thrashing vigorously as the men restrained her. Her mouth was a gappy void – Friedas were not entitled to false teeth – and her stringy hair was coming loose from her bun. She was shouting, her voice clear and educated, ringing out among the mediaeval facades.

'Take your hands off me, you louts!'

Her tone took Rose straight back to school and the figure of Miss Price, a maths teacher at the Clapham School for Girls. A mini martinet, in pebble glasses and a steel-grey bun, Miss Price was known not to suffer fools gladly and the sternest of men withered in her glare. Miss Price had been the bane of Celia's life, but when she taught Rose, a glint of humour softened the icy rigour. It crossed Rose's mind to wonder where Miss Price would be now. In some distant Widowland perhaps, fenced in and draped in black?

The burliest policeman was gripping the old woman pincer fashion by the back of the neck, his face rigid with anger, his jaw jutting and skin flushed with the effort of restraining his more violent urges.

'I am not Class Six subsection C or any other kind of class.'

Faces began to turn. Interest quickened and a thrill of diversion ran through the crowd.

'I'm an individual. My name is Adeline Adams.'

Her voice, hoarse with shouting, retained the timbre of command. Presumably some Friedas had once been more used to giving orders than taking them.

'I'm a British citizen and I demand to be treated with respect. Your behaviour is despicable. I said, remove your hands.'

Only a Frieda would dare to be so subordinate. It was almost as if Friedas didn't care what happened to them. The policeman gave an aggressive laugh.

'If that's what you want.'

He thrust her forward onto the ground, where she fell awkwardly on her forearm, and pinioned her with a foot on her chest. Attracted by the commotion, children turned away from the singing and with tribal excitement began pointing and laughing at the woman's predicament.

The sound of a motor closed in as a car, closely followed by a dingy van, swung round the corner and came to a halt at the kerb. Instantly, the mood amongst the onlookers changed and the children's teachers attempted physically to block their view. Out of the back of the car a man in civilian clothes emerged. The policeman removed his foot from the Frieda's chest and straightened up. Rose strained to hear the conversation.

'What the hell's this about?'

'Suspected guerrilla action, sir.'

'Evidence?'

'Eyewitness, sir.'

'And the reason for this?'

The newcomer gestured with distaste at the woman, now sitting on the ground, cradling her arm.

'Resisting arrest, sir.'

The suited man looked around at the three police officers.

'And that took three of you, did it? What was she in her previous life? A professional wrestler?'

'She's stronger than she looks, sir,' said the policeman in an injured tone, casting a vindictive glance at his elderly victim, who was now dusting down her black serge dress with meticulous care.

'Well, Sergeant Johnson, you know the form. Get her in and take the witness statement. Don't for Christ's sake make more of a spectacle of yourself than you have already.'

With a sigh, the man clambered back into his car, and the three policemen set about shoving the old woman into the back of the collection van with some extra kicks for good measure.

The morning that had seemed so pure was spoiled. It was starting to drizzle. Water was speckling the sheet music of the trumpet players and the children were shifting restively, focused on getting out of the rain. Moisture dappled the shop windows and the Alliance flags hung limply against their poles.

Turning away, Rose checked again the address of the hotel. The Red Lion. Judging by her map, it was only a few streets away. Hurrying off, she turned left down a slip of a cobbled passage called Magpie Lane squeezed between two colleges. It was so narrow that it set her mind wandering back to the past again – how ancient carts might have squeezed through its rough mediaeval walls and very likely got stuck there. Now, the only transport in evidence was a couple of bicycles leaning against the wall of a student lodging house.

Then, towards the end, at the point where the lane measured no more than ten feet across, a vivid scrawl of paint leapt out at her, arcing across the brickwork like a spasm of blood.

Lock up your libraries if you like; but there is no gate, no lock, no bolt that you can set upon the freedom of my mind

The Commissioner was right. It was everywhere.

CHAPTER TEN

The Red Lion hotel was shabby and tired, with a receptionist who matched the decor. She had obviously rouged cheeks and ringlets hanging down each side of her face, like a china Staffordshire dog that had lost its pair. Her sweat-stained Magda's tunic dress was as worn as the upholstery and her perfume fought a losing battle with the aroma of mothballs, mingled with the scent of that evening's dinner drifting up from the kitchens.

The Red Lion had certainly seen better days. But the same was true of England now.

'Will that be one breakfast or two?' she enquired nosily. It was not her place to ask direct questions but framing it as a technical query was just about permissible. She glanced down at Rose's left hand as she signed the register, then up again, lips puckering into a smile. Rose considered reprimanding her for such an intrusive question, but common sense overtook her.

'It's just me.'

She smiled and accepted the key.

On the wall of room thirty-seven, directly opposite the bed, hung a portrait of the Queen. Despite the softened lens and the cloud of ivory tulle that caressed her cadaverous form, her Majesty did not look well. In fact, even the sight of her was stressful. Her complexion was chalky, the wide jaw clenched like a trap, and the elaborate tiara on her blackened hair seemed to claw her skull like the talons of some great jewelled bird. *She looks her age*, thought Rose. At fifty-seven, Wallis Windsor could have been a poster woman for Pervitin, the nerve tonic that was so popular among the lower castes.

A Pervitin a day takes your worries away!

Not for Wallis and Edward, it wouldn't. Not with the Leader on his way.

Rose lay down on the bed and immediately regretted it. The mattress might have been stuffed with tennis balls. It was no more than three feet wide, caved generously in the centre, and the rusty springs complained at the slightest shift.

She considered the Magda's surprise to see a woman like her travelling alone. Celia was right. At the age of twenty-nine she ought to be more worried about the implications of her failure to find a man. She should be settled now, with three or four children instead of a job, and a nice house somewhere in the suburbs. Entertaining her husband's friends. Discussing menus with the Gretl. Shopping, gardening, playing bridge. By staying single, she ran a big risk of being reclassified. The duty to reproduce was even more important for Gelis, because of their quality.

It wasn't as though she hadn't tried. Men had come and gone, but she had never felt deeply connected to any of them. Not the way Jane Eyre felt about Mr Rochester. Or Catherine about Heathcliff. Not even the way that Queen Wallis must once have felt towards the King. Rose had experienced no bolt of lightning, or *coup de foudre*. Once the early rush of infatuation had faded, her feelings towards Martin were a muddle of curiosity, apathy and guilt. Every emotion was splintered with questions. Was Martin being honest when he said the relationship between himself and Helga was more that of brother and sister than man and wife? Did Helga know of Rose's existence and hate her, or was she blissfully unaware as she went about her *Hausfrau* life in the Berlin suburbs, meeting her friends for *Kaffeeklatsch* and nagging her children about their music lessons?

Martin had begged a photograph of Rose to keep by his bedside and told her he was in love. Yet whenever he asked about her own feelings, she evaded the question.

Perhaps it made no difference. She could never have rebuffed Martin's advances. It was not as if she could have turned him down. There was no way a Geli could refuse a senior man. His embraces were as much a cage as a comfort.

As the rain slapped against the window and drummed on the roof overhead, Rose fixed her eyes on the ceiling and thought of another bed, in another country.

★

It was probably – no, certainly – the most exciting time of her life. Foreign travel was banned outright to all women beneath Geli status, and even then was permitted only in exceptional circumstances. Rose had never dreamed she would get the chance. She knew no other woman her age who had ventured abroad since the Alliance was formed, and her only first-hand knowledge of Germany was her father's memories of being in a prisoner of war camp in Karlsruhe, which was not much to go on.

It was a Thursday morning in September, four months on in their relationship, and she had been engaged in a routine but time-consuming edit – downgrading the intelligence of Margaret Hale in *North and South* – when the moon face of Ludwig Kohl, Martin's secretary, with his fleshy, wet, curiously female lips, loomed over her.

'Kreuz's office.' He had onion breath and a nasal Saxon accent, which made any utterance sound snide. 'Now.'

She followed Kohl's fat, breeches-clad bottom up to the second floor where Martin was seated, wearing a pair of pince-nez and his most serious expression. Once he had closed the door, he leaned back in his chair.

'I have something very serious to say to you.'

He took off his spectacles and frowned.

She stiffened with alarm, but tilted her head enquiringly.

'It's about your work.'

'My correcting work?'

'I'm afraid I'm going to have to take you off it for a while.'

Her heart skipped an anxious beat. She had been found

out. It was true, her recent correction of *Little Women* had been unusually lenient. She had loved the character of Jo March, the novel's ambitious, precocious, complicated rebel, and had been reluctant to strike out some of Jo's attempts to rise above her gender and class, not to mention her heart-felt support for women's voting, which was outlawed for females in the Alliance.

Women should vote, not because we are angels and men are animals, but because we are human beings and citizens of this country.

Rose decided to leave the sentence in.

She did it partly because at the end of the novel Jo March ditched her dreams of being a writer, burned her own stories and married a German. Then she set up a school, for boys only. That, in several ways, made the text entirely appropriate for the Alliance's senior school curriculum.

All the same, it might take some explaining. Staring at Martin, Rose assembled a defence.

'If it's *Little Women* you're talking about, I would say that the end is entirely in accord with Rosenberg ideals and—'

'It's nothing to do with women. Little or otherwise.'

'Then perhaps Mrs Gaskell?'

Martin gave a dismissive wave.

'I don't give a damn about Frau Gaskell, whoever she is. And your work is perfectly satisfactory.'

She frowned. 'Then . . . ?'

'The fact is, I'm engaged in a short-term project a little further afield and I require an assistant with the correct qualifications.'

'I see. Can I ask what qualifications?'

'The qualifications are to be very beautiful and in love with me.' His face broke into a grin. 'Don't look so worried! You're coming to Berlin!'

He got up, wrapped his arms around her, and flourished an envelope with the official passes.

'It's the dullest of bureaucratic duties. I have to visit the Office of the Control of Literature to compile a briefing paper for a speech the Protector is giving at the Germania cultural summit. I'll need secretarial assistance, so I put your name forward and your pass has been issued. Pack a bag. We leave from Croydon tomorrow.'

As soon as the Dakota aircraft touched down at Tempelhof, it was clear that Germania, the newly named capital, would be everything Rose had heard and more. The airport itself was enormous, milling with impossibly well-dressed travellers touting calfskin suitcases and valises on small wheels that they pulled along a floor of Saalburger marble, blood red and white veined, like giant slabs of steak. Vast stained-glass windows were inset with images of Rome, Prague, Vienna and Budapest, and outside the terminal a monumental eagle with stretched wings and imperious beak peered loftily over the forecourt, where an official car with an SS driver was waiting for them.

As the limousine swept into the centre of Berlin Rose was astonished at the cleanliness and richness of the city. It reminded her constantly of the biblical phrase *a land of milk and honey*. From the creamy facades, all sparkling and soot-free, to the boulevards lined with towering ivory stone columns surmounted by dazzling gold eagles, the city shone. Municipal parks and flowerbeds bulged with geraniums and begonias whose very petals seemed more vivid and fleshy than those at home, and every windowsill contained tubs of trailing flowers.

On the streets, dazzling Volkswagens and BMWs circled traffic policemen in white gloves and on the pavements prim couples accompanied by packs of children strolled in the sunshine, the women with fur stoles around their necks and well-cut suits in silk and tweed, the men in smooth, expensive camel-hair coats and fedoras or green alpine-style hats. The people here looked like a different species.

Rose puzzled to work out why. It wasn't the fact that they were tanned, as though from regular hiking or skiing, or that their clothes were filled out with healthy curves. It wasn't even their confident demeanour. It was . . . their similarity to one another. Unlike Britain, with its range of female castes, its different races and mix of native and foreign males, there was a quality in the faces and figures here that made them all alike.

As they crossed a bridge over the Spree canal, busy with stately barges filled with tourists, she gasped.

'That's the *Schloss*!'

A photograph of it hung on the Ministry walls, as well as one of Unter den Linden, the elegant boulevard under whose lime trees they were now cruising. Martin smiled, as if indulging the excitement of a child.

'There's plenty more to see.'

As the car passed under the Brandenburg Gate and up a central alley, Rose was struck by a different kind of déjà vu. A high Corinthian column, with four lions at its base, surmounted by a one-armed figure in a bicorne hat and naval uniform, towered above them.

'Is that . . . I think I've seen that column before. Isn't it . . . ?'

'Nelson's Column? That's right. The Leader admired it very much so it made sense to bring it to the greatest city in the world. Wait till you see what's in the north–south axis.'

The limousine turned left into a boulevard faced by a row of disparate buildings, made up of a variety of styles that seemed at once alien and familiar.

'That town hall was in Rochdale. The Leader liked it so much that he had it taken apart brick by brick and reassembled here. And that's the Paris Opera House.'

'It's just . . .'

'Wonderful. I know. The best architecture in Europe is here. It's the capital of the world, after all. After libraries, architecture is the Leader's greatest passion. He often says if the burden of leadership had not fallen on his shoulders, he would have been an architect.'

He squeezed her hand.

'We'll have time for more sightseeing in the morning. Before then, we have work to do.'

★

The Amt Schrifttumspflege, the Protector's Office for the Control of Literature, was at Margarethenstrasse, west of Potsdamer Platz. In an effort to prepare, Rose had looked up the establishment before she came and discovered that its mission was 'to monitor and control the portrayal of the Party in literature from the standpoint of ideology, artistry and popular education, as well as to support deserving works.'

It was a mouthful, of course. The regime never used one word where a whole dictionary would do, but Rose was a practised translator of Party jargon and it sounded plausible. They had an office for everything and there was no reason why literature should not be processed and cultivated and bureaucratized as much as steel or cardboard or coal.

'This is where it all began.'

Martin led the way towards a high-ceilinged space, elegantly appointed with brass lamps, heavy wooden tables and thick carpets. It smelled of leather and beeswax and hummed with subdued activity. A fat woman in white gauze gloves was dusting the first ever copy of the Leader's autobiography, complete with his signature, a heart attack in cardiograph.

To the people of Germany

'This place is simply incredible. Rosenberg's Confiscation Squad has gone through libraries all over Europe to get these books. Occupied countries and private collections. Homes and bookshops. Since 1940, his people have collected more than three million volumes by Catholics, Poles, homosexuals, Roma, Jehovah's Witnesses. You name it.'

'But why? Why would he want to keep so much degenerate literature? Surely he can't update all of it?'

Martin paused, as though she was a bright pupil who had asked the correct question.

'Because he's a genius. What do you do if you want to study your enemy's psychology? His inner thoughts? His very motivations? You study his literature. These may be dangerous texts but they help the Security Service understand the nation's enemies in greater depth. As I said, books are intellectual weapons.'

He beamed at her and straightened up.

'I'm off to see the Controller, Herr Hagemayer. Why don't you take a look around?'

Rose wandered among the books. Generally, she adored the complicated perfume of libraries, scented with paper and polish, the most ancient volumes beautiful with their decorative brass clasps, silk endpapers and gilt-edged leaves. Yet the stacks here had a far more clinical air. Beyond shelves labelled *Freemasonry* and *The Slav Race* she came to a series of glass cases housing a display dedicated to the life of Alfred Rosenberg.

Curious, she peered in.

The Protector had been born in January 1893 to a family of Baltic Germans. He studied architecture and engineering in Riga before moving to Munich, where he had the great fortune to meet the Leader and instantly became one of his closest allies.

This event was illustrated by the familiar visage of the

Leader, looking younger and more forceful, and the Protector, whey-faced and shifty, hovering just behind his right shoulder.

In 1933, Rosenberg visited London to discuss the possibilities of an Alliance between the two great nations. Cue a photograph of the Protector laying a swastika wreath at the Cenotaph.

More promotions followed, as the Protector assumed an overarching cultural mission to confiscate degenerate texts from libraries and homes throughout Europe. This was illustrated by a photograph of stormtroopers removing boxloads of books from a library in Prague.

The Confiscation Squad operates in close co-operation with the Wehrmacht and Security Police in the occupied territories. Its officers have the authority to appropriate all writings by and on subversives. These materials are preserved as items of value for propaganda and research purposes.

The last picture recorded the Protector in London outside 10 Downing Street, the traditional home of the British Prime Minister, which he had now assumed for his own use. Alongside him Oswald Mosley stood ramrod straight, in his high-necked black uniform and brass belt. For the first time, Rose thought she glimpsed a look of uncertainty, perhaps even apprehension, in Mosley's forceful demeanour.

She drifted through the stacks until she came to an area labelled *Jewish material*, picked up a volume by a man called Henry Ford entitled *The International Jew: The World's Foremost Problem* and put it down again. Next to it was a badly damaged volume bound in cracked, cherry-coloured leather, its pages coming loose from its binding. It looked like a diary of some sort.

She turned to the frontispiece and read the words *Agatha Kettler, aged fifteen, 1941*. The schoolgirl handwriting was neat and regular, each page filled to the brim. Flicking through, isolated phrases leapt out.

Father was always talking about his dreams of creating a world, but Mother says he should have realized that other people have dreams, and it's their dream that has come to pass.

Curiously, she read on, her eyes skimming the mottled pages.

This morning they arrested another thousand Jews. I'm keeping this in a safe place in the hope that it might survive me.

The words made her stomach clench. Why would they arrest Jews?

Into her mind came the face of Sophy Freeman, who Rose had known at school. The Freeman family were Jewish; Sophy's father was a doctor who had fought alongside her own father in the war, and because the two men were friends, their daughters gravitated towards each other. Rose and Sophy had spent an entire summer together at the age of fourteen, exploring their local neighbourhood, camping in the nearby woods, laughing and reading and gossiping. Only recently, Dad had mentioned that he and Dr Freeman had met up for the first time in years, sipping pints at their favourite pub, The Moon Under Water. Sophy sent her love. Rose felt a momentary pang that she had allowed her childhood friendship to fade.

She caught the sound of footsteps approaching from behind. Guiltily she shut the book, as if she had been trespassing in forbidden territory. Martin was returning, swinging his briefcase jauntily, like a holiday bucket and spade. He was always tactile, but now he reached for her hand and linked fingers, like a boy with his first girlfriend. The heaviness and perpetual gloom that seemed to surround him in England had vanished, as though a physical load had been lifted from his shoulders. He kissed her cheek as they got back into the car and slung an arm around her.

'Mission accomplished. Now, my darling, the fun begins.'

'So, what exactly is it you're doing here?'

Two hours later, and they were lying in a vast, snowy bed in the Hotel Excelsior. On the back of the door hung two freshly laundered towelling dressing gowns. A bowl of fruit, glossy purple cherries and sable grapes sat on a side table, alongside a plate of *Lebkuchen* – sweet spiced biscuits that Rose had to stop herself devouring on sight. The tray had, to Rose's surprise, been delivered by an English Gretl – a pallid girl with a northern accent who must, like so many others, have applied successfully for a transfer to the mainland.

'How do you like it here?' asked Rose, as the girl busied herself with depositing the tray, arranging plates and trying not to look at them. But before the Gretl could reply, Martin flicked his wrist and with a look of speechless terror, she fled.

In the bathroom, a fat globe of ivory soap, rather than the curling sliver of carbolic found at home, rested in the dish next to a glass jar of bath salts which smelled divine. That evening, Martin had told her, they would have steak, grilled asparagus and a bottle of Châteauneuf-du-Pape. Then they would go to a nightclub patronized by Party VIPs. You had to be careful with these places – the Morality Office were jumpy about an SS officer out with someone who wasn't his wife – but the Ciro would be safe, or the Eldorado. Goebbels went there and he was the kind of man who had no problems seeing Culture Ministry officials with pretty girls. The only danger was, he might want Rose for himself.

Martin leaned back against the plush velvet headboard, lit a cigarette and savoured the rich Turkish tobacco.

'What am I doing? I'm writing a speech for the Protector. As Eckberg can't string two words together, the task generally falls to me, but this time I don't mind. It's interesting, actually. It's called "Achieving Perfection". Rosenberg holds England as his ideal expression of the perfect society where all his ideas about Aryan supremacy and social hierarchies have been put in place.'

'Wait . . . he can't possibly think England is more perfect than here?'

Rose stretched out on the crisp, clean cotton sheets. Her toes did not even reach the end of the mattress and the linen itself was softer than any she had known. Bolstered by goose-down pillows that smelled of laundry starch, she was cosseted in a fresh, silky nest that caressed her naked flesh. Every one of her senses was heightened by the sights and sensations around her.

Luxuriating in this glorious bed, anticipating a delicious supper, she mused out loud in a way she would never have done at home.

'I've never seen anywhere like this. The buildings, the food, the cars, the people. Even the flowers look more beautiful here. Those roses . . .' She glanced across at the plump apricot blooms, still pearled with water droplets, that had materialized at her bedside. 'And the coffee. Real coffee, not *Muckefuck*.'

Muckefuck was fake coffee, whose name translated as 'brown earth'. It looked like horse feed and tasted worse. No one in England could remember anything different.

'It's paradise here. I mean, I love England, but . . .'

Martin chuckled tolerantly. He adored explaining things.

'You don't understand. When the Protector talks about perfection, he's not talking about food or coffee or cars. He's talking about ideas. Alfred Rosenberg, you see, is the ideological heart of the Party. He's its genius and presiding spirit. He spent years thinking and planning for the implementation of a revolutionary society and when the Alliance was formed, Britain provided him with a blank slate. A *tabula rasa* that was all his to draw on. So the first thing he got in place was the caste system.'

'Why was that so important?'

'Social hierarchies are the bedrock. They're everywhere. All human societies organize themselves into castes. The better they're organized, the more smoothly a society functions.'

'Female castes, you mean.'

'In this case, yes. Female castes were first envisioned by the Indian Brahmins, whom Protector Rosenberg admires very much. Indeed, he holds the Brahmins to be fellow Aryans. A caste system works perfectly in India. Gandhi himself called caste "the genius" of society.'

'I've always wanted to ask. Why should it apply only to women? What about men?'

'Because women are special! They do something that men can't do. They produce children! How many times have you heard the Leader say the most important citizen in his society is the mother? If we want a pure-blooded nation, we need to focus on that. We need to regulate breeding. Ensure that we keep control of the national stock. The strength of any nation depends on its purity. That's obvious, right?'

'I suppose . . .'

'Besides' – he leaned across to cup her breast in his hand – 'you, Rose Ransom, are an elite. You're a Geli. And I don't hear any complaints from you about that.'

'Would you sleep with me if I wasn't?'

'Darling, if you weren't a Geli, you wouldn't be you. But as you mention our sleeping arrangements . . .'

Martin was careful and tender in bed. He positioned himself above her and rearranged her limbs as though conducting an orchestra playing silently in his head. He engaged in diligent foreplay, paying scrupulous attention to her breasts and kissing the length of her body with mathematical precision, as if he worried about leaving an inch untouched.

His approach to sex reminded her of the woodwork classes he talked about so fervently from his boyhood. He was meticulous, detailed, forensic almost. Acutely concerned for her pleasure. Keen to achieve a perfect result. Always asking, *Is this good? And this?*

And yet she could never relax. Not for a second did she forget the power that he held over her.

Every atom of her recoiled at his touch.

CHAPTER ELEVEN

Outside, the light was fading over Oxford's weathered steeples and domes. Rose sat up and pulled out her briefcase to study the list of questions she had compiled. She had brought a writing pad and pens to carry out the research for the Protector's book, and some notes she had already made on Rosenberg's views of a mythic past.

The past had always been a minefield, but never more so than in 1953. It was not only the Time of Resistance that remained under a veil. Citizens were instructed not to talk, and preferably not even to think, about what was popularly called the Time Before – the decades preceding the coming of the Alliance. Dwelling on the recent past, so the official line ran, could trigger all the paralyzing toxins that infected a decaying society – nostalgia, false consciousness, sentimentality. Old people with failing memories were given too much credit, in place of younger people with dreams and ambitions. The Protector railed against Jewish psychologists who advocated 'talking therapy'. *I prefer the famous British stiff upper lip*, he (or his speechwriter) said.

Rose was familiar with all this. She had once been trapped at a canteen table by Oliver Ellis, who had given her a lengthy disquisition on the Protector's theory for as long as it took him to consume a plateful of macaroni cheese and a dish of stewed prunes. Old-style history was outlawed, he explained, to be replaced by History with a capital H. Thinking about distant history was healthy. It helped Alliance citizens better understand their roots and connect with their ancient bloodlines.

None of this changed Rose's immediate dilemma. She could discuss ancestral beliefs, and she had no doubt that the Friedas would talk to her – to disobey a Government Ministry official was unthinkable – but how on earth would she discover any hint of insurrection? She certainly couldn't ask the old women directly. Short of seeing a pot of paint in the corner, there seemed no chance at all that she could discover if these Friedas had had a hand in daubing subversive graffiti on public buildings.

And if she didn't find something, God only knew what would follow.

Restlessly she put her notebook down and massaged her neck. It was too early for bed. Perhaps a walk would relax her.

Oxford's streets were almost deserted. Compared to the bustle of London, they might have been in another age. Dusk had consigned Oxford to mediaeval times. A group of dons, shrouded in flapping, academic gowns like the habits of ancient monks, vanished through the door of Trinity College. The narrow, gabled houses, the quadrangles and cloisters were plunged in silence. Soft light glowed from upper casement windows, and through gates set into ancient walls, manicured gardens could be glimpsed: herbaceous beds filled with cobalt-blue iris, lush violet wisteria, orange tulips and blush-pink musk roses, their colours flaring like jewels in the fading light.

Unthinkingly, Rose found herself heading for Magpie Lane, the place she had seen the graffiti that morning. The alley was drowned in darkness, yet by the light of an iron lantern affixed to the side of a building she could see that every trace of the words had already disappeared. Only an unnaturally clean patch where the wall had been meticulously scrubbed provided a ghostly echo of what had been scrawled there before.

Nothing else remained.

Except on the ground hard up against the wall, half hidden by a stump of cobble, was a splash of colour. A few stems of primroses, loosely bunched with string. So frail, they might almost have been dropped by accident, as if anyone dropped flowers by accident now. Because in the Alliance, flowers were always meaningful. Like Victorians, the English had rediscovered their language. From the drooping chrysanthemum tied to the railings where an insurgent had been apprehended, to the wilting rose on the bridge from where a suicide had plunged or the freesias left on the doorstep of a family who had disappeared, flowers were powerful. They spoke. And their message was always the same.

As was the colour. Always yellow. Their blaze displayed the defiance that no one dared express.

Even as she bent to look at the primroses, Rose realized how foolhardy she had been to return. There was every chance that the place would still be under police surveillance and simply being here was enough to bring suspicion on herself. Casting the most casual look behind, she scanned the end of the alley and caught the muzzy silhouette of a man in a trench coat passing at the top of the lane. He might equally be a citizen or an employee of the university, but whoever he was, something told her it would be better if he did not see her.

Hastening on, she turned a corner blindly and, attracted by the peal of bells sounding the half hour, slipped through an arch, across a quad and into the sanctuary of a chapel.

It was a long time since she had entered a church. Nobody used churches much anymore, except for community gatherings, Mother Service classes or Classification examinations for women. Yet the flickering candlelight and hushed gloom were instantly familiar. The colours of the stained-glass windows fell on the floor in patterns of sapphire, emerald and ruby. Her father had once told her that the symbolism of stained glass was to make the invisible manifest, in the same way God had made himself manifest in flesh, but stained glass was like art, too, he said, in the way it transmuted the world, how it framed and coloured what would otherwise go unseen.

Rose could tell that this chapel was especially ancient. Stone plaques set in the wall commemorated bishops and deans who had died in the Middle Ages. Faces of forgotten saints peered from their niches, and the floor was covered by memorials inscribed in tarnished brass to other, unremembered dead. The chill prickled her skin, and she couldn't help but think of the mouldering corpses, decaying in their tombs and sepulchres all around her. Yet the place was comforting too. The sweet, dank, musty smell was evocative of early childhood, of hymns and Christmas, of prayers and a mythical God who loved All Things Bright and Beautiful. They still sung that hymn in community centres, though the words had been changed.

The Magda in her kitchen,
The Gretl at the grate,
The Leader made them lowly
And ordered their estate

The church was cool and dark, laced with shadows of furled stone. As she advanced up the aisle towards the altar, her footsteps sounded unnaturally loud on the worn slabs. The air was thick with incense. She approached a lectern in the shape of a golden eagle with outstretched wings, where for centuries the Holy Bible would have been displayed, and now the Protector's book lay, open at a random passage of mystic rambling.

Today, a new faith is awakening – the Myth of the Blood, the belief that the divine being of mankind generally is to be defended with the blood. The faith embodied by the fullest realization, that the Nordic blood constitutes that mystery which has supplanted and overwhelmed the old sacraments.

In front of the lectern was a row of candles. Finding one that was yet to be burned, she held the cool wax in her hand for a second, before touching its wick to another and setting it aflame. Kneeling at the altar rail, she shut her eyes.

'Be safe till I come, Dad. Wait for me.'

CHAPTER TWELVE

Tuesday, 20th April

Rose had logged her request with the district Gauleiter and had been told that four Friedas would be located and assembled for interview at the address provided. All Widow-lands were encircled with fences, designed to enforce the curfew regulations that applied to Friedas, but these barriers were mostly ill-maintained and had fallen into disrepair, as though any money spent on widows was a waste. When Rose arrived at the guard post she saw plentiful gaps in the concrete and barbed wire.

A thin, official face squinted at her, and waved her through the gate.

The tightly packed rows of run-down cottages were situated on the far outskirts of the city, set between train lines and the marshy flats of a canal. The narrow terraced houses, two up and two down, had been built originally for boatyard workers and employees of the nearby ironworks foundry. Some were sunk into themselves, roofs half collapsed, propped up by their nearest neighbours. Being close to the canal had made them prone to flooding, and poor drainage led to disease. Even before the Alliance, the area had been notorious for poverty and overcrowding.

Picking her way through the cratered streets, Rose looked nervously around her. A woman passed, draped in regulation black, carrying a bucket towards a water pump erected on the street corner. A face appeared at a window, then vanished swiftly behind a tattered curtain. A mangy cat skittered over a wall. Car tyres and mattresses mouldered in yards. Where doors had been left ajar, she peered inside to catch glimpses of cracked tiles, ramshackle furniture and candles. Many of the windows had had their glass replaced with cardboard, and in places walls had been shored up with timber, tacked haphazardly across gaping holes in the brick. An advertising hoarding for Van Heusen depicting a woman kneeling before a man in his new shirt – *Show her it's a man's world!* – had been repurposed for the side of a henhouse.

With a jolt of pain, Rose stumbled on a pothole and wished she had worn her older, sturdier pair of lace-ups instead of the polished Mary Janes. She felt as if she had entered a foreign land, or rather, a land that was slowly and steadily being reclaimed from the grasp of man. On each side of the road, and in cracks in the tarmac, weeds and wildflowers shot up unchecked, insects buzzing and dipping around them. Gutters were silted and overgrown.

It had rained in the night, and the scent of herbs – nettles, dock, mint and wild thyme – rose from the damp ground. A hawthorn in full bloom had scattered its blossom like blown snow across her path and its musty odour evoked a sudden evanescent transport of memory – of walking with Celia down the street towards their childhood home. It was over as swiftly as it had begun.

The streets were sunk in a deep quiet, almost oppressive in its intensity. At this time of day, the Friedas must be mostly at work with only the oldest and most frail left at home. As if to confirm this, through the window of a house she glimpsed an elderly woman sitting beside a spinning wheel, operating the treadle with one foot while twisting the skein of wool expertly in her hand. Rose had heard about this. Spinning was a personal enthusiasm of the Protector, who believed it made work for idle hands and provided a link to a purer past. He had reinstated the manufacture of spinning wheels and had them distributed to the lower orders.

She pressed on. Somewhere, a cock crowed. Dogs scavenged in a rubbish heap. In a yard a tethered cow lifted its huge gentle head to observe her steadily as she passed.

If the Protector cherished a simpler, more primitive time, then this was its perfect expression. In Widowland, time had slipped as swiftly as a stone sinking to the bottom of a well.

She had been told to look out for a square brick church tower, and soon it reared up ahead like an Italian campanile, its green copper roof towering over the squat, terraced rows.

Beyond it, towards the canal, a flock of rooks drifted like flakes of soot onto a cluster of elm trees.

The house itself was on the corner of two streets, its frontage laced with ivy and its windows cracked. Around the door frame a vigorous climber tangled, and from the chimney stack, a thin plume of woodsmoke braided itself into the misty air.

Rose approached the door and knocked.

The widows were used to being interrogated. That was immediately obvious. They sat tightly upright on their frayed and battered armchairs, hands folded in their laps, wary and composed. The oldest, Kate Wilson, seemed the self-appointed leader. With her sharp grey eyes and shock of white hair above the shabby black clothes, she might have been a bird of prey, wings folded, hawkish and attentive to Rose's every move. Her skin was old paper, lined around the mouth and crinkled at the eyes, and her glasses were held together with tape – Friedas weren't eligible for new spectacles. The woman beside her, Sylvia Hancock, was neat and self-contained, with hair brushed into an earmuff braid around her head in one of the fashions prescribed for Friedas. She wore an unreadable expression that might just have been sardonic. Vanessa Cavendish was a slender woman in her late fifties with a porcelain complexion and dark hair liberally threaded with grey. Mild and shy, she had been married to a vicar. The fourth, Sarah Walsh, must have been a raving beauty once, and she was still eye-catching, with high cheekbones, a straight nose and full lips. The watchful expression in her deep-set eyes made her somehow ageless – as much a wary teenager as a sceptical widow.

'Do all four of you live in this house?'

'Five,' said Kate, tersely. 'Another woman lives here too, but she's away right now.'

Rose rubbed the ankle she had twisted on a pothole.

'I hadn't realized it would be so . . .'

'Run-down?' queried Sylvia. 'We do try to see the benefits, Fräulein Ransom. It's true the Government spends very little on Class Six residential areas, but that does mean we're spared the luxuries of more elite places.'

'Luxuries?'

'No loudspeakers, no agents hovering under street lights or in shop doors. We don't have any street lights or shops for them to linger in.'

Rose was offered the best seat, a deep wing armchair covered with a torn William Morris Liberty print that had evidently been salvaged from a tip. The walls were plastered with prints that looked as though they had been cut out of old books set in cracked frames, and the terracotta floor was covered with a threadbare Persian rug. The mismatched furniture included a coffee table made from an old orange crate and a worn sofa, upholstered in emerald silk, while a pair of china shepherdesses chivvied sheep on the mantelpiece. The creeper-clad casement windows admitted only a greenish, ethereal light and the air was saturated with the odour of damp timber. To combat the lack of heating all the women wore several layers of clothes, whereas Rose had come dressed in only a thin coat that she pulled more closely around her.

Despite the cold, however, the cottage had a distinct feminine cosiness. In the corners of the room hung bunches of dried lavender tied with string, and against a wall stood a tin bath with a copper jug to one side.

'Will you have a cup of tea?' asked Vanessa, in a cut-glass accent, like the vicar's widow she was. 'It's mint tea, actually. I don't know if you've ever tried it, but it's awfully good. We grow it ourselves. And we have honey, too.'

She gestured outside to the backyard, where a narrow brick path fringed with fruit bushes – redcurrants and goose-berries interspersed with raspberry canes – led to a beehive at the end.

'Herbs are the salvation of a limited diet,' she continued brightly, producing a teapot and a mismatched set of willow-pattern cups. 'We have no meat, but we do have thyme, sage and rosemary. We have apple trees. We grow nettles and sorrel, nuts and mushrooms, but the bees are our pride and joy.'

As the fragrance of mint rose up around them, fresh and revitalizing, Rose explained her mission.

'I'm here to ask about history.'

'I understood that was *verboten*,' said Kate. It was hard to discern whether there was a sliver of contempt at the edge of her remark, or if it was merely caution. They were so careful, these women, as though weighing out their words with their own tin teaspoons.

'Not recent history, of course. Not the Events, or the Time Before,' said Rose, quickly. 'I'm talking about real history. The Protector wants to explore the roots of the Anglo-Saxon Alliance. He's interested in folklore. Traditional family beliefs that have come down through the generations.'

She launched into the questions she had noted down. Basic information about the women's lives and their childhoods, as well as the superstitions and folk beliefs of their parents.

Were your parents religious?

What superstitions do you recall from your youth?

Which fairy tales did you know as a child?

As they talked, Rose transcribed their comments in her book, squinting in the dim light. Observing her difficulty, Sarah rose to light an oil lamp and its guttering flame threw a lacy shadow onto the ceiling.

'We used to have electricity, but when it failed, nobody was going to mend it.'

'Really?' No electricity meant no wireless or gramophone. Nothing for entertainment.

'What do you do in the evenings?'

'We meet and we talk.'

'About work?'

'Books, mostly. Novels. Just in groups of three, of course,' added Kate, with deadpan emphasis. 'According to the rules.'

Puzzled, Rose surveyed the scant furnishings around her.

'I don't see any novels. Where do you keep them?'

Kate laughed, flashing teeth as mottled as ancient piano keys, and pointed a finger at her temple.

'Up here, most of them.'

Looking down at her notes, Rose searched for something to say. So far nothing subversive had emerged from any of the women's observations about their lives. They had recounted, dutifully, their childhoods, marriages and the events that led up to their widowhood. Vanessa's relationship with a minister of the church might be considered suspect, as might Kate's former employment as a journalist, or Sylvia's work for an organization called Marie Stopes that promoted birth control for the purpose of limiting families. Kate's husband had died of a botched operation, Vanessa's husband had been consumptive and Sarah's husband had died during the formation of the Alliance, timing which marked him as a resistor, but that was hardly unusual.

She turned to Sylvia.

'How did your husband die?'

Sylvia was around sixty, with the keen eyes of a punctilious civil servant. On the surface she appeared calm and self-contained, yet now her anger flared like a struck match.

'He killed himself. I don't think it was to escape me, but you never know.'

Discomfited, Rose closed her notebook. Nothing in these women's present life, or their childhood memories, could possibly be considered offensive to the regime. How was she supposed to discover what the police and the Gestapo combined had failed to find? If any of these Friedas was involved in seditious behaviour, they would hardly volunteer it.

Yet once again she pictured the sweaty scowl of the Commissioner, and his threat sounded in her mind.

If you don't want to end up in a camp, it's in your interests to make this work.

She tried another tack.

'The Protector loves books, as you know. He's a great friend of literature. He sees literature as the cornerstone of Alliance society.'

'Is that so?' said Sylvia. It was hard to tell from her tone if this was a genuine enquiry, or if she was being ironic. Rose recalled what Martin had once said. *Irony is a weapon for you English. To say one thing and mean another. Your Jane Austen knew that all too well.*

'Yes. He's especially interested in reading material for schools. He's always taken a special interest. In Berlin he established an Office for the Control of Literature.'

'Why would the Party need to control literature, Fräulein Ransom?'

Rose tried to remember what Martin had explained, but the words seemed to crumble as she grasped them.

'It's obvious, isn't it? The Alliance is not against creativity, but it needs to be kept within certain boundaries.'

'You believe that, do you?'

'You can't allow artists free reign. No society on earth has ever done that.'

'I suppose that's true,' allowed Sylvia. 'Think of the Pope. The Catholic Church created a list of heretical texts in the sixteenth century. Any book which ran counter to the Church's teaching was forbidden. Galileo was banned. And Martin Luther and Immanuel Kant. In fact . . .' – she made a little frown – 'I seem to remember that when the Protector's own book was first published it was placed on the Vatican's Index of Prohibited Books. I think I'm right about that.'

Clearly, Sylvia knew all too well. Sarah cut in, as if wary of where the conversation was leading. The cadaverous cat Rose had glimpsed earlier had settled beside her and she was stroking it absently, its tortoiseshell fur sticking up in clumps.

'I'm lucky. I work as a cleaner in the Bodleian Library which means I get to spend all my time with books. Personally, I'm glad the Protector values reading. Reading preserves empathy and without that, we're not connected anymore. We lose that feeling of stepping into other lives.'

Rose was used to this argument. It was a problem that cropped up endlessly in the classic texts. Their authors seemed obsessed with the value of reading because it enabled people to experience the lives of others. She had mentioned it to Martin once and he was scornful. *Why would anyone want to experience the lives of others? Aren't our own lives interesting enough?*

'I agree,' said Vanessa, who had caught the tail end of the conversation as she returned with the teapot which she had replenished with freshly cut mint leaves and hot water. 'Judicious books enlarge the mind and improve the heart – isn't that what Mary Wollstonecraft said?'

A shiver travelled between the other three women, so transient it was almost undetectable, before Sylvia seized the teapot and busied herself with passing it around.

'Mary Wollstonecraft?' asked Rose.

Woll Stone Craft. The woman whose sentiments had provoked Commissioner Eckberg to such violent rage. With a lurch of anticipation, Rose proffered her cup.

'I'm not sure I've heard that name. Could you tell me about her?'

For a beat nobody spoke. Then Kate shrugged, and pushed her broken glasses up on the bridge of her nose.

'She was a writer. She wrote a book in 1792 called *A Vindication of the Rights of Woman*. It advocated that women were the natural and intellectual equals of men, and they should have equal treatment and opportunities.'

'All women?'

'Precisely.'

Rose sipped her tea, her heart thudding. That this Frieda had expressed openly heretical views, or had at least repeated them in front of others, was a felony in itself. But the fact that they had mentioned Mary Wollstonecraft was infinitely more significant. The very same woman whose seditious words had been inscribed across the facade of the British Museum only last week. Merely to repeat them was probably enough to land you in a camp.

Rose was duty-bound to report it. At the very least she should take notes.

Even so, Mary Wollstonecraft's heretical words hung in the air.

Women are the natural and intellectual equals of men, and they should have equal treatment and opportunities.

As she wondered how to proceed, a violent banging sounded on the door and the women looked around as one.

Before any of them could answer it, the door was thrust open, the rusty hinges of its upper half yielding easily from the rotten timber so that it lurched drunkenly into the small front room, causing a jam jar stuffed with bluebells to crash to the ground. Darkened silhouettes loomed against the light.

Three men in heavy leather jackets were standing at the threshold.

'Move!'

With no more than a single command, the policemen stepped over the splintered wood and, wielding short knives, began systematically tearing the house apart. The William Morris chair was sliced along its back, unleashing a spray of horsehair, and the dresser was tipped forward, sending its contents spiralling onto the ground. One of the men tramped up the rickety staircase and his heavy boots could be heard crunching methodically through the narrow rooms, along with the heave of mattresses being levered off the beds and the clatter of cupboard doors opening.

The four Friedas had sprung up instantly and pressed

themselves against the wall. Kate was ramrod straight, beads of sweat on her brow. Sylvia retained an expression of sardonic calm, although her fists were tightly clenched, and Sarah put a protective arm around Vanessa, who looked petrified. All the women seemed rigid with shock, if not surprise.

Only Rose challenged the intruders.

'What do you think you're doing?'

'Stand against the wall.'

'Why?'

The policeman dismembering the armchair paused. He had a face made for a pub fight: a shiny bowling ball with a squashed nose and jutting brow. He was the kind of man, Rose recognized, for whom cringing deference to superiors was balanced by ugly brutality to underlings. She noted the glint of calculation in his eye as he registered that Rose was a Geli, yet also that she would prove no impediment. Without comment, he seized her by the upper arm and shoved her violently against the wall, banging her head painfully in the process and bringing a reproduction of *Venice* by Canaletto crashing to the floor.

'You can stand there or you can stand in a cell. Your choice.'

From the kitchen came the smash of china, where the second man was removing cups hanging by their handles above the stove and running a rough hand along the shelves. The ugly policeman aimed a kick at the cat, which vanished in a streak of tortoiseshell fur, and proceeded to empty two vases of flowers onto the floor.

It seemed at once impersonal, and deliberate, this evisceration of the house, as though it was designed to create as much disorder and damage as possible. None of the men asked what a Geli was doing in this run-down habitation, and although Rose was itching to intervene, the policeman's threat was enough to prevent her.

What would the Commissioner say if she managed to get herself arrested on the first day of a highly confidential mission?

It took no more than a few minutes for every inch of the tiny house to be rendered even more broken than before. Then, without comment or explanation, the three men left as swiftly as they had arrived.

CHAPTER THIRTEEN

The Cherwell café was a shabby place to the south of the city, overlooking a mediaeval stone bridge that crossed the River Thames. Frilly nylon curtains sagged across the middle of the windows, as though they knew that nobody actually wanted to look in and had given up halfway. The name of the café was inscribed in peeling script on the glass and a couple of flies had expired on the sash. Old gas brackets were still fixed to the walls, but instead of gas lights, someone had inserted candles that painted the wall with a halo of soot. Smeared bottles of brown sauce and ketchup stood on each table and a card on the bar said, *Sugar available on request*.

Only one customer was there when Rose arrived. He was sitting at a corner table, chin cupped in one hand, tracing his finger along the maze of cracks in the table's linoleum as though they spelled out some fiendish puzzle if he could only discern it.

As the bell clanged he sprang up and offered his hand. 'Fräulein Ransom! How nice to meet you.'

Bruno Schumacher was unlike any other German she had seen. He appeared, in fact, more like an Englishman. He had none of the Germans' height or self-assurance. His complexion was as pitted as orange peel and he had a five o'clock shadow that looked like it had no regard for punctuality. His suit was a forensic inspector's dream, with specks of breakfast clinging to his tie and Rorschach ink spots on the upper pocket where his pen had leaked. He was, Rose assumed, the same age as Martin, and thus in his early fifties, but cigarettes and alcohol had gifted him another decade. His face was mournful and his frown lines deep, yet his eyes, true to his name, were as brown as a bear's and arrowed at the edges by laughter.

He gestured at the pint of beer that was already half drunk.

'When you asked to see me, and said you knew Martin, I thought this might be a more pleasant place to meet. And somewhat less overlooked. I hope this isn't inappropriate.'

'It's fine.'

'The police station is a perfect environment for conversations, if you like the kind of conversations that require you to repeat each question several times until you get the right answer.'

Rose edged onto the stained velour bench opposite him.

'I'm sorry to hear that my men might have been more forceful than necessary.'

She looked at him cautiously. Men, especially policemen, outranked all women in the Alliance, but she was a Geli, and an authoritative tone was probably the best approach. Flirting would have been Helena's way, but the scene Rose had just witnessed, watching impotently as the police combed the Friedas' cottage, overturning furniture, knocking out the backs of cupboards, ripping the undersides of cushions and sending feathers flying, had sobered her.

'I asked to see you because I was shocked by what I've just witnessed. I was on direct business of the Protector.'

'Apologies again. Our men are on edge. It's a difficult time, as I'm sure you appreciate, with the Leader's visit in ten days. In fact, I've never known anything like it. The city's on lockdown. The administration has drafted in three hundred troops as back-up, and all leave for my men has been cancelled. So when we get certain low-level . . . annoyances . . . a sense of frustration runs through the ranks. My men become overzealous. I suspect that having a German as their senior officer makes them especially eager to impress. Can I offer you something more than an apology? What will you drink?'

After the day she had had, the prospect of a drink was almost irresistible, but Rose needed her wits about her.

'Coffee, if they have it.'

'Ah! I like a woman who appreciates coffee. Most English girls confine themselves to tea and, I confess, I've never seen the point of warm water flavoured with dust. Though if you don't mind, I ordered myself something stronger on the grounds that it's almost six o'clock. Cocktail hour. That's one English tradition I do applaud.'

Schumacher called over to the Gretl to order the coffee and then tipped back in his chair, as if the day itself had physically pummelled him into submission. He smiled.

'So, you're a friend of Martin's.'

He was speaking English, but the word friend carried the ambiguity of the German – *Freundin* – where it might suggest a romantic relationship.

The underlying implication made her reply more sharply than she'd intended.

'We're colleagues at the Ministry. He gave me your name in case of trouble but I never imagined I would need to use it.' Then, more softly, and because she was burning with curiosity about this childhood friend of Martin's, she said, 'He told me you'd been in Berlin together.'

'Berlin. A place where beer still tastes like beer. And a cigarette lasts long enough for you to smoke it.'

Schumacher pulled a National cigarette from his pack in demonstration. As he held it up it sagged, then came to pieces in his hand.

'I've been here for twelve years now and I still miss everything about home. I miss the food, the entertainment, the weather, even the wit. Berlin wit is as dry as a widow's . . . Sorry. I mean, it's the kind of humour you don't encounter much around here. Martin's one of the few people I can still joke with. How is he?'

'Well. Very busy, of course.'

'I haven't seen him in years. Is he still the handsome devil I met on the first day at school? I remember him coming into class that day, planting himself down next to me and declaring that we would be best friends, just like that. And so we were.'

That was easy to believe. Martin, blessed with a blithe personality and sunny good looks, had an absolute confidence that whatever he wanted came to pass. If he declared someone would be his best friend, there was every chance they would be.

'He was always bright – he shone in anything he turned his hand to. Absolutely the teacher's pet. I wasn't bad either, but I was lazy. The cleverest thing I did was not getting caught. When we left school, Martin was on the fast track to law school. Anyone who's anyone in the Party has a law degree whereas I joined the Kriminalpolizei. We did our SS initiation ceremonies together. We were best men at each other's weddings, only he and Helga are still married . . .'

Rose winced inwardly. Though part of her was ravenous for information about Martin's wife, the other part recoiled at the thought. Almost always now, when she and Martin were in bed, Helga's face came to her, transmuting Rose's guilt into a kind of sisterly solidarity. It was almost as though Helga was in bed with them. When Rose kissed Martin, she imagined Helga kissing him too. When she ran her fingers along his chest, she wondered if Helga did the same. The fact was, Rose thought more about Helga than Martin himself.

'What's she like?'

'Helga? Sporty. Came top in her year in the Bund Deutscher Mädel athletics and went on to run for Germany in the '36 Olympic Games. Retired after marriage, of course. Four children, holder of the Bronze Mother's Medal. Enjoys skiing. Would infinitely prefer that her husband worked for the Strength Through Joy Leisure division.'

He said all this quickly, yet still Rose got the impression that gymnastics and skiing were not the activities that Schumacher himself prized. Sensitively, he hastened on.

'Whereas my wife left me for a Luftwaffe pilot with a better uniform than me and clear blue sky where his brain should be.'

'I'm sorry.'

'Don't be. It meant that when this job came up, I had nothing to keep me. It was this or a posting as Kripo chief in Wuppertal, so it wasn't much of a choice.'

'Do you enjoy England?'

'I wouldn't go that far.' He grinned. 'But it has its advantages. If, for example, like me, you need to lose a little weight, this is an excellent country to live in.'

He gestured at the table before him, where the curled remnants of a cheese sandwich sweated on a plate.

Rose couldn't help smiling. In a burst of intimacy, she confided, 'I visited Berlin last year to help Martin with a speech. The food was incredible. I've never tasted anything like it.'

'Don't get me started. The only useful thing my ex-wife

learned at Bride School was her cooking skills. I will say that about her. I miss Ursula's schnitzel much more than I miss Ursula.'

'Is it a problem for you being divorced? Professionally, I mean? I assume you have no children?'

With a morose shrug he rolled another cigarette between his fingers.

'It's true. As you know, all Kriminalpolizei have the rank of SS-Sturmbannführer and Himmler insists that his Schutzstaffel have four offspring. If they don't, they are required to adopt. So far, the gorgons from the Family Promotion department have left me alone, but it can't last. Perhaps they think I'm just not cut out for marriage. Ursula certainly did.'

He lit the cigarette and smiled.

'I'm sorry about earlier. As I said, we're on red alert. The Leader's visit is the biggest event this city has ever seen. I'm implementing a ring of steel around the city centre, no cars or buses will be running, and I've had to draft in help to erect the barriers. Gun emplacements to be established in All Souls, Hertford and Brasenose colleges. Dog handlers to go into the Radcliffe Camera half an hour before his arrival. Snipers authorized to shoot to kill. I've been making plenty of precautionary arrests and evening curfew for all orders was tightened to six o'clock from last week.'

So that was why the city seemed so eerily quiet when she had ventured out the previous evening.

'Then after the Coronation, the Leader, the King and

the senior men are congregating near here at Blenheim Palace.'

'Martin mentioned that the Leader was staying at Blenheim. He said he needed to check everything right down to the cutlery and the swans on the lake.'

He chuckled.

'So Martin takes care of the decor, while his oldest friend does the policing side. Who would have thought it?'

The notion seemed to please him.

'There's a bit of professional pride at stake for me too. The chief of the Reichskriminalpolizeiamt will be in attendance. A man called Arthur Nebe. My ultimate boss. He's been Kripo chief since 1936. He's a god to us detectives. I met him once. Want to see?'

He opened his wallet. Inside, where a picture of a sweetheart might be, was a tattered print of the younger Schumacher shaking hands with a wiry old man, on whose cap the glinting silver death's head shone like his own silver hair. His face was a blank canvas pierced with eyes like shards of ice.

'He should have retired years ago, but nobody's going to tell him that. Nothing escapes Nebe, so I don't want anything blotting my copybook.' He tilted the glass of beer towards her. 'This, therefore, is my last drink for a week.'

'Hope you enjoy it.'

'Oh, I will. But that's beside the point. It's no excuse for misconduct by my men. Can you tell me what happened?'

Rose took a sip of her coffee – a mouthful of tepid mud.

'I went to the Widowlands to question the Friedas about their early lives.'

'Can I ask why?'

'It's Ministry business in connection with a book that the Protector is writing.'

'Fascinating.'

'Yes. And I was just winding up my interviews when your men arrived. They barged in without asking and acted very forcefully. When I protested, one of your officers pushed me against a wall and hit the back of my head. But worse than that was what they did to the Friedas' house. It can't have been necessary. They ripped up the furniture and kicked through the doors. Those women have little enough as it is. It was shocking. I assured them I'd lodge a complaint about it.'

Schumacher bent his head to his glass of beer, as if some cryptic answer was inscribed in its watery foam, then looked up abruptly.

'Have you ever been to our Class VI residential area before?'

'No. Why would I?'

'And you say your visit was to, remind me, *question the Friedas about their early lives*?'

'As I told you, research. For the Protector's forthcoming book.'

'It's not often we get people coming to our Widowlands wanting to talk to Friedas about their childhoods.' He motioned a cartoon scratch of his head and frowned. 'In fact, now I think about it, it's never happened before.'

'Really.'

'Whereas there *is* a lot of interest in the Friedas at the moment for quite another reason.'

'Because of these low-level annoyances you referred to.'

Schumacher sipped his beer thoughtfully.

'Miss Ransom. I'm not sure if you have any idea of what's been going on. Normally this city is a pretty quiet place. In a typical week we might have a pair of drunken students in a brawl, a Magda who is pulled out of a restaurant where she's been flaunting herself with a married man, or a husband who's beaten up his wife – we get a lot of that.'

Rose knew all too well. Violence behind doors was endemic now. Native men who felt emasculated by their position in the hierarchy liked to take out their anger on those closest to them, and that was usually their wives.

'We might see a Leni whose clothes outrage public decency' – Schumacher ticked off imaginary offences on his fingers – 'and so on. That's pretty much normal. But these are not normal times . . .'

He sighed and gazed across the bar, where the Gretl was rearranging a pyramid of buns as if the magic of geometry might make them any less stale. Catching Rose's eye, she abandoned the doomed enterprise and disappeared.

'I can't tell you much, of course, but in return for the actions of my overzealous men, I owe you a little explanation. We picked up a woman yesterday on suspicion of sabotage of a public building. Specifically, graffiti. It's been cropping up everywhere.'

'And you think the Friedas are guilty?'

'Almost certainly. When it first happened, we assumed it was a student prank, but calls began to come in suggesting that it was happening in every big city. These examples of graffiti, you understand, are taken from degenerate texts. Listen, I have no views either way about literature – the most I ever read is the back of a cornflake packet and when I get home I fall asleep the second my head hits the pillow, so if they outlaw reading tomorrow, it's not going to bother me. But there are, as you know, specific laws governing the discussion of literature.'

'Always use regulation texts and never in groups of more than three people, unless in an authorized setting.'

'Exactly. Schools. Tick. Alliance Girls and Boys groups. Tick. Anything else, it's going to come to our attention.'

Rose recalled what Kate had said. *We talk about books. Just groups of three.*

'We've known for a while that these old women regularly meet to talk about literature. In large groups, and most likely *verboten* texts. Now, I'm just here to keep the peace, so the idea of some ancient Friedas boring each other to death isn't going to keep me awake, but when it comes to defacing public buildings, that's another matter.'

'How can you be so sure it has anything to do with the Friedas?'

He gave her another crinkly-eyed smile.

'Are you questioning the ability of my detective department, Miss Ransom?' Then he laughed. A deep, gurgling smoker's laugh. 'Only joking. You wouldn't be the first. But believe me, we know it's them, though we've not been able to catch any of them red-handed. Once we do, we can round them up and administer justice.'

'But you have no proof.'

'Unfortunately not.'

'Why would they do it?'

'We assume it's linked to the Leader's visit. They know the crowds will follow wherever he goes, so they want to get their half-baked message across, whatever that message is supposed to be. They seem to have no idea how ineffective it is. Nobody wants to hear. No one knows or cares.'

'What happened to the Frieda you arrested yesterday?'

'Let's just say she was un-cooperative.'

'Did she tell you anything?'

'Nothing I can make out. But she's a devious character. Turns out she was in prison until recently on charges of sedition. A Frieda called Adeline Adams. As a matter of fact,' said Schumacher, 'I have her statement here. Want to see?'

'Certainly.'

He reached into a battered leather briefcase and withdrew a piece of paper.

My name is Adeline Adams. I am sixty-five years old. I studied literature at London University and became a teacher. In 1937 I left my place of work to visit Spain where I participated in the Civil War. This is on my file, and well known to authorities. I was swiftly disenchanted with the fighting and returned the same year to teach at a high school for girls on the south coast. When the Alliance was formed, like all teachers, I was approached for a list of my pupils and asked to provide remarks concerning their personalities and their political attitudes. I was told that I would be given privileged treatment if I complied. My response was that divide and rule is a hallmark of all totalitarian societies and therefore I would not provide the necessary information. Shortly afterwards I was relocated and I have lived in Class VI districts since then.

In January this year I was arrested at my home on unfounded allegations of sedition. I was imprisoned and interrogated at the Alliance Security Office, as you can see.

[Suspect shows her fingernails. Nails on right hand are missing.]

Despite this encouragement, no charges were brought against me.

I have nothing more to add except this.

You ask me who has influenced me. If I model myself on anyone, it would be Aphra Behn, and I assure you there is no hope of arresting her.

Rose scanned the statement silently, then passed it back to him.

'So what did you do?'

'We've had to let her go. But before we did, we looked up her address and it was decided that the place should be searched for anything that might incriminate her. The rest you know.'

'Why are you telling me all this?'

'As I said, any friend of Martin's . . .' He grinned. 'Besides, why would I pass up the chance of a drink with a beautiful woman?'

Rose sensed in Bruno Schumacher a deep loneliness. More than sensed it – she recognized it, from one loner to another. She saw at a glance the endless nights, the half-hearted single meals, the alcoholic excess, the solitary watchfulness, and she felt an answering ache inside her.

It was a mystery to her, why she should feel this way. Did she not have everything she could ask for? An elite home, a fulfilling job? Friends, family and a senior man who professed himself in love with her? Surely, she was not so different from Celia or Helena or Bridget, or any of the other women she saw regularly. Why could she not share their pleasures and excitements?

Why did she long for something else?

She didn't need to ask. It went back to her father and the grimy, oil-stained 'office' in his garage, where he would con- jure worlds and try to share with her his love of history and poetry. Celia belonged to their mother and liked nothing more than donning an apron and baking or pretending to clean the house. Celia even resembled their mother, with her heart-shaped face and wide-set, implacable blue eyes, but Rose had always been her father's child.

Schumacher got up and pulled on an ancient trench coat that made him look more than ever like a tortoise longing to retire into its battered shell.

'The curfew's on now, so I'm going to issue you with a pass.'

He scrawled on a piece of paper and handed it to her.

'Anything else you need, just ask. I mean it. And send my regards to Sturmbannführer Kreuz. I'm pleased he's met a lady like you. Really, I am. Helga never understood him. But that's the thing about Martin, he was always able to look after himself.'

If there was a wistful note to his voice, it was immediately covered by a prolonged bout of coughing which made it sound as though he had a truckload of gravel in his throat.

'And if you ever fancy a wild night on the town in Oxford, you know where to come.'

Rose walked slowly back through the deserted streets. A couple of bicycles passed, lights winking, and a bracing wind shivered scraps of litter down the cobbled alleys. The smell of jasmine and lilac floated over a college wall and she glanced through a gate to see long, striped lawns draped in shadow. As she passed Christ Church she was stopped by a sentry on duty and produced her identity card along with Schumacher's pass.

Further on, outside the gates of St John's, a police car was parked, and a pair of plain-clothed policemen was escorting between them a tall man with wire-rimmed glasses and a shock of white hair. His trailing, scholar's gown caught in a gust of wind like a sail, and as he turned his face, she saw his eyes, wild with rage and fear. But his empty protests were carried away on the night air. Presumably this was one of the 'precautionary arrests' that Bruno had mentioned. The man was shoved swiftly into the police vehicle, and Rose watched his head jerking through the back window as the car crunched away.

In the Red Lion's dining room, supper was almost over. The narrow tables were set with tablecloths and single carnations jammed in vases. A scrap of typed paper pinned to a green baize board announced that the evening meal was a choice of pickled beetroot and tinned pilchards, fish, or slices of cold ham and peas. Pudding was a type of fatless apple flan.

A resentful Gretl came up.

'Ham's off.'

She smelled overpoweringly of cheap scent. The perfumes used by lower orders had a sharp, astringent fragrance, far from the sophisticated French perfumes of the 1930s. Gelis were more discriminating with perfume because the Leader was known to disapprove, and those that did have tiny quantities of Dior, or Guerlain, or Chanel left over from before the Alliance used them only sparingly.

'What fish is it?'

'Nothing particular. Just fish.'

The Gretl flicked a pointed glance at the clock, as if to convey the immense inconvenience caused both to the kitchen staff and herself of still serving dinner at almost nine o'clock.

'I'll have that then.'

The anonymous fish, when it arrived, lived down to expectations. Rose consumed it in silence and declined pudding. She got up and left the dining room with relief. Yet as she crossed the lobby she felt a prickling sensation she had long learned to trust.

She turned, and to her astonishment saw a familiar figure.

CHAPTER FOURTEEN

Oliver Ellis was leaning against the reception desk, a suit-case standing at his feet, as though he was in the process of checking in. He was wearing a trilby and mackintosh and looked wearied by travel. When he saw Rose he had the grace to look startled and a flush rose to his cheeks.

'Rose! What on earth are you doing here?'

In her surprise, she had to grope for the ostensible reason.

'The Commissioner asked me to conduct some interviews for him. In the Widowlands here.'

Though she remained outwardly calm, shock and alarm collided within her. There was no possibility that Oliver Ellis's arrival, at the precise time she was here, at the very hotel she had chosen herself, could be sheer chance. Who had sent him, and why? Plainly the Commissioner dis-trusted her, but was it possible that he had sent an emissary to monitor her while she was on his own secret mission? She wouldn't put it past him, but whatever the reason, she thanked God she had come into the lobby at that moment. If she had not had the good luck to catch sight of Oliver Ellis, she would have been entirely unaware of his presence.

Quickly, he recovered himself and smiled.

'How intriguing.'

'What about you?'

His story would be off pat. Of course it would.

'I have some books to access in one of the libraries. I'm looking for certain historical texts.'

There was no doubt he was a good actor. He seemed entirely natural.

'Matter of fact, I was delighted when I discovered that the texts I needed were here. Getting out of the office in the current madness is especially pleasurable. If I hear any more vapid chat about Coronation robes or tiaras, I may go insane.'

Rose was still standing, heart thudding, calculating what to do or say.

'I call this an extraordinary coincidence.'

'Isn't it?' Oliver scrawled his signature on the ledger and the receptionist slid a key across the counter. Pocketing it, he smiled. 'But it's serendipity too. Seeing as we're here and off duty, what do you say to a drink?'

Rose opened her mouth to refuse. She had every excuse. It was late. She had notes to write up. She had no desire to indulge in office gossip. Yet the shock of the police assault on the widows' house, and the conversation with Bruno Schumacher, had combined to produce a deep weariness.

Even if Oliver Ellis was here to shadow her, the idea of a drink seemed suddenly irresistible.

'Just one.'

He led the way to the hotel's wood-panelled bar where a few battered leather armchairs were clustered around a fireplace. A clutch of charred sticks shifted listlessly in the grate, giving off a faint warmth. A tattered carpet covered the flagstones, and the walls were panelled in planks of splintered oak. The only other occupants of the room were an ancient couple consulting a large guidebook on Tudor architecture.

'To be honest, it's a treat to be here,' Oliver said. 'You have no idea how pleasurable it is to visit these fabulous mediaeval buildings after the archives I've been working in recently. Have you ever seen the Rosenberg Documentation Unit?'

She shook her head.

'No.'

'Well, don't. A hundred miles of vaults and shelving. You could die down there and no one would notice.'

He ordered two glasses of Scotch and leaned back against the clubby leather armchair, to all appearances a man relieved to be out of London and on an enjoyable mission. Perhaps he did enjoy shadowing Rose. Maybe sharing a drink with her was some kind of double bluff.

'Being here takes me back to my student days, even if they were in Cambridge rather than here. In some ways, my undergraduate days were perfect preparation for the Protector's work.'

'How so?'

She was relieved that he was so keen to talk. Perhaps he was lonely, or maybe it was designed to relax her guard, but either way, he seemed to require little input from her.

'I studied historiography. That's the study of the way historians reinterpret the past. When you read the great historians – Tacitus, Machiavelli, Gibbon – you see that there's nothing new about adjusting history. The past is always being remodelled to reflect more accurately the views of the present. Every generation interprets history to its own agenda.'

'I would have thought the job of a historian was to reveal the past as it really was.'

He gave a slight, wry laugh. 'That's what everyone thinks. Each historian believes they're revealing things as they really were. They'll give you a load of detail. What the Romans ate. How the Georgians built their ships. Victorian coins. Edwardian stamps. But the truth is, we can never know how things really were. Everything we think we know about the past is determined by what historians choose to tell us.'

'It doesn't alter the facts, though.'

'Depends what you call facts,' he said airily. 'There was a saying by the traitor Churchill . . .'

Reflexively, Rose glanced around her. Churchill's name was not mentioned lightly, and preferably not at all, but Oliver Ellis seemed unconcerned.

'Something along the lines of, *History will be kind to me, for I intend to write it*. Whatever you may think of him, he got that right.'

'Shh.' Rose couldn't help herself. 'I try not to think of him at all.'

'Sure.'

Oliver rubbed his thumb against the tumbler and broke off to stare into the flickering coals in the grate. Rose could not help studying him. The firelight shadowed the cliffs of his cheekbones and his jaw was hazed with stubble. His hair was at least an inch longer than the prescribed length for men and a shock of it tumbled frequently into his eyes, prompting him to run his hands through it in an unconscious reflex. Off duty, in shirtsleeves and braces with his tie loosened, he seemed more boyish than the buttoned-up suited figure who sat beside her every day in the office. She realized she had never had a proper conversation with him – little more than a few tame jokes and the routine, guarded exchange of pleasantries.

She knew nothing about him at all.

'What part of history are you adjusting at the moment?'

'Mediaeval. In particular, a book about King Alfred. The Protector's a big fan of mediaeval history. He likes their way of doing things. He wants me to show how the English and the Germans share the same racial soul. That's what fascinates him.' He grinned. 'Nobody else, though. I'd guess the only people who will ever read this book are me and the Protector, and the Protector has other things on his mind.'

'In that case' – she faltered, but was too tired to stop herself – 'is there any actual point in correcting history? I understand the case for literature, of course. People are so easily influenced by novels. You have to watch what goes into people's minds. But if no one is reading all those historical tomes, then why exactly?'

'Because we owe it to future civilizations to explain the evolution of the past. People will always look to history to understand the present. There's a saying: *Those who don't know history are condemned to repeat it.* That's why we need to make sure history is cleansed of false and erroneous views.'

'It must be strange, spending all your time on something nobody might ever read.'

He paused, as if exhausted by the magnitude of the Protector's ambition.

'That's true. And it's an enormous task. The Protector won't rest until all the history books in libraries and public spaces across Europe have been corrected. He sees it as an ideological battle. If we can control what people know of history, we control memory too.'

Across the room, mention of the Protector had piqued the attention of the elderly couple and caused them to glance in their direction. Rose wondered what they made of them – a couple of business associates? Or, God forbid, given that she and Oliver were roughly the same age, a pair of lovers, sharing a romantic nightcap before bed? Either way, Oliver seemed unconcerned. In the office, he always appeared something of a cold fish, but now he was animated, almost physically charged with excitement. The reflection of flames lit up the depths of his eyes.

'It's extraordinary, isn't it? When you think about it.

History takes such shaky steps. So little determines whether it goes one way or the other. Just imagine, if things had gone differently, it might be a different monarch being crowned next week. We could have a Queen Elizabeth instead of a Queen Wallis.'

'I'd rather not think about hypotheticals.'

'Why? Gelis are permitted to think, aren't they? Encouraged, in fact. Doesn't the Faith and Beauty School train its Gelis in philosophy and logic?'

The Faith and Beauty School was another institution imported from the mainland. It was open only to elite young women likely to marry into the SS. Just three branches existed in England – one in Knightsbridge, another in Chelsea, and the third in a stately home in Sussex. They provided residential training in a host of accomplishments: music, tapestry, weaving, painting, classical philosophy, conversation. Everything necessary to mould fitting companions for the cream of German manhood.

Fortunately, the elderly couple had finished their drinks and were making their way fussily up to bed, forgetting first their spectacles, then the guidebook, then the need to request an early morning call. Once they had finally gathered their possessions and left the bar, Rose shook her head in amazement.

'Frankly, Oliver, if I'd gone to one of those places, which I didn't, I might also have learned discretion.'

Oliver seemed undeterred. He stretched his legs out, crossed his hands behind his head and regarded her thoughtfully.

'You know what happened to Geli? The original one?'

'She died tragically young. Everyone knows that.'

'Angela Raubal. The Leader's half-niece. She killed herself. Shot herself through the heart in the Leader's apartment in September 1931 with his own Walther PPK pistol. She was just twenty-three. She'd come to Munich to be a medical student and moving in with her uncle must have seemed the most natural thing in the world, but there was nothing natural about what happened next. The idea was that he would look after her, but in effect, he controlled her every move. He was crazily possessive. Wouldn't let her have a boyfriend. Went mad if she spoke to other men. Eventually, she formulated an escape plan. She would go to Vienna and train as an opera singer – but the Leader wouldn't hear of it. He wanted her with him, always. This was his own niece we're talking about. He was infatuated with her.'

Despite the warmth of the bar, Rose felt a chill go through her. She had never heard such a scandalous tale. To her, as to every female in the Protectorate, Geli was the apogee of womanhood. A secular saint, pure and perfect, to be honoured and emulated. Her brief life story was taught to five-year-olds. How she had grown up in Linz, the Leader's home town, a model child and then a faithful follower and supporter of her uncle. Photographs of her round, slightly pudgy face, with its unruly bob of brown hair and broad smile, beamed from the windows of department stores. It hung in classrooms and replaced the Virgin Mary in churches. Often, Geli was seen alongside the Leader's own image, as twin male and female ideals.

Rose thought of the day she and Helena had posed arm in arm beneath the statue of Geli on their Classification Day, trying to look suitably sober beneath her stately bronze form. That this same girl had taken a gun to herself at the age of twenty-three in an emotional crisis prompted by the incestuous behaviour of her own uncle was incredible. Horrifying.

'Her suicide almost pushed the Leader over the edge. His men feared that he would give up politics altogether. He was sunk for months in a pit of depression and rage. It was touch and go whether he would desert his career. His niece was said to be the only woman he ever properly loved.'

Oliver would not unlock his gaze from her eyes.

'Sad, isn't it?'

'I don't know.'

'You mean, you don't know if Geli Raubal's death is sad?'

'I mean, I don't know if what you say is true.'

'I do, and it troubles me to think about it.'

'The mind must know its bounds,' she murmured. It was one of the endless mottos the Ministry pumped out for posters and public information campaigns. Don't think beyond your own shores. Don't presume to speculate on other cultures. 'Cultural Misappropriation', it was called, trying to imagine you could understand how other people thought.

'Of course. The British like being an island, don't we? *A*

precious stone set in a silver sea – isn't that Shakespeare's phrase? Makes us feel safe.'

Why was he talking like this? Almost certainly it was designed to test her, but even so, it was reckless. The bar might be ostensibly empty, but waiters were hovering, buffing tables and polishing glasses. Gretls passed, with brushes and piles of sheets. No public space in the Alliance was free from prying eyes and keen ears. If Oliver was trying to draw her into some kind of treachery or indiscretion, he would need to try harder.

But he seemed to recover himself. He shrugged, pleasantly.

'So how did you find the Friedas?'

'They were . . . co-operative. Intelligent. But their homes . . .'

'Yes, what *is* Widowland like? I've never seen those places.'

'You wouldn't believe it . . .' The events of the day were catching up with her. She reached for a sip of whisky, but her hand trembled so much she put it down again. 'It's like a different world. One that's going on right under our noses, but we never see it. The Friedas are very poor. They make do, but they have almost nothing. No electricity even. Very few possessions. It's the kind of place I'd never dreamed of.'

He was silent for a moment, still monitoring her intently.

'What *do* you dream of?'

'Me? I never remember. How about you?'

'You don't want to know my dreams.'

The spell was broken. Oliver shook his head and grinned.

'But as far as my aspirations go, I have it pretty good. A lovely apartment. Congenial working companions . . . Another Scotch? It's doing me good, even if they do water it down.'

He looked like he was planning on talking all night so she feigned a yawn, and signalled her imminent departure.

'Actually . . .'

'You look tired, Rose.' He leaned forward solicitously. 'I would have thought time out of the office would be a relief for you, but—'

'It's been a trying day.'

'I'm sorry. I'm here for a while. Until Friday at least. How long will you stay?'

Three days, she had planned. There would be further interviews to conduct and notes to write up, and after that, the report to file for the Commissioner. All in a frighteningly brief timescale. The Leader arrived in ten days. She had until then to unravel the insurrection of the widows, or she – and, even worse, Martin – might be referred to the Morality Office. She had to find something. At the very least provide some names. Yet the thought of doing it under the observation of Oliver Ellis, with his restless dark eyes and searching gaze, was unbearable.

'I'm leaving in the morning actually.'

His face fell. No doubt she had thwarted whatever plans he had laid. Perhaps he too was operating under a tight deadline.

'Must you?'

'I must.'

He lifted his arms as if to protest, then dropped them again.

'Shame. No night on the town for us then.'

'Sorry.'

'Maybe sometime back in London . . . ?'

But she was already getting to her feet.

'Maybe. I'd better say goodnight now. I have an early start.'

When she closed the door to her hotel room behind her, she was shaking. The events of the day had left her in a state of nervous shock. Her head was throbbing, her ankle hurt and her back ached where the ugly policeman had pushed her against the wall, yet these physical aches were nothing compared to the trauma in her mind.

The encounter with the Friedas had profoundly unsettled her. She could not forget Kate's forthright gaze, or the sceptical way Sylvia questioned her entire *raison d'être*. *Why would the Party need to control literature, Fräulein Ransom?* Then Oliver's dreadful, scandalous suggestion about Geli, which had opened dark doors in her mind.

If she was to make any sense of it, she needed both time and space.

Leaving for London early meant that she may need to make a return journey to the Widowlands if she was to find enough information for the Commissioner. Yet the urge to slip away from the scrutiny of Oliver Ellis and return to familiar surroundings felt suddenly overwhelming.

As she undressed and crept between the chill sheets, she longed for all the little rituals that represented the sacred in her ordinary life. To open the creamy pages of her notebook and sit, head bowed, lost in concentration as the ideas flowed from her. To make tea and curl up in the armchair, listening to the trams trundling past, or the shouts of the children in the street or the birds singing in Gordon Square. To take a walk through the streets of Bloomsbury and imagine herself back in historical times. Or, even better, to catch a bus to Clapham and cuddle up with Hannah in her candy-striped bedroom, reading the latest instalment of their secret story, until, mouth open and eyelids heavy, the child finally fell asleep.

PART TWO

PART TWO

CHAPTER FIFTEEN

Wednesday, 21st April

A busload of tourists, faces agog and cameras at the ready, sailed up Piccadilly. They exclaimed at the tall stone columns that stood on either side of the street, each bearing the Alliance symbol on top: a mangy lion, surmounted by an eagle. They photographed the sentries standing guard outside the SS headquarters at the Ritz Hotel as though they had never seen soldiers before, and they marvelled at the advertising slogans spelled out in stuttering neon in Piccadilly Circus as if they were Wordsworth's finest. *Guinness is Good For You! Gordon's Salutes Our King and Queen!* Even the statues had them in raptures. The leaden figures on horseback with their bird-limed uniforms had, in most places, been replaced by members of the regime, and that morning in the centre of Piccadilly Circus, an immense bronze of the Leader, modelled by his favourite sculptor, Arno Breker, was being hoisted into place. Some of the tourists saluted.

As the open-top bus passed, Rose could hear the tour guide, an aged, port-faced man whose booming, aristocratic voice had evolved over the centuries to give orders in gentlemen's clubs, but was now reduced to advertising the buildings that had, until recently, been occupied by his ancestors.

'The royal couple will proceed to Westminster Abbey in the gold state coach. It has been used at the coronation of every monarch since George IV. It weighs four tons and is lined with velvet and satin. It is always pulled by eight Windsor Greys. When we say greys, we mean white horses. The King and Queen will be preceded by a cavalcade of Mercedes, in which we can expect to see a host of foreign dignitaries including the Protectors of Bohemia and France and Ministers Beria and Khrushchev representing the Soviet Union. Yes, madam, the Leader's route is being kept under strict wraps but that is part of the fun of the occasion. Now, if you look to your left you will see Cambridge House, once the home of Prime Minister Palmerston, later known as the Naval and Military Club, and now the private residence of Minister von Ribbentrop. Cambridge House was built in 1756 . . .'

Rose crossed the road and walked south towards St James's Square.

Access to the London Library, a lofty, mellow-bricked Georgian building in the northern corner of the square, was strictly controlled, due to the number of heretical texts that were stored there.

Rose, like everyone in the Correction team, had special authorization and went as often as she could. It made a change from working in the Ministry, with its soupy light and dingy warren of corridors, and besides, she loved the library's thick, dust-filled air and its metal stacks several storeys high that reached up on each side like a precipitous forest. If you looked down between the iron-slatted floor, you glimpsed thousands more books piled beneath your feet, like an ever-receding cavern. Whole stalactites and stalagmites made entirely of literature.

This was where it had started.

When she told Martin Kreuz that she had no time to read, she was telling the truth. As a young teenager she had read avidly, stories about orphans who turned out to be heiresses, adventurous animals, and hearty tales set in girls' boarding schools. But after the excitement of becoming a Geli when she was sixteen, life had been far too busy for any solitary pursuit. Immediately after the Alliance was formed, a great push towards community activity began. Scouts, Guides, chess clubs, and sporting societies expanded their ranks, each of them seeded with informers. Under the new dispensation, busyness was more than a virtue, it was a manifestation of patriotism. As on the mainland, any female over the age of ten would attend Alliance Girls meetings in the evenings and holidays, right up to the time she transferred to the Women's Service and ultimately Mother Service classes.

Where would anyone find the time for books?

That all changed when reading became work. When Rose was appointed to the Correction team (Fiction) her days were spent immersed in work that was ideologically toxic. Page after infectious page must be read, and in parts rewritten. Like an industrial chemist, Rose's job meant coming into contact with substances that the regime had pronounced dangerous.

And she was not immune.

Approach the job like a mundane task, Martin advised. Think of it like gardening. Spotting heresies like weeds. Pruning, chopping and tidying the text. If all else fails, remove entire paragraphs, chapters even.

Rose tried, really she did, but as she went on, it got harder. No matter that a novel's spine was cracked or its pages torn, the words breathed out of the book like a soul. Going home after a long day's work, she found she could not get the writers' voices out of her head.

She came to love the sensation of the writer's mind against her own. To feel the touch of another intelligence, jokey, tender, serious or preachy. To hear the breath of the author's voice in her ear. To know what it was to be alive in the eighteenth century, or the fifth century BC, or roaming the Yorkshire Moors. To ask questions, to experience the sounds and smells of a hundred imagined worlds. Living with an author meant, at times, becoming them. The writer's voice – be it calm, urgent or insistent – sounded in her mind like the voice of a friend. Rose came to appreciate their subtlety. The way the writer let her know not only what their character was thinking, but what they, the writer, thought of the character.

And then another thought arose.

Martin didn't know her. He had certainly misjudged her. Did he really think that she could read all this and remain unchanged? Was he so convinced of her stupidity and her incurious nature that he thought she could spend every day with these texts and see them as mere words – as weeds – rather than ideas that would take root and blossom and flourish within her?

Rose's ostensible reason for a visit to the London Library that morning concerned a corrected version of *Jane Eyre* that was shortly to be issued to schools and libraries. The text was problematic in all kinds of ways. The love story concerned a lower born woman who fell in love with a rich man from the higher orders and aspired to marry him. Yet when she finally won his affections, she left him. The narrative was riddled with assertions of female self-sufficiency. Empowerment, independence, self-awareness. Practically every page required an edit.

Rose had come to the point where Jane berates Edward Rochester, wrongly believing he plans to marry a higher caste woman.

Do you think I am an automaton? – a machine without feelings? and can bear to have my morsel of bread snatched from my lips, and my drop of living water dashed from my cup? Do you think, because I am poor, obscure, plain, and little, I am soulless and heartless? You think wrong! — I have as much soul as you — and full as much heart!

There was not much to do with this subversion, other than strike it out.

The fact was, as time went on, Rose found that her task of editing was getting increasingly difficult. The more she read, the more she liked to think of herself as a collaborator, rather than a corrector. She felt herself growing close to the writer, breathing the same breath, linking hands, as if the writer herself had entrusted Rose with this enormous task. And this made crude censorship impossible. When Rose corrected, she tried to maintain the tension and clarity of the text, keeping the narrative flowing, remodelling paragraphs, emulating the style, preserving its rhythms and fluency. She became attuned to the beat of the syllables and the internal music of a phrase. Perhaps this meeting of minds was what editing was supposed to be.

At the best times, Rose saw herself slipping invisibly like a spy behind the novel's lines. An agent operating from within.

Anyhow, it turned out that the aristocrat, Mr Rochester, was already married and keeping his existing wife hidden under the care of a nurse due to her mental illness. Rose would have to check this. Was keeping a madwoman in an attic quite as reprehensible as Charlotte Brontë made out? Rose was unsure about the correct depiction of female insanity, but she suspected that Mr Rochester's treatment was broadly in line with Alliance protocol. She never encountered mad people in daily life. No one did. Presumably there was little mental illness in the Alliance, but she supposed if it happened, it made sense that the patients were not left to roam the streets. And yet . . . even as she edited, Celia's words about their father sounded in her mind.

Those fits he has. It's madness. And it's been getting worse.

She carried on through the text, deleting lines, occasionally improvising a subtle dialogue change – *Reader, he married me* – all the time keeping one eye on the clock.

Although she had right of access to the stacks, this right did not extend to any kind of generalized exploration. Every area required a specific permission slip, stamped and signed, attesting that the holder had reason to examine the texts involved. Very little escaped the chief librarian, a gimlet-eyed Leni who manned the desk like a gorgon at the gates of hell. Past visits, however, had told Rose that the Leni took a short break at precisely one o'clock.

That day was no different. As the muffled peal of the bell from St James's Church dissipated through the London afternoon, the Leni levered her bulk to her feet. None of the other correctors, craned over their texts like mediaeval monks, even looked up.

Rose left her desk swiftly and trotted up the wide staircase, whose walls contained bleached rectangles where the photographs of degenerate writers – T. S. Eliot, Henry James, Virginia Woolf – had once hung. It was bad enough that their work should remain here, under conditions of rigorous control, but nobody needed to look at their faces as well.

Two floors above were the stacks marked *Degenerate Literature: Female Non-Fiction*.

Before she could examine them, however, she needed to get past the archivist, another Leni, but this one by contrast was young and cheerful, wilting in the library's deathly hush like a plant deprived of light and air. She had glossy brown hair in earmuff plaits, apple cheeks and a sweet, friendly demeanour. Going by looks alone, she might have qualified as a Geli, so there must be something in her background that told against her. Rose could imagine her at weekends, meeting her friends in coffee bars, idolizing film stars and experimenting with the most daring interpretation possible of the Leni's standard scratchy grey worsted.

At Rose's approach she brightened.

'Can I help?'

Definitely not.

'Got your permission slip?'

A wooden box containing a ream of stamped permission slips sat on the desk in front of her. Collecting them was the girl's chief, and not very taxing, job.

Rose shifted her bag from one arm to the other, as if in prelude to finding the necessary scrap of paper, and hunted for a question of her own.

'Looking forward to the Coronation?'

It was rare, but not forbidden, for Gelis to make idle chat with women of a lower caste. The girl blushed accordingly.

'I can't wait! A gang of us are going to watch the parade.

We're just wondering what position to take on the route for the best view. What do you think?'

She froze, as if this question might constitute an attempt to exact classified information.

'Not that . . . I mean—'

'No, of course not,' Rose reassured her. 'Everyone wants the best view and the authorities will ensure that all citizens get a good look wherever they are. But if you wanted my professional opinion . . .'

Here she hesitated slightly, as if uncertain whether to divulge sensitive material, and lowered her voice. 'I'd say St James's Street is the perfect spot. It's very near the palace and fairly narrow, so you can get close up. You'll see all the dignitaries. You won't regret it.'

Gratified, the Leni beamed.

'Thank you. I'll tell my friends.'

'I'm just . . .' – Rose mimed directions to her left – 'going to be a minute. I have a reference to check. It only just came up, so I didn't . . . Don't tell on me!'

Before the girl could protest, Rose slipped through the stacks and followed the alphabet around the corner.

She moved along the shelves, noting the perfectly filed volumes with their corresponding reference numbers marked above; the aged binding of their spines, polished leather in autumnal shades of golden brown, moss green, ochre and faded yellow, not to mention a whole case of reds – claret, merlot, cabernet sauvignon. Carefully she ran her finger over their ridges and indentations. In the past she had sometimes picked up a book and breathed it in, as if the emotions of the past could seep out from between the covers.

A whiskery man with glasses suspended on a chain around his neck was squinting at record cards. Another Leni further up was wheeling a trolley along the stacks, returning books to their correct places.

She ran her finger along the books to help her focus. *Political writing. Pre-Twentieth Century.*

Frances Burney, Harriet Martineau, Frances Trollope.

Rose pulled the odd volume out at random. Much of the writing focused on the importance of female education in a way that was directly in conflict with Alliance ideals. It was a familiar trope of nineteenth-century women's fiction, too, she had noticed. Elizabeth Bennet defending her education because *we were always encouraged to read*. Anne Elliot, the heroine of *Persuasion*, urging the importance of reading because it could *rouse and fortify the mind by the highest precepts*.

These reflections, however, were not what Rose had come for.

Feverishly, she scanned the shelves until her gaze caught on a small, slim volume covered in pale blue linen, badly foxed.

A Vindication of the Rights of Woman, Mary Wollstonecraft

She was in the act of levering it out when she saw him. A portly man, wearing a tweed jacket, with an enamel Alliance pin on one lapel and a navy and white spotted bow tie that marked him out as an intellectual. His name, she knew, was Oscar Stephenson.

Stephenson had been a political journalist originally, and his bulbous visage and pink scalp with its crinkly strands of tow-coloured hair was familiar to any reader of the *Radio Times* – the magazine that listed wireless broadcasts – illustrating the programme that he compèred called *Men of Distinction*. Its format was simple. The guests – always male – debated moral philosophy or the rights of man, along with the occasional light-hearted problem. For example, should women be permitted to play chess against men in public places? Or, was the Alliance ban on girls wearing trousers excessive? Occasionally, a debate would be held on the ethics of Widowland. What good were these useless people to society? Women who had contributed no children to the nation and whose withered frames were incapable of most manual labour? Technically, Stephenson adjudicated, but in reality he preferred the sound of his own opinions, issued in a blustering manner, which he used to patronize or batter his opponents, especially when they had the better argument.

Rose's mother loved him. She always referred to him by his nickname, 'the cleverest man in England'. It was a soubriquet Stephenson had popularized, if not actually invented.

He had been an early and vocal supporter of the Alliance: when he detected a lack of political enthusiasm in his guests, or a debate became especially complex, Stephenson would make the argument personal, suggesting that his guest was in some way questioning Alliance beliefs. Being invited onto *Men of Distinction* was a poisoned chalice, but turning Stephenson down was equally hazardous. Soon he would be even more prominent. Rose had read that *Men of Distinction* was to become a programme on the new television service.

Now, he was staring openly in her direction. She froze and tried to focus her eyes on the pages in front of her, but she could tell he was attempting to see the book's title. Much as she was yearning to open it, she felt uncomfortable reading a work of such heresy under his blatant gaze.

Casually, she glanced over her shoulder. Stephenson was still squinting at her so, covering the book's spine, she replaced it, and tugged the neighbouring volume forward a fraction to conceal it.

Next to Mary Wollstonecraft, and upsetting the alphabetical order, was another Mary. Mary Shelley. The archivist must have gone momentarily mad, and mistakenly shelved the women under their Christian names. As Oscar Stephenson's eyes burned into her back, she opened it at random. Looking down at the page, a phrase caught her eye.

The beginning is always today

The words sent a curious sensation up Rose's spine. A stirring of recognition and a creeping sense of déjà vu. She *knew* this phrase. She had heard it before. It felt like a riddle, or a call to arms. She had no idea what it meant.

A cursory glance told her that Stephenson was still watching. In a split-second judgement, Rose decided that on her way out she would make it clear that she knew his face. Encountering occasional celebrities through the Culture Ministry had taught her that famous people detested being approached by members of the public and obliged to make small talk or, worse, to prove that they were really who they resembled. She would confront Stephenson with delighted semi-recognition, question whether it could really be him, and then heap praise on one of his recent guests.

Smiling broadly in Stephenson's direction, she pivoted fractionally towards him and drew breath to speak. To her relief, the ruse succeeded. While he didn't actually retreat, he did at least turn his face away.

Heart quickening, Rose pulled out her pen and scribbled Mary Shelley's line impulsively on the back of her hand.

CHAPTER SIXTEEN

Thursday, 22nd April

The five sisters might have had their individual quirks, but the wide-set blue eyes, bobbed flaxen hair and porcelain complexions, not to mention their shared reputation for upper-class eccentricity, were recognized everywhere. They were said to have created their own private language, in which they planned practical jokes. Their exploits were faithfully followed by the newspapers' society pages, and the eldest had already made a wealthy and advantageous engagement. The second sister had a penchant for wild parties that embarrassed her parents and often ended with the police being called. The middle sister was writing her first novel. Whenever they got into scrapes, or were seen out with unsuitable companions, or had to be rescued from rowing boats at dawn, the establishment chuckled and rolled its eyes. The sisters' disdain for convention was the preserve of the elite, and it was also what made them household names.

Everyone had heard of the Goebbels girls.

The five daughters of Joseph Goebbels and his former wife Magda — Helga, Hildegarde, Holdine, Hedwig and Heidrun — had grown up in the bosom of the Party. As the First Family of the Reich, the image of them as children, outfitted in identical white smocked dresses and lined up in order of size, was seared on popular consciousness and reproduced in glossy magazines and propaganda posters everywhere. When they were younger, pictures of the Goebbels girls frolicking in the garden with the minister and his wife had been used in a sheaf of propaganda campaigns. Their suntanned bodies were juxtaposed with stark shots of mentally and physically handicapped children during a national drive to popularize the Elimination of the Weak. Once, there had been another VIP child to rival them: Edda Goering, who had grown up as a Princess of the Party, showered with gifts from crowned heads around the world. But Edda was now living in exile on a pig farm in Silesia, whereas the Goebbels girls were in England on a jaunt that had already taken in the best nightclubs, and several days' hunting at their father's country home.

That night, Rose observed them assume centre stage in the ballroom of the Grosvenor House Hotel where the reception for the delegation of American film-makers was being held. The walls billowed with cream satin lining, and on the dais, behind the band, a portrait of the King and

Queen was propped – Edward small and crumpled in his regalia like a child in fancy dress, and Wallis a matchstick in taffeta with a helmet of raven hair.

The Party VIPs were out in force for the Coronation. They had flown over and block-booked the best hotels and their loud, well-fed, self-confident voices jingled through the ballroom, like a cash register of Alliance marks. Their hair was sleek and their complexions soft as butter. The light of the chandeliers reflected off a roomful of diamonds and jewels, not to mention the silver insignia of a hundred SS dress uniforms. All the visiting women wore couture. The two elder Goebbels girls were dressed by the Parisian couturier Madame Grès, in bold patterned evening gowns with cut-out backs, one in silver stripes and the other in scarlet and black. The native women had resorted to whatever could be cobbled together with coupons and a lot of imagination.

Rose had agonized about her own outfit, in the end choosing an old evening dress donated by Celia that bared her shoulders, and the pearl necklace that Martin had given her in the early days of their relationship and which she had worn every day since. The dress's narrow waist flared out to a full skirt that flattered her slim figure and the purple silk complemented her complexion. She had waved her hair and pushed the ends back behind her ears, and her cheeks were already tinged with excitement. Yet as she stared into the mirror on her dressing table past the ancient bottle of Givenchy perfume that had belonged to her mother and the round tin of Max Factor Crème Puff, it was her father's eyes that stared back at her in scrutiny.

What would Dad make of her partying at the heart of the Alliance? Just occasionally she was grateful that his situation spared him the details of his daughter's life.

Bridget Fanshaw was standing alongside Rose, people-watching from the sidelines. Although Bridget was not naturally pretty like Helena, she compensated through the sheer effort she put into her appearance. Her moss-green dress was as low-cut as possible while keeping just within the demands of female modesty that applied even to Gelis (cleavage to be covered and skirts below the knee, nothing that excited sensuality or lascivious thoughts). Bridget routinely flouted the general disapproval of make-up by wearing both lipstick and rouge, despite regular admonishments. That evening her eyebrows were plucked into twin brackets of surprise, although thanks to her job in the Press department, very little surprised her.

'Not much love lost there.'

She folded her arms and nodded at the two elder Goebbels girls, who were ostentatiously ignoring their stepmother. The woman was, in fact, their second stepmother, being Goebbels' third wife, and although she had plenty in common with the sisters – she was practically their age – relations were frosty. The attraction between Suzy Ziegler and the powerful elderly minister had been instantaneous. They had met, in time-honoured fashion, in a casting session, and within a few months the bleached blonde and the wizened cripple acknowledged their love publicly in marriage.

Now, blotting out her surroundings with her fourth glass of champagne, her bosom encased in a froth of lace, Frau Goebbels was modelling the one Alliance fashion that trumped all others.

Pregnancy.

Being pregnant, producing a child for the Leader, was the highest honour of womanhood, so Suzy Ziegler, hanging on Goebbels' arm, had every reason to feel pleased with herself. Nonetheless, it was impossible to ignore her new husband's wandering eye as the cream of British female society drifted past in wasp-waisted dresses modelled on Dior's New Look. Their dresses may have been run up by backstreet seamstresses using synthetic nylon and cardboard instead of taffeta and satin, but it had been done so skillfully that it was hard to tell them from the real thing.

By contrast, Rose had no difficulty telling the nationalities apart. The German men took every opportunity to wear uniform and observed the minute gradations of correct dress with military precision. A sea of black serge was sprinkled with the appropriate insignia: daggers, cufflinks, death's head badges. The Americans, on the other hand, were almost horizontally relaxed. Some of the Hollywood men hadn't bothered with evening dress at all, but had come in lounge suits and ties, handkerchiefs in top pockets. In one case, Rose even spotted a pair of brown suede shoes. The nearest these men got to regalia was a Rolex.

'The Commissioner's delighted with the turnout,' whispered Helena. 'They've netted some pretty senior film executives here tonight. Eckberg thinks a slate of co-productions is ideal for cementing friendly relations between the Alliance and America.'

Could it be true? Was the relationship between America and the Alliance genuinely thawing? Avidly, Rose scrutinized the guests. The way that Alliance citizens were encouraged to think of Americans was carefully controlled by the Propaganda unit of the Culture Ministry. In the past, the general line was that America might be called the Land of the Free, but in fact it was a chaotic melange of organized crime, alcohol and pop music. Recently, however, more positive images of the United States were being propagated. Hence the appearance of *Little Women*, the tale of ordinary, good-hearted American girls, on the school curriculum. And the appearance of grander German women at the reception tonight.

Rose glanced across at von Ribbentrop's wife Annelies, in a gown the colour of dried blood. She was in deep discussion with Robert Ley, the Labour leader, who had met the King and Queen when they visited Berlin on honeymoon, his face as mottled as a slab of spam. Rose had never been in a room with so many senior Party members, and was relieved that Heinrich Himmler, who had famously vowed to shoot his own mother if the Leader asked him, was unable to attend. In the middle of the throng, a towering German with a lantern jaw was lecturing a squat, balding American in thick glasses.

The pair was almost comically mismatched, and the German was using his advantage of height in overbearing conversation.

'That's Rudolf Hess.' Bridget had been eavesdropping. 'He's telling the head of MGM about his aeroplane.'

Rose gawped at the Deputy Leader. Just being in the same room as him, a few feet away, should have impressed, even overwhelmed her. Instead his heavy brows and flashing eyes made him look almost . . . enthusiastic was the polite word but deranged would be more accurate.

'He has a vintage Messerschmitt Bf 110 apparently. It's all he talks about. He's telling them precisely how long it takes to fly from Germany to his estate in Scotland. He always flies solo.'

'Isn't that dangerous? What if he crashed?'

'He's never crashed. He says it's not his destiny.'

Restlessly, Rose looked across to Martin. They had arrived together, but he had left her immediately. For some time he'd been deep in conversation with a strikingly handsome officer with a curve of Brylcreemed hair brushed back from his broad face and wide, sensual lips. In contrast to his gentlemanly appearance, a coiled aggression emanated from the neck of his tightly compressed black SS tunic down to his glimmering patent leather shoes.

As Rose watched, the man's eyes flickered towards her, taking in every detail in a moment's chill appraisal. He knew about her, she could tell. He knew she was not Martin's wife.

Breaking off, Martin approached and drew her to a corner where they were shielded from sight by a vast urn of lilies and ferns.

'Who's that?'

'No one you want to know,' he muttered, taking out a cigarette. She noticed that his fingers were trembling slightly.

'What does that mean?'

'Walter Schellenberg. Remember I told you about him once? Head of the Reich Security Service. He learned his art at Heydrich's knee. After Heydrich died, he became Himmler's closest confidant. He's come over to take charge of the security arrangements. The Leader insisted on it.'

Rose couldn't stop herself glancing back at Schellenberg. He had been joined by a much older woman dressed entirely in black, whose porcelain complexion was traversed by a vivid slash of scarlet lipstick. With her kohl-blackened eyes, garlands of pearls and darkly lustrous hair, she resembled some frail, exotic bird. In stark contrast to the other women in the room, her outfit was acutely slim-cut to accentuate her toothpick figure. They made an odd couple, the elegant older woman and the bullish younger man. When he put his arm round her, she looked as if she might snap.

'Isn't that . . . ?'

'Coco Chanel. Yes. She's an old friend of the Queen. She's doing the Coronation robes.'

'Gosh. That's a big secret, isn't it?'

'Secret? I wish. The woman won't stop talking about it. I've been subjected to ten minutes on the subject of the design symbolism of the dress. The robes are going to be stark black and white with the Alliance emblem picked out in pearls and an androgynous twist – whatever that means. Lots of ermine and no colour.'

'No colour! The Queen's going to look like a Magda!'

'It's what she wants apparently.' Martin lifted another drink from a passing tray. 'He thought *you* were attractive.'

Rose frowned. She never knew what to make of her own looks. Throughout her childhood she had always been seen as a foil to Celia, whose beauty was acclaimed by everyone, so that eventually it became her defining feature. Rose, therefore, was thrown back on other qualities. And despite his endearments, Martin had never made her feel beautiful. Sometimes he would undress her and hold her by the wrist as he stood back to observe her, but the way he scrutinized her body made her feel like a machine part on a production line.

Now he drained the drink and looked around for another one.

'Not sure how I'm going to get through the next few days. You have no idea of the preparations I've been landed with. The Leader's meals – how that comes under Culture

God knows, but it does – and the detail is mind-boggling. I've been sent a diagram of his breakfast table with the correct placings for his plate, bowl, teaspoon and salt cellar. Can you believe it? He doesn't drink coffee. He must have apple juice. No meat. No alcohol. His favourite dish is cheese noodles. And he wants linseed oil on his bread. Linseed oil! I ask you. Then there's his travel, and his sleeping arrangements.'

Something had changed. Was Martin wearying of his loyalty? Rose had never heard this tone before, suggesting fraying nerves and ideological fatigue.

'Surely you can delegate that.'

'As if I haven't a thousand other things to do with a week to go before the Coronation. It's madness. And all this on top of the Blenheim conference. We're about to stage the most important conference for a decade, for which I'm co-ordinating the agenda, and here I am being sent memos about table settings. I ask you.'

'You never mentioned any conference.'

'It's scheduled for the day after the Coronation. But frankly, it's the main event.'

'Why didn't you tell me?'

'It's nothing you need to know about.'

'Even so.'

'I'm telling you now, aren't I?'

'Is that what's making you stressed?'

Another sigh of exasperation erupted.

'Actually, that's not what's stressing me.' He was staring at the wall as if he wanted to punch it. 'The graffiti's getting worse.'

Her throat tightened in alarm.

'What's happened?'

'Reports are coming in from all over the country. There've been incidents in Birmingham and Leeds. In Bristol they scrawled something on a factory wall yesterday, right where the Magdas come out. It must have been seen by hundreds of them, even if it was absolute gibberish. Something like, *She is too fond of books and it has turned her brain*.'

Rose recognized the quotation at once. It was a remark made by one of Louisa May Alcott's characters, Christie. Irony again.

'They also daubed some nonsense on one of the Cambridge colleges. King's, I think. The Fellows were livid.'

'What did it say?'

'Does it matter? It's not what it says, it's the fact that it's there at all.'

'Tell me.'

He rolled his eyes.

'It said, *I am no bird; and no net ensnares me: I am a free human being with an independent will*.'

Martin growled in frustration at the urn of scented lilies, as though he might rip their heads off. 'It's all so . . . *trivial*. This idiocy of desecrating public buildings. Foolish, worthless old women who contribute nothing to society but trouble. They're certain to pop up somewhere on his visit. I can just imagine how the Leader's going to react when he's confronted with some degenerate trash plastered across the country's finest buildings. Makes it look as if we can't keep our own Protectorate safe from a bunch of toothless old witches.'

He paused, and tried breathing deeply.

'The question is, how do we prevent it? Schellenberg's told me he wants to hold off from anything that might unsettle the populace before the Coronation, but at the same time he says it's essential that we crush any rebellious behaviour before it escalates. How exactly does he propose we do that?'

Extinguishing his cigarette in a glass of champagne, he lowered his voice.

'I've told him, there's only one way. Executive measures.'

Why should these bland, bureaucratic words have such an effect on her? 'Executive measures' was not a phrase Rose had heard before, but at the sound of it, the hairs rose on her skin, as though a chill wind had blown through the ballroom all the way from some barren, eastern plain.

'What does that mean?'

'What do you think it means? We go into the Widowlands, round them up and get rid of them once and for all. After all, we have the experience.'

'What experience?'

'It's not as if it hasn't been done before.'

Rose opened her mouth to respond, but before she could, Martin had taken her arm and moved her closer to the silk-covered wall.

'Listen, forget that.' He looked into her eyes as if registering her properly for the first time that evening. He had aged visibly in the last couple of weeks. The cheerful, confident man who first seduced her was now burned out and irritable. His complexion was jaundiced, the skin around his eyes bruised from lack of sleep and he seemed to have shrunk slightly within his evening dress. She felt a sharp pang of sympathy.

'I'm going up to Blenheim for a couple of days but l need to see you as soon as I get back. I have something to tell you, Rose, and I can't explain it here.'

Her ribcage constricted.

'Is it something I should worry about?'

'No. Yes. It's important. It's something you need to know.'

It was a relief to escape the reception.

Martin was obliged to go on to dinner with the VIPs. Goebbels and Frau Goebbels the third were hosting a banquet for eighty at Apsley House, where Rose's presence would be mercifully inappropriate. As soon as Martin told her, she slipped away.

Outside, a faint shower had brought down a line of bunting whose sodden paper flags squelched underfoot. The lights of the hotel spilled out onto a line of limousines, gleaming Mercedes and shiny Adlers, waiting, engines idling, for their

VIP passengers. Chauffeurs loitered together, smoking, raindrops speckling their caps.

Across the road, campers in Green Park, determined to secure a good position on the Coronation route, crouched beneath the trees or huddled under makeshift tents. In their hooded coats they looked like strange dun-coloured gnomes, watching the pageant from their place in the shadows. Further on, the long red and black Alliance banners draping Marble Arch and the department stores of Oxford Street stirred in the darkness.

Rose turned right, heading up Park Lane, turning Martin's words over in her mind.

It's not as if it hasn't been done before.

What was he suggesting? Was he referring to the relocations? Everyone knew the labour force was required on the mainland, and although mothers desperately missed their sons and husbands, they presumably saw that Extended National Service was in the Alliance's interest. Or did he mean the arrests, earlier, of political dissidents? *Get rid of them once and for all.* There must be hundreds of thousands of women in the Widowlands. How could you possibly do that?

She was so deep in thought that it wasn't until she was quite near them, turning down Upper Brook Street towards Grosvenor Square, that she noticed two figures ahead of her, a couple in close conversation standing beneath a street lamp. Even though Rose could only see her from behind, and the collar of her coat was turned up, something about the woman's lithe frame, and bouncy hair with a small upwards flick at the ends, was familiar.

Then she turned slightly, and the opalescent lamplight illuminated her face.

Sonia Delaney was more lovely, if possible, than her air-brushed photograph. Her perfectly framed profile showed a straight nose and a high forehead. In the spill of street light the garnets round her throat seemed to glow like the russet streaks in her hair. It was the kind of colour that came with a romantic name on the box: Autumn Gold or Honey Caramel or Chestnut Whisper. Her coat was belted at the waist and her hands were plunged deep in the pockets.

Even from a distance, Rose could see how animated the conversation was. The lean, dinner-jacketed man was gesticulating, hands upturned, as he bent forward to make a point, running his fingers through his hair in a gesture that Rose recognized.

Oliver! Two days ago she had left him in Oxford, working in the archives, and preparing to spend several more days buried in a library. Yet here he was, not only in London, but fraternizing with an American actress, their heads together and their bodies close, as if they were engaged in an intense and confidential argument. How had Oliver Ellis plucked up the courage to approach Sonia Delaney? He wasn't even interested in showbusiness. It seemed so out of character. What had he called the last film they'd seen? *Anodyne schmaltz*.

For a moment, Rose could not wrest her eyes from the sight of the couple, intimately absorbed in their conversation, and she felt a prickle of something more than curiosity; an emotion she couldn't quite name.

Oliver Ellis and Sonia Delaney. What on earth could they find to talk about?

CHAPTER SEVENTEEN

Friday, 23rd April

A scrum of journalists bobbed around the lobby of the Culture Ministry waiting for the Friday press briefing. With a week to go until the Coronation, a steady diet of news stories was being drip-fed to satisfy the raging appetite of the populace for all things royal. The items ranged widely, from the exact number of steps the monarchs would take to the altar and the precise part the Leader would play in the ceremony, to pure froth such as that the King enjoyed his breakfast eggs lightly boiled and Elizabeth Arden had given the Queen an exercise bicycle for Buckingham Palace.

The previous day's papers had been full of photographs of England's ancestral crown jewels. Altogether twenty-three thousand precious stones would be on display, including the largest diamond in the world, weighing five hundred and thirty carats, embedded in the royal sceptre. The most precious of the treasures were the St Edward's Crown, which was made for the coronation of Charles II, and the Imperial Crown that had been worn by Henry V at the Battle of Agincourt.

The whole lot had been crated up and brought over from Berlin in a Lufthansa plane all of their own, symbolically accompanied by six members of the Leader's own personal bodyguard, the Leibstandarte SS, as though they were guarding the King and Queen themselves.

The journalists jostled and chatted as Rose and Helena walked past. Journalists always seemed a race apart, more daring and confident than civil servants, waving notebooks and greeting each other in familiar, joshing tones. They gave each other nicknames and made jokes about the ministers. Yet this carefree demeanour, Rose knew, was an illusion. Journalists were scrutinized even more closely than ordinary citizens. They trod a daily tightrope of compliance.

On the mainland all press and broadcasting came under the control of the Party Press Chamber. Every workplace from 1933 onwards had been cleansed of employees who were ideologically inappropriate. The system had been transferred seamlessly to the Alliance. Every journalist was assessed before being given a job, but the scrutiny didn't stop there. Those who overstepped the mark in their daily work were sent for re-education, their fate recorded prominently in their own publications. Times *correspondent admits perfidy. Sentenced to two years' hard labour.* Or, Daily Mail *writer in false story shock. Judge jails him with warning.* When a journalist walked into their newsroom they were effectively entering a minefield.

A hum of expectation ran through the press posse. One of the photographers, pushed backwards, knocked over the Ministry noticeboard where daily announcements were displayed in Government font, a Gothic barbed wire of black officialese. Generally, these notices announced some fresh regulation, but when there was nothing new to ban, the default was a quote from the Protector. That day a functionary had plumped for one of Rosenberg's platitudes involving artists.

It is beyond question that the true culture bearer for Europe has been in the first place the Nordic race. Great heroes, artists and founders of states have grown from this blood.

Even as the photographer scrambled to prop up the noticeboard, that day's particular artist, whose honey-blonde hair and startling sapphire eyes attested to her undiluted Nordic blood, unfurled her long legs from a Government Mercedes and strode through the brass doors. She wore a cream cashmere coat with a silver fox collar and walked with the supple gait of a wild cat that might at any moment unsheathe its claws. As she passed, her image was bathed in the photographers' flash, to be reproduced for the evening papers, preserved in silvery aspic.

Leni – the original Leni – was here.

Leni Riefenstahl's groundbreaking documentary *Triumph of the Will*, charting the Leader's visit to the Nuremberg Rally in 1934, still played in cinemas across the land. Most citizens knew its opening scenes by heart – the camera panning along the cobbled backstreets of Nuremberg, the fog over the mediaeval squares, the massed ranks of storm-troopers assembled in the rally ground awaiting their leader. And then the Leader himself descending from the skies, his plane dipping and diving through the clouds, to emerge in a burst of sunshine above the Gothic spires.

The movie's success had sealed Leni's status as the Leader's favourite film director, and she had followed it up with a celebration of the 1936 Olympics, *Olympia*. In the 1940s, she had documented the conquest of other European countries with her epic *Europa,* and the building of the Leader's grand library in *The Eighth Wonder of the World*. So it made perfect sense that she, above all other film-makers, should have been awarded the rights and access to record the Coronation of Britain's King and Queen.

Now, at the age of fifty, Leni Riefenstahl was at her zenith. Lauded throughout Europe, afforded every privilege, her every move was saturated with her own publicity – and it was publicity that she very much believed.

Needless to say, there was not a Leni in the building who did not want an excuse to catch sight of their name-sake. Some clustered shyly, peering out of doors; others loitered brazenly on the stairs, star-struck and jittery with excitement. Mentally mirroring their heroine as if hoping to absorb her nonchalant glamour and make it their own.

'You have no idea how much work that woman has caused the Film department,' said Helena, whose status as a

Geli meant that she remained untouched by the office girls' excitement.

She folded her arms and pursed her lips.

'She has a production staff of a hundred. Sixteen cameramen plus their assistants, aerial photographers and special dollies for tracking shots up the nave of Westminster Abbey. Scores of sound operators, not to mention strict rules surrounding other cameras, which has led to a frightful row with the Americans.'

'What does it have to do with them?' Rose asked.

'The Americans are making a documentary about Wallis Windsor. *American Queen*, I think it's called. But Fräulein Riefenstahl insists that exclusive filming rights to the Leader's tour belong to her. No long lenses. No unauthorized shots along the route. The Americans are up in arms. They say the Coronation is an international event and they never tire of reminding us that the Queen is, after all, one of them. We've had to compromise.'

'You overruled Leni Riefenstahl?'

'They've been given permission to cover the Leader's visit to Oxford as a kind of compensation. Leni gets the Abbey to herself and the Americans can shoot outside. But even then, I see trouble ahead. Leni's got Albert Speer to design the lighting, and massed ranks of stormtroopers will be lining the aisles.'

'Sounds fun,' said Rose.

Helena narrowed her eyes as the subject herself stalked past the press posse towards a set of double doors.

'And she's demanded that the King and Queen present themselves for a run-through at the Abbey on Wednesday morning so she can work out positions and discuss angles with her cameramen.'

'I can't imagine the Queen allowing anyone to order her around,' said Rose.

'And I can't see Fräulein Riefenstahl taking no for an answer, so it should be good to watch. Probably more entertaining than the Coronation itself.'

The doors slid open and Commissioner Eckberg could be glimpsed, extending a greasy welcome. Bridget Fanshaw detached herself from the caravan of flunkeys buzzing round Fräulein Riefenstahl like flies around a picnic and joined them.

'Hope all this takes their minds off it,' she said.

The journalists filing into the briefing room seemed more subdued than usual.

'Off what? Is something wrong?' asked Helena.

Bridget nodded. 'One of the reporters was arrested this morning.'

'Who? What happened?'

The penalties meted out to journalists were especially harsh. Indeed, the Fleet Street office block belonging to the *Daily Mirror* was nicknamed 'Suicide Tower' because of the number of journalists who'd jump off it, rather than submit to official punishment.

'A feature writer on the *Chronicle*. Eddie Davies. Apparently he wrote a piece on Fräulein Riefenstahl's plans to make a film about Russia after the death of Stalin.'

'Is she? What's wrong with that?'

Rose knew, though. It would come under the label of 'political speculation'. In the Time Before, this topic alone had filled acres of newspaper space. Yet since the Alliance, discussing the political scene was deemed unhelpful. No one wanted journalists looking into the future, especially the kind of future that didn't bear looking into.

'It wasn't published, of course. The editor spotted it at once and insisted it would never have made it into print.'

'And he reported his own journalist?'

'Not this time. The Security people had someone in the newsroom. Actually, because the editor was so co-operative the Commissioner's decided to go easy on the paper. He instructed us to offer the *Chronicle* some kind of exclusive. I had to dig one up.'

'What did you give them?' asked Rose. 'Or shouldn't I ask?'

'Oh, it's top secret classified information. I could tell you, but I'd have to kill you.' Bridget gave a derisory laugh. 'Actually, I cobbled together a leak about the Queen's Coronation bouquet. It'll have lilies and roses to represent England, stephanotis from Northern Ireland, orchids from Wales and Edelweiss from Germany.'

'What about Scotland?'

'God, I don't know. Can't remember. Thistles probably. Something prickly.'

The populace of Scotland was considered the most recalcitrant of any Alliance territory. Most of the acts of terrorism were said to stem from there.

As they made their way reluctantly back to work, Rose held open the door and Bridget said, 'What's that on your hand?'

Rose looked down. A faint violet smudge of the line she had scribbled in the library was still there. She cursed herself for not scrubbing harder.

'Just something I needed to remember.'

As soon as she got back to her desk she looked around, grabbed a piece of paper from beside Oliver's typewriter, tore off a small strip and wrote down the phrase. Then she folded the paper to the size of a postage stamp, rolled it into a cylinder like a matchstick and slid it between the edges of the lining at the bottom of her bag, before covering it with the usual detritus of handkerchief, notebook and hairbrush. After that, she hurried to the cloakroom and scoured her hand fiercely under the tap.

Back at her desk, she couldn't focus. The typewriter blurred before her eyes and leaning over to a nearby Geli, she said, 'I think I need some fresh air.'

'Too much champagne at the reception last night?'

'Something like that. I'm over at the library if anyone asks.'

Grabbing her bag, she clipped down the marble stairs to the street outside.

She had no idea where she would go. She just wanted to walk, while the thoughts milling in her brain settled in some kind of order. She had an idea to head towards Embankment Gardens where she could sit on one of the benches, watching the sparrows, but she hadn't gone a few steps before she felt a touch on her shoulder and jumped.

'I thought it was you!'

A beaming figure had detached himself from the straggle of journalists leaving the Culture Ministry, and sprinted to her side.

Members of the British press were not notable for their looks. Indeed, most were identifiable by the physical infirmities that had made them unsuitable for Extended National Service. With their tea-stained teeth and smokers' complexions, they were not a handsome crowd. Yet amid the drab jackets and dishrag ties, Laurence Prescott stood out. Even in his forties, his springy gait and flung-back shoulders exuded a boyish confidence. His pinstriped suit was Savile Row and his shoes came from Church's.

Not for the first time Rose wondered what services Laurence's aristocratic mother had performed for Joachim von Ribbentrop to secure her son such favoured status.

'Laurence!' She proffered her cheek for a kiss. 'You must have been in the press conference. How was it?'

He groaned as they walked along Whitehall in lockstep.

'Same old, same old. Should the Queen wear a tiara that once belonged to the Russian royal family? How touching it is that the Coronation cake was made by some old Magda in Wales. Can you explain to me why women actually care who styles Her Majesty's hair? I mean, really, can anyone tell?'

The clatter of a helicopter overhead jogged Rose's memory.

'Apparently there was an incident the other day. At the Rosenberg Centre. What was it, did you hear?'

'You know I can't talk about things like that, Rose. You shouldn't even be asking.' Laurence wagged a finger. 'On the record, it never happened.'

'And off the record?'

'It never happened.'

He shrugged cheerfully.

'Anyway, much more important, how are you? Still with your Sturmbannführer?'

'Don't ask.'

She knew Laurence disapproved. She could see the mixture of concern and curiosity in his eyes.

'What about you?' she said quickly. 'Is there a girlfriend on the scene? Any wedding bells on the horizon?'

'You know me, Rose.' He laughed. 'Once you'd turned me down . . .'

This was a charming and inaccurate version of their break-up. Laurence was never going to marry. Why would he need to? Men like him could have any woman they wanted, provided an Alliance officer didn't want her first.

'Besides, I'm too busy. They've parachuted in a new editor so I need to make a good impression. I'm in the office all hours.'

'What's he like?'

'He's called Douglas Powell. Highly thought of. His sister's married to one of the Leader's aides, apparently. Seems a good chap. So far we seem to have hit it off. In fact, he's put me in charge of co-ordinating a big story for next week.'

'You mean, after the Coronation? I thought that *was* the big story?'

'Apparently we've been put on standby for a major Government announcement. It's all hands on deck.'

'What do you think it is?'

'No idea.' Laurence winked. 'But I don't imagine it's going to be a royal pregnancy.'

CHAPTER EIGHTEEN

It was getting dark, and the plane trees outside threw a fretwork of shadows on the linoleum floor, but Rose didn't switch on the overhead light. Instead she sat in her chair, staring at the wireless, contemplating turning the dial.

The urge had become greater recently, batting like an insistent moth at the edge of her consciousness until it was almost irresistible. Everyone knew shortwave radio broadcasts emanating from America encouraged dissidents and ordinary citizens to resist the regime. With the right radio set, it took only the minutest twiddle of the dial to find a bright Atlantic voice engaging in a chat show, or a political discussion, or a historical documentary. Freedom Radio, it was called. Mostly the Alliance administration refused to recognize the station's existence, but in the Ministry corridors, where it was acknowledged, Freedom Radio was denigrated as propaganda, or psychological warfare. The penalty for listening was harsh. Imprisonment, at the very least.

None of this would have mattered had not Celia, a few months ago in a fit of home renovation, acquired a brand-new Bakelite Volksempfänger – the official Alliance wireless with its pre-set stations – and offered their cast-off Roberts Radio to Rose. Nobody wanted old-style English sets, least of all Geoffrey, who fancied himself a technology buff, and Rose's own transistor was a primitive thing. The Roberts had a fresh set of batteries, which should not go to waste.

The first time she touched the dial, she sprang away from it, as if scalded. The second time, she had summoned her courage late at night and turned it sufficiently to catch the whisper of a talk show, fading in and out from the fog of static. Voices rose and dipped, and once they settled enough to make anything out, she discerned that the format was not unlike *Men of Distinction*. Yet in another way it could not have been more different. For a start, the panel appeared to be made up of both men and women, but the more astonishing aspect of it was that the females spoke entirely without deference. One woman in particular, who got annoyed by a fellow male panellist, said, '*I'm afraid, Professor, you don't have the faintest idea what you're talking about!*'

Just like that.

Now, moving towards the set, Rose reached tentatively for the dial, and stroked it towards the position she had memorized, keeping the volume as low as possible. A susurration emerged, like the faintest whisper of wind, carrying with it a trace of two voices, one male and one female, that resolved into a fuzzy dialogue.

'. . . *the Britain problem.*'

'*Oh, the Britain problem! Britain can look after itself. Don't we have enough problems on our doorstep?*'

'*I call that a most regressive viewpoint considering that our new president Eisenhower has specifically set his face against isolationism. Didn't he say all free nations have to stand together? There's no such thing as partial unity?*'

So absorbed was Rose in this exchange, she almost missed a sound from the next-door flat. It might have been no more than a chair shifting, or the tread of a footstep, or the slight rearrangement of a timber floorboard, but as soon as she heard it, she turned down the volume.

It was foolish to underestimate Elsa Bottomley.

Elsa Bottomley could hear a bat-squeak of conversation. She knew when Rose woke and when she went to bed, and almost certainly every detail of her private life. She was wasted in the Transport division. She should have been one of those women in the Alliance Secret Communications HQ, with headphones on their ears, charting every illicit conversation, every breath of dissent.

Her ear must be perpetually pressed to the wall.

Rapidly, Rose swivelled the dial to the BBC and the jocular tones of an announcer filled the room. '*This one's for Hubert Smith from his granny, Mrs Sandra Smith. Hubert is ten tomorrow and going to his first ever meeting of the Alliance Boys. Congratulations Hubert, and your granny has asked for a marching song to get you in the mood!*' The BBC evening request show, an institution. Nothing suspicious there.

Rose got up and paced around her room. The exchange she had heard on Freedom Radio made it impossible to settle. What did the panellist mean about free nations standing together? More importantly, what exactly was *the Britain problem*? Did it mean that Americans knew the truth about life in the Alliance? That they saw the oppression, the surveillance and the deprivation Britons suffered and believed them to be wrong?

The questions would not go away, resounding in her head as she supplied her own, inadequate answers. Restlessly, she made toast, then tea, tidied her clothes, took up a piece of mending and put it down again. Eventually, to quieten her racing mind, she turned off the wireless, settled herself down and picked up *Middlemarch*.

Without doubt it was Rose's status as star of the team that meant the correcting of George Eliot's masterpiece had fallen to her. She had only just begun the work, and already she knew she had never faced a challenge like it.

When she first picked up the nine-hundred-page volume, her heart had sunk a little, but Rose set about approaching the task in her usual meticulous fashion – perusing the entire text and, as she went, diligently marking out with a pencil her first impressions of those passages that would infringe the Alliance line on feminine portrayal. No female protagonist should be overly intelligent, dominant or subversive, no woman to be rewarded for challenging a man, and no narrative should undermine in any way the Protector's views of the natural relationship between the sexes.

To begin with, *Middlemarch* was straightforward. Astonishingly so. The story was set in the nineteenth century at a time in England when women could not vote, had no rights, and their status was wholly dependent on that of their husband. The nineteen-year-old heroine, Dorothea Brooke, wanted to marry a severe, elderly scholar called Edward Casaubon so as to support him in his literary endeavours. This seemed wholly commendable. The twenty-six-year age gap between the pair was scarcely unusual in Alliance terms, and Dorothea's justification for learning Latin and Greek to assist her husband was entirely appropriate. *It would be my duty to study that I might help him the better in his great works.* Dorothea quelled her naturally passionate nature to become a model of self-sacrifice, dedicated to providing Casaubon with secretarial aid. All this was fine. Even the title of Casaubon's great work, *The Key to All Mythologies*, seemed to carry a ghostly ring of the Protector's own magnum opus, *The Myth of the Twentieth Century*.

And yet . . . as Rose read on, the novel took a different turn. Somehow, George Eliot managed to show that Dorothea should aspire to learning for its own sake, for herself, and not to assist her husband. That she should live in tune with her own noble, intelligent nature, rejecting passive submission to a male intellect. That she should take responsibility for her existence on her own terms.

As with many of the novels she read now, Rose began to see her own life refracted through its pages. In Dorothea, who sought to devote her life to a cause and a passion, who yearned for a life beyond the strictures of femininity, who thrilled to the idea of opening books and hearing voices she had never expected, Rose saw herself.

The more she became engrossed in Dorothea's story, the more her heart expanded.

She was so deeply absorbed that she no longer heard the grumble of the traffic outside or the sounds of her neighbours around her. Curled up in her armchair, under the glow of the desk lamp, she read on and on until the pencil dropped from her hand, and outside, the last vestiges of light gave way to a starless night.

CHAPTER NINETEEN

Sunday, 25th April

'I understand the Leader arrives in Britain on Friday.' One of Geoffrey's golf acquaintances had a brother who worked at Heston airport. 'It's all very hush-hush.'

'Then perhaps we shouldn't be speaking about it,' replied Rose tartly, if only to shut him up.

In the car mirror, Geoffrey flicked her a look of pure hatred. She hoped Hannah didn't see.

'Is that an official reprimand, Rose? Only I understood Alliance citizens were still permitted to discuss national events in their own cars.'

'Oh, Geoffrey, don't fly off the handle. Rose was only being careful.' Celia gave a tight smile from the front seat of the Jaguar and resumed staring out of the window. 'If we're going all this way, we might as well try to get on.'

Hannah, sitting in the back seat next to Rose, squeezed

her hand. The child's other hand trailed in the thick fur of their father's dog, Rollo, who was seated between them. Geoffrey had been reluctant to bring the dog, objecting that it would be sick on the leather of his Jaguar, and even if it wasn't, would make the car smell for weeks, but Hannah had protested, and faced with a journey leaden with his daughter's tears, Geoffrey had given in. Swift capitulation to greater forces was a hallmark of his character, and just occasionally everyone benefitted.

Rose and Celia's mother had opted not to accompany them, preferring instead to take a bus ride to Oxford Circus to 'look at the crowds'. Celia, who would have loved to accompany her, was sympathetic to this choice, but Rose was incredulous.

'How could you turn down the opportunity to visit your own husband, Mum? You've not seen him for more than a week. He must be desperate to see you.'

If her mother felt uncomfortable or guilty, she wasn't showing it.

'I don't want to overexcite him. Dad needs expert care. It's what the doctor said. You've no idea what a strain it was, Rose.'

'But he's all alone in a strange hospital. He must think we've abandoned him.'

Her mother's face took on a pettish expression. 'I love your dad, God knows, but the trouble with your father, Rose, is he could never avoid a row. He never knew how to keep quiet. You have to know when to keep your mouth shut in life, don't you?'

Rose adored her mother. With her pillowy cheeks and petal-soft skin, her girlish beauty echoed the fact that, in many ways, Mum had never much matured. She hated confrontation and was happiest singing along to the piano, listening to her favourite wireless programme, *Music While You Work*, flicking through women's magazines or doing jigsaw puzzles. Apart from Oscar Stephenson, she couldn't bear any discussion of politics, or what she called 'unpleasantness'. Their father had always indulged her like a child and their happiest times were when he would take her dancing, or to the seaside. His 'episodes', however, had increasingly intruded on this peaceful existence, and Rose had to accept that her mother was relieved to have him tidied away.

Abandoning the argument, Rose allowed herself to be drawn into a discussion of plans for the street party Geoffrey was co-ordinating like the Battle of the Somme.

All morning, she had been sick with anxiety. A week had passed, and still she had no answer for the Commissioner. Bruno Schumacher had seemed certain that the Friedas were at the bottom of the insurgency, but even if one person was caught red-handed, that would still not prove who was co-ordinating the action. Yet if she had nothing to tell the Commissioner, he might seriously carry out his threat to have Rose and Martin investigated by the Morality Office. What might the consequences be? Not only to Martin, but to Celia and perhaps even Hannah?

There was only one course of action, and it weighed on her with a mixture of dread and fascination.

As soon as possible she would have to return to Widow-land.

The nursing home, in Midhurst, was a stolid Edwardian house with bars on the lower windows. The Jaguar crunched down a long drive, flanked with elm trees, and pulled up on a semi-circle of gravel. From the distance came the sound of a lawnmower and the smell of cut grass, while a gardener trudged around the beds, poking the earth with a hoe.

They were greeted in the entrance hall by a tight-faced Paula dressed in nurses' whites and rubber shoes. Her wire-wool hair was clipped beneath a starched cap and her face was as pinched as a pair of surgical pliers. She led them down an endless corridor of repeated arched doorways, a sea of herringbone parquet reeking of polish and some indetermi-nate but sinister chemical. A doctor in a white coat strode by officiously. Swing doors banged as Paulas manoeuvred trolleys laden with drugs. Glancing through an open door, Rose caught sight of a ward lined with supine patients. She flinched as she saw two orderlies prop up an old man and administer a glass of what looked like milk but almost certainly wasn't.

The smell, and the faceless corridors, gripped her with dread. What kind of nursing home had bars on the win-dows?

'Mr Ransom was a bit unsettled when he arrived, but he's calmer now the doctor has adjusted his medication,' said the Paula, by way of conversation. As they progressed, Rollo's meaty tail began to wag and he pulled on his lead, padding faster, his paws clicking on the parquet.

'Extraordinary how they know,' observed Celia. 'You'd think he actually wants to be here.'

'Just as well. None of the rest of us does,' murmured Geoffrey, who had relinquished his morning round of golf with exceptionally bad grace.

The nurse opened a door.

'He's not talking much, but he's very thoughtful, aren't you, Mr Ransom?'

Rose's father was seated in an armchair, staring at a stone slab of sky that lay beyond the barred window. He did not turn immediately. He exhibited that subtle change in appearance common to all patients, which makes a week in hospital seem so much longer. His hair was brushed differently, in lanky strands, and hollows had appeared in his cheeks. He wore his own shirt, but the braces had been taken from his trousers and he had no tie. A thin crust of saliva ran down the side of his mouth and his posture was slightly slumped. There had been times, in the past, when Dad travelled to another place, and could not be reached, his eyes glassy, like a mannequin. Was this one of those times, or was it the medication?

'Morning, Father,' boomed Geoffrey. There was no response.

Celia went over to her father and kissed him and at the same time the dog, wild with excitement, jumped up and put his paws on the chair, licking the old man's face.

'We've brought Rollo,' said Celia, redundantly.

Mr Ransom turned his milky eyes, bent down and buried his face in the dog's fur and kept it there. When he lifted his head, Rose saw that Rollo's fur was wet. She had never seen her father cry. She had never, in fact, seen any man cry, but the poignancy of seeing her valiant, beloved father reduced to sobs made tears prick her own eyes. She leaned down, rubbing her face across his cheek. He smelled strange, of unwashed linen and carbolic soap.

'Dad.'

Gently, he pushed her away and gruffly broke his silence.

'There are plenty of people who should cry, but not you, Rosalind.'

'Why d'you call her that, Grandad?' demanded Hannah. 'She's called Rose.'

'I always wondered,' said Geoffrey, with the air of someone determined to change the subject, 'about those names.'

Rose turned towards him. 'Dad loves Shakespeare. He named us after Shakespearean heroines. Celia and Rosalind.'

Drowsily, their father murmured,

> *Thus Rosalind of many parts*
> *By heavenly synod was devised,*
> *Of many faces, eyes, and hearts*
> *To have the touches dearest prized.*

'Very appropriate,' said Geoffrey. 'I don't know about a heavenly synod, but Rose is certainly admired in the highest places.' A spiteful smirk. 'Or so we hear.'

'It's a play called *As You Like It*,' Celia explained to Hannah. 'It's a bit unusual, because it has heroines at the centre of it, rather than heroes. Celia and Rosalind are two girls who are escaping from court. They go out into the Forest of Arden and they have to dress in disguise. It's a journey of discovery.'

'We don't need the entire plot, thank you, Celia. We get the gist.'

It was easy to see why Geoffrey had been attracted to Celia. He was, as someone said, a cage in search of a bird.

Rose proffered the bunch of daffodils she had brought.

'Got you some flowers, Dad.'

She cast around for a vase. The room was almost bare. Just two chairs, a bed and a minute cabinet provided for inmates to store their paltry possessions. Spectacles, pills, hand cream. An empty vase was there too, next to a photograph that Rose recognized.

It had been taken in the summer of 1939 – a time of foreboding, when the country seemed poised on the edge of war, uncertain if Chamberlain and Halifax between them could save it. The four of them were pictured on a bench in the garden – the glimmer of the greenhouse just behind. Her father, in shirtsleeves and braces, a smile on his handsome, good-natured face. Mother, even in her drab pinafore and bundled-up hair, as lovely as she was at twenty-one. To one side Celia, arch and knowing, head angled for the most flattering shot, and on the other, Rose, a hand draped lightly on her father's shoulder.

Rose squinted curiously at her fifteen-year-old self, recognizing at once the expression of watchful detachment, and the sense that she was apart from everything that went on around her.

'You're looking well, Father,' Geoffrey lied.

Rose filled the vase and plunged the daffodils in it, then sat beside her father, her fingers linked through his.

'Geoffrey's right, Dad. Which means they can't keep you here long. There's nothing wrong with you that a bit of rest won't cure.'

'Why does Grandad need to rest?' demanded Hannah.

'Shh, Hannah,' said Celia.

'I don't,' said their father shortly.

'Tell you what, sweetheart.' Geoffrey summoned a tone of bonhomie that must have cost him dear, and smiled at Hannah. 'Why don't we give Rollo a run in the garden?'

As the pair of them disappeared, Rose continued holding her father's hand and Celia chatted about the plans for the Coronation.

'First we're going to the golf club where they've set up a television. I can't wait to watch the parade. You've no idea how many crowned heads are coming. The Sultan of Zanzibar. The Crown Prince of Japan. The Queen of Tonga. Isn't that funny? I didn't even know that Tonga had a queen. She's six foot three and frightfully fat, apparently. She's come over in a canoe. Then we're expecting two hundred people for the street party. Geoffrey's organizing all the Gretls to wash the pavement and we're having trestle tables down the middle of the road. He's hanging posters of the Leader from the windows. And the King and Queen, of course.'

Celia's conversation ran on and on, as fluffy as fake whipped cream in a sponge cake. Their father stared blearily into the distance, but his fingers twisted incessantly in Rose's hand, as if in agitation.

'Don't know what we'll do when it's all over. Nobody's talked of anything but robes, tiaras, postillions, coronets and tea towels for weeks. Somebody's even invented a new dish called Coronation Chicken. Cold chicken, mayonnaise and two tablespoons of curry powder – to represent the Indian colonies, you see. It's going to be served at the royal banquet, so somebody – well, Mrs Herbert from next door – said why don't we make it ourselves? That way we can really feel in the swing.'

Outside, the garden was bathed in brilliant sunshine. Through the barred windows came the breath of recently mown grass, lying in faded stripes on the lawn. A strange fractured cry, like that of a wild bird, echoed across the herbaceous borders, and looking out, Rose saw a woman tussling between the arms of two Paulas. Behind them a couple of patients in wheelchairs were being pushed along the paths, their bodies silted with drugs, their posture as stiff and motionless as Guy Fawkes dummies. Rose could not stop thinking of something she had come across a couple of days ago – a discovery that brought fear, like a wash of acid, to her mouth.

★

It had arisen when she tried to work out how to deal with the mad woman in *Jane Eyre*. Charlotte Brontë's portrayal of Rochester's first wife, Bertha Mason, was directly in line with Alliance protocol. It might have been made for the posters and propaganda films that had been circulated for many years by Minister Goebbels' department. From the 1930s onwards, short information films produced by the Racial and Political Office played in cinemas throughout Germany to illustrate the problem of subhumans. Imbeciles and idiots were portrayed as terrifying figures, grovelling on filthy floors, raging with haggard faces and empty eyes. In that respect Jane Eyre's terrifying encounter with Bertha Mason seemed right on target.

What it was, whether beast or human being, one could not, at first sight, tell: it grovelled, seemingly, on all fours; it snatched and growled like some strange wild animal: but it was covered with clothing, and a quantity of dark, grizzled hair, wild as a mane, hid its head and face.

Rose's problem came when correcting Jane Eyre's reaction to Rochester's dilemma. Surely a true heroine would pity Rochester for his ties to a monster and congratulate his attempt to keep her under the care of a nurse? Instead of which, Jane Eyre abandoned him. To leave such a noble, high-born man was not only selfish, but unfeminine, and contrary to every model of female behaviour.

Mentally, Rose posed herself the question that was supposed to solve any tricky edit.

What would Minister Goebbels do?

There were no set rules for Fiction Correctors – they operated on instinct and a general understanding of Alliance attitudes – but short of calling up Minister Goebbels himself, Rose had to cast around for other guidance.

She found it eventually, in a document that had been compiled back in 1939 on the mainland, entitled 'Hereditary Health and Racial Hygiene'. It had been authored, apparently, by the Leader's own physician, Dr Karl Brandt, and its guidance was therefore impeccable.

In the first instance, various categories of madness including imbecility, schizophrenia, epilepsy and social deviance merited compulsory sterilization. Yet, the document continued, *those patients in care homes and special hospitals who, after a most critical diagnosis, on the basis of human judgement are considered incurable, would be deemed unworthy of life and granted Gnadentod.*

Rose had to read it several times.

Gnadentod. Merciful death.

Mad people beyond cure were granted merciful death.

Now her thoughts returned anxiously to her father, slumped in his chair. Dad wasn't mad. He might be drowsy and disorientated, but he was in full possession of his faculties. He was highly intelligent and could recite Shakespeare from memory. Anyone could see that. Couldn't they?

Celia was still chatting about the street party, filling the emptiness like someone inflating balloons, unleashing every bright thought that floated into her head.

'The lovely thing is that everyone comes together in a proper community, Geoffrey says. He's given everyone a task. I'm making fish paste sandwiches. And all the children are to have fruit gums and Spangles.'

At last their father stirred.

'Sounds quite a festival.'

'Oh, it will be!'

'Can I come?'

Celia shot Rose a panicky glance.

'I don't think . . . I mean, the doctors think . . . that you need to stay here for a while, Dad. For treatment.'

Rose looked at the medication on top of the cabinet and picked up a brown bottle.

'What exactly are they giving you, Dad?'

'Those are just aspirin. They're not going to leave anything there,' said Celia soberly. 'They don't want people taking their own pills.'

'They're to help me sleep,' their father replied.

'Do you have trouble sleeping?'

'No, I don't.'

He struggled to sit up straighter, propping himself with effort by gripping the arms of the chair and staring ahead, as if trying to focus.

'Too many of us are asleep. That's the problem. We need to wake up.'

As he spoke, the dog dashed back into the room followed by Hannah and Geoffrey, who clasped his hands together decisively, as if preparing to snap a neck.

'Well, fat chance of any sleep for me. I've a thousand things to do before next week. No rest for the wicked.'

'You're not wicked, Daddy, are you?' queried Hannah. 'Are you? Is Daddy wicked?'

'Don't talk nonsense, Hannah,' said Celia.

'Time waits for no man,' said Geoffrey, reaching deeper into his personal collection of clichés. 'We'd best be off, Father. Bye for now.'

Mr Ransom gave only an inarticulate snort, and a half-hearted wave of dismissal.

Celia, Rose and Hannah kissed him and followed Geoffrey out of the door.

They made their way down the long corridor and onto the drive where Geoffrey's navy blue Jaguar glinted in the sun. He ran a proprietary hand along the bonnet, like it was a racehorse.

'I think that's proof if you needed it that we did the right thing. He's in the proper place for an old man with his problems.'

'Oh, do stop it, Geoffrey,' said Celia, more sharply than Rose had ever heard. She fixed her headscarf with a savage tug. 'Just for once. Let's just get going, shall we.'

'Wait.' Rose stopped. 'Rollo's lead. I left it in Dad's room.'

Geoffrey sighed theatrically and turned, but Rose stopped him.

'No. Don't worry. I'll get it.'

Before he could object, she retraced her steps swiftly through the corridor towards her father's room.

Dad was still sitting exactly as they had left him, hands gripping the arms of the chair, gaze fixed on the daffodils whose gilded blaze lit up and transfigured the room.

As she closed the door his eyes flickered towards her. Kneeling down by his face, she put her mouth to his ear.

'I'm going to get you out of here, Dad. I promise.'

The eyes were keen now, and the face animated. He looked quite different. Almost his old self.

'Rosalind. I knew you'd come. There's something. There.'

She followed his gaze.

'Is it this you want?'

It was the family photograph in its ornate gilt frame.

'Pass it to me.'

He took it, but instead of studying the photo he turned it over, withdrew the picture and laid it down. Then he slid his thumb beneath the frame and edged it away to reveal, inside the moulding of the frame, a tiny cavity.

'Some time ago it occurred to me to prepare something for my quietus.'

It was a glass phial, no bigger than a baby's thumb, containing a white powder.

'Remember Dr Freeman? He gave it to me.'

'Sophy's father?'

'He was helping all his friends.'

'What is it?'

Her father didn't answer directly, but held it out on his outstretched palm.

'Let's just call it a gift. I won't need it now, so I'm giving it to you. It's all I have. You may never need it either, but if you're my daughter, you just might.'

Rose took the phial and plunged it into her pocket. She had a good idea what it was, but she couldn't bear to ask any more.

Kneeling, she took her father's face in her hands.

'I remember the poetry, Dad. All of it. I think of it all the time.'

He smiled. The moment of lucidity was over, and he was retreating somewhere she could not follow.

As she straightened up, he said, 'Be careful, Rosalind. They know everything.'

'What do they know?'

'Where you go, who you are, what you eat and drink. They know your dreams.'

'My dreams?'

'Of course. Why do you think they're so frightened?'

CHAPTER TWENTY

Monday, 26th April

At the guard post the sagging, chain-link fence was still tangled and twisted, but beside it a new concrete pillar had been erected, with a coil of barbed wire snaking like savage bindweed up its length. On the top a spotlight fixed Rose with a glassy eye.

Inside the guard hut, a sentry was studying the *Oxford Mail*.

Excitement mounts as Leader's visit approaches. City selected as first attraction on whistle-stop tour

He laid the paper aside reluctantly as Rose slid her ID through the window.

'What's all this for?' she said, gesturing at the spotlight.

'Extra security.'

'Really? Why?'

'Curfew violations.'

Beside him, a hunched Alsatian with patchy fur issued a low growl. The sentry prodded the dog with the tip of his jackboot.

'So better make sure you're out by dusk. Unless you want to get stuck here.'

He gave Rose's photograph a perfunctory glance before returning it with an ironic grin.

'Welcome to Widowland, Fräulein.'

The route to the widows' house was deserted. Rose knew the houses would be largely empty because most Friedas left in the early morning for their factories and places of work. Yet all the same, she found herself glancing over her shoulder, as though even in these mean streets she might be observed.

Nothing looked back. Except for a rat, which paused its exploration of a baked bean can to stare at her boldly, before disappearing beneath a bicycle with broken spokes.

Rose had telephoned ahead to ask the authorities to ensure that all the previous interviewees stay at home for another session of questions. Even before she had knocked, Kate opened the door, and gestured her inside.

The destruction of the previous week's raid was still evident, but the Friedas had made valiant efforts to put the damage right. The ripped sofa had been carefully draped with a blanket. In place of the smashed china shepherdesses, an old jam jar filled with buttercups, twigs and birds' feathers sat on the mantelpiece and the spot on the wall where the Canaletto had hung was now occupied by a painting of a wheat field.

Rose settled on the William Morris chair, whose lacerations had been neatly stitched, while Kate, Sylvia, Sarah and Vanessa gathered around her circumspectly.

'About that police visit the other day,' she began. 'I was shocked. I want you to know I made an official complaint. I saw a senior officer and informed him how badly his men had behaved.'

'Thank you,' said Kate. 'Though if you'd asked us first, we would have preferred you not to. We'll be targeted more than ever now.'

'Oh, don't say that, Kate!' Vanessa intervened soothingly. 'It was kind of Fräulein Ransom.'

'Rose. Please call me Rose.'

It was strange how comfortable she felt talking to these Friedas, when just a few weeks ago she would have been horrified to find herself in the same room as them. She knew she should correct them for addressing her as an equal and she should certainly not invite them to use her Christian name, but nobody was watching, and besides, a relaxed atmosphere was likely to generate more information, which was essential if she was to compile a report for the Commissioner.

As she pulled out her notebook, the cat jumped up and kneaded its head against Rose's hand, asking to be stroked.

As she caressed the ripple of fur along its spine the animal purred and arched its back, and a memory returned of her family's pet cat Tom, an impish tabby they had owned before the Alliance. He had disappeared shortly afterwards and she had not thought of Tom for years.

'Oh, I almost forgot. I brought you this.'

She took a package from her bag and placed it on the orange box table. It was a small container of silver cardboard featuring a garishly painted belly dancer hiding coyly behind purple veils amid a crowd of lascivious men in robes. Across the lid ran the scrolly legend *Turkisches Entzücken*. A gift from Martin after a recent trip.

'Turkish delight!' exclaimed Sarah, in girlish excitement.

The widows' eyes gleamed.

'I haven't eaten that in decades,' said Sylvia. 'My parents used to buy it for us every Christmas.'

'I had it once in Turkey,' commented Kate. 'In a bazaar in Istanbul, just after the war.'

Vanessa picked the box up reverently.

'All right if I open it?'

'Of course.'

Inside, a clutch of translucent ruby cubes, glistening with dusted sugar, nestled in pink tissue paper. All four Friedas stared at the treasure. It was almost certainly more sugar than they had seen for years. Rose had been hoarding the gift for the Coronation celebrations, but that seemed less important now.

'We haven't had sweets since we've been here,' said Sarah,

examining the box with pleasure. 'We don't have a sugar ration. We have to rely on the bees.'

'I'm glad you like it.'

'Mind if we eat one now?' asked Vanessa eagerly.

'Go ahead.'

The women handed the box around and each took a cube, allowing a solemn silence as the sweet melted slowly in their mouths. When the box was passed to Rose she declined swiftly.

'Oh, no thank you. I don't have a sweet tooth.'

For a short while a companionable silence reigned until the kitchen door opened and another woman entered carrying a pile of logs. She was about to cast them into a basket, when she caught sight of Rose and straightened up.

She was older than the others, in her late sixties perhaps, yet she exuded the energy of a woman half her age. She had a broad, almost mannish face, a strong nose and a commanding air. She must once have been beautiful, but her greying hair was straggly now and a bloodshot vein spidered the white of one eye. She wore a torn shirt, a pair of men's trousers and scuffed tan gloves.

Rose recognized her immediately. The Frieda in the street who had been arrested on suspicion of painting graffiti and whose police statement had been shown to her by Bruno Schumacher.

'This is Adeline Adams,' said Kate, closing the lid of the Turkish delight and surreptitiously sliding it beneath a pile of papers. 'Adeline, this is Fräulein Ransom.'

Adeline fixed Rose with a sharp, appraising glance before crossing the room, and removing her glove to clasp her hand in a firm grip.

'I'm pleased to meet you, Fräulein Ransom. I heard about your previous visit. It sounded eventful. I'm sorry I wasn't here.'

'I've heard about you too,' said Rose. 'In fact, I think I saw you being arrested.'

'Did you? It was annoying, considering I'd only just got out of their clutches. Though I hasten to add,' she said with heavy emphasis, 'that no charges were brought against me.'

As if to forestall further insubordination, Sarah leapt in.

'Fräulein Ransom's undertaking research concerning some particular interests of the Protector.'

Adeline looked unimpressed.

'I've always wondered what the Protector is particularly interested in.'

Rose chose to ignore the undertow of sarcasm.

'He's keen to know more about ancient English superstitions.'

'You mean like this?'

Adeline reached for a buttercup from the jar on the mantelpiece, plucked one out and brought it up close to Rose's face. Her proximity felt uncomfortable.

'My mother always said these flowers would reveal if you liked butter. A soft gleam on your skin if you do. If you don't like butter, then nothing at all. But I think that's a crazy superstition, don't you, Fräulein Ransom? How could a little yellow flower signify anything?'

Rose sat immobile. She understood the implication instantly; anyone would. This was a direct challenge, if not a taunt, to see if she would acknowledge the fact that yellow flowers were the symbol of resistance. Every citizen knew that, but to admit it would be to acknowledge the very fact that the regime might be resisted, and that was a crime in itself.

'I'll take a note of it.'

Frowning, she bent her head and leafed stiffly through the pages.

'I wonder if I could ask some more questions about your memories. The Protector is especially interested in ancestral folktales. He believes they have their roots in an ancient time when our two nations were more closely joined.'

'I'm sure we'd all like to help, Fräulein Ransom,' Sylvia interjected coolly, 'but I wonder. Are you sure you should be asking this?'

Rose was surprised at such impertinence. But instead of reprimanding Sylvia for asking a Geli a direct question, she said, 'Why on earth do you say that?'

'I was led to understand that memory is treacherous.'

Memory is treacherous. The familiar motto resounded instantly in Rose's brain. It was like that with all Government catchphrases. They stuck in the mind like rags on a barbed-wire fence, fluttering, distracting, ineradicable. Simple slogans that became mental roadblocks which you needed to dodge round to reach any original thoughts. Like advertising jingles, they were sandwiched between programmes on the wireless, and chanted in schools and community meetings. *Memory is treacherous.* Especially memories of the Time Before.

Technically Sylvia was right, though questioning a Geli on official Protectorate business could not be more reprehensible. Rose hesitated for a second, wondering how to proceed. She ought to persist, but her questions about childhood memories were, after all, only a cover for her actual, more pressing investigation. She had just a few days to discover if these women were involved in criminal activities that could affect the Leader's visit.

The urgency of the mission brought a fresh lurch of nerves and she changed the subject.

'I noticed, when I came in, that a new searchlight has been installed at the guard post.'

'The authorities do seem to have a curious fear of older women,' commented Adeline. 'Perhaps it's justifiable.'

'The sentry said it was due to curfew violations.'

'Extraordinary,' commented Sylvia. 'As if anyone would want to escape Widowland.'

'I suppose it's for show, but I can't understand why they've bothered,' said Sarah. 'There are plenty of holes in the fence for anyone who really wants to get in or out after hours. There's no way the authorities are going to waste scarce resources on repairing an entire boundary.'

'I for one would prefer they spent the money on our

housing,' ventured Vanessa. 'These places really are very cramped.'

'But at least you have company,' said Rose. 'No Frieda is condemned to live alone. You have companions.'

'Not that we get to choose,' said Sylvia.

'How do they select who goes with whom?'

'I heard the authorities allocate women on the basis of whether they are likely to get along,' said Adeline.

'That's something, I suppose.'

'I think what Adeline means,' said Kate with icy deliberation, 'is that they choose people who *won't* get along. Characters who might rub each other up the wrong way. They're not looking to foster happy friendships.'

Even as she said it, Rose saw that it was true. It was entirely plausible that the authorities would select groups on the basis of incompatibility. Adeline and Kate were a prime example. Two strong women who seemed perpetually to clash. Merely talking to them made Rose feel like Odysseus navigating between the mythical female monsters Scylla and Charybdis. As for the others, Sylvia was reserved, but sceptical and spiky. Vanessa was kind-hearted and obviously hated conflict and Sarah was the peacemaker. They were all very different, and that difference was designed to reduce strong bonds. Primary loyalty must always be to the Alliance itself.

Her gaze fell on the oil painting on the wall opposite. Something about the landscape transfixed her. What should have been a pleasant and harmless subject, a field of wheat beneath an open sky, was rendered dark and menacing. The sky writhed disturbingly and the blazing gold seemed to throb from the frame.

'Who painted that?'

'I did,' said Vanessa. 'It's a poor copy, I'm afraid. After Van Gogh.'

'Van . . . ?'

Rose recognized the name, but could not place it. She suspected the painter was degenerate. On the mainland, from 1937 onwards, a tranche of artists had been outlawed and their works removed from public display. Painting, like fiction, was subject to a blizzard of regulations and one of Rose's colleagues in the Art department had once taken her through the checklist. No colours to be used that were not from nature, no painting the sky green or the sun purple or the trees blue. No art that distorted the human figure or deviated from the Nordic ideal. Once the Alliance was formed these rules were imported to Britain and degenerate artists dealt with accordingly.

Yet even if he was degenerate, Kate seemed determined not to let the subject drop.

'You must know Vincent Van Gogh!'

'I don't see why,' said Vanessa defensively. 'Fräulein Ransom's a busy woman.'

'He's not the kind of artist you forget.'

'I do forget things, though,' Rose admitted. 'Increasingly.'

Memory was like a muscle. The less you used it, the less it worked.

As Kate opened her mouth to reply, Sarah leaned forward.

'It's the same for me. Sometimes, I can hardly remember my husband's face. I wonder, would you like to see our garden?'

As they walked down the narrow brick path, fringed with ramshackle cold frames and raised beds crafted from old timber, Rose sensed the others standing at the window, their eyes burning into her back. Sarah touched the shrubs as she went, trailing her fingers along their leaves as though they were living companions.

'Our lovely Cox's Orange Pippin,' she murmured, caressing the bark of one tree as though it produced globes of gold rather than, as Rose suspected, a harvest of gnarled and bird-pecked apples.

'And this one's a Bramley. Isn't that lucky?'

'I guess so,' Rose allowed.

'We trade among ourselves,' Sarah said. 'Some households grow potatoes or onions. Others grow strawberries and soft fruit. We have leeks and carrots. We're only eligible for very short rations, you see, and strictly we're supposed to hand in what we grow ourselves, but they very rarely check, and besides, there's no choice. Otherwise we wouldn't survive.'

She looked at Rose warily, out of the side of her eye, as though she was determined to nurture the frail trust between them like one of her own tender plants.

'What Kate said, about us not getting along . . .'

'I won't mention it.'

'I know you have your important work for the Protector, and other things that we can't begin to understand . . .'

She didn't need to elaborate. Rose realized that Sarah knew, and all the widows knew, that she was a Government spy.

'But you see, a comment like that would count as subversion. Any complaint about the nature of our accommodation risks severe penalties and we're none of us young and vigorous. Vanessa has her arthritis. Kate gets all sorts of headaches because of her eyesight and even Adeline is taking a while to recover from her recent interrogation.'

What were these penalties to which Sarah referred? What punishment could be worse than living in these dilapidated habitations, with their creeping mould and flaking plaster and damp brickwork? Yet no sooner had she asked herself the question, than Rose began to imagine the answer.

'I won't say anything. I promise. You have my word.'

'Thank you. And not that you will ever need it, but we're in your debt.'

When Rose reached home that evening, she began the letter.

Findings of research into insurgency in Oxford Widowlands
Category: Highly Confidential
Herr Commissioner,
I am writing to report on my two visits to Oxford, with regard to the ~~alleged~~ suspected insurgency by Class VI females. I met a Fräulein Kate Wilson, who was aware of the author Mary Wollstonecraft and repeated several lines of her heresy in my hearing. Fräulein

Wilson is a former journalist who appears to know the work of this degenerate writer by heart. In addition, I encountered a Fräulein Adeline Adams, recently arrested on grounds of suspected defacement of public buildings, who suggested that the authorities were rightly in fear of older women. With reference to the availability of painting materials available at the address, another of the household, Fräulein Vanessa Cavendish, showed me a work by the degenerate artist Vincent Van Gogh that she had recently reproduced . . .

At that point, however, she stopped. Nauseated, she put down her pen, screwed up the paper and threw it in the bin.

CHAPTER TWENTY-ONE

Tuesday, 27th April

'OK. Listen up, you two. Today I have an exclusive of my own.'

Bridget Fanshaw assumed the mock demeanour of a minister delivering a scoop at the morning press conference.

'The news is, I'm applying for a transfer. To the mainland.'

She took a sip of milkshake, sat back and savoured the reaction as her announcement sank in.

'You're joking,' said Helena.

'You have no idea where you'll end up,' said Rose.

Bridget looked around her. Coffee bars were all the rage, and the Soho Bar, with its booths of flaking, varnished wood and egg-yolk clapboard walls, was typical of its kind. The crimson leatherette seats felt stylish and modern, as did the cigarette machine, even if it was empty. The sound of 'Crazy Man, Crazy' by Bill Haley & His Comets issued from the jukebox and neon signs optimistically advertising Coca Cola and Pilsner beer jittered above the counter. The fact that the bar was a pastiche of its American counterparts made it an edgy venue – its very existence implied that America might offer better recreation than any Alliance paradise. Yet the Soho Bar and others like it were tolerated as the mark of a confident regime. Even if everyone knew that in America there would be hamburgers with melted cheese and chocolate milkshakes, whereas here the Krups espresso machine was almost certainly fake and the cappuccinos were made of *Muckefuck*.

'Wherever it is, it's got to be better than here.'

Just as Jane Austen's spinsters hankered for Bath, and Chekhov's Three Sisters pined for Moscow, so a great many women in the Alliance dreamed of life on the mainland. They had never been there, so they had no idea what awaited them, apart from what they'd seen on newsreels and in magazines. It was a gamble; a step into the unknown, from which there was no return.

'You'll never get a job like you have here,' said Rose.

Bridget rolled her eyes.

'I don't care. Think of the food. The sausages. The beer!'

Here, they were always hungry, even for the soggy toast in front of them, spread with margarine pungent with petroleum and a mauve chemical slime that passed for jam.

'What's to keep me?'

Perhaps Bridget was right. Her accommodation in Kings Cross might be elite, but it was a gloomy basement, reeking of hops from the nearby brewery, and with walls that shook every time a train passed. Her parents were dead, and her only brother had been relocated.

'Anyhow, Rose, you told me Germania was wonderful.'

'That was different,' Rose said awkwardly.

'Because you went with a senior man.'

'I mean, I've heard worrying things.'

'What have you heard?' demanded Bridget.

It was hard to explain. Certainly, there was a snob factor attached to English staff. Rudolf Hess had employed English nannies for his children. The von Ribbentrops kept a library of English books. Yet . . . she had heard whispers. Gossip. 'Pavement radio', some people called it. And she remembered the terror in the eyes of the English Gretl who'd brought the tray to their room in the Hotel Excelsior.

'They don't always treat foreigners with respect. Even Gelis. Once you're there, you have no rights.'

'People will always spin tales to stop other people going. I can look after myself.' Bridget hoovered up the foam from her glass. 'Besides, I'll have a friend when I get there. I've met a man.'

Rose and Helena exchanged glances. With Bridget, it was always a man.

'At the Grosvenor House reception the other night, I met an attaché with the Press Ministry there. His name's Friedrich Bauer. Frightfully handsome. Single. I went back to his hotel. Don't look at me like that! I'm not married.'

Ostentatiously she drew out a packet of German Roxy cigarettes from her mackintosh pocket and offered them round. Roxys were made of good tobacco, aromatic and strong. They tasted of privilege.

'Smoking?' enquired Rose. Cigarettes were strongly discouraged for women, especially elite women, because of the Leader's conviction that they damaged health and breeding potential. Some restaurants and bars carried tin signs banning women from smoking, but the Soho Bar, in its attempt to appear glamorous, presented a more relaxed facade.

'There won't be any smoking on the mainland.'

'Who cares? Friedrich said I'd love it there. With my experience, I could maybe get a job on a newspaper. And I must be sure to look him up.'

Rose took a cigarette and inhaled thoughtfully.

'Do you remember Violet? From the Astrology Office?'

A couple of years ago, Violet Thomas, a cool blonde who dreamed up daily horoscopes for syndication in the national press, had expressed a sudden yearning to go to the mainland. She had promised to stay in contact. She would write, and use her status as a Geli to make a return visit. Her aged parents, after all, would want to see their only child. She had never been heard of again.

'Violet never came back,' said Rose.

'Maybe. And perhaps I won't either. We can't all be like you, Rose, smooching with a senior man who treats us to expensive dinners. Where is it this week? The Dorchester? Claridge's?'

It was true, as it happened. Martin had telephoned that morning to inform Rose that they would be dining together the next day.

'He's taking me to his club, actually.'

'Well, I hope you enjoy it. You deserve it. But as far as I'm concerned, it's too late to change my mind.' Bridget's eyes sparkled with excitement for the future. 'I've handed in my cards and I've been issued with the papers. Come on! Be happy for me!'

'It's just . . .' Rose stopped herself. Who was to say she was right anyway? Helena saved her the trouble, throwing herself on her friend, and squeezing her in a fierce hug.

'We'll miss you.'

Bridget checked herself in her compact, then snapped it shut.

'And I'll miss you too, but I won't miss much else. The problem with us is, we don't have enough fun here. I intend to dance myself silly at the office Coronation party. It'll be a lark.'

Rose could see there was no point in trying to dissuade her.

'Tell you what,' Bridget beamed across the table. 'That rehearsal at Westminster Abbey tomorrow morning. There'll be a hundred film operators around the place and the Press team needs to check that the positions for the commenters and producers are hidden from view. The King doesn't want technology spoiling a timeless event, I think that's what he said. He'd really rather it wasn't televised at all, but he's no match for Fräulein Riefenstahl. How would you two like to come and watch? Even if I do get reprimanded, I don't care – I'm demob happy.'

CHAPTER TWENTY-TWO

Wednesday, 28th April

It was like being on the battlements of some ancient castle looking down on a tattered brocade of bloodlines, tradition and deference. A pageantry of flags and banners hung between the tapered arches and French Gothic pillars, and unfurled over the marble statuary, obscuring every sightless saint. Filtered through the stained-glass windows, lozenges of light shimmered against the pale stone.

Rose, Helena and Bridget had signed themselves out of the office on the pretext of Coronation preparations, which covered almost anything. Following Bridget's lead, they clambered up a cramped spiral staircase into a small recess between two fluted pillars that looked down on the cavernous vault of Westminster Abbey. The camera to be positioned here would focus directly onto the spot where, in a ceremony descended directly from King Edgar in 973,

Edward VIII would become the thirty-ninth English sovereign to be crowned. Nobody mentioned the thirty-eighth – the King's younger brother, George VI, who had been crowned after Edward abdicated back in 1936.

That was all blood under the bridge.

The three women rested their elbows on the cold stone, gazing a dizzying way down at the small party that had assembled to practise the Coronation ceremony. Directly below them stood the King, his strangely blank face with its deeply indented lines between nose and jaw giving him the appearance of a ventriloquist's dummy. Already a diminutive figure, he looked even smaller from above – boyish almost, his hair lightened and his skin tanned from his recent Caribbean holiday. After golf and bridge, holidays were said to be his favourite thing.

'I can hardly believe I'm here,' whispered Rose.

'Is that the actual King?' said Helena.

'Shh. Yes.' Bridget rolled her eyes. 'Keep as quiet as you can. I'll be banged up if anyone discovers you're here.'

Rose shrank further behind a pillar, without tearing her eyes from the proceedings below.

The nave was bathed in arc light and a series of podiums and gantries had been erected to hold the dozens of cameras that would be preserving the events for posterity. The abbey's magnificent acoustics, designed by generations of mediaeval stonemasons to carry the voice of prayer to heaven, now enabled them to hear snippets of a distinctly less pious exchange.

A figure in flowing robes of white and red bustled into the arena rubbing his hands in an ecstasy of supplication.

'I'm really most awfully sorry to keep you waiting.'

The Queen's voice floated upwards, as sharp as a shard of glass in a Martini.

'We've waited fifteen years, Archbishop, so I suppose a few minutes more won't hurt us.'

She wore a pale pink satin evening dress stitched with velvet chrysanthemums and a pair of high heels that clicked like gunshots on the ancient floor.

The Archbishop's apology, however, was directed elsewhere. He was gazing earnestly at a figure in long grey flannel trousers and a jockey cap who was approaching up the nave, a bunch of cameramen and her own personal photographer trailing in her wake. Leni Riefenstahl went up to the ancient oak throne in the manner of an actor scrutinizing a theatrical prop.

'Can we move this chair?'

She nudged it with her toe. The throne, battered and carved with the initials of ancient visitors, looked especially shabby in the phosphorescent light.

'Ideally not,' prevaricated the Archbishop. 'It's the Coronation throne. It goes back to 1296.'

Leni Riefenstahl tossed the golden coils of her hair. The Protector might be obsessed, but history cut no ice with her.

'Well, it needs to move. Here is awkward. It doesn't go with the choreography.'

The Archbishop winced. 'The throne is central to the ceremony, Fräulein Riefenstahl. It's named after Edward the Confessor. It's only been moved from the abbey once, and that was for Oliver Cromwell.'

With an exasperated snort, Leni turned aside and began to discuss takes, filters and apertures with the flock of cameramen tailing her.

'I want the camera to pan from the crown and dissolve to the face of the Leader. He will look simple, dignified, modest. Above all this . . . flummery.'

At that moment a figure who seemed the human embodiment of flummery entered the abbey.

'That's Fruity Metcalfe,' whispered Bridget. 'The King's equerry.'

He was hailed with obvious relief by the monarch.

'Fruity! D'you have a light?'

Fruity Metcalfe was wearing an outfit of frogged velvet that was as ridiculous as his name. Rose knew he had been best man at the King and Queen's wedding, during their brief French exile in 1937. Now, many thousands of country weekends and golf games later, he was about to play a prominent role in their enthronement. Seizing a votive candle from a rack, he proffered its flame.

'Thanks.' The King shifted impatiently, fiddling with his cuffs. 'This rehearsal is taking a godawful long time. If it goes on any longer, I'll be up there with my forebears.'

He nodded to the abbey walls, encrusted with the tombs of other, more memorable monarchs.

'Let's get on with it, Archbishop, shall we?' said the Queen, in her trademark Baltimore twang.

The cleric began a lengthy mumble about the timetable of the ceremony – the recognition, the oath, the anointing, the enthronement, the investiture and the homage.

'I will place St Edward's crown on the King's head and before the anointing I shall say a few words along the lines of the fact that the Leader is the first from overseas to sit here since William the Conqueror, and how proud the nation had been then. Et cetera, et cetera.'

Wallis paused to take a drag of a cigarette and looked around her. She was bored already and this wasn't even the real thing. In search of diversion, she lit on the director with a malicious glint.

'David and I enjoyed your movie, Fräulein Riefenstahl. *Triumph of the Will*. Frightfully theatrical. All those handsome soldiers in Nuremberg. A hundred and fifty thousand, wasn't it? Can't imagine how you got them all to stand still.'

'That is the gift of a great director,' replied Leni, briefly.

'Well, I'm simply longing to hear what surprises you have planned for my lil' old Coronation.'

'Thank you, Your Majesty.' Sarcasm glanced off Leni Riefenstahl like raindrops off a Panzer. 'I have many plans.'

'Oh, do tell.'

Leni Riefenstahl folded her arms, signalling that her patience was an expensive commodity, and running short. She was a rival queen, glorious in her haughtiness.

'Already, the entire structure of the film exists in my head. An oratorio to the majesty of monarchy and the glory of the Leader. We begin with the Leader's car, gliding along the parade route like a Roman emperor, the footage intercut with faces in the crowd expressing their joy. Then we move to the golden carriage that contains you, the Queen and King. When you make your way up the aisle, some of my cameramen will be wearing roller skates so they can film the moving shots. I will have them dressed in uniform so they can blend with the crowd.'

'Congregation,' corrected the Archbishop. 'On the subject of which, Fräulein, your request to pack the pews with massed ranks of the Schutzstaffel does, I confess, worry me a little. We have royal heads from around Europe and the world attending the service. Eight thousand guests in all. Dignitaries, presidents of local associations and so forth. Representatives of ancestral faiths – Zoroastrians, Muslims, Buddhists, Catholics and, er, Jews.'

'Jews?' enquired Leni Riefenstahl. Her voice curled like dry ice.

'Are you kidding me, Archbishop?' Wallis joined in. At last, a subject on which they could unite. 'In a Christian church? I don't really think they can expect to attend.'

'Absolutely beyond the pale,' added the King. This was no ventriloquist's dummy speaking now. His eyes were a blaze of anger. 'We saved our Jews, didn't we? They ought to be damned grateful. What more can they ask?'

At this point the conversation was obscured by the shouts of workmen erecting gantries for the television cameras, amid a clatter of scaffolding and the whine of an electric drill. One of the construction team pointed up towards the women's cubby hole and they were forced to duck their heads for cover before climbing shakily back down the narrow stone stairs and emerging into the bustle of Parliament Square.

'How's that for a private view?' said Bridget. 'I never thought I'd get that close to the genuine King and Queen.'

'What does he mean, he saved the Jews?' said Rose.

'No idea,' said Helena absently.

'Saved them from what?'

'Don't ask me,' said Bridget. 'But I'd better be getting back to the coalface. The *Daily Mail* wants to know the number of seed pearls used in the Queen's Coronation robe and I have a story for the *Mirror* about how many baby girls born this year have been called Wallis. Who says the Press Office doesn't perform a vital public service?'

Rose and Helena walked on through the clear spring morning, dallying in the warm sunlight and delaying the moment they had to return to the Culture Ministry and the stack of work that awaited them. In Victoria Tower Gardens, a small park next to the House of Lords that overlooked the river, a squad of soldiers were drilling, their officer's bark of command slicing the peaceful air and setting the pigeons aflutter.

'You've been different these last few weeks, Rose. Like your mind is elsewhere. Or you're worried about something.'

'Have I?'

'Yes. It's as though you're constantly preoccupied.'

Helena was about to ask Rose to reveal her terror, and Rose was about to lie. But instead Helena said, 'I noticed, because I've been trying to tell you something. And there's never been a good time.'

'What is it? Something important?'

'Kind of. 'Do you have to rush back?'

'I should, really.'

'Would you come with me somewhere? Right now?'

'Where?'

'It's not far. Wait till we get there.'

The house was one of those faceless wedges of Belgrave Square where wealth and power had solidified over generations into immaculate cream stucco. It was set on the corner of a block and protruded into the square like the prow of a battleship, its black door so glossy you could see your face in it. As they watched, a smart young Geli, visibly pregnant, her honey hair trained in a chignon and her swollen belly draped in a maroon coat, emerged from the building and clipped down the steps. She glanced at the girls with a knowing smile before heading off down the street.

'Do you know what this place is?' said Helena.

Rose went closer. The wall was bullet-scarred – a leftover from the Time of Resistance – but next to the door was a smart brass plaque etched with the word *Lebensborn* and underneath in curly italics *The Fount of Life*. She couldn't remember where she had heard the name before, but it echoed in the ether like a fragment of a bad dream.

'I think I've heard of it but I'm not sure what it is.'

'Me neither. Well at least I wasn't, until last week.'

Helena chewed her bottom lip and a frown appeared on her perfect brow, like a breath of wind on a millpond.

'Can I trust you?'

'Helena! If you can't trust *me* . . .'

'I'm pregnant.'

Rose received the calamitous news as calmly as she could.

'Congratulations. Are you happy? Is it . . . ?'

'Rolf's? Yes. I've told him.'

'How did he take it? He's married, isn't he?'

'He was fine. Perfectly fine and not angry at all.'

'You mean, he wants . . . ?'

'No.' Helena paused, her eyes glinting with tears. 'He doesn't want to marry me, if that's what you're asking. Or to be a father for the fifth time. The thing is, Rose, Rolf said, when it's time, he wants me to come here. It's a place where women of the right stock can have their babies without prying. He says there'll be no problem. We have proof of racial purity on both sides. And it's wonderful for the mothers, he says. They have extra rations, cream and meat and all sorts, and specially trained Paulas to look after the children.'

Rose squinted through the long windows at the ghostly shapes of women dressed in white moving around behind them. Distantly came the howl of a child, and the fast, gulping sobs of a young baby wanting milk.

'After the birth you can stay for weeks . . .' Helena tailed off.

'And then what?'

'Rolf says babies with Nordic attributes are highly valued by the Lebensborn. If your kid has blond hair and blue eyes, then it will have a fabulous life.'

'What's that supposed to mean? How do they know it will have a fabulous life?'

Helena bit her lip, and kneaded her hands, frowning at the ground. Maybe it was the glow of pregnancy, but to Rose she had never seemed more beautiful. Her waist was tightly cinched in a red leather belt that complemented the flowers of her skirt, and small pearl buttons marched down the front of her cardigan. She stared at the pavement with her head gently inclined, like the soft face of a woman in a Vermeer portrait, or a Renaissance Madonna.

'You don't understand. Rolf's not like Martin. He doesn't have a romantic bone in his body.'

'Are you saying . . . you don't get to *keep* the child? They take your baby away?'

Helena looked at her straight.

'What other choice do I have?'

A barren womb spells doom. That was one of the sayings they taught in the Alliance Girls. Gelis, on account of their superior racial characteristics, were expected to bear children, but only within marriage. An unmarried Geli who was foolish enough to have a baby alone faced rapid declassification. She would be relegated immediately to the lowest sector of Class III womanhood, moved out of her elite accommodation and she would have her rations dramatically reduced. The only way to avoid this was to find a man prepared to take on a pregnant bride and raise a child that was not his own. Those men, understandably, were vanishingly rare.

'And it's not as if I can . . .' Helena left the unmentionable act hanging in the air, but Rose grasped her meaning instantly. Abortion was out of the question. It was a crime, punishable by death. Desperate women might procure one, dangerously, in city backstreets, but it was outlawed for all but Class V females. Class VI would be exempted too, but they were assumed to be beyond childbearing.

'I'm not sure I want kids, anyhow,' said Helena, brushing her tears away roughly. 'I don't know the first thing about them.'

Celia had said the same. Rose remembered her grappling with the newborn Hannah, saying, *Infants aren't really my thing*, as though babies were a pair of kitten heels that you could take back to the shop.

'It's not what we imagined, is it, when we were kids?'

'I can't remember what I imagined,' said Rose automatically, before adding, 'No. Nothing like it.'

She thought of Hannah, her hair bright cinnamon gold, her sandy freckles and sweet, round face, playing with her stuffed toys. Hannah still lived in a world of possibility, where anything might happen. Not only that animals might speak, or nymphs live in trees, but that girls could grow up to be anything they wanted. A parallel universe, so close that it almost touched the real one. Rose dreaded the time when that world of possibility would end.

At that moment the door opened and a vast pram emerged, two rosy, bonneted toddlers peering curiously over the side, like first-class passengers on a cruise liner. A pudding-faced Paula proceeded to bump them down the steps and push them up the street with a flat-footed tread, glancing neither left nor right.

'What about you, Rose? Do you want children?' said Helena, looking after them.

'I'm not sure.'

'God forbid one might ever be a Klara. I always thought I'd be like my own mum. Marry a nice man and move somewhere in Surrey. Have a Labrador that wouldn't be allowed on the sofa. Four kids, I thought, two boys, two girls. Not . . . this.'

There was an edge of anguish in Helena's voice and she turned away, blinking. A pang of pure love went through Rose and she took her friend's arm protectively.

'Hush. Is there anyone who might . . . ? I mean, my sister knows some older men. She has a dentist lined up for me. I could give her a call.'

Helena gave a sniff and braced herself. 'It's all right. I've already decided.'

'Don't come here.'

'Easy for you to say.' With a last look at the Lebensborn, Helena linked arms with Rose and pulled her along the street. It was as though they were sixteen again, skipping out of the Rosenberg Institute, marching into a sunlit future of friendship and fun.

'Rolf's right, you know,' Helena said. 'We're lucky to be Gelis. Better food. Lovely clothes. Kind men to spoil us. We have the golden ticket, remember? So what if we don't get to keep our babies? We have a wonderful life.'

CHAPTER TWENTY-THREE

Martin's club, in Garrick Street, lay in the tangle of streets around Covent Garden and although she had never set foot inside, Rose had heard plenty about it. Behind its portentous facade, speckled with soot like ash down a dinner jacket, generations of men had enjoyed billiards, port, cigars and a warm sense of entitlement. All the London clubs were popular with the regime – von Ribbentrop had joined the Athenaeum in 1936 and was now its president. Robert Ley was in the RAC. Goebbels felt happier at the Reform. But unlike their rivals, members here considered themselves a cut above the rest by virtue of their enlightened interest in literature and theatre. Perhaps that was why it had been commandeered by a group of Culture Ministry men wanting to replicate the *Herrenklub* culture of their homeland with social gatherings of like-minded males, garnished by old wines and young women.

When, in the taxi, Martin told her they would be having dinner with his friends, Rose was astonished.

'I imagined we'd be alone. You never let me meet the people you know.'

'I thought it was about time.'

After they first became lovers, when Rose was seized with curiosity about her handsome seducer, she had longed to meet his friends, if only to discover more about the enigmatic Assistant Commissioner who had laid claim to her. Yet in all their time together, not once had Martin suggested socializing with his associates. They had attended events together, they had frequented the Ritz bar and the Savoy Grill, but never in a private setting. Rose knew she should have felt gratified to meet these men now, yet she was also alarmed. Did this mean that Martin had decided to publicize their relationship? If so, why?

'Evening, sir. Miss.' The porter nodded to Martin as he took their coats, adding for good measure, 'Pleasure to see you again, *Mein Herr*.'

The club's dining room was a place of heavy mahogany and oil paintings, with a carpet the colour of green chartreuse and oppressively dark red walls. Soft lamps and candelabras lit a long table furnished with stiff linen napkins and thick silver cutlery, its length groaning with plates of beef, roast potatoes, vegetables and fruit. The very air smelled expensive – of perfume and polished wood and lavish food with elaborate sauces. Beneath a dense fug of cigar smoke, a group of men in SS dress uniform lolled in their chairs, and between them, dainty as foals, sat several Gelis, their hair waved and nails polished. Their dresses looked expensive and foreign, Rose thought. Their fingers bristled with cocktail rings and one had pear-shaped diamonds hanging from her ears.

'So, this is your girl, Martin. You kept her well hidden. And I can see why.'

'Rose, this is Obersturmbannführer Hans Kinkel.'

Kinkel was claret-faced and looked badly drunk. His eyes glittered with savage laughter. Martin continued with a list of Sturmbannführers and an Oberführer and she nodded as these plump and gleaming men ran their eyes over her. There was a pug-faced officer from the Film Copyright department and a couple of the men from the Ministry who would stride the corridors with a Leni or two fluttering at their heels. Here they had a couple of women apiece, and none was providing secretarial assistance.

'And this is SS-Brigadeführer Ulrich von Aachen.'

This man was not drunk. Lanky, and arrogant, he inclined his head very slightly towards her. There was a silkiness to his menace that matched the fine lawn of his grey uniform with the three silver oak leaves on the collar.

'Good evening,' he said.

Kinkel leaned back in his chair, arms clasped behind his head. Malice hung in the air.

'A real beauty, this one, Martin. I take it she's not for sharing.'

Rose sensed a frisson among the other Gelis and was reminded that Martin was considered more courteous and reserved than his colleagues. A true gentleman. He was seen as a man of rare sensibilities and she guessed the other men knew that too.

'Or is she? Come and sit next to me, sweetie.'

Kinkel beckoned her, a Havana cigar between his sausage fingers, and the Geli next to him made room.

'Our friend Martin's very popular with the ladies. I've often wondered why. What is it about him that you girls like?'

The Geli with the diamond earrings laughed.

'It's his artistic temperament.'

'Is that it? Then let's have some of it. Give us some music, Martin. There's a piano in the corner.'

Without protest, Martin complied. He got up, sat at the piano and began to play some Rachmaninov, his face rigid. Unreadable.

Kinkel turned his attention more closely to Rose and placed a hand on her cleavage. She was wearing a low-cut evening dress with a black velvet bodice and his splayed fingers thrummed a tattoo on her skin as though she, too, was an instrument to be played. Her entire body clenched, defensively, yet she remained rigidly still. Kinkel sloshed wine into a glass and pushed it towards her. Alcohol seeped from his every pore.

'Perhaps Sturmbannführer Kreuz is romantic. Is that it?' His voice assumed a falsetto. 'My *Liebling*, you're the only one for me!'

The other men were laughing uneasily. Rose sensed that the veneer of civility was tissue-thin and beneath it swelled a bridling aggression.

Kinkel gripped her chin and tilted her face to the light. 'You Gelis will believe anything. You're all the same.'

The conversation moved on to a debate about the contrast between British and German culture. The pug-faced officer was holding forth.

'The Leader is on record as saying that the English cannot tell the Germans anything about culture. He says, a single German, like Beethoven, achieved more in the realm of music than all Englishmen of the past and the present together.'

This disquisition was interrupted by a raucous cheer, provoked by another man slapping his passing girlfriend on the bottom. It was a sharp assault that caught her off-balance and sent her careering into a Gretl who had just entered with a steaming china tureen. The shove sent the tureen and its contents – a scalding Mulligatawny soup – crashing to the ground, splashing the trousers of some of the men as the china smashed into pieces on the edge of the fireplace.

The Gretl, stoop-shouldered and aged, with fearful eyes, bent immediately to the floor, as if she could physically sweep up the tide of liquid with her hands.

The commotion diverted the attention of the quiet SS-Brigadeführer. His demeanour barely changed but he leaned over, plucked a billiard stick from a rack and brought it down on the Gretl's fragile back.

'Careless whore.'

The blow was crippling – a professional hit designed to exert maximum pain. The elderly woman arched her back in agony and staggered backwards, hands raised in self-defence.

For a moment it looked as if von Aachen would repeat the assault until he said with deadly quiet, 'Get out.'

Rose couldn't take any more. A wave of nausea swept over her and she jumped to her feet. Leaving the room, she hesitated in the hall, trembling violently, but Martin was hurrying after her.

'For God's sake, Rose, what are you doing?'

'I'm leaving.'

'Don't be a fool.'

He gripped her arm and led her through a sweeping hall to a small side room. It was a library of some kind, its walls lined with books and a maroon leather Chesterfield sitting in front of the fireplace. A green shaded lamp spilled a pool of light onto a side table set with crystal decanters and glasses.

'Calm down. You're hysterical.'

Rose shook off his hand and tried to sort the thoughts racing through her brain. So, this was how they thought of her. Not only her but Helena and Bridget and all the other women who imagined that being singled out by men gave them a special status. That their classification by a male-dominated regime made them elite. *Elite*. What empty mockery that sounded. *We're lucky to be Gelis*, Helena had said. How was this lucky?

'Is that how you see me? Like one of those women?'

'Of course not.'

'Why did you bring me here then? To show you could be just the same as them?'

She had no idea what possessed her. She had never spoken

to Martin as directly as this. Revulsion at seeing the old woman beaten had unleashed a rage that forced her words out, unfiltered and raw.

'I told you. We need to talk.'

'We could talk anywhere. At your flat. Or mine. There's no reason—'

He gripped her arms to interrupt.

'I'm being transferred. Away from here.'

A rush of relief ran through Rose. A sudden lightness, which lifted her almost physically, so she stood taller as she faced him. She checked herself, forcing herself to remember how happy Martin had once made her. Those few days in Berlin when they had visited Clärchens Ballhaus, a vast imperial ballroom, moulded with creamy stucco and parquet floors, where they danced the foxtrot, the tango and the waltz. Whirling around in Martin's arms, she had thought herself properly in love. Yet whenever she tried to hold on to it, the feeling faded as fast as the music.

'Helga will be pleased.'

'I'm not being sent to Germany. It's Paris.'

'But that's good. You always loved Paris, didn't you?'

'Yes. No.'

His face was creased with worry.

'It's a demotion. I don't understand why. I worked myself to the bone here and I always assumed the Protector appreciated me. It's almost as if the Commissioner wanted me out of the way.'

Rose felt a clutch of fear. She should tell him what she

knew, but the terror of revealing the Commissioner's threat was overpowering.

'Tell me what happened.'

Martin sank onto the arm of the Chesterfield and rubbed his brow.

'Eckberg called me in just before the reception last week. He thanked me for my work but said that immediately after the Leader's visit I should prepare for a move to Paris where I would henceforth work as a meaningless functionary. Those weren't his actual words, of course. *Deputy Supervisor of Cultural Cleansing* was how he put it. Making visits to private homes to check for hidden works of art. Chasing up valuables not declared by greedy householders. Seizing degenerate paintings. Low-level stuff. One up from a rent collector.'

'So you told him no?'

'It wasn't a question.' He drew a deep breath and blinked. 'Anyhow. I've decided. When I take the Paris position, I want you to come with me.'

'How's that possible?'

'We'll marry.'

She stared at him, uncomprehending.

'But how . . . ?'

'I'm going to ask Helga for a divorce.'

Instantly, she was shaking her head.

'Divorce is hard for senior men. Unless you're Goebbels. The Protector thinks it should be outlawed. The Party doesn't like it and it smacks of moral turpitude. You'd need permission.'

'If they don't allow me, I'll invoke SS privilege and take a second wife.'

The SS was Himmler's personal fiefdom and its members enjoyed special dispensations where women were concerned. In Himmler's view superior men should be permitted two wives, both because they possessed a natural excess of vitality and because they were valuable breeding material.

'Helga would hate that.'

'She'll have to live with it. She knew what she was getting when she married me. Besides . . .' – his eyes clouded – 'I don't think she would entirely mind.'

With an effort he attempted to conjure some brightness into his voice.

'Think of Paris, darling.'

'How can I think of it? I've never been there. I've got no idea what it's like.'

'Well, I'm telling you, you'll love it. I can take you shopping down the Champs Elysées.'

Suddenly into Rose's mind came a line she had recently eradicated from *Jane Eyre* in which Rochester promised the same thing. He would take Jane shopping for dresses of amethyst silk and pink satin.

I told him . . . that he might as well buy me a gold gown and a silver bonnet at once: I should certainly never venture to wear his choice.

Involuntarily, she touched her neck, where the pearl necklace Martin had given her hung like a millstone.

'I don't want to go shopping. I'm not interested in that.'

Martin tensed.

'You'll love the art. And the architecture. There are plenty of good buildings left. You know the Leader approves of Paris for holidays. He believes it to be culturally edifying. We can be together publicly, without worrying about what people think.'

She struggled for a response. The blood-red library walls seemed to be closing in, squeezing the breath from her lungs, and she had a desperate urge to escape. So this was why Martin had wanted to show her off to his friends tonight. The relief she had felt a few moments ago turned to mutinous despair.

'I know what you're thinking. You don't want to be with me publicly. When you walk out with me you see people flinching at my uniform. They see nothing beyond it. It swallows you, this uniform. You have no idea how it feels to wear it.'

'Do you have any idea how it feels to see it?'

In the dim firelight, he could not read her expression, but his tone darkened.

'I don't think you appreciate the immensity of what I'm doing, Rose. Senior men simply never marry their . . .'

'Their what?'

He shrugged.

'Their concubines? Their mistresses? Their Gelis?'

'Call it whatever you like. Words don't matter.'

'You're wrong, Martin. Words matter very much. You told me as much. Remember?'

Stiffly, he stood and faced her.

'So you refuse to accompany me?'

'I'm sorry, Martin.'

'I won't ask you again.'

He hesitated another moment, and receiving no answer, turned on his heel and left the room.

Rose realized she was trembling. She had crossed some kind of rubicon. She had no idea what to do, but she guessed she might as well leave. Collecting her coat from the doorman, she walked out and paused for a moment to get her bearings.

The evening murk was sequinned by the lights of the West End shows. All around, people were flooding out of the theatres, patting their pockets for cigarettes, thronging up St Martin's Lane and Long Acre to Leicester Square, trying to prolong the escape from dour routine that an evening's entertainment provided. Rose had an intense burst of longing to be among that crowd, caring for nothing but the play they had just seen and the prospect of the Coronation to come.

What happened next was so fast that she barely registered what was going on.

A car pulled up at the kerb beside her. Two men got out, one in front and one behind her. They wore the grey-green livery of the Alliance Security Police and their faces were as nondescript as their uniforms. Each man grasped one of her arms and they lifted her slightly, sandwiched her between them and then bent her like a doll into the back of the car.

Wildly she looked around for Martin, or anyone, but the eyes of the club doorman slid discreetly away and passers-by averted their gaze, as they always did when police appeared.

'What's happening? What do you want? Where are you taking me?'

The car jerked off with a squeal of rubber, forcing her back against the seat, and one officer leaned over from the front.

'You'll know soon enough.'

CHAPTER TWENTY-FOUR

The Romanesque towers and Gothic turrets of the most feared building in London, the Alliance Security Office, sliced the South Kensington skyline like a sheaf of knives. In previous times this building had been a citadel of education, behind whose spiky, idiosyncratic facade, studded with the reliefs of birds and animals, scholars and archivists probed the origin of species.

Now the place existed to examine one species alone. Man.

The building once known as the Natural History Museum was now familiar to every Londoner as the Honeycomb. It wasn't named for the intricate pattern of its honey-coloured facade, nor the thousands of cells in its basement designed to contain the defunct bodies of insects and other creatures. Now that the dinosaurs, dodos and blue whales had been relocated, its cathedral-like spaces and labyrinthine corridors were dedicated to another use. ASO was the hive to which foragers of information brought their nectar: the reports, and nudges and whispered denunciations. These findings would be meticulously filed away in the system of rotating stacks devised by Heinrich Himmler himself for the Sicherheitdienst in Germania, and later installed here in a network of tunnels that coiled for miles beneath the intricate marble floor. The ASO was the living brain of the Alliance, its deep memory and dark, beating heart. It was an ever-replenished battery of information, essential for the Alliance's continued survival.

In a strange way, it made sense. Society was like nature, the Leader had once said. A vast inter-related organism in which every part was connected to another, watching, monitoring, informing. *The perfect society must remain in a state of perpetual alertness*. Humans, therefore, under Alliance rule, were only conforming to their most primal instincts.

Once past the glass security booth, where a guard scrutinized her identity documents, Rose walked between the two officers across the vast, vaulted atrium and through a concealed panel leading to a corridor painted industrial green, where fly-flecked lamps cast an underwater light. Even at this time of night, the building was pulsing with activity. Night and day seemed to have no meaning here. Frosted-glass doors led off the corridor. The sounds of women's voices, telephones and typewriters emanated from behind them. The atmosphere was one of dull bureaucracy. Lenis, with clipboards and pencils behind their ears, clipped along, chatting to each other. The corridor was lined with forgettable, low-grade reproductions of cityscapes: Berlin,

Cologne, Paris, Vienna, Prague, and one of London that looked as though someone had spilled brown soup over it. The dust of long-extinct animals that had once been displayed here seemed to choke the air, as though the dinosaurs and whales were still present, floating in a phantom, particulate trace in the atmosphere.

One officer peeled off and the other led the way down a flight of steps, and then another flight, moving further and further from ground level until they came to a corridor flanked on either side by steel doors. Once, Rose thought, these must have been storerooms for something beautiful – African butterflies or rare, exotic birds – but they were now a holding area for frightened living creatures like herself.

A prisoner passed, pale-faced, sandwiched between two officers. His eyes dragged over her in desperation and an answering sweat broke out on her in a cold film of fear.

Wordlessly, the guard pulled a key from the bunch attached by a chain to his waist, opened a door and pushed her inside. The key turned in the lock.

The cell was ten feet by six. A wooden bench was fixed to the wall, as was a steel lavatory, and high in the side wall was a rectangle of frosted glass. Three thick bolts were slid across the other side of the steel door and in one corner the mark of a boot, like a child's potato print, was etched in dried blood. She had no idea how long her wait would be, but she could guess what lay at the end of it.

Rose knew about interrogation. Once, during her

relationship with Laurence Prescott, he confided that he had been invited to a top-level ASO conference at a mansion north of London. The place was like a country house hotel, he said, and along with the silver trays of tea and the plush furnishings, one might have taken it for the annual get-together of an accountancy firm, were it not for the number of SS uniforms around the bar. The discussion centred around enhanced interrogation procedures, but to Laurence's surprise, he himself had been summoned to discuss his journalistic interview techniques.

They said they knew how to do the heavy stuff, but it was the subtlety they were after. How a journalist gets a person to open up despite themselves. They thought, because I interview actresses, I could tell them how to beat the truth out of some poor sod who'd resisted their knuckledusters. I'm not sure if I told them anything, but I did learn a couple of tips myself.

What did you learn?

They said, no prisoner needs anyone else to betray them. They will betray themselves. Just like a doctor knows that a patient's diagnosis will announce itself, if only he listens properly.

For once, Laurence's natural jollity had evaporated, and she could tell how deeply his brush with ASO had shaken him.

Thing is, Rose, in those interrogations, you can't win. They not only want you to say black is white, they want you to explain why black is white. They're remorseless. They have all the time in the world. They can see behind every shadow in your mind.

She tensed as a pair of boots thudded down the corridor

and panic rose like bile in her throat, constricting her chest and forcing her to take breaths in tiny gasps. But the thumps passed the door without stopping, the heavy tread receded and her heartbeat gradually slowed.

Hugging her knees to her ribs, she tried to tamp down her emotions and think rationally. In particular, about Martin. One question worried her. When they were at the reception, and Martin had been complaining about his workload, he had said, *The graffiti's getting worse*.

The Commissioner had instructed her to keep the graffiti a secret, and Rose had obeyed him. So why did Martin assume she knew all about it?

Slowly the night passed. Dawn announced itself in a slice of light from the frosted window that crept slowly across the stone floor. At some point the door was opened, and a shaft of cold horror pierced her, but it was only an unseen hand that pushed in a tray containing water and a single slice of bread, smeared with margarine.

She shivered. Beneath the navy evening coat she was still wearing her sleeveless black dress, satin with a velvet bodice, flimsy shoes and Martin's pearl necklace at her throat. She couldn't imagine how she must look. Or how long she would be alone.

Human beings can only tolerate so much solitary confinement, and the citizens of the Alliance were less equipped than most. Solitude was discouraged. Every moment of a citizen's life should be spent in productive or social events. Once, during one of Celia's inquisitions about marriage, Rose had echoed Greta Garbo's appeal in *Grand Hotel*.

I want to be alone.

Her sister was furious.

Don't say things like that. You spend far too much time alone as it is. You're not even in the Women's Service. They notice these things.

Now, Rose had her wish. She was truly, deeply alone. Yet even solitude was not enough. Was there any corner of her mind where she could crouch unseen?

It wasn't until the slice of light had passed the central point of the floor that the scuffle of boots and crank of keys told her she was finally being summoned.

To her surprise, the interrogator was younger than her. He must have been in his early twenties, with tow hair shaven like a freshly cut lawn. Like every institution in the Alliance territory, most of the staff members were native-born and this one reminded her of her baby-faced cousin Paul, right down to the tiny wound on his neck where he had nicked himself shaving.

Her breathing calmed. Perhaps she could take him on.

The young man slid a piece of paper across the desk, with a pen. He looked nonchalant. Bored even.

'Sign.'

Rose had heard about this. Under the system imported from the mainland, prisoners taken into custody, without judicial proceedings, had to sign their own *Schutzhaftbefehl* – the order requesting imprisonment. Once she had scrawled her signature, he said, 'Sit on your hands.'

She knew about this too. The hands would sweat and they could remove the rough material from the chair seat, in case they ever needed scent for dogs to follow.

Every fibre of her body was tense as she waited for the interrogation to begin.

And waited.

The officer tapped his fingers on the table. When she lifted her eyes to his enquiringly, he looked away. She realized she was not the only one waiting; he was waiting too.

Then the door slammed open and another man entered.

Ernst Kaltenbrunner's irises were as pale as concrete and the whites resembled boiled eggs. Half his face was scarred like a collapsed candle. Albert Speer, the Leader's architect, had described his look as 'curiously mild' but others detected in him a low, patient cunning, like a snake biding its time. Perhaps in emulation of the Leader, he carried a bullwhip casually dangling from one hand. He addressed her in German.

'Miss Ransom, this can be difficult, or it can be easy.'

He had a soft, slippery voice, which made her want to confide everything she knew. She felt it penetrate, reaching for the secrets that might lie buried beneath her every instinct and inhibition.

At Kaltenbrunner's nod the younger man rose and scurried out of the room, with every sign of relief.

Rose focused hard on the desk in front of her, tortured

with cigarette burns. Her mind was spinning with the implications. The chief of the ASO himself had arrived to interrogate her. There had to be a reason.

He came close and touched the strand of pearls around her neck, rolling one between his fingers. She forced herself not to recoil.

'You're a friend of the Assistant Culture Commissioner, SS-Sturmbannführer Kreuz, I hear.'

'Yes, sir.'

'What do you discuss with him?'

'I report to him for my work.'

'And your work is . . . ?'

'I correct literary texts to align them with Alliance ideals.'

'What rules do you follow in that correction?'

It was a tricky question. While in every other area of life there were enough regulations to fill a library all of their own, the Alliance's rules on female subordination largely existed unwritten. Unwritten rules were more powerful. They made people check themselves. Self-censorship was always more effective than any other kind. Why police people when you can scare them into policing themselves?

'I often refer to the Leader's Table Talks.'

She had found the collection of Table Talks given by the Leader a useful reference. He was known to despise 'intelligent' women. A woman should never aspire to better a man in education or conversation. She should never assert her individuality.

'Do you discuss politics with Herr Kreuz?'

Martin? Could it be that their interest lay in Martin, and not her?

'Never.'

'Come, come. Not even harmless tittle-tattle? You never chat about the Commissioner's new haircut, or the arrival of the Leader, or . . .' – a soft chuckle – 'the dismal quality of senior staff in the Culture Ministry?'

'No.'

Kaltenbrunner perched on the edge of the table and changed tack. This was like a dance, she understood. An interrogation must have a rhythm and a progress. Maybe the idea was, he would step forward, then step back, and eventually she would step into his arms.

'You've been visiting Oxford. What were you doing there?'

She recalled the Commissioner's face. *Tell no one.* But nobody, not even the Commissioner, was above the ASO.

'I was asked to visit the Widowlands there to interview some women about their lives.'

That much was true.

The ASO chief's snarl deepened, as though he was personally offended.

'Explain.'

'The Protector is writing a book about the mythic traditions of ancient England and the connections between the German and English people. He wants a section on superstitions and he believes that old women will be the best source of knowledge for that.'

It was so plausible. The Protector's enthusiasms were enough to make even Ernst Kaltenbrunner glaze over.

'Why Oxford?'

'It was the Commissioner's suggestion.'

'Who did you associate with there? Apart from Friedas?'

The face of Bruno Schumacher came into her head. Then Oliver Ellis.

'Nobody.'

'Is that a lie?'

He had the kind of mild voice that could make a person jump better than any scream.

'Surely a man of your experience would know a lie when he hears one.'

The slap of his bullwhip on the table stung the air.

'Don't try to play with me, Fräulein Ransom. I assure you we are much better at games than you. We have interrogated people in the London Library. A Leni there gave you unorthodox access without permission.'

Poor girl. She would be out of a job. There would be no happy Coronation party with her friends. What horrors could Kaltenbrunner's cold imagination fashion for her?

'She tells us you showed an interest in certain volumes of degenerate historical work. A reader in the stacks where you browsed recalled seeing you.'

The man in the tweed suit. Oscar Stephenson.

'What exactly were you looking for?'

What could she say? That she hardly knew herself? She thought fast.

'I'm correcting a text of *Jane Eyre* to be placed in schools. Sometimes we write an addendum. I wanted to provide examples of degenerate attitudes to female education.'

It made no sense, but nor did anything in Alliance literary policy and it seemed to satisfy Kaltenbrunner. Abruptly he rose, brushed imaginary dust from his sleeve and said, 'Right then. You can go.'

Could that really be all? Relief weakened Rose's limbs. She could barely stand up.

Kaltenbrunner walked across to the door and opened it a fraction, then paused, hand on the handle, as if a thought had just struck him.

He closed the door again.

'Just one thing. We found this in your possessions.'

Removing an envelope from his pocket, he extracted a small, thin square of paper, rolled up to the size of a matchstick. Rose had hidden it so carefully right at the bottom of her bag between the join in the lining. But her bag had been taken from her the moment her arm was seized and they could find anything if they put their mind to it.

Kaltenbrunner opened the scrap of paper, and read ponderously, '*The beginning is always today*. What's this gibberish?'

'It's a motto . . .' Rose cast around for inspiration. 'It's like, every year the Ministry sends out calendars and we have uplifting messages on special days. You know, Alliance National Day in August. April, the Leader's birthday. We were doing a souvenir brochure for the Coronation and I thought it would go well.'

It was all true. Entirely checkable. Utterly plausible. Almost certainly the ASO had been sent some complementary copies of their own. Probably they lit the fire with them.

'Mottos?'

'Just simple lines, really. *The future is together. State before self. Memory is treacherous.*'

It was hard to imagine any of the Culture Ministry's anodyne exhortations hanging on these walls.

'I see.' Kaltenbrunner looked down at the piece of paper in his hands, as though he longed to ball it up and bin it. Or tear it to tiny fragments.

'And what precisely about this trite – some might say meaningless – sentiment makes it suitable for a commemorative brochure?'

Rose shrugged. 'I don't know, really. It could mean a number of things but to me it seemed to echo the Party idea of eternal change. Minister Goebbels himself has written that he favours a state of permanent revolution.'

'And the paper?'

He held the scrap up between his thumb and forefinger in demonstration.

'Where did you get it?'

For a second her mind was blank. Where had she found it? Mentally she retraced her steps. She was in the office and had just returned from watching the arrival of Leni Riefenstahl. Bridget had noticed a smudge of ink on the back of her hand. Looking round for somewhere to jot down the words, she had grabbed a scrap of paper from Oliver's desk.

'I found it on the desk next to me.'

When she walked out of the building she went down into the underground and pressed her back against the wall, gulping in the dusty air until a train arrived. The carriage was warm, the windows smeared and stuffing was seeping out from the chequered claret and green upholstery, yet it was comforting to be in this familiar, anonymous place. As the train rattled into the tunnel, the wooden slats shook beneath her feet and she had a vision of all that lay beneath – the cables and trenches, the debris and the live rail – as though her mind had reset itself and was now striving to see under the surface of everything.

She had no clear idea why she had been arrested. Whether it was curiosity about the book she had been reading in the London Library, or a report from the odious Oscar Stephenson that she had been acting suspiciously. Or was the true focus of the ASO's interest really Martin? If so, she dared not contact him. They would be observing her closely now.

Studying her reflection in the train window opposite, she attempted to see herself as others might see her, focusing intently on any aspect that could possibly single her out. Everything about her was appropriate, from the navy wool evening coat pulled over her smart Geli dress, to the dark blonde hair styled in an appropriate blunt bob. She had friends from the correct caste. Her romantic relationship might transgress Party guidelines, but no more than a thousand other relationships between Gelis and senior men.

Yet the truth was, she did feel different. She didn't fit in. Could it be possible that the officers of the ASO perceived what she had barely acknowledged herself?

The dim light from the glass-shaded lamps painted the other occupants with a lurid underwater tinge. No one looked at each other. Every person sat immersed in their own world, sunk in their own private thoughts. They must all have their secret hopes and dreams, but who could say if they yearned for a different world, or had lost the ability even to imagine it?

Rose closed her eyes. Her old life felt ripped and torn up now, like a scrap of newspaper rolling along the carriage floor. This was her new existence. Plunging into darkness, with no sight of what might lie ahead.

CHAPTER TWENTY-FIVE

Thursday, 29th April

The red-brick Victorian edifice of Kindergarten 237 had, until a decade ago, been surrounded by ornate iron railings, safeguarding the generations of children who played netball and hopscotch and tag on its tarmacked forecourt. Now, like all quality metal, the railings had been transported to the mainland, leaving only the brick structure of a gate, around which every afternoon a bunch of Klaras obediently clustered. Yet in other ways everything about the kindergarten was the same: the same blackboards and stick-man paintings tacked on the wall, the same line of hooks with art smocks hanging on them and shoes below, the same scent of chalk dust and lunch in the air. It was as if nothing had changed, instead of everything.

When the bell rang, the children burst out, dancing round their mothers like sparkling insects around slow-moving cattle. Klaras were, indeed, nicknamed *Milchmädchen* – milk maidens – or more rudely *Kuhfrauen* – cow women – because they were obliged to pump regular quotas of excess breast milk into bottles for donation to sickly children on the mainland. Those who didn't meet their quotas had their rations cut, which had the effect of reducing their milk supply even further, so generally the only thing they could do was produce another child.

As soon as Hannah saw Rose her face broke into a smile, showcasing the fresh gaps in her teeth.

'Auntie Rose! What are you doing here?'

'Your mother sent me to fetch you.'

'For a treat?'

'Yes.'

The moment Rose had got back to her apartment, she had stripped off her clothes and bent over the basin to wash every inch of her body with a gritty sliver of soap, as if to scrub the last trace of the ASO from her flesh. Then she changed into a skirt and blouse, pulled on her mackintosh and telephoned Celia to suggest that she collect Hannah from school.

'Why aren't you at work?' Celia demanded.

'Coronation preparation.'

'Lucky old you. Well, it would be useful actually because then I can get our Gretl to clean the silver. She's frightfully lazy and I have a host of things to do before Sunday, not to mention some girlfriends coming over to tea. You've met Judy and Lettie, haven't you?'

Rose had, and would rather never meet them again. But she had an urgent, panicky need to see Hannah's face. To stroke the slender childish neck, like a young gosling's, and the invisible down on her cheek. To breathe in the innocence of the child, hold her trusting hand, and immerse herself in normality again. To read their secret stories and seek refuge in their private childhood kingdom.

Hannah skipped alongside her, running one hand along the wall and pushing her fingers into the tiny dips and holes.

'Why's it spotty?'

The wall was bullet-scarred and pocked by shrapnel.

'It's just old.'

'Old is bad,' Hannah repeated dreamily.

That was one of the sayings they learned in school. *Old is bad*.

Towards the end of the street, the damage to the wall intensified and in one place the mortar had entirely crumbled as though from a fierce barrage of shots aimed directly at one particular spot. Nobody had attempted to mend it. Rose stared at the scatter of gunshot, wondering exactly what horror it recorded. Then, on the ground beneath, she saw a trail of tulips, egg yolk yellow, littering the paving – and her chest tightened.

Them.

Already the petals were bruised by passing feet, and in an hour they would be mulch in the gutter, every bright trace of their beauty gone.

*

Judy Leadbetter and Lettie Hodges, like all of Celia's friends, were genial and uninspiring Gelis, fully immersed in the lives of their husbands and children. Neither was as pretty as Celia, which was probably why she liked them so much. Judy was dissolving into premature middle age, her flesh slack and chin sliding down into her tortoise neck, a clutch of pearls at her throat. Lettie was going the opposite way, becoming narrower and sharper like an old kitchen knife. Back in the Time Before they would all have been firm adherents of the Women's Institute, meeting every month in a draughty church hall to discuss the perennial issues of jam making and baby care. The annual outing to the Royal Academy Summer Exhibition and the charity bazaar would have been the highlights of their social calendar, the tennis club, jumble sale, school and their husbands' office would have marked the limits of their known world.

Now that the WI had been outlawed as a criminal organization and replaced with compulsory membership of the Women's League and the Mother Service, any frank or honest exchange of gossip required them to meet in each other's homes.

When Rose arrived with Hannah, the women looked up with inquisitive glances.

'Not often we see you out of the office, Rose,' observed Lettie.

'It's a busy time. All our shifts are up in the air.'

'Are you coming to our street party?'

'Can't wait.'

'You look tired,' said Judy, with an accusatory frown. 'What have you been up to?'

Where should she begin? That the previous evening she had turned down a proposal of marriage? Or that she had spent the following hours crouching in the claustrophobic basement cellars of the ASO, cowering before Ernst Kaltenbrunner and his bull-hide whip? Or that now, in a daze of fatigue and fear, she was trying to make sense of her entire existence?

'I saw the King and Queen the other day. At Westminster Abbey.'

The effect was electric. All three sat up like children promised a treat.

'What *was* she like?'

It was always Wallis who interested them. Nobody wanted to know about the King. The poor man elicited no more excitement than his own valet.

'Regal, I suppose.'

'I'll bet.' Judy's cup was poised halfway to her mouth. 'How far away was she from you?'

'About a stone's throw.'

'She's awfully beautiful, I imagine,' said Lettie, more than ever like a bedraggled hen in her tweedy plumage.

'Very elegant certainly.'

'I was just showing everyone this,' said Lettie, burrowing in her bag and producing a commemorative plate of the King and Queen – a waxwork and a gaunt geisha in poorly produced porcelain. 'It's art really. Not for actual use.'

'They're so good-looking,' cooed Celia. 'Such a shame they never had any little ones.'

There was a minute hiatus at this remark. The fact that Edward and Wallis were the last of the Windsors was rarely aired. Though the subject was not officially off-limits, that didn't mean people dared openly speculate as to what might happen when they were gone. Would an ancient branch of a German royal family be drafted in to do the job, like the Hanoverians in the eighteenth century? Or, as seemed more likely, might the British monarchy be allowed to wither and die?

'D'you know,' announced Lettie, deftly changing the subject. 'If I had to work, which thank God I don't, I think I'd take *your* job, Rose. I'd absolutely love to meet the Queen.'

'I didn't actually—'

'In fact, there's only one thing I'd like better.'

Rose saw it coming, even as Lettie pinked girlishly, and her voice lowered to a breathy gush.

'And that is to meet the Leader.'

Rose read a couple of stories to Hannah, but the magic of her imaginary kingdom had faded. Ilyria was too fragile to provide any refuge from real life. For Rose, if not Hannah, the spell of their secret world was broken.

Bidding a brusque farewell to Judy and Lettie, she headed for the front door. Celia followed her.

'You might try a bit harder with my friends, Rosalind. That was bordering on rude.'

'I'm sorry. I have a lot on my mind.'

Celia brushed her cheek with an air kiss.

'I suppose you're forgiven. Matter of fact, I was going to tell you – the hospital telephoned. They want to let Dad out soon.'

Rose flushed in delight.

'Oh, Celia. That's just fantastic. The best news I've had all day.'

'Isn't it. Only, don't make a fuss, Rosalind, please . . .'

'About what?'

'Geoffrey's asked them to keep him in for a while longer. Just for a few weeks. Maybe a month or so. For Mum's sake. He says it's the least we can do.'

A squall of rain had come and gone, and as Rose approached her apartment block, she noticed wet footprints leading up the pale stone steps and into the tiled hallway. They continued up the stairs and came to a halt outside her door.

Danger sang in her ears.

Opening the door cautiously, she strained for the sound of an intruder, but the air of the flat felt empty and her movements echoed in its vacancy. Moving swiftly, she went over to the hiding place in her bedroom wall, levered off the plank behind the leaf-stencilled wallpaper, carefully extracting the bricks and placing them on the floor, before reaching inside and feeling for her notebooks.

They were still there.

She laid them out on the floor beside her. She had

completed seven notebooks now, each one meticulously dated and filled with the loops of her own hand marching neatly across each page. As she flicked through, Rose wondered yet again at this writing urge that had arisen from nowhere and taken possession of her. Perhaps writing was a way of separating herself, and staying separate, from the world around her. Of withdrawing to some inner location that even she did not properly understand. Or maybe, like Jane Eyre on the moor, straining to catch the phantom voices swirling around her in the misty air.

Rose didn't discriminate: the notebooks contained everything from musings and random thoughts to stories, fragments of poetry, journal entries and sometimes no more than a string of words or a sentence that appealed. They were also the place she charted her shifting feelings about Martin. In the year they had been together she had scrupulously avoided discussing the relationship with friends or family – not even Helena enjoyed full disclosure – and consequently the diary had become the only space where Rose could analyse her own conflicted emotions. There they lay in front of her: the passionate entries from when they first met and kissed, to the bewilderment when she and Martin had first made love.

I thought it was supposed to feel more exciting than this.

As the relationship progressed, her guilt towards Martin's wife had intensified.

Helga would hate me if she knew. But she couldn't hate me more than I hate myself.

And later: *Why must Martin constantly ask what I'm thinking? Whenever he does, my instinct is always to conceal the truth. The closer we are, the further away I want to stay. Is this normal, or a fault in my character?*

Leafing through, she reached the most recent entry; the enigmatic line that had caused a frisson of excitement to run through her when she stumbled across it in the London Library. The line that Ernst Kaltenbrunner had discovered rolled up at the bottom of her bag. She had jotted it down without comment, so she would not forget it.

The beginning is always today

Crouching there, exhausted, her fingers itched to start writing again, even if only to record the dreadful events of the previous twenty-four hours. She knew that articulating them would help to tame and make sense of what had happened. Maybe she could turn the whole of last night's experience into a story of some kind, or at the very least record every detail she could remember.

That was what she would do. It was the nearest she could get to a plan of action. She would make coffee, strong and black, and a sandwich, then settle at her desk and write.

She was still kneeling on the floor when a creak sliced the silence. She tilted her head and strained to filter the ambient noise. From the pub on the corner came the distant chink of bottles, and far beneath the ground the vague rumble of an underground train. In the flat above, a sewing machine whirred, and next door, Elsa Bottomley barked like a seal with her interminable cough.

Rose waited, frozen as a hare on her haunches. A minute passed. Every one of her senses detected nothing, except for her sixth sense, which roared like tinnitus in her brain.

Scrambling to her feet, she scooped up the notebooks, bundled them into the cavity, adjusting the plank and wallpaper and pushing the bed back against the wall. Then she took a deep breath to steady herself, and with a jerk, flung open the door.

'Hello. I'm glad you're in.' Oliver Ellis emerged from the darkness of the hall and moved forward to lean against the door frame. 'I hope I didn't startle you.'

'What do you want?' she demanded.

'I wondered if now might be a good time.'

'For what?'

'Don't you remember?'

The blood rushed in her ears. Disorientated by shock and fatigue, she frowned at him fiercely.

'No, I don't remember. Remember what?'

'That drink I mentioned.' He smiled. 'If you still feel like it, that is.'

PART THREE

CHAPTER TWENTY-SIX

In a greasy alley off Chinatown, down vertiginous steps to a basement, where a trail of water from a leaking drainpipe glistened on the brick, a black door faced them, the name *Jazz Town* stencilled roughly on its peeling paint. It was a place people went when they wanted to pretend they were citizens of the world.

It must have been a cellar once but now the sooty corners had been whitewashed, and a tiny wooden dais erected on which a gramophone was playing. Oliver explained that although it was policed regularly, the ethos of Jazz Town was that customers should feel they were enjoying a little subversive liberty.

The music was American, which was allowed, but it pushed at the boundaries of Culture Ministry regulations, which still proscribed swing, or anything by black performers. Only Gelis were permitted, and the male clientele contained a high proportion of Culture Ministry employees, who liked to consider themselves more relaxed in their outlook than their colleagues in more straitlaced departments. Very occasionally two men could be found together, enjoying a late-night camaraderie that was more than platonic and anywhere else would get them thrown into a camp.

Against the wall was a series of curtained booths. On each table stood a small pink shaded lamp that threw out a pool of light – just enough for two people to see each other while casting the rest of the place into shadow.

Oliver ushered her onto a seat and settled himself opposite.

Cigarette smoke drifted over shafts of lamplight. Rose was aware of couples dancing around them, the bare flesh of the women's arms gleaming in the ceiling chandelier, along with the flash of paste diamonds and insignia on the men's uniforms. The booth had the effect of cutting them off from the world, as though just the two of them existed, in a warm, rose-tinted cocoon.

He poured her a glass of Alliance gin. It tasted oily and bitter, as though it was drugged.

'Sorry, again, if I surprised you. I don't make a habit of it. I was just following on from that suggestion I made back in Oxford, that we might have a drink together.'

'You didn't mention the drink would be Alliance gin.'

'You wouldn't have come if I had.'

He tipped his glass at her.

Rose smiled wanly. The events of the past twenty-four hours had pulled the ground from beneath her feet, but this warm, smoky basement felt like a refuge from the chaos of her existence.

'How d'you know this place?'

'I have a drink here some evenings. When I want to blot everything out with the aid of alcohol.'

She wasn't surprised. Alcohol was the fuel that the Alliance ran on and for most people regular oblivion was a necessity.

Rose stared around her, wishing she had worn something more appropriate than the blouse and pencil skirt that she had thrown on, when all the other Gelis in this place were decked in the latest evening gowns.

She fixed on a man who was moving from table to table with a pack of cards.

Oliver followed her gaze.

'That's worth watching. He's a close-up magician.'

The man was a shabby character, in his fifties, wearing a threadbare velvet smoking jacket and a bow tie. A cigarette dangled from his lips and on his briefcase in fading print were the words *Magic Stan. The Card Man.*

Magic Stan's hands were deft and flexible, shuffling, flicking and cutting the deck before fanning the cards out in front of his customers, who craned over them, watching every move, determined to spot the trick.

'I used to love magic tricks when I was a boy,' said Oliver. 'At one point – probably about the age of eleven – I thought it was all I wanted to do in life. Be a full-time magician.'

A delighted cry came from the table as Magic Stan retrieved a card from a Geli's sleeve.

'It's the three of diamonds! The three of diamonds!'

'That's incredible,' muttered her companion, a perspiring Bavarian in a double-breasted dinner jacket. Rather than impressed, he looked angry that he'd allowed himself to be tricked.

'You try again, my friend, you won't catch me out.'

Sensing the bridling violence, Stan bowed and moved swiftly on. As he approached their table, he leaned towards Rose.

'I can never resist a beautiful lady.'

Rose smiled. Close up, Stan reeked of sweat and there were ebony smudges on his neck where his hair dye had run.

'Does the lovely lady have a photograph? Your identity card perhaps?'

Rose took out her wallet, placed it on the table and removed the card that by law she carried everywhere with her, identifying her as an Alliance Female Class I (a). Two pictures of herself stared out, front and profile, rosy-cheeked, with a slight, vigilant smile.

'What a face!' Magic Stan clutched a hand to his chest and feigned a stagger like a stage Italian. 'I am smitten.'

He took her hand and kissed it, then reached an imploring hand out to Oliver.

'Sir, with great respect, this lady's beauty has overwhelmed me. In fact, I must make her disappear. Do I have your permission?'

Oliver shrugged, and Magic Stan closed his eyes and

grimaced in concentration before gesturing to Rose to check her wallet.

In the place where her identity card had been was a playing card. Astonished, she slid it out.

'The Queen of Hearts.' Magic Stan beamed. 'How appropriate.'

Rose frowned at the playing card, then began to cast around for her ID.

'Ah, so now you have my Queen, but you have no ID. You are a lady without a name, and without a classification. How does that feel? A little frightening perhaps?'

Magic Stan's patter was practised and smooth. It was a trick he had performed many times before. His tone darkened with mock menace.

'What will a lovely lady like you do without an identity? Are you worried?'

'Should I be?'

'Let me think.' His brow creased, then he darted forward and pulled something from the chest pocket of Oliver's jacket.

'But it was here all along! I might have known. He was keeping you close to his heart.'

Oliver smiled, reached for an Alliance mark and pushed it in Stan's direction. Pocketing the money, the magician bowed and shuffled off.

'How on earth did he do that?' said Rose, taking her ID card back from Oliver and stowing it safely.

'Sleight of hand. He's worked out the science of attention.

You can pull off anything if you distract people. It's called misdirection.'

'But I was watching him the whole time.'

'You watched him kiss your hand, right above your wallet on the table, then reach out to me. You focused on his theatrics and failed to see what was really going on. When people are consumed by one thing intensely, they're blind to anything else. They see only what they're expecting to see. It's like the Coronation.'

'Huh? How?'

'All the tea towels and the bunting. The talk of carriages and coronets. The television. It's just distraction.'

'From what?'

'From what really matters.'

For a moment, she thought he would go further, before he smiled and changed the subject.

'So this is what I do when I want to get away from it all. What do you do?'

'In the evenings?' Rose hesitated for a second. The gin, on her empty stomach, was having its effect on her. The horror of the previous night, and her encounter with Kaltenbrunner, had chipped away at the barricade of her caution.

She took a brief, fortifying sip and said, 'I write.'

'You take your work home? I might have guessed.'

The words Rose had never spoken clamoured in her mind. She felt as giddy as a parachutist, about to take a step into the unknown. She tipped up her chin and said, 'No. Not my work. I write for myself. That's what I was about to do when you turned up outside my door.'

Once she had begun, she was unstoppable. The wall that she had built so carefully in her head, brick by brick, to stand between her thoughts and her words, was beginning to crumble. The booth became her confessional, its formica table her altar, its draped curtains her sacred space.

'I don't know why I do it. Writing would never have crossed my mind until I started this job, but now, it's as natural as breathing. In fact, I don't know how I would have carried on without it. It began when I was given my correcting job. The Assistant Commissioner told me that literature was dangerous, that it could infect minds. Those who did it might need to protect themselves psychologically from what they would read, but he was sure I could deal with it.'

'He underestimated you.'

'Martin . . . I mean, Assistant Commissioner Kreuz . . . had such faith in me. He asked if I was a reader, and I told him I hadn't read books since childhood.'

Oliver's expression hardened.

'He must have assumed you were deaf and blind if he thought you would be able to read the classics and remain unaffected.'

'I don't know.' She was fiddling with her glass, running her finger along the rim. 'I feel I don't know anything anymore. Do you think writing is . . . reprehensible? I know the Party disapproves.'

Oliver drained his gin, cast a quick look around him and frowned.

'The Party hates writing for the same reason they hate reading. Because it involves being alone, in contact with an unfettered human imagination. That's why they fear it.'

'I don't quite understand why I do it.'

'Why does anyone write? Because all our lives are heading for the night. By writing we preserve our brief snatch of life. Like placing a star in the darkness of the past.'

His eyes were intent on her.

'Good job you write, frankly. There's been nothing worth reading published in the last thirteen years.'

'Nor will this be. It's only short stories, and thoughts and fragments. No one's ever going to see it.'

'I hope you let me read it.'

He reached across and took her hand in his own – an electric brush of skin that ran through every nerve in her body. It was the first time they had ever touched, yet the momentary contact was enough for her to register the large palm, the long fingers and the strength of his grip. The warmth of him surprised her. Everything else about him seemed cool.

'Martin says nobody will read much of anything after this generation. After television gets going.'

'Perhaps we should allow for the possibility that some-times, just sometimes, Herr Martin Kreuz could be wrong.'

She turned her face downwards, to hide her smile, then said, 'What about you? I feel I know nothing about you.'

'My mother's dead. My father lives in New York.'

The information astonished her.

'So you have dual nationality? You're half American?'

'That's right.'

'Then you can travel. You could leave. You could go anywhere!'

'I suppose I could.'

'Yet you don't.'

'To start with, I didn't want to go. Now, I don't go because if I did, I could never come back.'

'Why would that matter?'

She felt the answer before he spoke it. She saw it in his eyes, green with flecks of flame in the iris, as they fixed her, and heard it deep inside herself.

'Why do you think?'

He took her hand again and she felt her blood quicken. Excitement pulsed through her, as though her body already knew what her mind had not yet recognized. Turning her palm, she interlaced his fingers tightly with her own, and returned his gaze.

After a moment she said, 'There's something I haven't told you, but I should tell you now. I was interrogated yesterday. At the ASO. They kept me in overnight, then they released me without charge.'

The vivacity vanished. Sombrely, he asked, 'Does the Assistant Commissioner know?'

'I'm . . . I'm not sure. He's very busy. He's organizing a big conference to be held at Blenheim the day after the

Coronation. Only, just before I was arrested, he told me he was being relocated to Paris.'

'Did they tell you why they pulled you in?'

'No. But the man who interrogated me was Ernst Kalten-brunner.'

Oliver's eyes widened, but he remained silent.

'They seemed to think I knew something. But I don't know anything! None of it makes sense.'

'Perhaps you do know something. You're just not aware of it.'

The atmosphere between them had shifted. He grasped her hand more tightly, and in an urgent whisper said, 'We can't talk here. And we need to talk. I have something to explain. Come with me.'

CHAPTER TWENTY-SEVEN

They walked in darkness south to the river. The Thames was a black mirror, dark and glassy, reflecting back a glittering necklace of lights from the opposite bank. All around them rose the soft murmurs of a spring night: the tide lapping against the hulls of the houseboats, causing them to knock gently together, and the faint hoot of a tug moving downstream. Crossing Chelsea Bridge, they passed a green cabman's shelter where taxi drivers were congregated, drinking tea and waiting for fares. A ribbon of canned laughter leaked from a wireless set. A little way further they came to an elegant red-brick mansion block overlooking Battersea Park, typical of an elite residence for a single man.

Through a tiled hallway reeking of Jeyes Fluid, Oliver led her up two flights of steps and unlocked a door. He stepped back to allow her in first before pulling the door shut behind them.

It was a generous sitting room, with eau de nil walls and

a tiled fireplace into which the fractured elements of a gas fire had been wedged. The paint was dappled with the odd damp stain and the plaster was cracked. Through a door she saw a hand basin and taps, and beyond it, a narrow bed. Even by the standards of most dwellings, where furniture tended to be shabby and carpets worn, this dwelling was unusually vacant. The floorboards were bare. No pictures hung on the walls. No cards or photographs on the mantelpiece. A lone kettle stood on the tiny workspace, next to an empty milk bottle. Curtains featuring blowsy chrysanthemums framed the window, and a faded Turkish rug lay between two chairs.

Oliver locked the door and threw his jacket on a chair.

'It helps to keep it simple. I go over it every day, top to bottom.' He gestured up to the light fitting, and the electrical sockets, and tapped the switch by the door. 'I don't think there are any microphones but you can never be sure.'

Then he nodded towards a stack of papers and magazines heaped in a corner, like a student's filing system, and next to them a desk, cluttered with more books. The top one, *Palgrave's Golden Treasury*, she recognized. It was a poetry book her father had owned.

'That's my little rebellion. This whole nation is obsessed with order. Ordering books, ordering women. So I figure a little disorder threatens their sense of control. Einstein said if a cluttered desk is a sign of a cluttered mind, what's a tidy desk a sign of?'

He paused at her look of puzzlement.

'You've heard of Einstein, right?'

'I'm not sure.'

'He's a friend of my father's. They knew each other in Berlin.'

Rose took off her mackintosh. Despite its shabbiness, the flat felt like a fortress. For the first time in ages, she felt safe.

'Tell me about your father.'

He put his finger to his lips, went over to the wireless and selected the Home Service. The room came alive with a burst of music and the patter of applause followed by the voice of a compère: 'Ladeees and Gennelmen, pray silence for . . .' It was a variety performance from London's oldest music hall, a faux Victorian repertoire awash with confected cheer.

Oliver came to sit opposite her.

'Dad was born in Berlin-Wilmersdorf. His name was Ellermann but he changed it to Ellis when he met my mother and came to settle here. In the late 1930s, sometime after the Leader came to power, my father wanted to move. He'd seen what happened in his homeland and believed it would happen here too, but my mother refused to leave. She loved England and said if her country was in trouble, she should stay and fight for it. My father went without her.'

'Were you an only child?'

'Yes, it was just my mother and me, and I hated him at the time for deserting her. On the night the Alliance was formed, before the telephones were cut off, my father tried to call her. He worried that she would act recklessly and get caught up in the fighting. I wasn't there, but eventually he managed to get hold of me and ordered me down to London to find her. I discovered she'd been killed on the barricades.'

Softly she said, 'Oh, how awful for you.'

'My father was broken when I told him. Their marriage was over but he blamed himself for leaving. At the time he believed he had no alternative. He's Jewish, you see.' He looked at her for a wordless moment. 'Do you have any idea what's happened to Jews on the mainland?'

A memory came to her, of the diary she had picked up in the Protector's library in Berlin. Agatha Kettler, age fifteen.

This morning they arrested another thousand Jews. I'm keeping this in a safe place in the hope that it might survive me.

'Not really. Do you?'

He was leaning forward, close to her, and his face had never seemed so intent or alert.

'I've heard things. Rumours of prison camps. It's hard to tell what's true.'

'Does your father know more?'

'If he does, he has no way of telling me. I can only communicate by letter and there's not much I can say in them. Nothing to excite the censors. I haven't spoken to him properly since that last telephone call in 1940. He urged me to come to New York as soon as I could. I thought he was overreacting. There was no way the Alliance would last. As it happened, plenty in the regime agreed with me.'

He gave a dry laugh.

'The fact is the authorities couldn't believe how smoothly

it went here. They expected a long, hard-fought resistance and instead they found the population was mostly placid. People liked the idea of a strong leader – they didn't much care what that leader stood for. What citizens wanted above all things was a quiet life. They didn't mind shrinking their horizons. They didn't object to not travelling, as long as nobody else was travelling either. They wanted an orderly life, with everyone knowing their place. Plenty of rules, the more of them the better. So that's what they got. The British didn't feel like collaborators, they felt like victims. And that's always much more comfortable.'

He jumped up to root in a drawer for cigarettes, lit two and handed her one.

'But the death of Stalin has changed everything. Tell me, when you saw the BBC newsreel of Stalin's funeral, what struck you?'

She recalled the immensity of Red Square, the black horses of the cortège, the banks of flowers and the flags at half-mast. And most striking of all, the figure of the Leader on the balcony and Helena's comment.

He's half-dead. Should be him in the coffin.

'The Leader. He's obviously not in good health.'

'Precisely. But any kind of comment on it is strictly censored. Why do you think the press has been issued with all those new instructions regarding long-range cameras during the Coronation?'

'Isn't it because Leni Riefenstahl has the documentary rights? The images have to be exclusive.'

He laughed shortly.

'The fact is, they don't want pictures of a sickly Leader getting out. Not before the invasion is launched.'

'Invasion?' Half choked, she repeated it. 'You mean, Germany is planning to invade the Soviet Union? They're allies!'

Oliver was pacing the carpet, smoking furiously.

'What do you think all those bullets are for? The ones the Magdas and Friedas are making in their factories? The Germans have long planned to overturn the Soviet pact. The Leader would have done it as early as 1941, only Goering and Hess discouraged him. They said Stalin was too fearsome an opponent. The Russian winter would defeat the Wehrmacht. Better simply to divide Poland between them. But now the Soviet leadership is weakened, it's the ideal time to act. The endgame is to expand eastwards. To level the largest cities and starve the population. Annex the entire Baltic region. Wipe Moscow off the surface of the earth by the creation of a giant lake, made by opening the dam gates of the Volga Canal. Make Crimea and large areas of southern Ukraine available for German people to move east.'

'How on earth would you know all this?'

He looked at her narrowly, as though trying to decide how much he might confide.

'I said I haven't managed to communicate directly with my father, and that's true. But there are channels. My father's part of a group — refugees from Germany and various British exiles. Some politicians who left England in a hurry in 1940. They have powerful factions in the US Government on their side. Recently, I was able to make contact with one of them.'

Slowly, Rose said, 'Sonia Delaney.'

He froze.

'I saw you together,' she explained. 'After the Grosvenor House reception.'

'You followed me?' His voice was suddenly chilly.

'Not intentionally. You were talking to her. I was surprised that . . .'

'That a man like me might have made the acquaintance of an American film star?' He smiled wryly. 'Sonia was born Sonia Dimitriova, in Berlin, to a family of Russian émigrés. They left in the early thirties when she was just a child, and moved to New York, but her family still has strong connections in the Soviet Union.'

He came and sat close to her and fixed her intently.

'Sonia is convinced that an attack on Russia is planned. Maybe not right now, or even in the near future – but it has implications for America and for us.'

'Which are?'

'It means there's growing support for American intervention here.'

Vaguely, Rose recalled the voices on Freedom Radio. The ones who'd talked about 'the British problem'.

'But surely America isn't going to help us? That's madness,' she protested.

'Is it? Perhaps with a royal figurehead at the helm . . .'

She shook her head in disbelief.

'What are you talking about? The King and Queen couldn't be more loyal to the Alliance.'

'I don't mean King Edward.'

He got up, went over to the window, tugged the curtains more tightly shut, then returned to sit next to her.

'When the Alliance was formed, the royal family were Vanished, and we assumed the two princesses too. In fact, Himmler ordered that Princess Elizabeth should be separated from the family. At that stage he wasn't sure if the Alliance would hold, and the day might come when he needed a high-value hostage. Unfortunately for Himmler, his plans went awry. A group of high-ranking German officers secreted her as far as Liverpool and from there she was taken to Canada. She'll be part of this.'

Rose sat immobile as she tried to process this information. It had been a long time since she had thought about Princess Elizabeth, whose face, along with her sister's, had once been familiar to every child in the land. Rose's mother had adored the young royals and put up a picture of them in the kitchen, standing side by side in velvet-collared coats and buttoned shoes, little felt hats tied beneath their chins, and a corgi at their feet. Celia and Rose were exactly the same age as the princesses and her mother had even dressed them alike, as if this way her own children might absorb the young royals' elegance and deportment.

Since the Alliance, her mother had never mentioned the

princesses again. Yet the thought that Princess Elizabeth was still alive, and living in Canada – that she might even return – was too much to take in.

'If she's still alive, why don't we know about it?'

'The same reason we don't know anything about life outside this country. Except, in this case, Elizabeth's life has been kept secret from everyone. It's too much of a risk. Relations between Germany and America have been too sensitive. God forbid the Princess became a pawn in some international deal. No, she's been held in reserve until the time comes.'

'Time for what?'

He looked at her for a moment, until something in his expression changed and Rose realized that he had taken a decision – to confide in her just as she had confided in him. He took a breath.

'For an uprising.'

'That will never be possible.'

'You could be right. But it doesn't stop us trying. We've had a network of units in existence for years, most of them in remote areas of the countryside, or in cellars and bunkers and hideouts stocked with arms and explosives. It's not been easy. They've all needed food, ration coupons, identity cards, money. Not to mention rifles, grenades, Molotov cocktails and a system of beacons. We have all kinds: young lads trying to escape Extended National Service, Jews, former soldiers. There are thousands of them.'

Them. The pronoun that ignited a tiny subterranean

flicker in the psyche of every citizen. The word that nurtured a quiet flame of hope.

Them.

Oliver corrected himself. 'Or I should say, us.'

He gave a little snort.

'I might curse the Coronation, but it couldn't have come at a better time. Remember the science of distraction? The regime's been operating it for decades. Now we plan to exercise it ourselves while the Party's focus is elsewhere.'

Thunderstruck, she whispered, 'When?'

'It's already begun. We had a code that would be printed as a signal when we were ready for action. A call to arms. The code was very simple: we used the name of a spy thriller. No such film existed, actually, but we got the line in a newspaper story about a slate of movies.'

Even as he spoke, it came to her. The sense of déjà vu, the stirring excitement. She murmured, 'The beginning is always today.'

Oliver recoiled, his face blanching in shock.

'How on earth do you know?'

Quickly, she said, 'I saw the story in the *People's Observer.* It was a list of the movies Sonia Delaney has made. That was one of the titles, wasn't it? A spy thriller? The line caught my eye. Then later, in the library, I came across the same line and remembered it, though I couldn't think where I'd seen it. But Oliver . . .'

She was breathless as the implications tumbled through her mind.

'I wrote that line on a piece of paper. Because I liked it and didn't want to forget it. The police found it.'

He shrugged.

'They couldn't possibly know what it meant.'

'I don't think they did. It's just . . .' She hesitated, trying to make sense of it, recalling the flicker in Kaltenbrunner's reptilian eye. 'I thought it was the words they were interested in. But they also asked me about the paper.'

'Why should that matter?'

'When I wanted to write it down, I grabbed a piece of paper. A thin, tissue kind of notepaper. They asked where I had found it.'

'What did you tell them?'

'I told them I found it on your desk.'

Oliver paused. His look was unfathomable. Then he shrugged, and in a sudden movement, he slipped out of his braces, unbuttoned his shirt and pulled it off. His chest was tanned, but hatched with two livid scars, long and jagged, that extended under his arm and round to his back. He reached for her hand and brought it gently to touch his bare skin.

'D'you mind these?'

With infinite gentleness she traced them with her finger.

'Where did you get them?'

'Nineteen forty.'

'I thought you didn't fight. You were a student.'

'My studies were pretty eclectic.'

'So you were a resistor?'

'It was before that. For a year I belonged to something called the Military Intelligence Research division. A division of the old War Office formed to support armed resistance in what was then occupied Europe. We engaged in all kinds of subversive activities and covert operations. I went over to Poland a couple of times in 1939. These scars are my personal souvenir of derailing a train and not getting clear in time. As it happens, they were key to my survival, because my injuries meant I couldn't fight in the Resistance. I had to go back to my books. Otherwise I'd probably have been killed. And then I would never have met you.'

He lifted her fingers up to his mouth and kissed them.

Softly, she said, 'Why did you wait so long?'

'I assumed you only had eyes for an Assistant Commissioner.'

'You might have given me a hint. I had no idea.'

'And there was me thinking you spent your days reading romantic literature.'

'How did you know you could trust me?'

'I did hesitate. Given that you're the girlfriend of a senior man.'

'Ex-girlfriend.'

'But the fact is, I trusted you as an act of faith. Because the authorities want to destroy all trust. If you can eliminate trust between men and women, even between parents and children, then there's nobody to trust but the state. That's why we have to trust each other. It's part of being human. No good society can exist without mutual trust.'

For a second Rose hesitated, then she reached forward, pulled him to her and kissed him.

Until then, she had physically shut down. To sleep with Martin required it. Even in the early days she'd never felt as she'd hoped she would. Yet now her senses came alive, and she was feverish, surging with excitement. She had never known how easy and natural it could be to want another person and have that desire reciprocated.

His arms were around her and then his hands were running over her shoulders and back, down towards her waist, drawing her closer to him. She felt the twitch of muscles as his body responded to hers, his mouth reaching to hers, and the weight of him as he pressed against her. How little she had acknowledged him. She realized she could not have told the colour of his eyes until that night, yet now every inch of him was imprinted on her senses. Even the dance band on the wireless serenaded them.

> *I may be right, I may be wrong*
> *But I'm perfectly willing to swear*
> *That when you turned and smiled at me*
> *A nightingale sang in Berkeley Square*

In their fervour and fumbled urgency, as he pushed back the blouse from her shoulders, her necklace broke and sent its pearls spiralling across the floor.

Eyes closed, she whispered.

'It doesn't matter.'

CHAPTER TWENTY-EIGHT

Friday, 30th April

Rose stirred first, still bathed in the afterglow of their love-making. It had been the kind of night she had never imagined. Nothing she had read properly described the way her body had flooded with pleasure when he touched her, or how their coupling felt not just a twining of flesh and limbs, but a connection of souls. Half awake, she relived every moment of it, awash with sensuous delight, astonished at how sex could encompass such a variety of sensations. How different the same act could be when it was with the right person.

Reaching over, she gently kissed his head. She barely knew him. But being there next to him, breathing the salty scent of his flesh, feeling his arm, heavy with sleep, flung over her, she was glutted with delight. She resolved to memorize every detail of the moment: the soft rise of his chest, the warmth of his slumbering body and the light seeping through the thin fabric of the curtains, making the orange chrysanthemums blaze.

He must have sensed her eyes on him because he woke up and reached a finger to her lips before springing out of bed and turning on the wireless. Then he came back, held her close to him and murmured in her ear, 'Get dressed. We have to leave.'

Then he pulled on a pair of grey trousers and a white shirt. He knotted his tie and grabbed his glasses. Muzzy with sleep, she watched him.

'We need to look as normal as possible. We mustn't stand out.'

She raised herself on one elbow.

'What? Why?'

'That paper you took from my desk – it was airmail paper. The kind you use for posting overseas.'

'That's not strictly illegal.'

'But it's unusual. Suspicious. All foreign communications are censored and I'm far too cautious to write anything reckless, but an airmail letter? That's going to get flagged up and the fact that they're already on my trail makes it a red flag. They won't ignore something like that.'

'What do you mean, they're already on your trail?'

'I've been aware of it for some time. They're almost certainly building a case against me. Using everything I do and say in preparation for an arrest.'

'If you realized that, why didn't you tell me straight away?'

He went over to the curtain and parted it a fraction, then he came and sat on the bed, pulled her face to his and kissed her.

'I didn't want to. I wanted this night. Because it's only just happened, after I spent so long thinking about it. And if anything goes wrong, I would have cursed myself if I hadn't spent it with you. I might need a treasure to hoard.'

He sprang up again and pulled an ancient khaki kitbag from the top of the wardrobe, unbuckled it and pushed spare clothes inside.

'Make no mistake, they'll be watching. We need to look as if we're going to work as usual. Not as though we're planning to escape.'

Rose's head was spinning. On any other Friday morning she would be heating a small saucepan of porridge oats and water, adding a pinch of salt, stirring it for a lazy moment before eating in a hurry standing up, washed down with a cup of tea. Then she would dress and head to the bus stop, walking swiftly to make it to the office by eight thirty because she was always a few minutes late.

Instead she was in a room with bare floorboards in Battersea with Oliver Ellis, who was stuffing a canvas kitbag and talking about escape.

'Where are we going?'

'I'll explain when we get there. But just so you understand' – he put a hand on her shoulder and frowned – 'there's no going back.'

★

Many years previously, in their walks around London, Rose's father had pointed out the elegant, eye-catching statue of Prospero and Ariel, carved in smooth grey Portland stone, that adorned the frontage of Broadcasting House. It was a triumph of Modernist sculpture, Dad explained; Shakespeare's draped and bearded wizard holding the naked body of the child spirit before him represented the power and magic of radio waves that emanated from this inspiring building.

That degeneracy was all hacked off now.

Since the BBC's home had become the Rosenberg Documentation Centre, a fresh figurehead had been commissioned and the portal was now graced by the official symbol of the Alliance – a lion overshadowed by an oversized eagle with spread claws and outstretched wings. Whether because the sculptor had too little talent, or too much, the lion had a distinctly nervous look on its face.

'Just follow me and say nothing. I've been in and out of here for the past three months,' said Oliver tersely. 'There's no reason for them to suspect anything at all.'

They had made their way to Portland Place barely speaking, Rose hastening slightly to keep pace with Oliver's stride. Above, the sky was plumped with a glittering swell of clouds, promising a fine day. At that time in the morning the whole city was waking up and the noise of buses and trams mingled with the clatter of metal shutters opening on shop windows. The streets filled with businessmen heading for the office, umbrellas rolled, Lenis clipping along in heels, and Gretls returning from night shifts, ready to snatch a few hours of rest. Outside butchers' shops and bakeries, women were beginning to queue. It was Friday, and the queues were always longer before the weekend, let alone a weekend like the one to come.

Oliver was right – the uniformed commissar merely nodded as the two of them flashed their Ministry passes and headed down a flight of steps to the basement.

A corridor wound sinuously beneath ground level, like some Minoan labyrinth to be navigated not by thread but by white-painted arrows on the wall indicating mysterious destinations: *Buro RAM files*, *Numbers D1-19*, *Foreign Office Secretariat Files*. It was a burrow of dirty cream paint and stone walls punctuated by open doors providing glimpses of steel shelves stretching from floor to ceiling, filled with boxes and files. Each room held a desk, or a couple of desks, at which people were working, heads bent over papers, while others stood searching the stacks. Unlike a library, with its beeswax polish and comforting smell of old, well-thumbed books, this was a sharper, more clinical place, of evisceration and classification, scented with the metallic tang of typewriter oil and ink stamps.

This was their natural habitat now, Rose thought. Document centres, archives, libraries. Places of the past that she and all the Correction teams laboured endlessly to control.

'I'm not sure if you know, but a large tranche of papers recently arrived from Berlin to be archived here,' said Oliver quietly.

'Actually, I remember Martin complaining about it. He said Berlin wanted to relocate half of the Foreign Office archive to London with no extra provision for it. He had to find space for hundreds of boxloads of documents.'

'I was seconded to help. It was intensely dreary work, sorting the files into their relevant epoch. But to my surprise, I found some very recent stuff amongst it.'

He diverted suddenly through a door into an empty room and glanced around before closing it behind them.

'It was a stroke of luck. This is the room housing documentation from 1937. It's divided into microfilm, Foreign Ministry files and papers. They range from the historic to the incredibly trivial. I've shelved Frau von Ribbentrop's party guest lists here, can you believe. And her dressmaker's bills.'

The place was a gloomy cavern, illuminated by a single bulb that cast a dismal light. Oliver was standing beside one of the stacks, pulling out folders and rifling through them.

'It's just a question of finding . . .'

His fingers were working quickly, running up and down the shelves, tugging files in and out, checking the numbers and letters that were pasted onto their spines, tunnelling into the mountain of documents, folders and papers like a miner searching for a fragment of gold.

'Look at this, the German–Russian treaties of the twenty-third of August 1939 and another from the twenty-eighth of September 1939, detailing the protocols of the Molotov–von Ribbentrop pact.'

He held them out to her with the wonderment of a historian, as thrilled as if they had been Bronze Age medallions plucked from the earth. Then he put them back.

'But those aren't what we're looking for.'

'So what exactly *are* we looking for?'

'The Berghof Convention.'

A growl of voices in the corridor outside grew louder, and the two of them froze as the approach of heavy footsteps made the metal stacks vibrate. Then the steps passed and faded, and a bark of command from far away uttered, '*Komm!*' Oliver continued.

'Back in 1937, the King and Queen visited the Leader at his home in Berchtesgaden in the Bavarian Alps. They were on honeymoon, but that didn't stop them talking about the shape of the future, should things turn out as they hoped. Specifically, an Alliance between England and Germany. This was the first time they had drawn up plans for how that might work. The agreement they made is known as the Berghof Convention, but as far as we know, it never actually physically existed. It remained unwritten and its protocols were always kept secret. Not even the Queen was allowed to be present during the discussions, and we had no idea of exactly what was agreed, until now . . .'

He seized a file and waved it triumphantly.

'Here it is!'

He brandished a couple of pages of tattered A4 notepaper, branded with an off-centre stamp of red ink forming the words *Streng Geheim*. Top Secret. The typing on it was blotchy and faded in places. It looked more like an aide memoire than a formal record of a high-level conference.

'I thought you said it wasn't written down.'

'It wasn't. A document of that sort would have been dynamite in 1937, with the King's brother on the throne. Can you imagine? If it had got out, it would have been *prima facie* evidence of treason. High-level talks with the leader of a foreign power about the prospect of usurping a king? By sheer chance, though, when I was going through all this, I came across the records of one of the interpreters on that day. According to custom, the interpreter always makes a record of verbal discussions, so even though it's not the finished article, you can see the specific lines of agreement. I'm guessing this should never have seen the light of day.'

Rose peered over his shoulder. From what she could see in the dingy light, the document appeared to have been hammered out on a personal typewriter from hasty notes. The entries took the form of disjointed sentences, as though the interpreter was recording faithfully every meandering part of the two men's conversation.

22nd October 1937

The notes began with an exchange of pleasantries about the visit and, despite current obstacles, the Leader's hope that one day the King would fulfil his destiny. This was followed by a statement of intent.

Under the Alliance, Great Britain will become a sister nation. Our two peoples will be entwined through their ancient Germanic brotherhood in a 'special relationship'. The British Parliament will be involved in the making of some laws, though overall the Protectorate will administer the territory to the benefit of all.

This vision had elicited a clarification, Rose noted.

The King insists that Britain would be no subject nation, required to bend the knee to a conqueror.

She skimmed the pages professionally. The paragraphs ranged from the trivial to the mundane.

Road signs will be written both in German and English. British vehicles will drive on the right-hand side of the road. British schools will carry out all teaching in German.

Halfway down the document her eye snagged on a paragraph about citizens' rights.

Jews and non-Aryans will be permitted to remain in society (subject to obvious strictures).

'We know all this, don't we? There's nothing new here. I still don't see—'

'Look at this.'

Oliver pointed to a paragraph towards the end of the paper.

The terms of the Berghof Convention will stay in place until the Coronation of the King, at which time, a fresh agreement will be drawn up.

'What of it?'

'You mentioned Martin Kreuz is co-ordinating a conference right after the Coronation.'

'At Blenheim. He's organizing the agenda. He said it was the most important conference for years.'

'If I'm right, Blenheim will be where the top-level men convene to decide the future of Britain. If only we could get our hands on the agenda, it would tell us exactly what our fellow citizens have coming to them. And my guess is, that's something the Resistance badly needs to know.'

He paused, took off his spectacles to rub his eyes, then shook his head in frustration.

'The maddening thing is, I can't see any way of getting into Kreuz's office. Not even with your help. You'd have to get past that secretary of his, Kohl, and that guy misses nothing.'

Rose stared at him intently, and said, 'SS-Brigadeführer Schellenberg warned Martin that offices are the least secure of places. Martin says Schellenberg rents a locker at the Lehrter railway station for his really important documents.'

'You're not serious,' Oliver said. 'You're telling me

that Assistant Commissioner Kreuz rents a railway station locker?'

'No. Of course not. He keeps the really important papers at his flat.'

Oliver drew a sharp breath and then bundled the interpreter's record back into its file and seized her hand.

'Where are we going?'

'To your old boyfriend's apartment. I take it you have a key?'

'We can't! What if he's in?'

'He won't be.'

'It's a crazy risk. What makes you so sure?'

'Because I have watched SS Assistant Commissioner Kreuz arrive at work on the dot of eight o'clock every day for the past three years. Like clockwork, I've seen that fat secretary fetch him a cup of real coffee, sugar and milk on a silver tray. There's no way on earth he would still be at home at ten o'clock in the morning.'

'There's a concierge at the apartment block.'

'Do you know him?'

'He's seen me coming in with Martin occasionally.'

'Then tell him we're from the Ministry. We're collecting some papers belonging to Assistant Commissioner Kreuz.'

'And what are we actually doing?'

'Precisely that.'

Martin was fond of touting the many amenities of Dolphin Square, which included a swimming pool, tennis court, croquet lawn, gymnasium and shopping arcade. But perhaps the most valuable amenity was Mr Percy Kavanagh, the concierge of Greville House, who dwelled in a glass cubicle at the entrance to the block. According to Martin, Mr Kavanagh was the equivalent of the maître d' of an upmarket restaurant, a compendium of confidential information who prided himself on knowing the names of every single occupant, not to mention the faces of their wives and mistresses.

He recognized Rose at once and smiled, revealing badly tobacco-stained teeth and an unctuous expression.

'Herr Kreuz is unfortunately out, Miss Ransom.'

His gaze strayed curiously towards Oliver.

'Yes, I know, Mr Kavanagh. He's sent my colleague and myself to collect some papers.'

'This is most irregular.'

'I'm sorry. It's a busy time, as you can imagine.'

Percy Kavanagh did not imagine. Imagining was above his pay grade and besides, in his line of work, allowing his imagination free reign would be overwhelming.

'I do have a key.'

'Strictly . . .' Percy Kavanagh hesitated and Rose could almost see his brain working. Strictly, it was against procedure to allow non-residents access, even with keys, and no tenant was permitted to lend those keys to anyone else. And although the SS Assistant Commissioner was generally perfectly genial, and generous at Christmas, he could be ferocious when crossed. Percy himself was coming up to retirement. God forbid his plans for pleasant hours on his allotment and the odd day trip to the south coast should be derailed by a moment of overzealous enforcement of the rules. Kreuz could be savage with underlings, and the approaching Coronation had thrown a lot of normal procedure into disarray. It may even be that some fresh rules had been issued, of which he was unaware.

'It really is a matter of urgency,' said Rose. 'The Protector's own business. You can see our Ministry passes if you like.'

She flourished her own, and Oliver fished a pass out of his top pocket.

Kavanagh scrutinized them, looking down at the photograph on Oliver's card and up to his face and back again, then adjusted the lapels of his ill-cut suit with its gilded Alliance pin.

'Would you need me to accompany you?'

'Of course not. We'll only be quick.'

Hastily, she and Oliver clipped up the carpeted stairs.

Like everything else in his life, bar perhaps his romantic affairs, Martin's sense of order was meticulous. Rose had watched him many times in the past, sitting at his desk, filing letters and documents in the lower drawer, locking it and concealing the key beneath the brass statue of an eagle that perched precisely midway on the mantelpiece between his SS medals and the pictures of his wife and children.

When she retrieved the key, Oliver strode rapidly over to the desk and began rifling through the papers. Then he was pulling the drawers out and feeling with his fingers into the space behind them.

Rose looked around her.

It was so familiar, this apartment. How many nights had she spent in this bed with its peach silk counterpane, or looking out at the river from this window? Making cups of tea in the kitchenette or luxuriating in the pink enamel bath? Sitting with her feet tucked up on the sofa while she waited for Martin to complete some Ministry business before they went out? From her early infatuation, to the increasing disillusion and dragging unhappiness, these walls had witnessed her every mood and emotion.

Yet now, bar a pair of Aristoc stockings in the drawer and a suggestion of Guerlain perfume in the bathroom, not a trace of her remained. She might as well never have set foot here.

'I think this is it. Look.'

Wonderingly, Oliver was staring down at a printed list, typed on an official Government typewriter equipped with the runic symbol for the SS, set out on the Ministry's heavy, expensive, ivory paper.

Blenheim Conference
3rd May 1953
Classification: Top Secret
List of Participants
Leader, Protector Rosenberg, SS-Brigadeführer Schellenberg,
SS-Gruppenführer Ernst Kaltenbrunner, Reichskriminalpo-
lizei chief Arthur Nebe

Other Representatives: Foreign Ministry, SS, Gestapo, Race and Resettlement Office, Women's Office

What do you notice about the list?
She looked up at him soberly.
'The King's not on it.'
'Exactly.'
'Why not?'
'Because of what they're discussing.'
He pointed to the body of the text.

Agenda
Harmonization of regulations in the Anglo-Saxon territories with mainland law

'There's no way anyone would organize such a gathering of Party top brass unless they were discussing something of the highest importance. I suspect the phrase "harmonization" means the gloves are off. Everything that applies on the mainland will apply here. Any protection that non-Aryans and other groups have had will be over.'

'But we don't know what applies on the mainland.'

'That's true. But what we do know from those notes is that under the Berghof Convention, King Edward was allowed a certain latitude in the way that the Protectorate would be run. The man was indulged, basically. Humoured. It's a weakness of people when they come up against kings, and I imagine the Leader is as susceptible as anyone to the allure of monarchy. Nonetheless, it was always clear that the convention was only ever a temporary arrangement. That was stated in the protocols of the convention itself. Once the King was crowned, they had every intention of replacing it.'

'Replacing it with what?'

'Whatever exists elsewhere.'

She didn't know – none of them knew – what existed elsewhere, but Rose felt the same shiver that came from a dentist's waiting room, that something terrible lay beyond the door, and she dreaded finding out. A thought came to her.

'I have a friend, a journalist, Laurence Prescott. He's on the *Echo*. He told me they're on standby for a major Government announcement next week.'

'That'll be it,' said Oliver sombrely. 'My guess is, they'll start with the Jews. The Protector is a violent anti-Semite. It must have required every ounce of that homeopathy he takes to keep that hatred in check.'

'How do you know that?'

'It's all there in his book. His views are in plain sight if anyone bothers to look.'

He was folding the paper into his kitbag.

'What are you doing?'

'I'm taking this with me.'

'You can't! Martin will discover it instantly. He'll know it's gone!'

Oliver stopped for a moment and took her face in his hands.

'Don't you think he knows everything already?'

What did Martin know? His proposal of marriage and Rose's refusal – all that seemed a lifetime ago, yet almost certainly he was nursing his hurt, and therefore would have no idea of her arrest, or the fact that she had not returned to her flat the previous night. He had been so persistent in his affections over the past year, however, and so certain that the two of them had a future together. Surely, he would at some point seek her out.

On impulse she went over to the drawer by his bedside. All rental apartments were provided with a copy of the Protector's book as standard, tucked inside a bedside drawer, in the way that a Gideon's Bible had been in the Time Before. The idea was that the work would console and inspire readers in the lonely reaches of the night. It was in this book, inside the red leather covers, sandwiched between the gilt-edged leaves, that Martin kept the photograph he had asked of Rose when they first met. 'Not much chance of anyone looking in here!' he had joked at the time.

She shook the Protector's book upside down, but nothing emerged. Like all the other ghosts of her past life, the once treasured photograph had melted into thin air.

With a last glance around the flat, she closed the door behind them.

*

Outside, on the opposite side of the street, a pair of men were waiting in a black Opel. They shifted fractionally as Rose and Oliver left the building, barely bothering to disguise themselves.

'They're watchers, aren't they?' she said.

'They're on to us sooner than I thought. That concierge is brighter than he looks. I'd guess he called them up the moment we walked through the door. There'll be others too. Probably another two ahead. We're very lucky.'

'Lucky?'

'If they'd sent the police, we'd be sitting in a cell right now. Instead of which they want to see where we're going. We need to lose them.'

Rose forced herself to walk normally, eyes on the pavement ahead, looking for all the world as though she was strolling to the office rather than leaving everything she knew for an as yet undisclosed location. There was no turning back, she acknowledged. The momentary comfort of an ordinary day hovered at the edge of her consciousness, then was dissipated by the sound of a car engine.

Behind them the Opel crawled into gear.

'It doesn't matter that we've seen them. It's straight from the ASO playbook. Two and two. They swap positions so one pair is in front and the other behind. In this case, I suspect, the other pair are on foot. Pavement artists. A forward party and a back-up team. They pass messages between them – with their hats, or the way they carry a newspaper – they have a whole lexicon of signals. We need to spot them but if we can lose the pair in the car, we stand a better chance.'

Fraught with nerves, Rose scanned the passing figures. A Geli, in a fur collar and tartan coat, two Magdas, carrying cheap plastic handbags, and a Klara dragging a pair of protesting twins in school uniform, their socks at half-mast. A couple arm in arm, the man with thinning hair and a chiselled, handsome face, and the girl – a Leni by the look of her neat heather-grey suit with its herringbone pattern – clinging to his side. Their mutual absorption and passionate closeness told her at once that they were not husband and wife, but lovers. Perhaps they, too, had passed a blissful night together and were making the most of their physical contact before separating for their working day. She felt a momentary longing to be that girl, arm in arm with her lover, face turned laughingly up to his, with no more worries than what they might see at the movies that weekend.

Towards the salmon-pink and cream cobweb of Albert Bridge, recently repainted for the Coronation, traffic slowed. Most London bridges had guard points now, to check cars and prevent those intent on suicide. A year ago, a bomb had been placed beneath Hammersmith Bridge, primed to explode as troops were crossing. News of it made the deep inside pages of the newspapers beneath the terse headline *Terrorist Outrage*, but the extent of the carnage went unreported. No mention of the dozen killed or the soldiers still maimed by the bomb blast. The bridge had subsequently been closed for months and the remains of an upended troop carrier still rested on the riverbank.

The Opel was picking up speed, weaving through the traffic so that it was only a few feet behind them.

'Where are the others?' muttered Oliver under his breath. 'Keep looking.'

Rose studied the pedestrians anxiously, peering into each face for evidence that they might be watching, checking their direction of travel. All the ordinary kinds of people passed by – men in suits and uniform, anonymous types in trilbies and mackintoshes; women of all ages and castes.

'I can't see anyone at all. Or rather, it could be anyone.'

'Look for those who are doing nothing. Anyone reading a newspaper on a bench. Girls window-shopping. Doing nothing is the hardest thing to pretend.'

All along the Embankment a series of coaches was parked and droves of fresh sightseers were climbing out, lugging camping chairs and rolls of bedding, backpacks and baskets containing sandwiches and thermos flasks. The tourists had come from all over the country, to judge by their mix of accents: Midlands, Northern and West Country voices mingling in the air, all of them excited for Sunday's big event.

Beside her, Oliver was walking briskly, yet forcing himself to keep to a steady pace. Tension radiated from him as he searched the road ahead for evidence of a tail, glancing down in car wing mirrors for a backward view.

Then, a break.

Behind them, a lorry carrying a consignment of troops

parked up, temporarily blocking the traffic as the soldiers jumped down, unlatched the tailgate and began to unstack metal crush barriers onto the pavement. Cars travelling southwards began to back up, and a swift glance confirmed that the Opel, too, was stuck in the queue.

'We're changing tack. We need to be quick.'

Darting across the road, Oliver led them towards the narrower streets that ran away from the river. As they passed a parade of shops, Rose noticed him glance in the windows, checking for repeated faces or any obvious surveillance.

Urgently, she tugged at his sleeve.

'I've had a thought. We should go to my parents' house. My mother is with Celia so it's empty.'

'You think they don't know that? They'll be waiting for us.'

Her throat constricted in alarm.

'Then perhaps my sister . . .'

'Your sister will also be due a visit.'

With horror, Rose pictured the police arriving in Celia's quiet Clapham street, Geoffrey at the door negotiating in a bluster of threats and denials, her sister cowering behind him and their mother sobbing and wringing her hands.

'Where can we possibly go then?'

'Nearest station, I'm afraid.'

'Is that wise?'

Although there were spies everywhere in the Alliance, railways stations, like anywhere that people might meet, were especially infested with them. In addition to those almost certainly on their tail, there was every chance that other watchers would be sprinkled among the railway staff.

'We have no choice. We need to get away. It's harder for them in a crowded area because they have to get closer. We should be able to lose them.'

A towering bronze statue of the original Klara stood on the forecourt of Victoria station, a pigeon on its head. To birds, there was no distinction between effigies of the regime and the pewter-faced statesmen who had populated London for centuries. Essentially, they made much the same perch, except that sitting on Klara was a little more troublesome. Among the women of the Alliance a superstition had arisen that the Leader's mother possessed supernatural powers to confer fertility and, for that reason, this particular statue had become an unofficial meeting point. Any pigeon seeking peace was regularly interrupted by passing women rubbing Klara's outstretched hand for luck.

'Here's a good place to wait. I'll get tickets.'

Oliver left and Rose positioned herself beneath Klara's maternal bronze arms. This day, the station seemed busier than ever, swollen with sightseers arriving with canvas bags and suitcases and Coronation hats. She watched as hundreds of people crossed the forecourt, weaving around the workmen erecting extra loudspeakers onto lamp posts, gantries and departure boards, preparing to broadcast an entire day's output from the BBC.

The appeal of Klara's statue was clear. For some women

the ritual appeared to be automatic – they brushed her burnished hand as they passed. Others darted forward quickly, as though shy of broadcasting their heartfelt desire to the world. Rose wasn't the only woman lingering, as if issuing a private prayer to the Leader's mother. On the other side of the statue another girl was standing, face squeezed in supplication, hands clasped across her heather-grey suit.

It was a suit Rose had seen before.

There was no time to alert Oliver. Turning sharply, she allowed herself to be subsumed into the crowd. She moved blindly, weaving in zigzag fashion left and right, dodging behind newspaper stands and shoe polish stalls, until she found an alcove in the brick wall, drab with decades of soot and pungent with urine. Pausing for a moment to look around her, she saw directly opposite the dingy white and gold frontage of an Alliance coffee house.

Back when Rose had visited these cafés as a child they were called Lyons Corner Houses. Now they had been liberated from their Jewish owners and rebranded, though their waitresses still wore the distinctive black and white uniform that had been created for Lyons' 'Nippies'. The Nippies were selected for their looks and deportment, so their marriage rate was higher than among the rest of the Gretl population and their friendliness made the cafés congenial places to linger. If you ignored the dismal offerings on the menu and the dishwater coffee, you might idly imagine yourself back in another age, had that kind of imagining not been expressly forbidden.

Rose chose one of the prestige tables reserved for men and Class I females. It offered a superior view, looking out over the station forecourt, rather than the lower caste tables squashed towards the back of the shop, and it was the only way she could think to look out for Oliver, while escaping the attention of the watchers.

In a corner of the bar, a television set had been installed and was broadcasting a programme of music specially selected for the Coronation: Wagner, Strauss and Beethoven – all conducted by Herbert von Karajan. It wasn't the perfect background for morning coffee, and as usual in public places, the volume was a little too loud. A constant wall of sound was the norm in the Alliance, almost as though the regime wanted to drown out any ideas people had for themselves. Whenever the loudspeakers in the streets and cafés stopped relaying speeches and ordinances, they switched to music, usually bands of every kind: dance bands, brass bands or marching bands, but on really special occasions, opera was called for.

Settling down beside a man who was consuming treacle sponge and custard, and concealing her face behind the menu, Rose scanned the station outside.

'I said, what would you like, miss?'

Rose jumped, as the Nippy beside her raised her voice against the rising strains of *Die Meistersinger*.

'Nothing. I mean, a cup of tea, please.'

She fixed her gaze on the flow outside, the dense mass of people moving like one organism, a single pulsing palette of greys and browns.

Nothing out of the ordinary.

Towards the end of one of the platforms she noticed a trainspotter, his flat cap and beige trench coat buckled tightly. He was holding a notebook and glancing up and down the carriages, as if registering their liveries and model numbers.

Except that he could not be a trainspotter, because that hobby had been outlawed on grounds of national security.

Even as Rose remembered this, she saw the man glance at a pedestrian making his way along the platform, then wave a notebook discreetly.

Oliver's anxiety was there in the set of his shoulders, but his face was a perfect blank as he walked purposefully towards the station entrance, glancing around him as if he were any other commuter, mildly irritated by the surging crowds who were slowing his habitual commute. He must have noted Rose's absence and drawn the obvious conclusion.

Leaving a five-mark note on the table, she slipped out of the café and made her way briskly towards him.

'Hey!'

The other half of the passionate couple – the man with the chiselled face and thinning hair – had broken cover and hailed her openly. Passers-by looked around in alarm.

Fear rose in her throat, but Oliver had seen her and sprinted in her direction.

Seizing her hand, he darted across the forecourt towards a train that was starting to move away from the platform and, wresting open the door, bundled her inside and followed.

'Don't look down. That's what my mother used to say. Like a tightrope. You'll manage if you don't look down.'

The train began to pull away and behind them the followers stalled, frozen with indecision, before hastening backwards.

As the train picked up speed Rose leaned back against the nicotine-stained upholstery, waiting for her heartbeat to slow. Her life had slipped its moorings now. Amid the sea of posters, advertising hoardings and Coronation flags she was adrift from everything she had known.

CHAPTER TWENTY-NINE

They were going to Oxford, Oliver said. He'd explain later. They had to change twice before they found the right train and this one seemed to be slow on purpose. It trundled along the line, stopping at every station and halt, hauling itself at glacial speed between them. Every station platform fluttered with bunting and every newsstand advertised commemorative editions of magazines and journals for the Coronation. At Reading, Rose even glimpsed one of the calendars she had helped compile, complete with an inspiring motto and a Technicolor portrait of a different senior man for each month: Joseph Goebbels relaxing on his yacht. Rudolf Hess leaning against his aeroplane. Hans Frank silhouetted against the battlements of a castle. April was Heinrich Himmler, harshly shaven and weak-chinned, his pale eyes staring myopically into the camera through his wire-rimmed spectacles.

There must have been plenty of households looking forward to turning that page.

Outside the smeared windows, the roads were crammed with cars, trucks and buses making their way towards London. Very little traffic was headed the other way. In a first-class carriage, reserved for men and elite females, Rose and Oliver found themselves alone.

He sat opposite her, so close that their knees were touching, and took her hands. He hadn't had time to shave and his chin was covered with a light stubble. The sight caused her a sudden, physical pang and made her wish she was still in bed, pressed against his naked form.

'I'm sorry about that,' he said. 'The station was a calculated risk and I thought it was worth taking. As it is, we can't count on evading them for long. They'll have circulated our pictures everywhere. Our details will have been telexed to every police force. They'll man the stations and ports.'

Although her insides plunged in fear, Rose attempted to keep her voice level.

'So, why Oxford? You said you'd explain.'

'When I was last there I told you I was researching in the archives. In fact, I was searching for something else.'

Along the corridor a compartment door slammed. Although they were alone, he started and looked around him. After a moment's silence, he said, 'I was searching out a good spot for a gun.'

Gun. The word fell leaden amid the soft chunter of the train's wheels. Oliver brought his face very close to hers.

'Specifically, a semi-automatic pistol. A Walther PPK with a .380 ACP calibre bullet.'

'What are you talking about? Are you saying you have a gun on you?'

'Not me. My Hollywood friends. The film crew who are making a documentary about the Queen. Except they're not, of course. Their camera is a modified Arriflex 35. The box where the film is kept has been fitted with a quick-open catch and clips inside to secure a gun and spare magazines. It's the perfect hiding place. No one ever looks inside a camera box because if you let any light in, it will expose the film. The cameraman in question has been training for months. He's an extremely accurate shot.'

Martin's words rang in her head.

Some charlatan astrologer has told him his life's in danger.

'The Leader was warned about this.'

Oliver sat back in alarm.

'What are you saying?'

'By his psychics. Martin said they'd forecast an assassination attempt. The Leader almost cancelled the trip.'

Oliver relaxed visibly.

'Is that all? People have been trying to kill him since 1933. You don't need to be psychic to predict that.'

'Was this your idea?'

'No. Not at all. The whole thing started last year. One of the big American studios got in touch with the Ministry about a slate of possible co-productions and there was a historical movie among them. Obviously, it was essential any potential movie should conform to Alliance historical theory so I was seconded to meet them. They were staying at Browns Hotel, just off Piccadilly, and this producer – at least I thought he was a producer – took me for a walk in Green Park. He said he wanted to see Buckingham Palace, but what he really wanted was to talk without anyone listening. He explained he was a friend of my father's and he had a message for me. As I told you before, there's a considerable lobby gaining support in the States for intervention in the British territories. He couldn't tell me how or when it might be, but he needed to know if I would be involved on the ground. To help smooth arrangements should the opportunity present itself. The time might never come, but if it did, they needed to be ready.'

Rose looked at Oliver and thought, the whole of humanity is divided between those who don't hesitate to act and others who stop and calculate the consequences.

'What did you say?'

He frowned. 'I said yes, of course. And from that time on, I was ultra-cautious. But a few months ago, I realized it wasn't enough. The authorities were watching me. They obviously had wind of something. Then, when Stalin died and the Coronation was announced, my American friends got in touch again. They had devised a plan. A small documentary crew would be coming over to make a film about Wallis. *American Queen*. It was the perfect strategy, and it very nearly went wrong.'

'Why?'

'Leni Riefenstahl began to complain about foreign camera crews in London, so I suggested they relocate to Oxford.

It's the Leader's first stop. He visits the Radcliffe Camera tomorrow at nine a.m. precisely. All traffic will have been halted from the night before. The whole city centre will be closed off, but the camera crew have authorization to film on the route.'

Rose sat very still as she absorbed what he was telling her. The immensity of the plan, and the ambition of its consequences, were almost too great to take in. If the Leader was to die, how would the police and army react? Back in 1942, when Heydrich had been killed, the regime's blood-crazed vengeance had consumed an entire village. What greater punishment would lie in store for those who assassinated the Leader himself?

The consequences were unimaginable.

Suddenly a crazy spirit of levity possessed her and she said, 'Do you know, when we met in Oxford, I assumed you were following me.'

His eyes widened for a second, then he broke into a grin.

'Officially, you mean? As an emissary for the Alliance Security Office? How could you have thought that?' He stopped himself, and shrugged. 'But of course you thought that. What else would you think? And why would you want to chance a drink with one of those low-lifes who lurk around spying on other people?'

'I'm sorry.'

'Don't worry. My evening wasn't entirely wasted, as it happens. After you'd left me that evening, something curious did happen. You see, I was restless – all stirred up and not ready to sleep – so I decided to chance the curfew and go for a walk. I went north, towards the parks. I thought there would be less chance of being stopped there. By sheer chance I came across someone I knew. A woman. It was dark, and she was wearing black, so I didn't see her in the shadows, but she called out to me. I almost didn't recognize her – in fact, I never would've if she hadn't addressed me by name. She used to live opposite our home in Kensington.'

'In the Time Before?'

He nodded. 'She's a Frieda now, living in the Widowlands. She was probably the last person to see my mother.'

'Were they friends?'

'My mother died in her arms.'

Rose saw a spasm of pain cross his face as he stared down at his shoes. Then hoarsely he said, 'She was shot on the barricades, alongside this woman's own husband. Apparently, my mother was brave. She ran out into the streets without a thought for her own safety.'

Rose was quiet a moment, then said, 'What was your mother called?'

'Marina. I have a photograph of her . . . Here.'

He reached into his chest pocket and pulled out a small leather case. The woman who looked out from the oval frame had full lips and a finely chiselled nose. Her glossy hair was parted centrally and pulled back low on her neck, and her dark, intelligent eyes were guarded.

After they had gazed at it briefly, he tucked it away.

'You remind me a little of her, actually. That's the first

thing I thought when I saw you. That reserve of yours. The way I never knew what you might be thinking, though I was always trying to guess.'

'So that's why you were staring at me. I assumed you were checking if I was wearing make-up.'

'Max Factor, Sweet Cherry. I know all your secrets.'

She ran her fingers lightly over the skin of his face.

'Not all of them.'

'Good. I want more.'

It was almost as though they were avoiding the subject that loomed over them, willing the clock to slow. The plan that was almost too audacious to imagine. Whatever happened, these would be the last hours that life would feel like this.

At Didcot, a couple came into the carriage and settled themselves opposite Rose and Oliver, obliging them to fall quiet. Oliver moved next to her so they sat, shoulders touching, and beneath the cover of her mackintosh she felt him reach for her hand. The intimacy of his presence was electrifying. Although she had so much more to say, they sank into their own kind of silence, communicating on a frequency only the two of them could receive. Fingers locked together, they stared at the framed photograph that hung on the wall opposite.

Side by side, they looked into the eyes of the Leader.

After they left the train, Oliver turned to Rose and said, 'You need to stay out of sight. Even though we'll separate, they'll still be looking for you.'

'What do you mean?' She was seized with alarm. 'We can't separate!'

'We must. Staying together is too risky. The people I'm working with – they have a safe house in the city. I'll go there.'

'But where will I go?'

He put his palms on either side of her face, brought her mouth to his and kissed her. It was a deep embrace, one that seemed to compress in its brief moment more tenderness and passion than she had ever known. Then he pulled away and surveyed her.

'I've thought of that. The Frieda I mentioned. The one who called out to me that night, walking in the park. My mother's friend. She told me she'd been visited earlier that day by a Geli. A pretty girl from the Culture Ministry, she said, come to do some interview for the Protector.'

'You mean, she was one of the widows I met?'

'She's called Sarah Walsh. And you need to find her. Widowland is the only safe place to be.'

CHAPTER THIRTY

Rose spent all day walking around the city, lurking in shops, dawdling down the high street, trying to remain inconspicuous. She sat in a café and peered past the twin posters of the King and Queen pasted on the window to survey the stream of shoppers outside, seemingly buoyed up by anticipation of the excitements to come. At one point she thought she saw a follower – a middle-aged man with a bloodless complexion, who lingered in Carfax, darting covert looks at her. He was in no hurry, and he wore the kind of buttoned trench coat that a watcher might deploy to look anonymous, but when she saw him directing similar glances at another woman of her age, she concluded he was merely seeking female company. If Oliver had been with her, his training would have told him instantly if the man was a threat, yet all she could do was be cautious, aware that the city would be saturated with policemen and crawling with spies. Even though she and Oliver had evaded the team shadowing them in London, there was every chance surveillance had been picked up once they arrived in Oxford.

She was haunted by the thought of her family. Was Oliver right to suppose that Celia and Geoffrey would be questioned? What would they tell Hannah? She couldn't help picturing her sister's face blotched with tears, and Hannah, clutching at her mother's skirt until she was pulled away. Geoffrey, in shirtsleeves and braces, blinking into an interrogation spotlight, alternating between accusations and appeals. Eventually, maddened by speculation, Rose went into a telephone box and dialled Celia's number. The receiver was picked up on the second ring, but instead of the Gretl or Geoffrey's booming tones, 'Clapham 2768,' a different voice answered. A male voice, German-accented.

'Hello. *Ja?*'

Terrified, she crashed the receiver back into the cradle, and walked swiftly away.

For hours, she loitered around the town, checking shop windows. A toy store had devoted its entire window display to a battlefield of Alliance soldiers, and she stared for some time at the plastic figures painted the colours of different regiments: field grey, khaki and black, ranged in serried ranks across a green-painted terrain, with no enemy to fight.

As dusk fell, she headed west, hugging the backstreets approaching the canal. A wind had got up and was thrashing the tops of the trees and harrying the fish and chip papers that littered the towpath. She felt a kind of hyper-vigilance to everything in her surroundings: from the pair of boys kicking a ball, to the man mending a roof and the pair of Klaras immersed in conversation over a fence. Anyone and anything was transformed into a threat. At one point a sharp sound made her jump and, looking round, she saw a dog chained to a fence. It was rare to see a pet dog now. Soon after the Alliance, the shortage of food meant that people had killed their dogs, and in some cases ate them. She'd even heard that people switched animals with their neighbours so as not to consume their own pet. The few dogs that remained tended to be working animals, and this one looked like a police dog, but if so, he was off duty. Instead of barking, he stayed low, his pointy muzzle and yellow eyes following as she passed.

Eventually, she reached the outskirts of Widowland.

Any worries she might have had about getting back into the district were unnecessary. Remembering what Sarah had said about the newly installed barbed wire being only for show, she headed some distance away from the guard post and found a place where the fence was full of gaps and holes, with some stretches entirely replaced by weeds. Once through, she hurried along the dreary, impoverished streets, inhaling the sour reek of drains and rubbish, keeping her head down. The route was familiar to her now. She threaded her way past soot-blackened houses with grimy windows and yards filled with iron debris and redundant machinery until at last she spotted the square brick church tower silhouetted against the marbled sky, clouds drifting like cannon smoke across a mother of pearl moon.

★

'When we met before, I still thought you might be a Government spy. So I wasn't as friendly as I might have been. Forgive me.'

'You were right to be cautious.'

Sarah Walsh had started when she opened the door hesitantly and saw Rose's face emerge from the gloom. But when Rose whispered that she needed a place to stay, and that Oliver Ellis had sent her, Sarah took her hand and beckoned her quickly inside.

The house was just as Rose remembered it, only this time the odour of woodsmoke, mildew and coal dust was overlaid with a savoury, spicy fragrance. Even though she was shivering from nervous exhaustion, the smell reminded her that she had eaten nothing all day.

'We're making dinner,' said Sarah. 'You must eat with us, Rose. But first I need to consult the others. I won't be long.'

She disappeared into the kitchen at the back of the house and after a few minutes of hushed conversation, re-emerged.

'They'd be honoured if you'd join us. I told them you'd explain everything later.'

In the kitchen, Sylvia was peeling potatoes, saving the skins for a pig, and Kate was stirring what smelled like a stew. Rose's stomach rumbled.

'Thank you so much for inviting me in,' she said awkwardly, glancing around her. Here too, she observed, the widows had done their best to create a homely space. Despite the curlicues of paint peeling from the ceiling and mould gathering in the corners, someone had carved flowers and animals into the wooden mantelpiece and arranged a series of battered photographs along the top.

'That smells wonderful. What is it?'

'Lobster bisque, boeuf en croute and black forest gateau,' said Kate.

'Take no notice,' said Sarah. 'We fantasize about the meals we'll have. We take turns constructing the menus. Last night was poached salmon with hollandaise sauce. Please, sit down. Actually, it's bean stew.'

Sarah, Vanessa, Kate and Sylvia assembled around the table, set with a range of chipped plates, and began to help themselves to food. If they were astonished at Rose's sudden appearance, they summoned every social grace to conceal it.

'This is delicious.' Rose was eating the stew ravenously and discovering it was unexpectedly tasty, even if it was accompanied by the lowest quality bread, black and crumbly, packed with sawdust.

'We've had to learn to cook with vegetables alone,' said Sarah. 'Because we have no meat or eggs or milk.'

'And I think we've done rather well.'

Adeline had come in from the garden. She had cast off the black serge smock in favour of a liberty print shirt, a pinafore and the same worn tan gloves. Her abundant hair was neatly tamed into a bun and even without make-up, her broad face with its high cheekbones was strikingly handsome. She gave Rose a penetrating stare.

'Fräulein Ransom. This is a surprise.'

'Rose has run into difficulties with the authorities,' said

Sarah, with quiet emphasis. 'She's asked if she can stay here tonight.'

'I'll explain everything,' said Rose. 'It's just for one night. I'll be gone in the morning.'

'That's for the best,' said Adeline briefly, sitting down and heaping her plate with stew. 'I don't want to appear inhospitable, but it doesn't do to underestimate them.'

'I'm sure Rose is aware of that,' said Sylvia.

Adeline flashed her a look.

'Maybe. But did I ever tell you how I was first arrested? Back in London?'

The others looked up curiously, as though this information was new to them.

'I was expecting a visit – aren't we all, constantly? – but I was complacent. When they arrived, I watched the Gestapo go over everything with a fine-toothed comb, but I still wasn't worried. I wasn't expecting to be caught out. I had no typewriter, obviously – I knew they were looking for anything that might suggest I could make pamphlets. But I was so certain that I'd been careful. That was my mistake.'

'How was that a mistake?' asked Rose.

'I underestimated them. Never underestimate them. Can you guess what they found?'

She looked around the table theatrically, as if waiting for an answer to her rhetorical question, her eyes blazing with a kind of steely rapture.

'A lid. Nothing more. An inch-square lid. I had a child's printing set – one of those things with little rubber letters and an inkpad – and I'd disposed of it meticulously – the letters, the stamp, the box. Yet for some reason, the lid of the carton that held the inkpad had fallen to the bottom of a drawer, and they found it. That was enough.'

She paused briefly to take a sip of elderflower wine, and closed her eyes, savouring it like a rare delicacy.

'When they took me in, they had a lot of questions. But believe me, I didn't furnish them with any answers.'

She flinched slightly, as though recalling the tortures she had endured, and glanced down at her gloved hands. Then she surveyed them benevolently.

'It was a great comfort to me, when I was in prison, to think you'd all be carrying on our work.'

Our work. Rose glanced at Kate and was startled by the flicker of cold dislike.

'Kate was our pioneer, actually,' said Sarah, as though reading Rose's thoughts. 'The slogans were her idea.'

'Such a clever idea,' said Rose.

Kate shrugged.

'Of course, I used to write at greater length. Back when I had a newspaper column, I'd complete a thousand words a day on issues of major national importance.'

The others laughed. This was clearly a joke of long standing.

'What kind of issues?' asked Rose.

'Oh, shopping, baby care, keeping house. How to polish a hob or clean your husband's shoes or mix a cocktail for him when he returns from work. How to refrain from conversation if he's feeling tired or make yourself seductive if he requires entertainment.'

She gave a rueful smile at the world she had left behind.

'All that changed when the Alliance began. Along with everything else, I realized that society was moving away from literacy and entering a slogan world. There were slogans everywhere. So I thought, if that's how it's going to be, then that's how we should fight back. With slogans.'

'Kate stole a pot of paint from the factory and daubed a line on the wall of Rhodes House,' said Sylvia. 'That's a building dedicated to Cecil Rhodes who founded Rhodesia.'

'I chose the words of Emmeline Pankhurst. *We have to free half of the human race, the women, so that they can help to free the other half.* And after that, the whole thing just took flight.'

'I did wonder,' said Rose, 'how exactly it spread.'

'How do any ideas travel?' asked Kate. 'Like a ripple on a pond? Or some invisible microbe on the air? All I know is, it was marvellously effective. No sooner had we begun than all over the country writing began to appear on walls, like the invisible hand at Belshazzar's Feast.'

Rose frowned.

'I'm sorry?'

'It's a story from the Book of Daniel,' explained Vanessa. 'The tyrannical ruler, Belshazzar, was holding a feast, when behind him a sentence appeared on the wall, traced by a hidden hand. It was a message prophesying that he'd die. The story's in the Bible.'

Rose nodded. The Bible was not degenerate exactly, but it was hardly the kind of book anyone would be caught reading.

'A few lines of graffiti might have been nothing in the scheme of things, but they rankled,' said Sylvia. 'They've never managed to catch anyone, though they suspected it was coming from the Widowlands. I suppose they assumed we were the only ones capable of it. They know older women enjoy discussing novels.'

'A truth universally acknowledged,' smiled Vanessa.

'On the subject of literary discussions,' said Sarah, 'we were engaged in one just now. There's to be a presentation to the Leader tomorrow. At the Radcliffe Camera. The head librarian wants to donate a special volume to the Leader's library in Linz. It's only symbolic, of course. The Leader could have the entire Bodleian shipped to the mainland tomorrow if he wanted.'

'What has he chosen?' Rose asked.

'That's what we were discussing. It's an interesting choice,' said Kate. 'I was surprised when Sarah told us about it, though on reflection I can see there's a certain significance in the subject matter. It's the first edition of a novel set in Ingolstadt, about a German genius who changed the world. Have you heard of *Frankenstein*?'

'I saw the movie, but I had no idea it was a book.'

'Written by Mary Shelley at the age of eighteen. She, Shelley and Byron were on a rainy holiday in Switzerland in 1816. While they waited for the weather to clear, they decided to hold a horror story competition. I've always wondered what the men made of the fact that a teenage girl came up with a work of such genius while their own efforts were forgotten. Not to mention that after *Frankenstein* was published, a lot of people assumed it was written by Mary's husband.'

'This is the actual, handwritten version. It's more than a hundred years old,' added Sarah. 'It's very fragile. You have to wear special gloves to touch it.'

Adeline snorted.

'I'd like to see the librarian who dares ask the Leader to wear cotton gloves.'

'I find it impossible to imagine that the Leader appreciates literature,' said Vanessa quietly, as if she was still uncertain of uttering such heresy in front of a Geli who, until only recently, had been engaged on Government business.

'It's not the appreciation of literature. It's the possession of it,' said Sylvia tersely. 'He sees books the way other people see diamonds. For ownership. Shutting up in vaults.'

Rose said nothing. She wanted to explain what Martin had told her about novels – that it was literature's power that the Party understood and feared – but in her hungry and disorientated state, such reflections were beyond her. She focused on finishing the food and allowing the warmth of the kitchen to seep into her bones.

Abruptly, Adeline said, 'You were going to explain why you were here.'

Kate leaned towards Rose and reached out a reassuring hand.

'Actually, don't.'

'No, I—'

'I mean, you don't have to tell us,' she qualified. 'Say as little as you want. But there's absolutely no need to say anything at all.'

Yet, for Rose, one look around the widows' concerned, intelligent faces was enough.

'Adeline's right. I owe you an explanation.'

As soon as she began, Rose found the events of the past forty-eight hours spilling out of her, almost as if she was trying to explain it to herself. As if she was still attempting to rationalize everything that had happened – her arrest, Oliver's revelations and their escape from London. She told them of the film crew and the assassination plan, yet for some reason she could not understand, she withheld her own extraordinary truth. That she and Oliver had become lovers.

It was as though she wanted to hoard that intimate secret for herself.

The widows' faces grew grave as they listened. The earlier atmosphere of warm-hearted banter evaporated, and a hush fell on the room, making the tick of a battered clock above the stove sound unnaturally loud.

'Where's your friend Oliver now?' asked Adeline quietly.

'I don't know. Somewhere in the city, I think.'

Outside, a mournful siren sounded the curfew.

'We need to sleep,' said Kate. 'The bus for the factory arrives at six thirty. Anyone who misses it is docked a week's rations.'

She got up, came over to Rose and kissed her cheek.

'You and your friends are very brave. I hope for all our sakes they succeed.'

One by one, the others disappeared upstairs, leaving only Sarah and Rose together, in the oily light of the kerosene lamp.

'Oliver told me you knew his mother,' said Rose.

'Marina.' Sarah's face broke into a smile. 'Yes. She used to live opposite us, in Kensington. As soon as I saw Oliver again, I recognized her in him. He has her eyes, and the same nose and brow.'

'What was she like?' asked Rose.

She found herself suddenly ravenous for any information about the man she had worked alongside for more than a year yet had known for the space of a single day. Their intimacy lingered in her body as much as her mind. Even now, her fingertips retained the precise feeling of his flesh, the hard muscle in his arms, the softness of his neck, his warm hands clasped around hers in the train carriage.

'Oh, self-possessed. Intelligent. Very beautiful. Marina could be quiet, but she loved wearing bright colours. Shot silk in vivid emerald and purple. I used to think Marina looked like a fantastic peacock among hens. She had a particular dress, with a nipped-in waist and a full skirt, that she'd copied from a painting. When I admired it, she said that actually it would suit me better, and the next time we met she brought it with her, folded in brown paper. And she was right, it did suit me. I thought of Marina whenever I wore it.'

'You were with her when she died.'

'She was expecting it.' Sarah's face grew solemn. 'Though not in the way it happened. For a while she had been talking about what she called her "exit plan". She believed we should all have worked out our own way of killing ourselves in the event of an invasion. She said she personally was storing petrol so that when it came to it, she could shut the garage door, keep the car engine running and die from carbon monoxide.'

Rose thought for a moment, and then reached into the pocket of her mackintosh for the small glass phial and placed it on the table between them.

'A few days ago, my father gave me this. He said I might need it. I think it was his own exit plan. I don't know what it is, but I suspect it's some kind of drug.'

'My husband was a chemist. Let me see.'

Sarah reached for the phial, rolled it in her palm, then very tentatively prised off the cap. She held it about six inches from her nose and immediately recoiled.

'It smells of bitter almonds. That's a tell-tale sign. It's potassium cyanide. It's fast-acting and will kill you in seconds.'

In a flash, Rose understood. Her father had told her precisely what the phial contained. *Let's just call it a gift.* Gift. The German word for poison. Dad had given her poison because it was the only present he was able to bequeath her.

'Be very careful,' said Sarah. 'It's extremely dangerous. A touch of it can permeate the skin.'

Rose replaced the stopper and stowed it back in her pocket.

'Will you sleep tonight, do you think?' asked Sarah.

'I'll try.'

'There's a spare mattress in Kate's room. I'll use that. You can take my bed.'

Sarah's room was a cramped space right up in the eaves of the house, barely big enough to contain a rickety iron bedstead. Rose sat on it tentatively.

'Do you ever think about your old home?'

'All the time. Wouldn't you? Mentally, I imagine going over my mother's Regency furniture with lavender beeswax polish or walking on our Persian carpets or looking at our Victorian oil paintings. When I lie in this bed, I think myself back into our marriage bed and the gorgeous Italian hand-embroidered sheets we bought on honeymoon.'

'What happened to your house?'

'It was made available to an elite family.'

'You must miss it terribly.'

'Do you know? The idea of a horde of strangers trampling on the carpets or using the Wedgwood china or stealing the cutlery ought to make me shudder, yet it doesn't. Once David died, I didn't give a damn for those things. I'd have given a whole street in Kensington for one more kiss of his lips.'

They were still for a while, listening to the clank of couplings and the guard's whistle issuing from the nearby railway tracks.

At that moment from the far distance came a fresh sound: the rumble of military trucks, followed by the drum of soldiers' feet disembarking, the clatter of equipment and muffled shouts of command.

'They're arriving!' gasped Rose.

'Where will you go tomorrow?'

'I have no idea. The city centre, I suppose.'

'Do you have any other clothes?'

Rose looked down at her outfit. The only clothes she had were the ones she was standing in and they were creased and grubby now. The white blouse and black skirt she had thrown on after she got home from the ASO. A light, belted mackintosh, and a navy pillbox hat. A pair of pale blue calfskin gloves.

'These'll do.'

'Wait there.'

Sarah returned with a garment of dense silky cloth, as blue as a summer's sky. She shook it out and held it up to Rose.

'This is Marina's dress. I've kept it for years. I smuggled it here, even though I knew I'd never wear it again, but I can see that it would suit you perfectly. Why don't you wear it for me?'

CHAPTER THIRTY-ONE

Saturday, 1st May

She couldn't sleep. All night a clamour of images thronged her brain: of Oliver, and Helena and her unborn baby. Of Hannah, Celia and their parents. Her body was rigid with tension and her muscles refused to relax. Memories that rarely escaped from her subconscious, even in the darkest reaches of an insomniac night, rose to the surface of her mind.

She began to remember the Time Before.

Alliance citizens were routinely discouraged from thinking about the Time Before, and all youth clubs, Mother classes and community groups taught mental strategies to prevent memories intruding in unguarded moments. *Build a wall in your mind, to keep the past behind*, went the popular refrain. Any stray remembrances should be quashed with thoughts of the future, until eventually they would fade, like photographs left out in the sun. Geoffrey was such a stickler for the rules that Celia refused to discuss with her sister any aspect of their youth, so the past had dwindled to a series of bright, unconnected cameos in Rose's mind.

Yet now, as she lay, a kaleidoscope of childhood revolved before her. Images that had lain long buried came back with all their vivid smells and sensations. The family eating fish and chips on the seafront at Brighton, or tramping up Box Hill as Dad strode ahead, recounting tales from history. She and Celia staging plays in the garden with her sister pirouetting in her sugar-pink ballet costume through every star role.

When she finally dozed, Rose dreamed of her father kneeling at the flowerbeds, weeding and plucking, with Rollo snuffling in the grass alongside him. Looking round to see a squad of policemen coming through the gate.

We have reason to believe your daughter Rose is an enemy of the Alliance and a traitor to the state.

Her father standing up, brushing the dust off his hands onto his old moleskin trousers, and turning to the policemen, beaming with pride.

Only then did she sleep, while the houseboats moored on the canal shunted softly against each other in the muddy pull of the water, and a pumice moon slowly descended the sky.

At dawn she climbed out of bed, and using the jug of water and the flannel left by Sarah, did her best to wash. Then she brushed her hair and pulled on the blue dress. Sarah was right – it did fit well and the colour matched her eyes, bringing out their depths.

It was strange to think that Oliver's mother had made it. For a second, surveying herself in a fractured washstand mirror, she allowed her vision to blur her into Marina herself and imagined what that courageous woman might have made of her. She wondered if her own parents, Dad particularly, would ever have the chance to meet Oliver, but almost immediately she dismissed these ruminations. They were as poignant as they were meaningless.

After throwing on her mac and fixing her hat, she quietly let herself out.

She picked her way through the fissured roads to the point where the houses gave way to a stretch of grassland leading to the canal and followed a path through the meadow. The wide, flat plains imbued her with a sense of infinite possibility, and she had a sudden yearning to walk away and escape into another existence. The future had never seemed so formless. She had no idea at all of what the coming day might bring.

The morning held the trace of the previous night's rain and dew, glittering on the grass, refracting light upwards towards a sparrowhawk hanging motionless in the sky. All around, cattle and horses grazed. She took a lungful of air. Everything seemed newly minted, as if on the first day of creation. As she walked, Rose sensed something watching her and, turning, saw a young, sandy-coloured deer standing stock still in the gentle mist, ears pricked, berry-black eyes unblinking, fixed on hers. For a few steady seconds she held the creature's gaze, allowing herself to be watched, and in a flash of understanding she realized it was the first time that she had ever been content to be observed.

Then the deer flicked its ears, spooked by someone coming, and bucked away to the far end of the meadow, into the tangled undergrowth.

She turned to see a figure dressed in black picking her way through the damp turf before drawing level.

'I come here sometimes too,' said Sarah. 'Before work. When I want to be by myself. I don't have long this morning because the cleaners need to be out of the library in good time for the visit.'

They continued in silence, weaving their way through the meadow, yet Rose was consumed by anxiety, and overlaying it something that had been troubling her since the previous evening. Or rather, someone.

Adeline.

Both times that they had met, Adeline had been wearing a pair of battered tan leather gloves. But the first time they met she had removed them for an instant to shake hands. Rose recalled her firm grip, and the fingers slender and perfectly formed. Yet in the statement she had given to Bruno Schumacher, her fingernails were missing.

I have been interrogated in the past, as you can see.

[Suspect shows her fingernails. Nails on right hand are missing.]

What else had Adeline's statement said?

You ask me who has influenced me. If I modelled myself on

anyone, it would be Aphra Behn and I assure you there is no hope of arresting her.

Slowly, Rose said, 'This may seem a strange question, but have you ever heard of someone called Aphra Behn?'

'Yes, of course.'

'Who is she? Does she live here?'

Sarah laughed delightedly.

'Hardly. She died more than two hundred years ago. She was England's first female playwright. She actually managed to make a living from writing, which was a feat no woman had achieved before and not many since. She's buried in Westminster Abbey.'

'I see,' said Rose uncertainly.

Sarah grinned. 'I always admired the fact that Aphra Behn said she lived a life wholly dedicated to pleasure and poetry. To me, that sounds like the perfect combination.'

Rose frowned. Somehow, this hedonistic ambition didn't fit with the steely rigour of Adeline Adams, who left a comfortable life in England to fight in a foreign war.

'Aphra Behn did have other occupations, though,' Sarah mused. 'One of her more exotic sidelines was working as a Government spy.'

It was as though parts of her brain were reconnecting. All Rose's questions were organizing themselves into a coherent pattern. She gasped.

'She's not safe!'

'Who?'

'Adeline's not safe. She knows about the plan and she's

going to inform on us. We need to find Oliver. We need to warn him.'

Sarah studied her with alarm. 'Slow down. What on earth are you talking about?'

'Adeline told the police that she modelled herself on Aphra Behn. That was her way of saying she's a spy. A Government spy.'

Sarah scrutinized her, the intense dark-lashed eyes puzzled.

'That's not rational, Rose. Adeline detests the regime. She fought in the Spanish Civil War.'

'On which side? There were communists and fascists in that war, weren't there? And both sides were riddled with double agents. When did Adeline come to Widowland?'

'A few months ago. Then almost immediately she was arrested and imprisoned. They tortured her, Rose. Badly.'

'They pulled out her fingernails, didn't they?'

'Amongst other things. She suffered terribly.'

'But her hands are perfect. When I first met her she took off her gloves. Just briefly, but long enough for me to see.'

Sarah was hesitant, calculating.

'She always wears those gloves . . .'

'Adeline must have been put among you because the authorities suspected insurgency. She was planted in Widowland as a spy. None of you knew her, but who could possibly suspect her, with a track record like that?'

Comprehension was dawning on Sarah's face.

'Kate suspected her. She never trusted Adeline. Kate said

being a journalist had made her a good judge of character and she tried to warn us, but Adeline's a strong personality.'

'As I've seen. She managed to get me to tell her everything. It was her who was asking, even though Kate tried to stop me. Kate told me I needn't explain, but I didn't take the hint. And now, Adeline knows about Oliver. We have to find him.'

'That's impossible. You don't even know where he is.'

Rose was gulping for breath.

'If Adeline betrays him to the authorities, it will all have been for nothing.'

'If she's going to do that, my guess is, she's done it already.'

'Then they'll know about the plan. They might even cancel the Leader's visit. They'll be arresting every camera crew on sight.'

Through Rose's mind flashed a multitude of images. Of Oliver and Sonia Delaney and the camera crew being executed, in that special way reserved for enemies of the regime who needed to die quickly. A bullet in the back of the neck.

The entire uprising compromised. Because of her own stupidity.

An anguished cry broke from her.

'There *must* be something . . .'

As she spoke, a thought stirred, so dangerous that she could scarcely breathe as it took shape. A proposition both terrifying and ingenious that she could not suppress. Reaching into the pocket of her mackintosh, her fingers searched out the phial of white powder that her father had given her. The one she had shown Sarah the previous evening. She brought it out on her palm.

'That book. *Frankenstein*. The one only the Leader can handle.'

The two women's eyes met. The same thought coursed like electricity between them. Sarah would be cleaning the Radcliffe Camera that morning. She would dust the lectern and the precious volume that had been selected for presentation to the Leader. This tiny phial contained a lethal poison that could permeate the skin. Suppose the Arriflex camera plan failed in some way. What then?

'Nobody would ask the Leader to wear gloves.'

Sarah's eyes met hers, level and calm.

'Do you dare?' Rose asked.

Carefully Sarah took the phial and put it in her pocket. 'I'll go now.'

CHAPTER THIRTY-TWO

For more than five hundred years, the city of Oxford had woken early on May Morning. By tradition, on 1st May, choristers rise before dawn and ascend the fretted turrets of Magdalen College to salute the arrival of spring.

On May Morning 1953, however, a rather more important arrival was awaited.

As the rising sun glittered off mercury-grey domes and towers and the bells of Magdalen College Tower rang out, Rose caught the faint voices of the choirboys tangling high above in exquisite counterpoint. Below the wheeling pigeons the whole city lay, slate spires glinting, college quads shining like emeralds set in pewter, towers and pinnacles cupped by the misty blue surrounding countryside. From the street, all that could be seen of the choristers was a line of heads, red-haired, blond and dark, and the white billow of vestments, as the traditional 'Hymnus Eucharisticus' floated into the crisp air.

Their song was almost drowned out, however, by the *thump thump thump* of helicopters circling over the city. Black uniforms were scattered antlike around the quads. The entire central area of Oxford, including Radcliffe Square, Catte Street, Holywell Street and halfway down Broad Street, had been roped off, guarded by a cordon of field-grey uniforms. Police dogs sniffed the sandstone courtyard of the Bodleian and the steps of the Radcliffe Camera, scrambled over the wooden dais that had been erected for dignitaries and snuffled behind rubbish bins and newspaper stands.

Rose pressed through the crowds, already sweating in her dress, trying to zone out from the blare of the military bands relayed by loudspeaker all through the city centre. As she went, she saw a knot of people divert around a spot on the end of a terrace facing a deconsecrated church whose noticeboard advertised meeting times for the Mother Service and the Alliance Girls. The whitewashed brick bore a message in orange paint.

Beware, for I am fearless and therefore powerful

The words resounded like the beat of her own heart. A moment later a soldier with a bucket and mop raked the words into a sloppy, terracotta stain as she watched and the crowd averted their eyes.

Rose passed the chequerboard red and ivory brick of Keble College, and opposite it, the Pitt Rivers Museum, its Gothic arches rising like the ribs of some extinct mammal. In the distance the cloud-grey dome of the Radcliffe Camera seemed to float above the commotion on the ground, as if testament to the loftiness of the generous imagination that designed it.

Scanning the stream of onlookers, glancing upwards at the roofs and church towers, she felt sick with nerves. Behind her ribs her heart lunged, like a giant bird in her chest.

Amid a crowd this size, how could she possibly find Oliver? She had no idea if he would be with Sonia Delaney and her camera crew or whether he would be acting as a lookout. Might he be hiding on one of the rooftops, in the eaves of Exeter College maybe, or behind some ancient, half-eroded gargoyle? Crouching behind a chimney stack or secreted in one of the narrow rooms of All Souls?

She prayed that even if the Americans were apprehended, Oliver himself would be safe.

As her eyes searched the skyline and probed the leaded windows and Gothic arches, her arm was grasped roughly from behind. She saw the flash of a black uniform and heard a voice.

'Come with me. Don't talk.'

She was pulled into the pink-washed entrance of a pub. Rose glimpsed the name – The King's Arms – and a flash of luminous dark wood and rough plaster. A dense cloud of beer and cigarettes engulfed her as she was hustled towards a door labelled *Dons' Bar: Women Not Permitted* and pushed inside. Her captor shut it with a kick of his boot.

'I suppose I should be surprised.'

Martin was transformed. The tenderness that had always softened his voice had gone and there was a hard light in his eyes. He looked paler too, as though his own human warmth had bled from him and calcified what remained.

'I'm here to accompany the Commissioner to the ceremony. I won't bother to ask why you're here. I don't care anyway.'

He cared a lot. That was plain.

'You know they arrested me?'

His silence confirmed it.

Incredulously, she gasped as realization dawned.

'It was you! You told them where I would be?'

Martin cast a longing eye across at the drinks. The festivities had prompted the landlord to stock extra supplies, and a stack of beer crates and cartons of Scotch were piled up behind the bar. Rose could see Martin fighting the need to drown his emotions, before losing the battle and leaning across to pluck out a bottle of whisky. Prising it open, he took a gulp.

'What could you possibly think I'd done, Martin? This is madness, and you know it. You know me.'

'I thought I did,' he said tensely. 'When the Commissioner called me in, he told me they had something on you.'

'And you too. We were guilty of the same crime.'

'Not adultery. It was far more than that. Eckberg said they had evidence you were a traitor. You've been a long-standing enemy of the Alliance. He gave me the choice to go to Paris, or stay and be humiliated with you. Imprisoned. Purged. Maybe worse, he said.'

'So you took me to your club and let the police know where I would be. You set a trap?'

He jutted his jaw pugnaciously.

'I have a family, Rose. Four children. Don't you think I have some responsibility towards them? Not to mention my wife.'

'Your wife? Since when have you shown such concern for Helga? You asked me to marry you!'

'I knew you'd never agree.'

Rose remembered what Bruno Schumacher said. *The thing about Martin is, he was always able to look after himself.*

'Really? How could you be so sure?'

'You wouldn't leave your family – your parents, your niece. You're always talking about that child. I could tell you loved her. She sounds sweet.'

He paused, then quietly, almost casually, said, 'Actually, it was the child who gave you away.'

'Gave me away? What are you talking about?'

'She's proud of you, Rose. She said, nobody writes stories like her aunt. The stuff they read at school is dull, it's all stormtroopers and Alliance Girls. Little Hannah wanted princesses and dragons. Magical talking animals. She told the teacher she should ask you for your stories about a place where there are no female castes or some such nonsense . . . Ilyria? Can that be right?'

Ilyria. It seemed like ancient history now. The fantasy world ruled by a benevolent queen, with talking leopards and fauns and fairy-tale cooking pots that produced any food you wanted. And Hannah, who still lived in a world of limitless potential, and had not yet learned confinement, watching with her solemn, dark eyes, sucking her thumb and nestling against Rose's arm.

Nothing, in retrospect, had ever given her so much pleasure.

She shrugged.

'They believed a child of six?'

'Not without evidence, of course. What do you take them for? The teacher, naturally, informed the authorities of Hannah's remarks and they were obliged to carry out a search of your flat. I've seen photographs of what they found in your file. Notebooks full of all kinds of forbidden material. Dreams, degenerate stories . . .'

Finally, she understood the rage pulsing through him.

'Some nonsense about me.'

So that was it. The core of his pain and anger. For Martin, Rose's diary had achieved what books never did, which was to enable him to see himself through another's eyes. Once he had read her merciless words, his love had shrivelled and died.

'So my crime is writing. Did that really make me an enemy of the state?'

'It wasn't only the degenerate muck or the lies about me. They found something else. Some kind of message. A line of words they know must be a code. They had no idea what it meant — only that it was significant. The ASO let you go, so they could see where you'd lead them.'

He hesitated.

'I wasn't going to show you this, but you might as well see it now.'

He pulled out a typed report. She noticed that his hands were trembling as he thrust it under her eyes.

'It was issued last night. It will go to all police departments.'

Her eyes refused to focus. All she could see was the words at the end.

Interrogation. All available methods. Liquidation.

'By rights, now I've found you, I should arrest you straight away.'

He took another gulp of Scotch and leaned heavily on the bar, sticky with spilled beer and wet ash. The alcohol brought back a touch of the old tenderness and he looked her up and down, noting the dress that brought out the blue of her eyes. He put his hands on her shoulders. They felt like dead weights.

'It might not have to be that bad. They could allow me to help you, Rose. If you told them everything you know: what that code is all about, how you've associated with traitors, what their plans are. I think I could arrange for you to be transferred. There are plenty of places that require more female stock and you are a Geli, after all. The eastern lands. In time, Russia maybe.'

She didn't reply. She could hardly bear to look at him. Everything that had passed between them, every embrace, every act of lovemaking had come to this. All their kisses had curdled into thin, cold air.

This man had taught her what love wasn't. But would she ever have a chance to discover what it was?

The face of Oliver came into her mind, and at the same time the wail of a police siren prompted Martin to check his watch. From outside came the restive hum of the crowd. He moved towards her and tipped her chin.

'You can't possibly evade them, you know? You'll be in custody within hours.'

'Are you going to help them, Martin? Will you give me away?'

He made no answer, only turned and left the bar.

Outside, the cacophony had intensified. The drumming of a marching band undercut the cries of news vendors in flat caps, bellowing their headlines. 'Leader's Visit Latest! Special Edition!' Someone in the crowd had got up a chant, 'We Want Our Leader!' and portions of the throng were raggedly following suit, while others remained grimly silent.

Gelis never had any problem with crowds. Obstructions melted and complaints died on the air when an elite woman approached. Anyone tempted to protest gave way instantly to a pretty female in a mackintosh and smart dress. Priority was always given to higher orders. Yet Rose decided to stick at the back of the throng, while she scanned the scene. A crush of people waving triangular Alliance flags strained at the barriers. Schoolboys in flannel shorts and schoolgirls in gaberdine tunics were at the front. Then came Klaras holding toddlers with chubby legs who clutched paper flags. The throng was seeded with watchers, easily identifiable by their trench coats and the binoculars they trained on sectors of the crowd. An area at the front had been cordoned off for the press, and journalists, with flashguns and cameras, notebooks out, were already jostling. She imagined Sonia Delaney's cameraman, levelling his Arriflex camera, squinting for the best possible angle. Hoping the target would be moving as slowly as possible.

One after the other, the bells of Oxford began to sound the hour with their habitual lack of synchronicity. As they did so, a ripple ran through the crowd, imperceptible at first, before rising to a low roar, and the distant thrum of motorcycles filled the air. Sightseers craned over the crash barriers and military music leaked from the loudspeakers as a line of limousines arrived and disgorged several uniformed figures.

Rose knew that anticipation and delay, even to the point of tedium, was essential to any celebrity visit. The honour guard was used to it, accustomed to standing for hours at rigid attention, poker straight, whether in blazing sunlight, their uniforms prickling with sweat, or freezing wind and rain. The troops didn't flinch, but Rose could feel the crowd becoming restive, like children at a birthday party who have consumed too much sugar. It was nine o'clock now. When would he appear?

A further fifteen minutes passed. She craned her head to see a range of figures enter the Bodleian's gates and proceed to Old Schools Quad, where a dozen dignitaries shuffled in their medals and ermine robes on a dais. A guard of honour lined up for the salute. She noticed a black and white cat staring dispassionately from a Hertford College windowsill.

Nine seventeen.

Then came the moment the crowd was waiting for. The Leader's car, a powerful beast, crunched over the ancient cobbles. It was flanked by four motorcycle outriders, two in front and two behind, and through the windows Rose glimpsed the pallid blur of a face. As the Mercedes moved down Broad Street amid a wave of cheers and a forest of salutes, she caught sight of a film cameraman with an Arriflex camera following its progress.

A second later the clang of shrapnel on metal cut like a scalpel through the din and sent flights of pigeons wheeling into the air. In a blare of sound, tyres squealed and members of the Leader's own bodyguard, the Leibstandarte, rushed into the road and, with a shout and a scuffle, knocked the cameraman to the ground. A second man, a stills photographer accompanying him, was seized, his camera smashed, and he was dragged, heels trailing, as guards scurried to collect the equipment he'd dropped. Dogs lunged against their leashes as police moved to surround the spot.

What did the pale-faced passenger in the limousine make of it? Perhaps he didn't even notice. Once the driver had taken evasive action, he pressed on through the mass of people, without stopping or reversing, and continued to the Bodleian Library.

The chatter of the crowd was as sharp as gravel in Rose's ears. The air was filled with the smell of rubber and metal. An obese Magda, with bad skin and hair teased into a lacquered helmet, pressed heavily against her, causing her to stumble on the kerb and clutch the woman's sleeve. The Magda turned angrily, then, seeing she was a Geli, managed a saccharine smile and made way for her.

It must have been a minute later, immersed in the thickest part of the crowd, that Rose sensed, rather than saw him. Before she properly perceived it, she registered the sleeve of Oliver's jacket next to her own and, looking down, recognized his black lace-up shoes. Seconds later his hand reached for hers and locked fingers and she heard his voice, barely audible in the din, his lips hardly moving.

'Don't look at me. Look straight ahead.'

She continued staring, unseeing, at the wall of flesh in front of her, and all the fluttering mayhem of armbands and hats and flags, and it was, in that instant, as though time itself had shifted and dissolved.

'It's over,' he said.

'It's not over.'

'We'll try again. We'll never stop trying. But I need to get away. I have somewhere safe. Promise me you'll leave now.'

'Don't go.'

'We'll be together. We'll get to America. If you go back to London, I'll get a message to you.'

'How?'

He turned very slightly then and, reaching into his pocket, offered her a National cigarette. He bowed his head in a swift nod, before looking away.

'Don't smoke it. The address is in the filter.'

His hand squeezed hers hard, then slipped from her own.

Rose glanced once, as he had forbidden. She saw his jaw clenched, and the knot of muscles in his neck, and she met his eyes, preserving the image of him for whatever might follow.

Then the crowd opened to swallow him and he was gone.

It was easy for Rose to push through the forest of flags to the crash barrier.

The Leader's car had parked. His route would take him firstly through the Great Gate and the Old Schools Quad to the dais where the Mayor and the Vice-Chancellor were standing, accompanied by their wives and a mass of field-grey uniforms. Greetings must be made. Medals and insignia glittered. The honour guard was clicking heels and pre-senting arms, smacking their rifle butts in unison like a thunderclap.

Rose saw a face she knew.

Bruno Schumacher, the man she had thought of like a tortoise beneath its shell, was just then standing at the crowd barrier. He must, she thought, be experiencing one of the high points of his life. Today was his chance to shine before Arthur Nebe, the man he had called his hero, who would finally recognize the organizational talents of the overlooked SS-Sturmbannführer Schumacher and convey a few words of thanks. Who would recognize that even in this distant corner of the empire, a police officer who had been inspired by Nebe's own leadership was right now repli-cating those diligent standards and ensuring that everything ran like clockwork.

And yet, Schumacher looked nauseous, as though he sensed that even now, at the eleventh hour, something might still go wrong. His brow was slick with sweat and his eyes prowled the crowd, looking out for any anomalous movement, any trace of dissent.

'Herr Schumacher!'

He started and took a second to focus on the pretty Geli in the sumptuous dress, tiny pillbox hat and powder-blue calfskin gloves standing before him, her complexion peachy and her eyes imploring.

'I'm Fräulein Ransom. Martin's friend.'

His face lit up. He must assume that Martin was here too. Maybe his childhood friend would witness him soaking up the praise from Reichskriminalpolizei chief Nebe for an operation that had gone like clockwork. It would be a rare opportunity for Bruno Schumacher to feel accomplished in front of Martin Kreuz.

Rose gave him a confidential smile.

'You have to help me, Herr Schumacher. I'm going to get in awful trouble. I'm supposed to be with the Culture Ministry group. But I got delayed. I need to be inside.'

A volley of shouts and cheers rang across the quad. The Leader had emerged from his limousine and was making his way to the dais. The crowd drew its collective breath.

He looked nothing like his posters.

Hunched in the familiar greatcoat, his gait was a slow shuffle. His body was pitched forward, his skimpy hair hidden beneath the cap, his skin the colour of cooked veal.

Halfway across he stopped to survey the domes and towers and spires around him with a look that seemed to say, *So this was what I fought for all those years ago. This is what has been waiting for me.*

What thoughts swam through that dark mind? Was Oxford, like Paris, an anticlimax?

The crowd surged and, in response, a wall of British police in high helmets, black uniforms and silver buttons instinctively closed ranks. Schumacher didn't hesitate.

Lifting the cordon swiftly and parting the policemen, he ordered, 'Quick. Let the lady through.'

Once inside, she took a brief, distracted glance around her. Gleaming shafts of light lanced down from the windows of the Radcliffe Camera, touching the gilt-stamped spines, buffing the ancient oak, turning the motes of dust to drifting gold. Beneath the pale green hexagons of the dome, eight pillars were arranged with repeating symmetry in a circle, each one interspersed with studded circlets of stone and a clotted lattice of stucco leaves. In the middle of the ground floor, space had been cleared for a welcoming party of senior dignitaries – if the prospect of SS-Brigadeführer Walter Schellenberg, Reichskriminalpolizei chief Arthur Nebe and Cultural Commissioner Hermann Eckberg counted as anyone's idea of a welcome.

Rose scanned the line of men. There was Nebe, wiry, with close-cropped silver hair, and Schellenberg in uniform with the army insignia above the breast pocket and eyes the colour of November rain as he stared straight ahead. The familiar figure of Hermann Eckberg, vast and irascible, standing to one side of a wooden lectern and right behind him Martin, with an expression of glazed fatigue, studying the floor. When he saw Rose, he gave a visible start, and the colour drained from his face, but it was too late to react. The Leader was hobbling in, summoning a smile that contained neither humour nor benevolence.

The head librarian approached with an unctuous salute, which the Leader returned with a trademark flip of his own, and the pair progressed towards the lectern where Mary Shelley's precious book lay open, tiny and fragile with its lethal trace of dust. Rose could not hear the conversation, but she guessed that the essence of the gift was being explained.

It's the story of a German genius who created something fantastical.

The Leader was eight feet away. His face was pale and waxy, like a candle lit from within, and his hands seemed boneless, as if made entirely of cartilage. He was not wearing gloves.

Three feet away.

He looked down at the fragile volume, its edges coppery with age, the binding dented and cracked, the filmy pages faded and crumpled as moths' wings. It was a dense tissue of words. Mary Shelley's neat teenaged hand was tightly compressed, with numerous crossings out, and in places, where a thought had struck her, a line of dialogue marched vertically up the edge of the page, disdaining natural order.

In 1816 Byron had called her book 'a wonderful work for a girl'. But what would the Leader make of it, this dreadful warning of the perils of hubris?

Murmuring appreciatively, he reached out and Rose's heart stilled.

Then, without touching the foxed pages, the Leader replaced his hand in the pocket of his greatcoat.

A roar of adrenaline filled her head, through which a line beat like a drum.

Beware, for I am fearless and therefore powerful.

The Leader was making to move away, pivoting towards the next section of the library, poised for a briefing on the history of the architecture and the millions of volumes that stretched out in the stacks above him.

Rose stepped forward, her feet unsteady beneath her, like a child who had just learned to walk. Fizzing with a rush of excitement and a cold sweat of fear, her entire body was shaking. Yet even as she moved towards him, the fear resolved into a great wash of exaggerated calm and a sense of release.

He must have heard her because he turned, and his eyes, twin pits of darkness, were all she could see. Their unnatural intensity rooted her to the spot.

The Leader was profoundly familiar with the mingled terror and delight that affected anyone who approached him. It had always been this way. Women would run up to him on the road, trying to get in his car. Dodging bodyguards, they would cast themselves in his path, begging for his attention. Sometimes, in their anguish, they would bare their breasts with cries of adulation and love. It seemed to be his destiny that beautiful girls should throw themselves before him with no thought for their own safety.

Benignly, he waved his aides away and nodded.

Rose picked up the book from its stand and, smiling, handed it to him.

AUTHOR'S NOTE

Although the setting is fictional, many figures in this novel existed, and the story is based on the genuine SS collection task force established by Alfred Rosenberg to loot Europe's libraries for books between 1939 and 1945. Tens of millions of books were plundered from libraries in every country of Europe and brought back to several archives, including Rosenberg's Amt Schrifttumspflege in Berlin. Rosenberg's approach to controlling literature went far beyond book burnings, and the team he established aimed to adjust certain aspects of history to reflect National Socialist beliefs about the past.

He was executed in Nuremberg in 1945.

SS-Brigadeführer Walter Schellenberg was tried at Nuremberg and detained for two years in prison before being released on grounds of ill health. He had had an affair with Coco Chanel and she paid his medical bills when he died in Switzerland in 1952.

Rudolf Hess flew to Scotland in his Messerschmitt in May 1941, probably to open peace talks with members of the British aristocracy. He crash-landed and was taken prisoner before being returned to Germany at the end of the war, where he died in Spandau Prison in 1987.

The five Goebbels girls and their brother died after being given cyanide by their mother, Magda Goebbels, in Hitler's bunker on 1st May 1945. Magda and Joseph Goebbels subsequently committed suicide.

Leni Riefenstahl was the pre-eminent film director of the Third Reich and produced many epic propaganda films for them. After the war she was classified as a 'fellow traveller' and denied knowing about the Holocaust. She continued making films and died in Munich, Bavaria, at the age of 101.

The Duke and Duchess of Windsor passed the war in the Bahamas, where the ex-King served as Governor, and they subsequently lived in France. The Duke did hold a private meeting with Hitler at the Berghof in 1937, but although the substance of their conversation has been much debated among historians, it was not documented. No record has survived.

ACKNOWLEDGEMENTS

Would that all writers had the support of agents and publishers like mine. My thanks go to Millie Hoskins, Olivia Maidment and Amy Mitchell, as well as others at United Agents, for generously reading and rereading drafts of this novel.

I could not have wished for more engaged and visionary publishers than Quercus and I'm especially grateful to Jane Wood, my fantastic editor, and Jon Butler for his knowledge and enthusiasm. Thanks also to Florence Hare, and to Lorraine Green for her meticulous copyediting. When I saw the fabulous jacket design, my heart skipped a beat. Thanks so much to Nathan Burton and Andrew Smith.

Lastly, Caradoc King, legendary agent and long-time friend, has been an unwavering source of interest and help in all the time that I've known him. He has happily engaged in endless discussions on fiction and character and plot, and the very least he deserves is that this novel is dedicated to him.